Irish author **Abby Green** ended a very glamorous career in film and TV—which really consisted of a lot of standing in the rain outside actors' trailers—to pursue her love of romance. After she'd bombarded Mills & Boon with manuscripts they kindly accepted one, and an author was born. She lives in Dublin, Ireland, and loves any excuse for distraction. Visit abby-green.com or email abbygreenauthor@gmail.com.

Jackie Ashenden writes dark, emotional stories, with alpha heroes who've just got the world to their liking only to have it blown wide apart by their kick-ass heroines. She lives in Auckland, New Zealand, with her husband, the inimitable Dr Jax, two kids and two rats. When she's not torturing alpha males and their gutsy heroines she can be found drinking chocolate martinis, reading anything she can lay her hands on, wasting time on social media or being forced to go mountain biking with her husband. To keep up to date with Jackie's new releases and other news sign up to her newsletter at jackieashenden.com.

T0337245

BABIES BEFORE VOWS

ABBY GREEN

JACKIE ASHENDEN

MILLS & BOON

First published in Great Britain 2024
by Mills & Boon, an imprint of HarperCollins*Publishers* Ltd,
1 London Bridge Street, London, SE1 9GF

www.harpercollins.co.uk

HarperCollins*Publishers*, Macken House, 39/40 Mayor Street Upper, Dublin 1, D01 C9W8, Ireland

Babies Before Vows © 2024 Harlequin Enterprises ULC

The Heir Dilemma © 2024 Abby Green

The Twins That Bind © 2024 Jackie Ashenden

ISBN: 978-0-263-32034-3

12/24

This book contains FSC™ certified paper
and other controlled sources to ensure responsible forest management.

For more information visit www.harpercollins.co.uk/green.

Printed and Bound in the UK using 100% Renewable Electricity
at CPI Group (UK) Ltd, Croydon, CR0 4YY

THE HEIR DILEMMA

ABBY GREEN

MILLS & BOON

I'd like to dedicate this book
to my favourite BBC soap opera, *Eastenders*.

And specifically to Cindy Beale, whose recent return
to Albert Square sparked the idea for this book!

CHAPTER ONE

QUINTANO HOLT SURVEYED the scene before him: a glittering party on the rooftop of one of Manhattan's most iconic hotels. Flaming lanterns and flickering candles bathed some of the most powerful, influential and beautiful people in New York society in a golden glow. Black-and-white-clad waiters moved fluidly through the crowd, offering a choice of beverages and canapés. A full moon hung low in the clear night sky. The air was balmy. All in all, a very exclusive and idyllic scene.

He savoured this moment he had alone to himself, before anyone noticed his arrival. He allowed the sense of satisfaction to settle in his belly. Tonight was the culmination of years of work. He'd floated his tech company on the stock market earlier that day for an astronomical amount of money. This was a celebration of the indelible proof that he could make it on his own. That he hadn't needed his family legacy.

A legacy that he'd sensationally walked away from over five years before, after discovering that his father *wasn't* his biological parent. Some other nameless man had been his father. Maybe the pool boy. Or his Brazilian mother's personal trainer.

Not that the man who had brought him up had tried very hard to stop him from walking away. He'd taken the news that Quin didn't intend to cash in on his inheritance or take up a role in the family business with a shrug of indifference which had pretty much summed up their relationship.

As for his mother... There were only two people in this world whom he despised and she was one of them. Buried deep inside Quin was the wound of her abandonment, something he'd always blamed himself for. He knew rationally that of course a three-year-old couldn't drive a mother away from her family, but Quin had grown up believing it on a cellular level because of the trauma.

She'd walked out on him and his older brother without a backward glance and she didn't deserve an atom of Quin's energy. He certainly wasn't going to let toxic memories of her infect this moment.

He shut out all unwelcome thoughts and focused on the crowd. He let his gaze wander over the women, each one as stunningly beautiful as the last. Blonde, brunette, jet-black hair, redhead. All poured into dresses that showed off willowy limbs and luscious curves.

All so tempting...and God knew Quin should be tempted. It had been years for him since—

No, not going there. That would be to invite a level of toxicity that went way beyond memories of his mother.

But the problem was that he wasn't tempted. Not even remotely. He looked at these beautiful women and not one caused even a frisson of interest in his blood or his body. He was flatlining.

A sense of desperation climbed upwards. It couldn't be the case that *she'd* ruined him for all women. On top of everything else she'd done. He let his gaze linger on the woman with red hair. She was the one who least resembled *her.* He willed himself to find her attractive, letting his gaze drop over her perfectly toned curves—no doubt honed in one of Manhattan's many sleek gyms.

But that only made him think of another body—equally slim and toned, but from surfing and jogging and walking fast. He'd used to tell her she reminded him of an irrepressible imp, full of kinetic energy. But she'd also been soft in all the right places, and plump in even better places. The way her breast had filled his hand, as if made especially for him… The sharp stab of her nipple… He could still recall how it had felt against his tongue, and the way she'd buck against him, spreading her legs, begging him to—

Quin cursed softly. He was finally feeling aroused and it was thanks to a ghost. Damn her to hell. It was time to move on with his life and if he had to fake it until he felt it then he would do whatever it took.

He was about to take a step towards the party when something made him hesitate. The little hairs went up on the back of his neck. A scent tickled his nostrils. Roses and something sharp. Citrus. Very unique. Only one woman had that scent.

Everything in him tensed. *No.* He would not let her haunt him like this.

Determined to push the past behind him, where it belonged, Quin took a step forward just as a voice said his name from behind him. It was so low that Quin wasn't sure if he'd even heard it.

He stopped, going against every instinct within him that urged him to keep moving forward. The voice came again, louder this time. Firmer.

'Quin.'

Slowly, Quin turned around, fully expecting to see nothing behind him because his mind was playing tricks. It had to be. Because it couldn't possibly be—

His gaze fell on a woman. *It was her.* The only other person he despised in the world other than his mother. And yet his first instinctive response wasn't disgust, or even rejection, it was something much closer to relief, and an almost overwhelming need to haul her close, touch her... feel for himself how real she was.

No way.

He hated this woman with a passion. It wasn't relief he was feeling. It was pure unadulterated rage and disgust.

And yet the maelstrom inside him wasn't so easily categorised as he took her in...

Slightly above average height. She'd used to love the disparity in their sizes. He was almost a foot taller. She'd run into his arms and wrap her legs around his waist, arms locked around his neck, pressing her mouth to his as if she needed him more than air.

She looked different, though, he vaguely realised through the shock reverberating through his body and brain. Her hair was lighter. Blonde, with reddish streaks. It was down past her shoulders, wavy. Un-styled.

She was pale. Freckles across her cheeks. Aquamarine eyes. Blue and green. Achingly familiar. Long lashes. Straight nose. Wide mouth. Plump lower lip that had made him want to kiss her the first time he'd laid eyes on her.

She wore a plain black evening gown. Strapless. Showing off a delicate collarbone and slender arms. No blinging jewellery. Minimal make-up. Something about that—about her understated appearance—landed like adrenalin in his gut, waking him out of his shocked trance.

And then he realised it wasn't adrenalin. It was lust.

'Sadie Ryan...' Quin breathed, not quite able to believe

he was uttering her name out loud, or that she above all women still had the power to bring his libido back to life after four years.

This was the woman who had betrayed him in the worst way possible—by making him trust her. *Love her.* No, he told himself now. It had never been love. It had been lust. That was all. But the assurance rang hollow, mocking him.

He blinked, hoping that she might disappear. But she didn't. She was all too real.

He said, 'What the hell are you doing here?'

Sadie Ryan looked up at Quin Holt and couldn't quite believe that she was standing here in front of him. And that she was still breathing—that she hadn't fallen, overwhelmed, into a mass of emotion at his feet. Blood was pounding through her body, drowning out the strains of music and the muted chatter of people coming from the party.

He looked as amazing as she remembered… *More.* Short, dark blond hair. Dark eyes. Stubbled jaw. Classically handsome, but with an edge that elevated him to truly gorgeous. Charisma oozed from every pore. As did pure, raw sex appeal.

Past and present seemed to blur into one another as the memory of seeing him for the first time flashed back into her head. He'd been standing against one of the wooden pillars on the porch that had wrapped around the little beach house in Brazil, drinking from a beer bottle. He'd been wearing nothing but long board shorts. Bare-chested. Utterly gorgeous. And then, as if feeling her gaze on him, he'd looked at her, and she'd felt the electric *zing* from him to her as if they were connected by a wire.

Sadie forced her mind back to the present. She couldn't

get lost in memories now. Her mouth was dry from nerves. She tried to swallow, to lick her lips but her tongue and mouth wouldn't function. She'd dreamed of this moment for so long that it didn't feel real.

Emotions churned in her gut and moved upwards, making her chest swell. Finally, *finally* she would get to see—

'I said, what the hell are you doing here?'

Quin's question cut through the emotion. Sadie realised that he looked angry. *No.* Livid. A muscle was popping at his jaw, reminding her of when she'd been in hospital four years ago, in intense pain, and no one had seemed to be listening to her. His jaw had popped like that when he'd been talking to the staff.

She concentrated on the present moment even as the past threatened to drown her in images and memories.

But instead of the rehearsed speech she'd been practising—*I know this must be a shock*—she heard herself blurting out emotionally, 'I'm so happy to see you.'

Quin frowned. Sadie had only barely taken in the dark suit and light blue shirt. The way that his clothes moulded to his tall, powerful body. She'd never seen him so formally dressed. When she'd known him he'd worn a uniform of T-shirts and faded jeans or board shorts, and more often than not he'd spent his time bare-chested. Or naked. Heat flooded her body at that memory.

'You're *"so happy"* to see me?' Quin's voice was incredulous. 'What is this? Some kind of sick joke?'

Sadie shook her head. She cursed her naivety. Of course he wasn't going to be overjoyed to see her. She'd walked out without any explanation. Vanished into thin air. Left him and—

'You were not invited to this party. You should leave.'

The hostility radiating from the man in front of her

made Sadie shiver. 'I tried calling you a couple of times recently, but your number must have changed...or maybe you blocked me.'

Quin was silent for a moment, and then he said tautly, 'I had the same number for a year after you left...when you didn't use it, I didn't see any point in keeping it operational. You're not welcome here.'

She said, 'I know I wasn't invited, but I saw in the press that you were due to be here, so I took my chances and they let me in when I said I knew you.'

Quin's dark gaze swept her up and down, nothing warm in it at all. He looked at her and said, 'You *"knew"* me a long time ago.'

Sadie's heart shrank inside her chest. He was looking at her as if she was a stranger and she knew she couldn't blame him.

'Four years isn't that long,' she said weakly, but the lie tasted like acid on her tongue.

The last four years had felt like a lifetime. Each hour crawling past torturously. Each day taking a little bit more of her heart and soul and crushing them to pieces. Until the glorious moment only a few weeks ago when she'd got the news that she could start living again.

Quin shook his head. 'You have some nerve, showing up like this. What do you want?'

'We need to talk.' Surely he couldn't deny her that?

Quin folded his arms across his chest and Sadie hated how aware of his biceps she was, bulging against the expensive fabric.

'Talk about what? How you disappeared without a trace? Leaving behind only a note with no explanation. How did it go again?'

Quin pretended to think for a second and Sadie wanted

to beg him not to say those hateful words that were engraved into her soul. But it was too late, he was biting them out with caustic relish.

'Oh, yes, that was it: *"Please believe me when I say I don't want to leave but I have to..."'*

The fact that he'd omitted part of the note was small comfort. Maybe he didn't want to remember the bit where she'd said, 'I love you.' Or the other part, which was why she was here...

'Quin.' She tried to appeal to the side of him that didn't want to vaporise her on the spot. 'We need to talk. We need to talk about—'

'We have nothing to talk about,' he cut her off brutally. 'You need to turn around and leave right now, or I'll have you thrown out.'

Panic clutched at Sadie's gut. He couldn't do this. But her limbs were turning to jelly at the thought that he might very well have her unceremoniously thrown out onto the streets, that she might not get to see—

She forced air to her panicking brain. She had to be rational and remember she had rights.

She forced herself to stand tall in the face of his white-hot anger and clear rejection of her presence. 'I'm not going anywhere, Quin. I've come here because I want to see my son. *Our* son, Quin. I want to see Sol.'

CHAPTER TWO

QUIN STILL COULDN'T believe that Sadie was standing before him. And uttering his son's name out loud. It was blasphemy, coming from her. The woman who had walked out on her days-old baby. Their son. *No.* His son. She'd given up her rights to be his mother the day she'd turned her back on him with such callous disregard.

He of all people should have realised it might happen. After all it had happened to him. In his world mothers wreaked nothing but havoc.

The need to protect his son from this woman and whatever she wanted was overwhelming. He said, 'How dare you even mention his name? You have no right.'

She went even paler in the dim light. Eyes wide. The colour of the ocean. He'd used to drown in her eyes. He'd fought it for a long time when they'd first met, having never really trusted anyone after his mother had walked out on him at such a young age. But day by day he'd fallen deeper and deeper under this woman's spell, until one day he'd woken up and realised that he'd die for her. She had become his world.

That was when she'd told him she was pregnant, looking as shocked as he'd felt. But then there had been an overwhelming surge of joy and hope. He was being given a chance to do things differently...to change the script. He'd naively looked forward to witnessing a mother who loved her child enough to stay. He'd relished the opportunity to show his child love and support. Not the indifference he'd experienced from his father.

Quin had grown up with unbelievable privilege—anything money could buy, but nothing of real value. He'd learnt about that value by carving out his own path, and the thought of being able to pass that on to his child had been incredibly cathartic.

Sadie had been so happy—they'd both been so happy. Talking long into the night about all the dreams they had for their child. And each other. They'd been married in a simple ceremony on the beach, when Sadie was seven months pregnant...

'I have every right, Quin. I'm his mother.'

Sadie's voice pulled Quin back from the far too vivid past. He forced himself to be rational when he felt anything but. In spite of her heinous actions four years ago, he knew that as his son's biological mother, she did have rights. Although he couldn't imagine a court in the land regarding her favourably when she'd walked out of their lives, days after their son was born, without a backward glance.

'What is it you want, Sadie?'

'I want to see my son. I want to be a mother to my son.'

Anger bubbled. 'You've had four years to be a mother to your son. Why now?'

Something occurred to him then, and it made his guts curdle with disgust. At one time he'd believed he'd known this woman as well as himself, but he'd been utterly naive.

She was opening her mouth, but he uncrossed his arms and held up a hand. 'No need to say a thing. Your timing says it all.'

'My timing?'

She looked genuinely nonplussed. Quin might have laughed if he'd felt remotely like it. Her acting skills really were superb. Another thing he'd never given her credit for, because he'd trusted her.

'You expect me to believe it's a coincidence that you appear back in my life on the day that I float my company on the stock market and it makes millions?'

Well, actually billions, but Quin wasn't going to be pedantic.

She shook her head, 'No, that's not it at all.' She blushed. 'I'd been following you in the news, to try and figure out the best way to contact you, and I read about your success…but I'm not interested in that side of it. I mean…' She stopped and then said huskily, 'I am interested in the fact that you've achieved everything you'd set out to achieve when I first met you. It's amazing, Quin, you must be so proud.'

His chest squeezed at the way she said his name like that, catching him unawares. He'd confided in this woman…all his hopes and dreams. Ambitions. He'd opened up to her in a way he'd never done with anyone else—not even his older brother—helplessly seduced by her open and loving nature, never thinking for a second that she would be the one to rip his world apart.

More fool him. At one time he'd imagined sharing this moment with her, but now the triumph felt somehow… tainted. As if trusting her with those nascent dreams was now invalidating everything.

The past was all around him, closing in, whispering in his ear and sending a kaleidoscope of incendiary images into his brain. He forced ice into his blood, but the throb of awareness was almost impossible to quench. It always had been. From the moment he'd laid eyes on this woman he'd wanted her with a primal need that he'd never felt before. He needed to push her back.

'You say you're only here to see your son? In that case I'll give you my solicitor's details and you can contact me through the appropriate legal channels.'

Sadie could feel her blood drain south, and for a second she felt dizzy. She must have swayed slightly or something, because Quin said, 'Are you okay?'

But he didn't sound concerned—he sounded irritated. Sadie nodded. She wasn't going to wilt at his feet like some sort of waif. Even if it had been hours since she'd eaten; she'd been too nervous. And she hadn't slept much since she'd arrived in New York from England the day before.

'I'm fine.' She needed to be strong, to appeal to Quin. 'Look, I don't have the kind of funds required to hire a solicitor to enter into legal proceedings to gain access to my son. I just want to see my son and spend some time with him.'

Quin shot back without hesitation, 'And then what? Disappear again without a trace? One advantage of leaving when you did the last time was that he was only a few days old. He's four now, and he has a mind like a steel trap. He notices everything and everyone.'

Emotion bubbled up at how he described Sol, stinging Sadie's eyes before she could stop it. Her knowledge of her son had been confined to very grainy paparazzi photos of Quin and Sol taken over the years, compounding her pain and loneliness at having left them.

When it had become apparent that Quintano Holt, son of legendary billionaire and industry titan Robert Holt, was a single father, the social columns had gone into a frenzy, speculating about where Quin had been for the past few years and how he'd become a single father.

Sadie hadn't known about Quin's own father—or, apparently, according to the gossip sites, the man who was *not* his biological father. She hadn't known that he had an older brother, or that he'd come from an incredibly privileged background, born into one of America's founding families.

Quin had never spoken much about his life before he'd met Sadie during the year they'd been together, only telling her that he wasn't close to his family. She'd sensed his reticence to talk about it and so she hadn't pushed. After all, she'd only known the full extent of her own past for a couple of days when she'd first met him...

But now was not the time to get into all of that. They had bigger issues. She forced the emotion down and said, 'I'm not going anywhere. Not again. I'm here to stay. I'm here to be a mother to Sol.'

Even though the thought terrified her. She'd been his mother for mere days before she'd known she had no choice but to leave, for Quin and Sol's safety.

Quin made a snorting sound. 'Based on previous behaviour, I'd say there are two chances of you sticking around: slim and none.'

Sadie needed to try and convince him somehow, and the only thing she could convince him with was the truth—but she could already imagine Quin laughing his head off. Disbelieving her. Even though it would be easy to prove.

She pleaded, 'Give me a chance to explain why I left, Quin—please. If you'd just—'

But he held up his hand and stopped her words. She watched him take a small phone out of an inner jacket pocket and press a button, then hold it up to his ear. He

turned away slightly, and even that attempt to hide himself from her was wounding. When they'd been together
he'd never hidden from her.

Except that wasn't true. Quin Holt *had* hidden a huge
amount from her—not least his significant family history.
In the year that she'd known him she'd assumed that he
was little more than a surfer boy and a tech nerd, travel-
ling and working remotely because he had no ties, or none
that he cared much about.

Not that Sadie could claim any moral high ground after
what she'd done and what she'd hidden about herself. But
right now she needed to gain his trust, not alienate him.

She realised he was talking Portuguese, specifically
Brazilian Portuguese. He sounded a lot more fluent than
he'd been when they'd been living in a small surfing beach
town to the east of Sao Paulo in Brazil. Evidently they'd
both had their reasons for being in such a place, where
one could get lost. Except she'd forgotten her reasons for
being there thanks to a head injury sustained while surfing, just two days after she'd first laid eyes on him. He'd
been the one who had pulled her out of the water and who
had saved her life.

For almost the entire year she'd been with Quin, in a
whirlwind, passionate and life-changing relationship, she
hadn't remembered a thing about who she really was. She'd
felt incredibly vulnerable after the accident, but he'd won
her trust by taking care of her and expecting nothing in
return. And then, over the days and weeks that had followed, their building attraction had finally become too
powerful to ignore and they'd become lovers, inseparable.

Somehow, the fact that she couldn't remember who she
was, or anything of her past, had almost faded into the
background. They'd been so caught up in each other, in

a dreamlike bubble. It had been easy to forget that Quin must have had a past too. He'd become her anchor. And the love of her life.

She'd only regained her memory after the birth of Sol. And that had led to her fateful exodus—the hardest thing she'd ever had to do in her life. And the most painful.

Quin had terminated his phone conversation now and was looking at her. Sadie tried again, 'Please, Quin—'

But he cut her off. 'I don't have time now to hear whatever story you've concocted to explain how you could have walked away from your own baby without a backward glance. I'm returning to Brazil.'

She hadn't walked away without a backward glance. Far from it. Every day since then had been an absolute torture. The only thing that had got her through those endless days had been the knowledge that she'd done what she'd done to keep Quin and Sol safe at all costs. And the cost had been huge. But worth it. Even now, in the face of Quin's hostility and anger. Even if he never forgave her.

The need to defend herself mixed with panic at the thought that Quin was going to just walk away. She focused on what he'd said.

'Brazil? What's in Brazil?'

'I live in Sao Paulo with Sol.'

Sadie's heart clenched. That was where he'd been born.

'Sol is there now?'

She wanted to ask him how he could leave their son behind, thousands of miles away, but she bit her lip. She didn't really have that right.

'Yes, he's there. With his very much adored and capable nanny, who has been with us since you left.'

Another poison dart to Sadie's heart.

Quin continued, 'I haven't even been gone twenty-four

hours. I was planning on staying in Manhattan overnight and returning in the morning, but I've decided to leave now.'

Sadie deflated. There was no way she could afford to travel to Sao Paulo and follow Quin. It had taken all her paltry finances to come to New York at short notice when she'd read that he would be here for the stock market flotation.

'Quin, I—'

'Look. I'm going to give you one chance.' His jaw was tight. 'Not that you deserve it. But, as much as I hate to admit it, you do have some rights, and when this comes to court—as it inevitably will—I don't want you to have any reason to lay accusations at my door that I didn't give you an opportunity to see my son. I won't take any risks when it comes to Sol and ensuring I remain his primary custodial parent, so if that means allowing you some initial access then I'll do it.'

Sadie surmised that the brief phone conversation must have been with his legal team. They would have advised him to tread carefully. She didn't much care, because all she felt was huge relief. 'I… That's amazing, thank you.'

But then she remembered her limitations, and her insides plummeted again. 'It's not that I wouldn't jump at the opportunity right now, but the truth is that I can't afford to go to Brazil at such short notice…'

She heard herself and winced. She sounded as if she was making excuses. No doubt Quin would jump on this to cast her off.

She waited for him to smirk and tell her, *Tough*.

But he didn't smirk. He just looked at her with unnerving intensity. Then he said, 'I will have to take your word for it when it comes to your means—after all who knows what you've been up to for the last four years? Are you married? Do you have more children?'

Sadie felt a bubble of hysteria rise up at the notion. She pushed it down and shook her head. 'No, nothing like that. Of course not.' She thought of something and asked, 'Do you? Have a partner?'

She hadn't seen pictures of him with anyone, but then he'd never been showy...

His mouth tightened, but he said eventually, 'Not that it's any of your business, but no, I'm not with anyone right now.'

But he had been? That was what he was implying. Sadie's insides twisted with something dark. Jealousy. A jealousy she had no right to feel. And yet she heard herself say, 'We *are* still married.'

Quin let out a curt laugh. 'Hardly. That beach wedding was ceremonial only. We never signed anything.'

Sadie flushed. Of course. They'd been due to have a proper, legal ceremony after Sol's birth...but then her world had been turned upside down with the return of her memory.

'Of course... I know that,' she said now, feeling gauche and naive.

She'd always believed that beautiful ceremony on the beach had been more binding than anything in a church or a register office. Clearly he hadn't. But at the time it had felt so real. The way he'd looked at her...as if she was the only thing in the world.

She hid her hands behind her back and removed the ring he'd proposed to her with—an emerald and sapphire ring that had become her single most treasured item, along with a picture she'd taken of Quin holding newborn Sol before she'd left. The thought of Quin seeing her still wearing the ring now made her skin go clammy with panic. As did the thought of him seeing the short unvarnished nails and careworn skin of her hands. They were evidence of her constant moving around and the only work that had been available to her, which had inevitably been menial and backbreaking.

'I can explain what I've been doing, if you'll let me.'

Except what if she told him and he thought it was so outlandish and unbelievable that he cast her out of his and Sol's lives for good? Her mind raced, thinking of that scenario—by the time she'd worked to make enough money to try and see Sol again he'd be a teenager.

She realised that she couldn't explain here, like this, with them facing each other like bitter adversaries. She blurted out, before Quin could answer, 'Actually, maybe now isn't such a good time.'

He arched a brow. 'You need more time to come up with the right story?'

Sadie swallowed. 'It's not like that…it's just a lot to explain…'

He glanced at his watch. 'I don't have time for this. I've instructed my plane to be ready to leave within the hour. You can come with me.'

Sadie stopped breathing for a second. He was going to take her with him? She was afraid she'd misheard him.

But then he asked impatiently, 'Where are you staying?'

Sadie quickly gave the address of the travellers' hostel near Central Station, afraid he might change his mind. Quin's eyes widened marginally at the mention of the hostel, and now that she knew of his background she could well imagine why.

He said briskly, 'I'll have someone go and pick up your things. They can meet us at the plane.'

Sadie thought of the mess she'd left behind as she'd hurriedly changed into this dress, which she'd bought in a discount store earlier that day. 'Is that really necessary? I can rush back now and pack…'

But he shook his head, already taking out his phone again, giving instructions.

This new businesslike version of Quin was a revelation to her. When she'd known him he'd been the quintessential surfer traveller. He'd also been a tech nerd, spending hours a day on his laptop, not issuing instructions like this.

But then that memory returned of when they'd gone to the hospital in Sao Paulo, for her to have Sol. For the first time she'd seen Quin in authoritative mode, and the way the doctors and nurses had meekly acquiesced to his instructions, as if sensing his innate authority. No wonder. He'd been oozing generations of privilege and entitlement.

She hadn't taken too much notice at the time, because she'd been in the middle of intense labour pains, but now it clicked into place like a missing jigsaw piece. As did the fact that he'd managed to get her into a private birthing suite at the hospital. At the time she'd wondered only vaguely how they could afford it…

She felt naive now. For not questioning him about his past more. For trusting him so blindly.

He handed her the phone. 'Tell Martha what she needs to know to pack your things.'

Sadie took the phone and turned away from Quin, not wanting him to hear her apologising for the state of the room before telling the perfectly polite woman on the other end where her things were. She'd always been messy, in contrast to Quin's almost fanatical tidiness.

She turned around again and handed back the phone. 'Thank you. I really appreciate you taking me with you.'

'I'm not doing it for your benefit, believe me. My driver is waiting.'

Quin put out a hand for Sadie to precede him out of the area leading into the party. She noted that he was careful not to touch her. She was grateful, even as she ached for his touch. She didn't need him seeing how attuned to him she still was after all this time.

In the back of the chauffeur-driven car, the air between them was frigid. Quin looked out of the opposite window, brooding. He must be irritated that she'd disrupted his evening. Sadie sat still, afraid that if she moved even an inch Quin would change his mind and throw her out onto the road.

But the car sped on, through the streets and off the island of Manhattan to a private airfield, where a woman in a smart trouser suit was waiting with Sadie's small wheelie case, which she'd been dragging around with her for years now. At that moment Sadie wanted to throw it into the nearest bin, she was so heartily sick of it and its reminders of what she'd endured.

But it would have one last journey to make—because she wasn't leaving her son's side ever again, no matter how she did it. Even if she had to camp outside Quin's home.

And at least she didn't have to worry about how to get there.

The fact that they were stepping onto a sleek black private jet was almost negligible to Sadie, she was so eager to get to her son. But once on board she couldn't help but notice the plush opulence. The softest carpet, and cream leather seats with gold trim. Quin was walking down the plane to some seats near the back. Not sure what to do, Sadie just followed him.

He sat down and looked at her. He waved a hand towards the other seats. 'Make yourself comfortable. It's a long flight—between nine and ten hours. We'll arrive in the morning. Sao Paulo is an hour ahead of our current time.'

Sadie became very aware of her dress. She gestured to herself. 'I'll change, then, into something more practical.'

Quin gestured behind him to a door. 'The bedroom and bathroom are in there. Be my guest.'

Sadie had disappeared into the bedroom with the small case that seemed to be her only possession. Quin was so tense he wondered if he hadn't burst a few blood vessels. Her scent lingered in the air, taunting him. He cursed and forced himself to relax as the crew prepared for take-off.

He still couldn't quite believe that she had appeared in front of him within the last hour, as if conjured out of his imagination. But the response in his body was an unwelcome reminder that she was all too real. His blood was still hot. Sizzling. His muscles were aching from the control it had taken for him not to reach out and touch her... See if she was real. See if her skin still felt as soft. Her hair as silky.

He'd been aware of every minute move she'd made in the back of the car, barely breathing in case her scent went too deep inside him.

He wondered if he was crazy to be bringing her with him. But his legal counsel, whom he'd spoken to on the phone, had told him to find out what she wanted. They'd advised telling her to contact them through the proper channels. They hadn't said to keep her close at all costs. That was his own decision. An instinct to keep an eye on her... In case she disappeared again?

No, he told himself. It was a practical move to make sure he knew what she was up to. If she was with him, she couldn't take him by surprise again.

He scowled at himself. She'd disappeared once before, and he had no doubt she would do it again. He just had to figure out what it was she was after. Because she might deny that timing had anything to do with it, but it was almost laughable that she'd chosen this exact moment to reappear.

He'd been independently wealthy for the last few years, once his startup had gained attention and traction, but the stock market flotation had put it and him onto another level. She'd obviously been biding her time. She'd known based on what he'd told her back then that this might happen one day. She was the one who had first encouraged him and told him it was a great idea.

Maybe—the thought occurred to him—she was going to try and claim some kind of ownership of the company? Make a case for him owing her something of the profits?

At that moment the door opened behind him and he tensed all over again as her scent preceded her. She walked past him and he noticed that she'd replaced the dress with faded jeans and soft pink short-sleeved top. She'd pulled her hair back into a messy knot. But he couldn't look away from where the material of her jeans lovingly cupped her heart-shaped backside. As pert and plump as he remembered. Small waist. Narrow torso. Firm breasts.

One of his last memories of her was when she'd been breastfeeding Sol in their bed, after they'd returned to Sao Sebastiao on the coast. She'd been pale. Distracted. He'd put it down to the stress of trying to get the baby to feed properly. He'd been fractious. As if he'd sensed that something was wrong… But how could he have known that his mother would walk out and leave him just a couple of days later?

Clearly she'd known something then too... After Sol was born she'd changed, become withdrawn, hadn't been able to meet his eye. Again, he'd assumed it was just to be expected after something as monumental as giving birth.

She turned around now, and Quin forced his gaze up and tried not to let those huge green-blue eyes unsettle him. Except he had to concede that every time his son looked at him with those exact same eyes he was reminded of his errant mother.

No wonder Quin hadn't felt remotely like pursuing another woman in the meantime. Sadie had been like a resident ghost. But she wasn't a ghost any more.

She said, 'I...ah...just wanted to say thank you...again.'

From behind her, Quin saw one of the staff send him a signal and he welcomed it. He said, 'We're about to take off. You should take a seat and buckle in.'

'Of course, yes.'

She looked around and chose a seat that put her facing away from Quin. That made him feel irritable—and then *that* made him feel even more irritable.

He buckled his own belt and focused on the plane taxiing and taking off into the night sky over New York—and *not* on the woman who was sitting just feet away. The same woman who had built him up only to tear him down and remind him that he'd been an utter idiot to believe in love or that trust could ever exist.

There were only two things he trusted in this world now: himself and his son. The sooner he knew what Sadie Ryan was up to, the sooner he could put her at a safe distance again.

CHAPTER THREE

SAO PAULO WAS full of tall, soaring buildings as far as the eye could see. They hadn't driven into the city itself. They were somewhere on the outskirts, on wide, leafy streets. As they'd stepped out of the plane a short while before, the early-morning sun had made the nearby city glimmer in the golden light.

A new day, a new dawn. Sadie had taken it as a sign of better days to come and clung on to that now.

Surely now she could start to rebuild her life? Make amends for what she'd had to do? Be a mother to her son…?

'You didn't sleep much on the plane. You could have gone into the bedroom.'

Sadie tensed at virtually the first words Quin had uttered since they'd taken off from New York. He'd noticed her restlessness. She'd been doing her best to try and ignore him and her awareness of him. He'd changed on the plane at some point—into khaki trousers and a short-sleeved white polo shirt. He looked dark and suave and ridiculously sexy, his clothes doing little to hide the powerful body underneath.

Sadie felt self-conscious. She knew she must look tired. And wan. A far cry from the golden tan she'd had the last time she'd known Quin…golden from practically living on the beach. They'd spent more time in the water than on land.

'I'm fine,' she said now. 'I'm not a great sleeper at the best of times.'

Although she knew that the truth of her restlessness had more to with Quin's proximity and the impending reunion with her son than with anything else.

'You slept fine when—' Quin stopped abruptly.

Sadie's heart thumped. 'When we were together?'

He didn't answer. He might want to pretend it hadn't happened…their relationship. But it had. They had a little boy as proof that once he'd loved her.

She said, 'I did sleep well with you.'

She blushed. When they'd actually slept. Usually around dawn, after spending hours exploring each other with a thoroughness that had left her wrung out and destroyed by pleasure. But it had been a beautiful destruction.

She'd felt so safe with Quin, in his arms. It had been a completely instinctive sense of well-being, as if as long as she was with him everything would be okay. No wonder her mind had been blank of the horrors—

'You used to have nightmares.'

Except for those. Her subconscious had provided images at night that she hadn't been able to understand, and it had only been when her memory returned that she'd realised the nightmares were based on reality. Her memory taunting her.

'I don't get them any more.'

Her reality had been enough of a nightmare for the last four years. Now her sleep was broken up with wondering if and how she'd get to see her son. And Quin. And now here she was. Moments away from meeting her son.

'Does he ever ask about me?' Sadie blurted out before she could stop herself.

Quin shot her a glance. 'He's only just started to recently. Since realising that he's the only one of his friends who doesn't have a mother.'

Sadie felt a little sick. 'What have you told him?'

'That you had to go away.'

Just that. So stark. No mention of the anguish and pain it had caused her to leave.

The car was slowing to a stop outside relatively inconspicuous-looking gates with lush greenery screening anything behind them from the road.

But Sadie could see the gates were tall and fortified. She also noticed the discreet security men just inside, as the gates swung open as if by magic to admit them.

The car proceeded up a long driveway, bordered on each side by thick vegetation, until suddenly they emerged into a vast open courtyard in front of a modern structure on different levels that somehow managed to blend in with the vegetation around it, as if it had been there for hundreds of years.

Lots of clean lines and glass—more glass than she'd ever seen on a building.

The car pulled to a stop, and before Sadie could prepare herself, the front door of the house opened and a blur of energy ran down the steps towards the car. Quin was out of the car, leaving the door open, and bending down with arms outstretched, ready to welcome his son.

His son. Their son. Her baby boy.

Sadie couldn't breathe. She couldn't move. She was frozen as she watched this tableau from inside the car.

Quin swung Sol up into his arms and she heard Sol saying ecstatically, 'Papa, you're home already! Lena said you wouldn't be back till later!'

'I wanted to surprise you.'

Shakily, Sadie somehow managed to get out of the car. The driver had opened her door. She stood up and could feel the sun beating down on her head. She looked across the roof of the car at her son and couldn't believe it. He was leaning back in Quin's arms now, grinning. He was all at once familiar and totally strange to her. Even though she could see he took after her with his strawberry blond colouring. He had her eyes. Light green-blue. But he had his father's darker-toned skin. Golden. He had freckles. And an impish smile.

As if feeling her avid gaze on him he turned his head and looked at her. He said, very baldly, 'Who are you?'

Who was she? She was a stranger. She was this little boy's mother. She was lost. She was drowning in a sea of emotions.

She opened her mouth. 'I—'

'She's a friend from work. She's come to help me with a project,' Quin interjected smoothly.

Sol seemed to take this with total equanimity. 'What's her name, Papa?'

Sadie didn't look at Quin. She could hardly take her eyes off her son.

Quin said, 'Her name is Sadie.'

Sol repeated it. 'Sadie… I don't know anyone with that name. That's cool.'

The little boy scrambled down out of Quin's arms and came to stand in front of Sadie. She wasn't sure how she was still standing when she couldn't feel her legs any more.

Sol looked up at her. She noticed he was wearing a T-shirt with a school logo and matching shorts. Scuffed sneakers. There was a scab on his knee. He was clearly active.

He said, 'Hey, do you want to see my bedroom? It's pretty cool. I've got posters of my favourite football players.'

Somehow Sadie found her voice through the blood rushing to her head at the enormity of this moment. 'You like football?'

He nodded. 'It's the best ever. When I get older I'm going to play for Sao Paulo.'

'You are? That's—'

'Come on, Sol, time to go to school. You'll see Sadie later.'

His eyes widened, mirror images of his mother's. 'You're *staying* here?'

Sadie dragged her gaze from her son to look at Quin helplessly. She hadn't even thought about what would happen when she got here. She had no money to pay for accommodation.

His expression was unreadable, and he just said to his son, 'Perhaps.'

And then an older woman appeared behind Quin, middle-aged, with a kind face and a shrewd gaze that went from Sol to Sadie.

Quin said, 'This is Madalena. Sol's nanny and my saviour.'

Sadie smiled weakly at the woman as Sol piped up with, 'But we call her Lena, 'cos it's shorter.'

Madalena came and shook Sadie's hand, smiling warmly. 'Welcome to Sao Paulo. Excuse us, but it's time for this young man to get to school.'

She took his hand and they walked away, Sol jumping beside the woman, unable to control his energy. When they'd got into a small car and driven down the driveway

Sadie almost sagged back against the bigger car, adrenalin draining down through her body. Quin was standing to the side, watching her carefully, hands in his pockets.

She shook her head. 'I don't know…what to say. He's beautiful…more beautiful than I could have imagined.'

'Yes, he is. He's turned out to be a happy, secure little boy…in spite of everything.'

Sadie absorbed the dig. She suddenly felt exhausted, the culmination of the last few days catching up with her.

'You look washed out.'

'Thanks,' Sadie said dryly.

'Come on, we'll get something to eat and then I'll show you where you can stay.'

'I am staying here?'

He looked at her. 'If you're sticking to your story of not having any money then I'm assuming you'll need a place to stay?'

There was no point trying to defend herself, so Sadie just said simply, 'I would appreciate that, yes.'

She followed Quin into the vast modern structure, eyes widening as she took in the open, airy spaces. Wood finishes softened the concrete walls and floors. Abstract art added splashes of colour, as did huge rugs with local designs. She caught glimpses of lush foliage all around them through the windows and a pristine green lawn in the distance.

Quin pointed out the dining room beside a massive open-plan kitchen where a man was working at the cooker. He greeted Quin with a smile and they exchanged a few words.

Quin turned to Sadie. 'This is Roberto, Madalena's husband. He's our chef. They both live just next door, through an adjoining garden.'

Sadie smiled shyly. 'Nice to meet you, Roberto.'

She'd spent so much time in the intervening years avoiding making much contact with people that it felt strange to be able to do this. The man was like his wife, his gaze friendly, but also shrewd. Sadie had the feeling it wouldn't take much for them to put two and two together.

Quin was striding onwards. Sadie had to hurry to keep up. Clearly he wasn't giving her this tour out of a sense of solicitousness. There was a sitting room off that area, and another one that could be closed off with sliding doors. There was a gym, and a vast home office.

Sadie asked, 'You work from home?'

'Sometimes, but I have an office in Sao Paulo. I employ close to a hundred people now and we're growing all the time.'

'That's really...cool,' she finished a little lamely, borrowing the word that Sol seemed to like using.

Quin was opening a massive sliding door that led off the open-plan space of the living area out to the garden. Sadie followed him. It was so tranquil. The only sounds were birds calling and the muted hiss of water sprinklers. There were portable goal posts set up—presumably for Sol to play football.

As she followed him down the lawn on strategically placed flagstones Quin said, 'The entire property is completely self-sustaining. We use solar panels and we have a well. We grow as much of our own produce as we can, and our housekeeper supplies a local homeless charity with the excess.'

Sadie's heart squeezed. They'd once talked for hours about how they would live sustainably, careful to consider the life of their unborn child. 'That's impressive.'

Quin glanced back at her. 'Sol is obsessed with the

planet and environment. His school is big into teaching them about sustainability.'

'Isn't four a little young for school?'

'It's a preschool class at the International School, until he's six. Then he'll be entering into the main curriculum.'

'Oh.' Sadie knew that Quin would not appreciate her opinion on how to school their child. Not after abandoning him.

Quin was disappearing down a path between the trees now, and Sadie followed him into a lush, quiet space where a separate building stood. It was in the same vein as the main house but smaller—lots of glass and wood and concrete, all on one level—yet it still managed to blend in with the background.

Quin said, 'This is our guest house. You can stay here.'

So she wasn't to be allowed in the familial space. Silly to feel hurt. But it was a reminder that when her memory had returned she'd realised just how alone she'd been all her life—first because of her parents' tragic premature deaths and then through years of a failed adoption and fostering.

No wonder she'd cleaved to Quin with such passion and blind trust. He'd been the first person to give her any sense of total security and *love*. A sense of home.

After the surfing accident Quin had offered to let her stay with him—the relative stranger who had saved her life. It had been nuts to say yes, but she'd known on some deep level that she could trust him.

Ostensibly it had been for practical reasons—the hospital had said they weren't going to release Sadie after the head trauma she'd suffered—and also because she'd lost her memory—unless she could be observed and cared for. There had been no friends rushing forward to offer to take care of her. Her mobile phone had been lost or stolen in the aftermath of the accident. She'd been on her own and vulnerable.

But by the time Sadie had fully recovered, there had been no question of her moving out. By then, she and Quin had embarked on a passionate love affair. All-consuming and life-changing.

She forced down the echoes of the past and moved forward to take in the sizeable property, hoping that her emotions wouldn't show on her face. 'This is more than generous, Quin.'

He was moving to the side of the property and Sadie followed him, even though it didn't seem as if he much cared if she did.

He stood at a break in the trees and pointed. 'The pool is through there, and the pool house is fully stocked with swimwear and robes, if you want to swim.'

Just looking at the pool made Sadie feel dusty and grimy. It was deliciously inviting, barely a ripple on the green-blue water as it glistened under the sun.

Quin was already moving back to the house, going up a couple of steps, opening the front door. He stood aside to let her pass him and his scent—hints of sea and leather and earth—made her want to close her eyes to breathe him in fully. She kept them wide open and held her breath.

This building was like a micro version of the main house—open spaces, flowing rooms. A massive bedroom suite with dressing room and bathroom. The bathroom had a shower area that was open to the elements, and a colourful bird flew past as Sadie looked up. It was whimsical and romantic.

She quickly diverted her attention back to Quin's whistlestop tour to crush such rogue notions.

There was a fully stocked kitchen, and a living area

that had a luxurious L-shaped couch and a massive TV, even a separate dining area. There was a utility room—the height of luxury to Sadie, who had been pretty much living out of her case and washing her clothes in laundromats for four years.

Again, there were colourful rugs and art to soften the stark modern lines. Sadie liked the style, she found it soothing.

Quin was talking. 'We have a housekeeper too—Sara. She's probably in town, shopping for supplies. She'll unpack your things when she returns.'

Sadie thought of her paltry belongings and said quickly, 'There's no need for that. I'll come and get my case.'

Quin shrugged. 'Suit yourself.' He glanced at his watch. 'We'll have something to eat and then I have to go into the office.'

He led the way back up to the main house through the garden, and Sadie once again hurried after him to keep up. A vivid memory assailed her of running to catch up with Quin on the beach in Sao Sebastiao, and how she'd jumped onto his back. He'd caught her legs under her knees. She'd wrapped her arms around his neck and kissed him, tasting the salt of the sea on his skin.

She stumbled on one of the flagstones, and was pitching forward with a small cry when Quin turned around and caught her.

She fell against him with a small *oof*.

An immediate wave of heat flushed through her entire body, bringing cells alive that had lain dormant for four years. Electricity hummed along her skin, raising the small hairs. Lust, immediate and raw, pooled in her belly.

She looked up, off-balance and helpless against the storm raging inside her at being so close to him. His eyes were unreadable, though. Two pools of dark obsidian. No chink of light. No forgiveness. Jaw tight. Nostrils flaring.

Before she knew what was happening Quin was putting her away from him with two strong hands on her arms and letting her go. Practically pushing her away. Showing his distaste for having any part of them touching.

Her face flamed. 'I'm sorry. I wasn't watching where I was going.'

He was already turning around and striding forward, saying, 'It's nothing. Don't worry about it.'

Sadie followed, and wondered if this man would ever look at her again the way he had on that beautiful day on the beach when they'd been married by a humanist celebrant. Joined by love and the baby growing in her belly. He'd looked at her as if she was the only precious thing in the world. She'd felt so loved…treasured. And she knew that she'd been looking at him the same way because he had been her world.

Still was.

No matter how she might wish otherwise, she'd never stopped loving him. How could she? He was the father of her child. He'd been her first lover.

It had been so perfect…and yet it had dissolved so easily. Yes, her transgression had been huge. Perhaps unforgivable, maybe even when he knew her reasons why.

All she could hope for was that when the dust had settled, and when they'd established an acceptable routine in which she could be part of her son's life on a permanent basis, one day Quin might not look at her with such abject loathing…

Quin picked up Sol from school that day, to give Lena a break, and all Sol could talk about on the drive back to the house was *Sadie*. It was unusual. Sol liked people, and wasn't shy, but he didn't usually fixate on someone like this. Clearly he'd sensed something about her.

The fact that when he'd stood in front of his mother earlier you'd have had to be blind not to have noticed the resemblance between them.

It had knocked the air out of Quin's lungs and then made his chest squeeze tight. He'd seen the narrow-eyed look in Lena's eye. Nothing got past that woman. Or Roberto. But they hadn't said anything. Yet.

Sol jumped out of the car now, when Quin came to a halt in the main courtyard, and ran into the house. Quin followed, feeling tense. Sol was in the kitchen, helping himself to the healthy snacks Roberto had left out for him—a little post-school ritual. Not for the first time Quin was endlessly grateful that he had such good support around him. Being a single parent was probably the hardest thing he'd ever done. And it had only compounded his anger at his mother for her abandonment.

And Sadie, for hers.

It had been the bitterest pill of all to swallow—the knowledge that he was subjecting his son to the same experience he'd had—growing up with no mother.

Sol spoke around the apple in his mouth and Quin put up a hand. 'Not with your mouth full, young man. Swallow and then speak.'

Sol did so, with such comic facial expressions that Quin had to bite his lip to stop himself from smiling.

As soon as he could speak, Sol said, 'Is Sadie gone?'

Quin felt a moment of trepidation. She might very well be gone. Maybe after she'd seen her son she had realised that actually, Quin's fortune notwithstanding, she didn't want to do this, and left again? Vanished into thin air.

There was such a mix of conflicting emotions at that idea that Quin said abruptly, 'Why don't you change out of your school clothes and put them in the laundry basket for Sara? If she has to pick them up from your floor again she said she's going to instruct Roberto to feed you nothing but zucchini for a whole week.'

Sol made a gagging sound—he hated zucchini—and ran to his room.

Quin put a hand through his hair. He went outside and looked towards the trees that shielded the guesthouse. He walked towards it, but as he did so memories rose up and threatened to swamp him. Memories of that fateful day when he'd returned to the little beach house where he and Sadie had lived together. He'd had days-old Sol in a harness, strapped to his chest. He'd taken him out for a walk to let Sadie get some rest after an early-morning feed.

When he'd returned to the house he'd been quiet, mindful of Sol sleeping against his chest, and also that Sadie might still be sleeping. But when he'd checked the bedroom, the bed had been empty.

Assuming she was in the bathroom, Quin had waited for a minute. But he'd heard nothing. Concern had grown and, imagining that something had happened, he'd called her name softly and opened the bathroom door—only to find that room empty too.

Maybe she'd gone to the beach?

Quin had gone out to the wraparound veranda and scanned the beach. No sign of Sadie. A sense of unease like nothing he'd ever experienced had crept along his skin. Somehow, he'd known in that moment that she was gone, and yet he hadn't admitted it to himself for some hours. Waiting. Feeding a fractious Sol with the expressed milk he'd found in the fridge.

It was only in the early afternoon that he'd found the note propped up against a mirror in the bedroom. The note that had struck him like a blow to the head, leaving him reeling.

Please believe me when I say I don't want to leave but I have to. Don't try to find me. Take care of Sol. I love you.

I love you. Quin let out a harsh sound. If that had been love then it had confirmed everything he'd been taught growing up. Love didn't exist. The only love he trusted now was the love he felt for his son.

Quin broke through the tree line and made his way to the guesthouse, telling himself that if Sadie had disappeared again she'd have done them all a huge favour. The fact that he was even feeling any kind of trepidation that she might be gone again irritated him intensely.

Sadie had finished unpacking her paltry belongings some time ago, after returning from lunch, during which Quin had mainly avoided her eye and said as little as possible.

She'd put a wash on—and it was embarrassing how much that had felt like such a treat. She'd explored the entirety of the guesthouse and been blown away again by its sheer opulence, albeit tastefully understated.

She'd showered and changed into soft, worn jeans and a clean T-shirt with short sleeves. She'd resisted the temptation to put her engagement-wedding ring back on her finger and instead had put it on a plain chain around her neck. She couldn't bear for it not to be touching her skin somewhere. It had become something of a talisman in the last four years, along with the picture of Quin holding Sol when he was a tiny baby.

She'd found a massive TV behind a sliding wooden door, along with a sound system. Books lined shelves—

thrillers, literary fiction, commercial fiction, non-fiction. Sadie's fingers had itched to pick up one of the books— she hadn't had the mental headspace to do something as relaxing as reading in years. Four years. When she'd been with Quin she'd read voraciously.

Now she was in the bedroom. It was like an oasis of calm, with dark polished wood and soft textiles. Earthen colours. The massive bed looked so inviting that Sadie had no choice but to kick off her shoes and crawl onto it, groaning a little at the way it cushioned her body. Weariness crept over her...a bone-deep weariness. She felt the adrenalin of the last twenty-four hours finally draining from her system.

She was about to close her eyes when she heard a sound, and looked up to see Quin standing in the doorway. Instantly any sense of peace vanished and adrenalin flooded her system again.

She sat up and scooted off the bed. 'Sorry, I was just—'

'You don't have to apologise,' Quin said tightly. 'This is your space, and while you're here you're our guest. I should have knocked.'

The way Quin had looked at her since they'd met again—with something veering between disgust and severe distrust—made her wonder how much control it was taking for him to be so civil. But she didn't want to give him any excuse to kick her off his property. Out of their lives.

'Thank you,' she said. 'I do really appreciate that you're letting me stay.'

'Sol was asking if you were still here.'

Sadie's chest tightened at the mention of her son. 'I'm not going anywhere.'

Quin glanced at his watch. 'We'll have supper in about an hour.'

'Okay.' Sadie watched Quin leave and disappear back into the trees.

She sat down on the end of the bed, deflating. Absurd to feel so hurt by Quin's coolness, especially after everything that had happened.

She was here now, and she was free to pursue a life with her son—that was all that mattered. Whatever bond she'd had with Quin was well and truly broken.

CHAPTER FOUR

QUIN DIDN'T LIKE the way it felt to hear Sadie's distinctively low-pitched voice mingling with Sol's more high-pitched excitable tone, both emanating from his bedroom, where Sol had demanded she come as soon as she'd appeared at the house a short while before.

It felt disturbing and arousing and a million things all at once.

He'd all but shut the door on Sadie ever being a part of their lives again. It was conflicting, inspiring too many things for him to unpick. But one stood out... The hum in his blood when he heard her now. The slow-burning lick of desire, coiling his insides tight.

It had been like that from the moment he'd seen her.

The first day he'd laid eyes on her would be seared onto his memory for ever, whether he liked it or not. He'd been living in Sao Sebastiao for a few months by then, and one day he'd noticed a young woman on the beach, in the water, surfing...or attempting to surf...inelegantly.

He'd been intrigued by her because she'd seemed to be by herself. No friends. Like him. He'd watched her attempt to catch waves, and fail, and then get up and try again. Her tenacity had impressed him.

As had her physicality. The slim, lithe limbs. Toned muscles. He'd been able to tell she was pretty, even from a distance, but he'd had no idea how pretty until he'd seen her up close a couple of days later.

She'd disappeared from the beach after that first sighting, he'd thought he wouldn't see her again, until he'd walked into the local barber shop and she'd greeted him.

As soon as their eyes had met he'd felt it like a surge of electricity, all the way through his body. And he'd realised, *She's not pretty...she's beautiful.* Those wide aquamarine eyes, that straight nose, wide mouth. Dark hair...darker than it was now. Framing her face and making her look pale, in spite of the sun-kissed glow and freckles.

She'd cut his hair and it had felt like a more intimate act than sex. He hadn't been able to take his eyes off her. Her hands were small and deft, nails short. Unvarnished. And, against every instinct within him that had always told him not to trust women, there was something about Sadie, uniquely, that had lodged under his skin from that first meeting and started to dismantle all those defences without him even noticing.

He'd asked her out. But she'd declined. Not meeting his eye. He'd come back and asked her out again the next day. She'd blushed, but declined again, looking genuinely conflicted.

It had been the following day when he'd seen her trying to surf again and had witnessed the accident. She'd disappeared under the water for too long. He could remember the sense of panic as he'd raced to find her and pull her out of the water, giving her mouth-to-mouth resuscitation. The blood had flowed from a gash on her head.

When the emergency crew had arrived they'd just assumed he knew her, and without even questioning it he'd accompanied her to the hospital. When she'd woken, she'd frowned at Quin and said in a cracked voice, 'Do I know you?'

He'd almost been insulted—he knew he'd made an impression on her—but then it had transpired very quickly that she didn't remember anything at all from before the moment of the accident. Not her name or where she came from. She spoke with an English accent. *He* knew her name and where she worked because they'd met at the barber shop. When no one had come looking for her, Quin had offered to be the one to watch over her for the first few days after she left the hospital.

She'd had to be supervised, in case of further after-effects from her head injury. But, apart from the memory loss and the nasty gash on her head, there had been no further injuries or trauma.

Quin had taken her to the barber shop, where they'd told her where she lived, and they'd gone there—a small, modest studio apartment a few blocks from the beach. There had been no identifying things there, like pictures. Her mobile phone was gone—lost or stolen. The number had been inactive when he'd tried calling it. They'd found her passport, listing her as Sadie Ryan, twenty years old, with no next of kin. Born in Dublin, Ireland.

This had confused Sadie, and she'd said, 'That doesn't sound right. I don't have an Irish accent…and I don't think I've ever been there.'

The doctor had warned Quin not to let her get stressed, so he'd told her not to worry about it too much and that he'd look into trying to trace her and her family. Then they'd packed up her things so she could stay with him, as his beach bungalow had two bedrooms.

While she'd slept in the spare room he'd looked her up online and found no trace of her. Nothing. No social media presence. No records. No one seemed to be looking for her. Odd... But then a modest-sized city on the coast of Brazil, more akin to a sleepy beach town, was full of such nomads. He should have known—he was one of them.

He'd offered to put her details online with a picture, to advertise that she was looking for relatives, but she'd had the oddest reaction—one of almost fear. She'd said that she couldn't explain why, but she didn't want him to do that. So he hadn't.

He'd put Sadie's reluctance to be found and lack of on-line presence and any obvious family down to something that she could worry about when she got her memory back. He'd been able to empathise with her wanting to escape from her family, if that was the case.

As the days had passed she'd recovered from her injury in every other way except for her memory. She'd never moved back into her studio apartment. Finding out about her past had become less and less of a priority.

She'd never left Quin's side during those early days of recuperation. They'd become entwined. They'd fallen in love. And the outside world had fallen away...

Sadie laughed now—a low chuckle, bringing Quin out of the past. He shook his head, angry with himself for letting those memories intrude. He hadn't loved her. It had been infatuation borne out of lust.

He walked to the door of Sol's room and stopped. Sadie was sitting cross-legged on the floor and looking up at Sol, who was standing on his bed, pointing to a poster of his current football hero. She was wearing jeans and a T-shirt and her hair was pulled up into a loose knot on her head, tendrils falling around her face. Quin was once again struck by her natural beauty.

Sol was saying, 'Someday I'm going to be even better than him!'

Sadie smiled. 'I saw the goal posts in the garden—you must practise a lot.'

Sol saw Quin and jumped off the bed. He came straight over, launching himself at his father, arms around his waist. 'My papa is the best—he's practising with me every day after school.'

Sadie got to her feet in a fluid motion. Quin's pulse throbbed. She'd always been so naturally graceful. Except when it came to surfing. She'd never fully mastered the art, and had been too impatient, no matter what Quin said to her.

More memories.

He shoved them aside and said, more brusquely than he had intended, 'Dinner is ready.'

He saw the way Sadie's smile faltered at his tone. But Sol didn't notice the chill in the air and let Quin go, skipping downstairs. Quin refused to let those huge eyes affect him. He turned away, but couldn't deny how acutely conscious he was of Sadie as she followed him down to the kitchen-diner.

Roberto had prepared a light meal of pasta and sauce with salad and bread.

Sol grabbed some bread and Quin said, 'Ah-ah—not so fast. Let's try and pretend we're a little more civilised, hmm?'

Sol put the bread back with a sheepish look at Sadie and sat down. Quin avoided looking at her. A part of him didn't want to see how she was reacting to being with her son. Because he didn't know how to deal with it yet. The most important thing was to keep her close, where he could be sure of knowing exactly what she was up to…

Once they were all seated, Quin handed Sol the bread and said, '*Now* you can eat.'

Sol fell on the food, demonstrating his ravenous appetite.

Sadie ate too, with the healthy appetite that Quin remembered, cleaning her plate.

He couldn't help observing, 'You still eat fast.'

Sadie looked at him, eyes wide, a faint flush stealing into her cheeks.

Sol was indignant. 'I eat the fastest in this house.'

Quin welcomed the distraction from looking at Sadie and remembering too much. His tone was dry. 'It's not a race.'

When he was finished, Sol emitted a barely concealed burp.

Quin said, 'Okay, that's enough, young man. Take your plate into the kitchen and have a piece of fruit for dessert. You can play one game, and then I'm coming to get you ready for bed.'

Sol jumped up, and then stopped and looked at Sadie. 'Will you still be here tomorrow?'

Sadie's eyes were huge. Mirror images of her son's. It was almost laughable how alike they were. She glanced at Quin and he had to clamp down on his body's response.

She looked at Sol. 'I think so. I'm hoping to stay for as long as you'll have me.'

'Cool! See you tomorrow! Do you know how to play football? I'll show you. Night!'

He disappeared up to his room in a blur of motion. Sadie looked at Quin. She seemed a little dazed.

Eventually she said, 'He's an amazing kid. You're a good father, Quin.'

'I had no choice.'

Her mouth tightened. 'Parents have a choice, no matter what the circumstances. You could have easily outsourced his care, but clearly you haven't. And Madalena seems to be almost like a grandmother to him.'

Quin made a snorting noise. 'There's no harm in that. He's never met his real grandmother.' He looked at Sadie. 'Either of them.'

She went pale. 'You know that I had no idea if I had any family or not…'

Quin arched a brow. *'Had?'*

He could see Sadie go even paler, visibly swallowing. 'Actually…that's what I need to talk to you about…to explain why—'

'Papa! The game isn't working! Can you make it work?'

Unnoticed, Sol had reappeared by the dining table and was holding up a console.

Quin cursed silently and stood up. He wasn't sure he'd ever be ready to hear why Sadie had left so precipitously, but he knew he had to. Maybe not right now, though.

He said to Sol, 'Go back upstairs. I'll come up in a minute.'

When Sol had left, he looked at Sadie. 'We can't talk about this now. I'll be busy getting Sol to bed in a bit, so help yourself to anything else you'd like from the kitchen. Lights will come on in the garden to guide you back to the guesthouse. I'll see you tomorrow.'

Sadie stood up and picked up her plate and Quin's, but he said, 'Leave them. Roberto will clean up in the morning. Sara would normally be here, but she's out of action.'

She put the plates back down. 'Your housekeeper? Did something happen?'

'She was involved in an accident today and she'll be out of work for a week. It shouldn't inconvenience you too much.'

Sadie looked genuinely concerned. 'That's awful…is she okay?'

Quin didn't like this reminder of Sadie's compassionate

nature. Because it had obviously been false. No genuinely compassionate person could walk away from their baby. Or the man they'd professed to love.

He said, 'Her car was totalled but she's okay—just shaken. I gave her a week off to recover...'

Sadie gestured to the plates. 'I'll do this. I don't mind—honestly. And I can do whatever else she was meant to be doing. It'll give me a way to say thank you...for letting me be here.'

Quin felt a strong sense of rejection at the thought of Sadie doing his domestic chores—but then this wasn't a regular situation. And there was also a little devil inside him that relished the thought of calling her bluff, to see if she really meant it. He had to admit, the notion of her doing menial work as some sort of recompense wasn't altogether undesirable. The rage inside him that still burned bright for what she'd done demanded to be appeased.

But he said, 'Are you sure? There's no need. Between me, Roberto and Lena we can manage.'

Sadie shook her head. 'I'm sure they're busy enough. I insist—it's the least I can do.'

Quin shrugged. 'Suit yourself. Roberto will fill you in on Sara's duties when he comes in tomorrow. Good-night, Sadie.'

'Are you sure this is okay?'

Lena was looking at Sadie with concern in her eyes. But Sadie couldn't have been more sure that she wanted to keep herself busy. What else was she going to do in her lush isolation among the trees?

She nodded. 'Honestly, it's fine. I'd like to help out.'

Lena obviously wasn't convinced. 'But you're—'

She stopped, clearly not wanting to state the obvious.

Yet. The fact that Sadie was Sol's mother, who had re-appeared after four years of abandonment. That, as his mother, she shouldn't be working like an employee.

Sadie forced a smile. 'I'm happy to be here. And happy to be of use.'

Lena finally gave in and pushed a Tupperware box to-wards Sadie. 'You can pack up Sol's lunch, then, if that's okay? And I'll make sure he's getting dressed.' She rolled her eyes, 'He's probably playing one of his games...'

Sadie's heart squeezed as the woman left the kitchen. That should be *her* job—chasing Sol to get ready for school. But she didn't have that privilege yet. Would she ever?

The way Quin had looked at her last night did not bode well. He'd tolerated her presence and that had been about it. She supposed she should be glad that he was even al-lowing her to come and eat with them. Not confining her to the guesthouse.

She'd come up to the house early this morning, hoping that she might get to continue her aborted conversation with Quin. Give him the explanation of why she'd left. But she'd found Roberto clearing up after breakfast. He'd told her that Quin was in the home office, making calls, and that Sol was getting ready for school. He'd looked at her quizzically when she'd told him she was going to fill in for Sara, but he'd said nothing—just told her that he'd go over her duties once Sol had left for school. Then he'd insisted on her having breakfast, and had made her a de-licious plate of scrambled eggs, ham and chives.

Sadie felt pathetically grateful that Roberto and Lena didn't seem to be judging her for her absence.

She'd just closed the lid on the Tupperware lunchbox when Sol appeared in front of her, as if conjured out of her imagination. He looked smart in his shorts and school T-shirt. Hair smoothed.

He smiled. 'You're still here.'

Her heart squeezed again. 'Yes.'

He touched a tooth in his mouth. 'I have a loose tooth.'

Sadie came around the table and bent down. She could see it wobble. 'If it comes out you'll have to leave it under your pillow for the tooth fairy.'

Sol frowned. 'What's a tooth fairy? We leave it out for the bird, and the bird leaves a gift. Your tooth has to be really clean, so I cleaned extra-hard today, but it still didn't come out.'

Sadie bit back a smile and stood up. 'Ah…where I came from the tooth fairy takes the tooth from under your pillow and leaves a surprise, but I like the sound of a special bird.'

'Where *did* you come from?'

That question hadn't come from Sol. It had come from someone much more adult.

Sadie looked up to see Quin. She couldn't find her breath for a moment…he was so stupendously gorgeous. Clean-shaven. Hair still damp from the shower. Dressed in a shirt open at the neck, sleeves rolled up. Faded jeans.

It had only been around thirty-six hours since they'd met again, and yet it felt all at once like years and no time at all. Apart from that reference to a grandmother last night, Quin hadn't yet mentioned her memory loss, or asked about it, but was he ready to hear what she had to say now? Was *she* ready?

'Don't you know where Sadie comes from, Papa?'

But Quin didn't look at Sol. Sadie swallowed. Did he really want to do this here? Now? In front of their son?

She was about to answer, but then Quin broke the intense eye contact and said, 'We'd better get moving, Sol. I'm going to drop you to school today.'

'Yay! I'll get my bag.'

'See you out front in five minutes.'

Sol disappeared again, and now it was just Quin and Sadie. He arched a brow. Clearly waiting for an answer.

Sadie said in a husky voice, 'I was born and brought up in England, just outside London.'

Something flashed across his face. 'So your memory came back…or was it ever really gone?'

Sadie gulped. She'd never considered that he might doubt she'd really lost her memory. 'Yes, it came back.'

'So, you're not Irish, then?'

'Well…my father was Irish. But I never lived there.'

'But you had an Irish passport?'

Yes, she had. But she hadn't grown up with an Irish passport. She'd actually grown up with *no* passport. She'd only got her first passport to come to Brazil.

She opened her mouth again but Sol reappeared, trailing a small bag. 'Okay, Papa, I'm ready.'

Quin's jaw clenched. But then he said, 'Okay, let's go.' And then to Sadie he said, 'Lena and Roberto will show you the ropes. I'll be out at a function later, and Sol is going to a sleepover, so we'll see you tomorrow.'

Sol was already running out through the door. 'Bye, Sadie!'

Sadie said a very faint 'Bye…' as she watched them leave, feeling all at once frustrated and relieved that her attempt to explain everything to Quin had been interrupted again.

Later that night Quin was not in a good mood as he took a swig of alcohol from the thick crystal tumbler in his hand. He was staring out through the massive glass wall of his living area, down to where he could just make out the guesthouse, illuminated through the trees.

He'd just endured a function in central Sao Paulo where all the women seemed to have made it a national sport to get his attention. His mouth tightened cynically. Amazing what becoming a billionaire could do for your eligibility.

Not that he'd ever *not* been eligible, he had to concede, with no sense of hubris.

He'd been distracted all evening—and not just by the women seeking his attention. He'd been distracted because he hadn't been able to get one woman out of his head. The woman who had haunted him for four years. The woman who was no longer a ghost but very much alive and breathing—and existing mere metres from where he stood now.

That night in New York he'd finally been ready to cut her ghost and her memory loose. To get on with his life, take a lover… Only for her to appear in the flesh, thwarting him and setting him back. Four years.

He'd just had a conversation with Lena, who'd told him, 'She knows her way around cleaning a house and doing laundry—that much is obvious. But, Quin—'

Before she'd been able to say anything more—like demanding to know what the hell was going on with this woman who had just appeared and who looked ridiculously like Sol—he'd terminated the conversation and she'd left to go back to her own house.

He didn't like it that his conscience was prickling with the knowledge that he was keeping something huge from the two people who had been more of a family to him than his own family, and the fact that the mother of his child had been doing menial chores around his house.

It all mixed together with the residual anger, hurt, confusion, distrust…and *lust*…to make a volatile mix.

He swallowed the rest of the drink and took off his bow tie. He opened his top button, feeling constricted. Restless. He could keep drinking and brooding, or he could go and confront the woman who was lodged in his side like a burr.

He pulled off his jacket, dropped it on a chair, then pulled back the glass door and went outside. The air was warm. Soft. When he felt hard. Prickly.

He walked down through the garden, and as he came closer to the trees and the guesthouse he could hear the soft strains of familiar music. But not that familiar… He hadn't heard it in four years.

He came to a stop in the trees as the sensual voice of a well-known Brazilian jazz singer washed over him. For a crazy second he wondered if he was losing his mind. Had he hallucinated Sadie back into his life and now he was hearing things? She'd loved this artist and had used to play her all the time. She'd given birth to Sol with this music in the background.

He kept moving forward until he could see the house. Low lights were on, but he couldn't see any sign of Sadie. He walked around and saw the front door was open. The music was louder now.

He walked inside and could smell her scent. Not a ghost, then. He went over to the sound system in the den area and pressed the *off* button. Silence enclosed him.

Then from behind him a voice said, 'You used to say that I played her too much.'

Quin turned around and the blood rushed straight to his head. Sadie was standing before him in a short, belted robe. Long bare legs. Pale. Hair damp and falling in golden-red skeins around her shoulders.

He dimly realised she must have been swimming, just

as she gestured with her hand behind her and said, 'I hope you don't mind… I had a swim.'

He shook his head, but everything had turned fuzzy. He couldn't take his eyes off her. Off the vee of skin exposed by the robe…the hint of plump cleavage.

Blood thundered through his veins. It had been so long. She'd tortured him for four years with X-rated dreams that had left him aching and frustrated. He'd been tortured by endless questions. *Why? Why? Why? Why? Why? Why?* Yet now she was here in front of him, and he could actually ask her *why*, Quin perversely didn't want to know. It was as if he'd intuited that once he knew *why* he would no longer have anything to hold on to.

The hatred. The justifiable anger. The pain. *The loss.*

He moved towards her as if pulled by a magnetic force. He couldn't *not*. She looked at him, eyes wide. That mesmerising shade of blue and green. Depths he'd drowned in. But no more. There would be no drowning this time.

She spoke. 'Quin…we should talk. Maybe now is good because Sol is away tonight. We have time—'

Quin put his hands on her arms and the words stopped. Good. He didn't want words. Except to say, 'I don't want to talk right now. All I want is *this*.'

He pulled her into his body, where she fitted like a missing jigsaw piece, slotting into place against him. He lowered his head and took a breath as he closed his eyes and slanted his mouth over hers, and everything inside him turned to heat and fire and longing and an almost unbearable demand for satisfaction. It had been so long…and he'd never stopped wanting her.

Any recrimination he might have felt for giving in to this weakness was burnt to ashes in the conflagration of their kiss.

CHAPTER FIVE

SADIE WAS RIGID against Quin for a long moment. It was the shock of being in his arms again after so long. The shock of his mouth on hers…all at once familiar and utterly new. But the shock was fast dissolving under his touch, being replaced with a desire and a hunger so deep and ravenous that within seconds she was pressing closer, twining her arms around his neck and stretching up as much as she could, so she could meet his kiss with a desperation that clawed up from the centre of her body and spread out to every limb, making her shake with it.

They ceased to be bodies. They were heat and need and intense burning desire. Quin's hands were on her robe, undoing the belt, pushing it off her shoulders so it fell to the floor. His fingers were under her swimsuit straps, pushing them off and down, then the wet material was being peeled from her body to fall to the floor.

He broke the kiss and pulled back, stood up straight.

Sadie was unselfconscious in her nakedness—she needed Quin too much. His dark gaze feasted on her flesh, taking in every dip and hollow. She was filled with urgency and reached for him, undoing the buttons on his shirt, breath fast, panicky with need, in case this moment somehow dissolved and she lost him again.

You didn't lose him...you walked away, reminded a little voice.

Sadie ignored it. Clearly Quin was not ready to hear what she had to say, and maybe she still wasn't ready to tell him either. There was so much unspoken between them and maybe this was the only way to defuse it. Then maybe they could talk like rational adults.

Quin was naked now. Sadie wasn't aware of having removed his trousers and underwear. Maybe he had. But she didn't care. She felt as if she could finally breathe again.

She reached out and touched his chest, putting her hands to his warm skin. Her fingers trapped his nipples, the light dusting of hair over his pectorals. Her gaze took in the lean muscles of his stomach and down, to narrow hips and the place where he was magnificent and proud. *Hard* for her.

She wrapped a hand around him and heard his indrawn breath. She looked up and felt dizzy. His face was stark with the same need that was coursing through her own blood.

He took her hand off him and said, 'No time. I need you now.'

He took Sadie's hand and she let herself be led into the bedroom. Quin let her go for a moment, disappearing into the bathroom. Sadie sat down on the bed, her legs weak. She was trembling all over. She couldn't believe this was happening. Was it a dream?

Quin reappeared, his tall, muscular body gleaming like burnished bronze in the low lights. He'd always been supremely at ease naked. That was helped by the fact that he was more beautiful than any man could be, but also because he had an innate confidence that Sadie had always envied.

Now she knew it came from being brought up as a member of one America's most venerated families. Something he'd kept from her. Her guts twisted. They had so much to discuss… But, weakly, she pushed it all aside and watched as Quin rolled a protective sheath onto his erection.

She hadn't known there was protection in the bathroom. Did he use this house when he brought lovers over? That had to be it. To keep his home and personal life separate. A little knife lodged in her heart as she thought of him taking lovers here, but of course she had no right to be hurt. Not after what she'd done.

Then Quin stood before her and every thought went out of her head.

He said, 'Move back on the bed.'

Sadie somehow managed to get her limbs to move. She lay back and watched as Quin came over her, muscles rippling. She remembered how it had always been between them. So intense. She quivered inwardly. Was she ready for this again? She'd never be ready… But she knew she needed it like she needed oxygen. To keep breathing. To stay alive.

Quin looked at her, and she felt the flush of blood rising to her skin under his gaze.

He said roughly, 'You haven't changed.'

Sadie would have refuted that if she'd been able to speak. She felt like a different person. She'd broken inside when she'd had to walk away from Quin and Sol, and she didn't know if those jagged pieces would ever heal. But he wouldn't want to hear that.

'You haven't changed either,' she said, feeling shy for a second.

His gaze met hers and she almost gasped at the swirling vortex of emotion she glimpsed before he lowered his lids and masked his eyes from her. Maybe he had changed too. Although, as much as he'd told her he loved her *before*, she couldn't imagine that he'd loved her more than she had him. And that love had certainly died with her disappearance.

He rested on his hands over her, his body long and sleek. Jaw stubbled. Mouth tempting. To stop any more thoughts intruding, and robbing her of this moment, Sadie reached up for him. 'Please, Quin. I need you.'

He hesitated for a moment, and Sadie had a few seconds of blood-curdling fear that he'd planned on bringing her to the brink like this only to humiliate her at the last moment. The old Quin she'd known wouldn't have ever done anything so cruel, but this man was not the same. Physically, maybe, but in every other way not the same.

But he put an arm under her back, arching her up to him. Sadie widened her legs around him, tacitly telling him what she wanted. She bit her lip. And then before she could take another breath Quin was sliding into her.

She gasped at the sensation. She'd forgotten what it was like...and yet she'd forgotten nothing. He was stretching her wide, and it had been four years, so it bordered on being painful.

Quin stopped. 'Sadie?'

But she could already feel the way her body was accommodating him, relearning his shape, accepting him.

Breathless, she said, 'It's fine... I'm fine. Don't stop... *please.*'

Slowly he started to move...in and out. An age-old dance. He was the only man she'd ever slept with, and she had to bury her head in Quin's shoulder for a moment, in case he saw the emotion bubbling upwards at the realisation that she wanted him to be the only man she ever slept with. Forever.

But that was a dream she had no right to now.

All she had was this present moment.

Mercifully, the sensations in her body were eclipsing the emotion as their movements became faster, more hungry.

Sweat slicked their skin. Desperation clawed at Sadie's insides as the shimmering peak of ecstasy appeared on the horizon, her body quickening and tightening in anticipation.

She vaguely heard Quin mutter something under his breath—some kind of curse… Maybe because he wanted to eke out this moment but couldn't. Sadie could well imagine that Quin would relish torturing her as long as possible.

But the frenzy was upon them, and Sadie knew from previous experience that all she could do was surrender to it and let it sweep her away.

And that was exactly what happened. Quin thrust so deep that Sadie arched her back and wrapped her legs and arms around him, breaking apart all over and splintering into a million shards of pleasure.

She clung on for dear life as she felt Quin's big body jerk against hers as he found his own release, before he slumped over her, his face buried in her neck.

In that moment, Sadie felt the first measure of peace she'd had in four years.

When Sadie woke, she felt as if she was climbing up through several layers of sleep. She cracked open her eyes and squinted a little at the bright sunlight. She took in her surroundings—the spacious room, lots of glass, teak.

The guesthouse. Quin.

Instantly she was wide awake and registering that she was alone.

She sat up, holding the sheet to her chest. The bed was very rumpled but there was no dent in the pillow beside her, so Quin obviously hadn't gone to sleep here.

It all came rushing back. She'd taken a swim and had come back into the house to see Quin standing in the room. He'd switched off the music.

Music that had made her feel emotional as she heard it again, transporting her back to those halcyon days in Sao Sebastiao in their little beach hut, so wrapped up in each other that the outside world had gone unnoticed.

The music that Sol had been born to at exactly the same moment her head had been filled with restored memories and images and a horrific realisation. Two profound things happening at once.

Obviously she'd had to prioritise devoting all her energy into giving birth, ensuring her baby's safe passage into a world that was suddenly not a benign place any more. But from that moment on she'd been on borrowed time.

Sadie shook her head to free it of the past. She was here now. With her son. Well, not exactly *with* him, but in his world. And last night had just been a conflagration of the tension between her and Quin. Not helpful to their situation. Quite possibly he would resent her for this. Maybe he would see it as a weakness—giving in to the chemistry that was still between them.

If emotion had been involved on Quin's side Sadie was sure it wasn't any positive emotion. For her, though, it had been incredibly overwhelming, reminding her of the pull she'd felt as soon as she'd met him face to face for the first time.

Although, as she well knew, she'd felt that pull after spotting him on the porch of his house on the beach a couple of days before that. He'd been a solitary figure. Like her. Tall, compelling. Beautiful. But she'd done her best not to look him, to pretend that he hadn't caught her eye. Because she hadn't been able to afford to make connections with anyone. It was too dangerous.

But then he'd walked into the little barber shop where she'd worked, and she'd had nowhere to hide nor time to pretend she hadn't seen him. Within minutes she'd had his head in her hands. Running her fingers through his hair. Trying her best to avoid those dark, mesmerising eyes in the mirror. That sculpted mouth that had made her press her thighs together to stem the heat rising deep in her core.

He'd asked her out and her heart had leapt. For the first time she'd resented her life. She'd wished she could say *yes*, even though the thought had terrified her because he was so intimidatingly gorgeous and sexy. In any case, she hadn't had a choice. She'd had to say no.

The next day he'd reappeared and asked her out again. She'd said no again, even more regretful.

And then the next thing she remembered was waking in hospital after the surfing accident…with nothing but a persistent fog in her head.

After that they'd never been apart again—until the moment she'd walked away. Out of his and her son's lives.

Sadie got out of the bed and pulled on a robe. Between her legs she felt tender. She blushed. Ridiculous. She took a shower and noticed the places on her body and skin where Quin's stubble had made it red, or where he'd squeezed her flesh.

She turned the shower to cold for a second, hoping to shock some sense back into her brain. Last night had meant nothing. Only that the desire between them was as strong as ever. Except…

Sadie shivered a little as she turned off the water. Maybe last night was all Quin had needed to exorcise her from his system.

When Quin returned from work later that day he wasn't prepared for the sight before him on the lawn. Sadie, in jeans and a T-shirt, battered sneakers, her hair pulled up, was playing football with Sol. She might have passed for a teenager if it hadn't been for her womanly curves.

He'd walked out of the guesthouse as dawn had broken that morning, telling himself that he wouldn't touch Sadie again. It had been a moment of madness. A build-up of four years of frustration and pain and anger.

He'd hoped that maybe now he'd feel some kind of peace.

But far from feeling any measure of peace, he'd been tormented by her all day. He'd kept having flashbacks to seeing her naked for the first time in four years. The way it had felt to slide into her body...the moment when she'd looked at him with wide eyes, reminding him of how she'd looked at him when they'd first made love because she'd been a virgin.

A question had buzzed in his head all day. Had she looked at him like that, had her body been so tight, because she hadn't slept with anyone in four years? Since him?

He hated it that he even cared.

Sadie expertly deflected the ball from Sol. Quin realised she was good. Sol was in heaven with such a worthy adversary, trying to get the ball back, and Quin could see the exact moment when she feigned missing it so that Sol could get it and shoot for the goal. He jumped up and down with glee and Sadie caught him around the waist and lifted him up. The two heads were close together, strawberry-blonde.

And suddenly it was too much—last night and now this.

Quin called out from the open door, 'Sol, time to clean up for dinner.'

Sadie turned around with Sol still in her arms and the two sets of aquamarine eyes hit him like a sledgehammer to the gut, compounding the sense of exposure he felt at having indulged in his lust for Sadie last night. And the way she'd dominated his thoughts all day.

He still didn't even know what her agenda was. Or why she'd walked out four years ago.

You didn't give her a chance to talk last night, reminded a little voice.

It made him call out again with uncharacteristic sharpness, 'Sol, *now*. I won't ask again.'

Sol slid down from Sadie's arms and came inside, looking at Quin warily, making him feel about two inches tall. He rarely, if ever, spoke harshly to his son.

He looked at Sadie and felt the impulse to blame her— but that wasn't fair either, in spite of everything.

She said, 'Sorry, that was probably my fault. I didn't realise how much time had passed.'

She had dirt on the knees of her jeans, and Quin could see a streak across one cheek. He couldn't imagine any of the kind of women he met now allowing themselves to get so dishevelled. But Sadie had never been concerned with her appearance—except for that weird habit she'd had, insisting on dyeing her hair once a month.

He'd asked her once, 'Why do you bother?'

If anything, it had only made her look more pale, and there was no reason to do it that he'd been able to understand.

She'd said, 'It's the weirdest thing, and I can't explain it, but I feel safer if I do it…'

Because of her memory loss they'd both put things like this down to quirks that might one day be explained.

He pushed the past back and said, 'It's fine.' And then, 'You should probably wash too…before dinner.'

Sadie put a hand to her face and blushed. She still blushed.

She said, 'Of course. But I just need to finish a couple of jobs first.'

She'd walked by Quin into the house before he could stop her, trailing her tantalising scent behind her—earth and roses and citrus. Clean, innocent...

Irritation and frustration prickled over and under Quin's skin at so many different things that before he could expose himself any more he set off to check on Sol—who was his priority above anything else. Or any*one* else. Especially her.

Sadie was left in no doubt that Quin deeply regretted what had happened the previous night. The look he'd given her when he'd found her playing football with Sol had almost cut her in half.

Maybe she shouldn't have indulged in playing with her son, but when he'd come home from school with Lena he'd asked if she could play football with him. She'd explained regretfully that she still had some housework to do, but Lena had pooh-poohed that and told Sol to get changed into his kit.

Sadie couldn't feel sorry, though, because the last couple of hours had healed so much of the hurt and pain she'd endured. Her little boy was a joy. Sunny and mischievous and kind and funny. More than she'd even imagined he could be. Talking non-stop, endlessly curious...

Now Sadie quickly finished up what she'd been doing—sorting clothes in the laundry—and went back out to the main living-dining area, steeling herself in case she bumped into Quin and his disapproving expression again.

But Roberto was there, smiling. 'Dinner will be ready in a short while.'

Sadie's heartstrings were plucked. She'd love to spend

more time with Sol, but she knew when she wasn't welcome. Sol had been away last night, and no doubt Quin would want to have him to himself.

She forced a smile. 'Thank you so much, but I'll eat in the guesthouse this evening.'

Roberto remonstrated with her, but Sadie insisted. However, he wouldn't let her go without giving her a portion of his stew in a Tupperware container. Sadie took it, touched again by his and Lena's kindness.

Before Sol had come back down earlier, still in his football kit, Sadie had said, 'I hope I'm not intruding too much on your routine with Sol?'

The older woman had shaken her head. 'Not at all. It's good you are here.'

Sadie had bitten her lip, and then blurted out, 'Thank you...you have no idea how much that means to me.'

Lena had taken Sadie's hand in hers and said, 'Some women are capable of walking away from a child, but I don't think you are. I'm sure you had a good reason to do what you did.'

Surprise at hearing her confirm that she did know that she was Sol's mother and at her words had taken Sadie's breath, and by the time she'd felt remotely able to respond Sol had returned and Lena had disappeared with a small wink.

Sadie said, 'Thank you,' again to Roberto, and left the house, walking back down through the garden to the guesthouse. She'd only been here for a couple of days, but the place already felt more like home than anywhere else she'd been.

Except for Sao Sebastiao.

Her and Quin's beach paradise.

She'd never wanted to leave. She hadn't even wanted

to go into Sao Paulo to give birth. But Quin had insisted, strangely paranoid about the risks of childbirth.

It was only in the last four years that Sadie had realised that maybe on some level, in spite of her memory loss, she'd known that it would be inherently dangerous to go out of their cocooned existence at the beach and into a big city. Maybe going into the city had been the thing that had precipitated her memory return, and then Sol's birth had brought it back completely?

She was inside the guesthouse now, and she set up a place for herself at the dining table and tried not to look towards the trees, where the lights of the big house were just visible. She'd spent too many days and evenings walking around towns and cities in the last four years, glimpsing scenes of families together, and she wasn't going to allow herself to wallow in that self-pity again. She was free, and she was here—near to her son.

She pushed down the rising panic at the thought that she might always exist like this, on the margins of their lives. It was enough. It would have to be.

But a couple of hours later Sadie couldn't settle. She'd tried watching TV, but couldn't understand Portuguese. She'd tried reading, but had thrown the book down when she'd realised she'd read the same paragraph ten times without understanding a word.

It was rising within her. The need to tell Quin what had happened. He had to know. *Now.* The lights were still on in the house, visible through the trees. Yet she felt reluctant to go up there—especially as Quin hadn't appeared to invite her to join them.

Or to make love to you again, whispered a little voice. Sadie cursed herself. That had been an incendiary moment, borne out of their tangled past and chemistry. An anomaly.

But in spite of her reluctance and misgivings, she pulled a light cardigan over her T-shirt and left the guesthouse.

All was quiet when she reached the house. No sign of anyone. She guessed Roberto and Lena would have gone home. Sol must be in bed. Maybe Quin was in bed too?

But then she heard a noise coming from the area where his office was situated and followed the sound. The door was partially open and light spilled out. Her heart thumped. She curbed the urge to turn and run. It was time to do this.

She knocked lightly on the door.

Quin's voice came. 'Sol? I told you that it's too late for—'

The words stopped when he opened the door and saw Sadie.

'Not Sol. It's me.'

He just looked at her for a long moment. 'Why didn't you come to dinner?'

She pushed aside the lingering feeling of loneliness. It was ridiculous, *she'd* made that decision to eat alone. In four years she'd not succumbed to self—pity and she wasn't about to start.

'I thought you'd appreciate time with Sol because he was away last night.'

And they'd made love. Heat threatened to rise at the memory. But then Sadie went cold inside as she wondered if she was so desperate for him to touch her again that *this* was the reason she'd come up here looking for him, not because she wanted to unburden herself about why she'd left.

He said, 'You would have been welcome.' Then he frowned. 'Is everything okay?'

Sadie swallowed. Whatever her reasons for coming

here, there was only one thing she really needed to do right now. 'I think we need to talk about what happened.'

Quin's expression turned to stone. 'That was a mistake. It won't happen again.'

Now Sadie frowned, confused. And then she realised what he was referring to. Last night. The recent past— not *the* past. A pain lanced her heart. Well, if she'd been in any doubt about how he felt about it, she wasn't now.

Feeling defensive, she said, 'You came to me.'

'I'm aware of that. Put it down to a certain level of frustration.'

Charming. He'd only slept with her because she'd been convenient, in spite of all of their baggage.

Forgetting momentarily why she'd come, Sadie said, 'So does that mean you haven't had any lovers?'

He looked at her. 'I told you I wasn't with anyone.'

A little rogue devil inside Sadie somersaulted. Maybe if he hadn't been with anyone then he didn't despise her as much as he wanted her to believe. 'I wasn't sure if that meant lovers or a relationship.'

'Like I said, I don't have much time to focus on a personal life.'

Sadie realised they'd got way off track. She shook her head. 'That's not what I came to talk to you about. You misunderstood me.'

'What *did* you come to talk about?'

She steeled herself. 'I think now is as good a time as any to tell you why I left.'

For a long moment Quin said nothing. She half expected him to say it was too late.

But then he stood back to admit her into the office and said, 'I guess it is.'

Nerves assailed Sadie as she walked into the large room,

but she couldn't back out now. She hadn't taken in all that much detail in when she'd seen the room before, but now she noticed the hardwood floors softened by colourful rugs. Floor-to-ceiling shelves groaned with books. There was a huge desk and a plethora of computers and devices. Touchingly, in one corner there was a kiddie-sized table and chair—evidence of Quin having Sol close by while he was working. Making him feel included.

Quin walked around to the other side of his desk and folded his arms and looked at her. 'Go on, Sadie, I'm all ears.'

He wasn't making this easy. Needing some courage in the face of his lack of emotion, not to mention his rejection of what had happened the previous night, she asked, 'Do you have anything to drink in here?'

Quin unlocked his arms. 'That's not a bad idea.'

As she watched, he went over to a cabinet in the corner of the room, and she saw him open a bottle and pour dark golden liquid into two small glasses. He came back and handed her one.

He lifted his glass and said, 'Cheers,' then downed his drink in one.

Sadie echoed his *'cheers'* faintly, and did the same as him, wincing as the bitter liquid burned its way down her throat and into her belly. But it had an effect, sending out a warming glow that automatically made her feel less…edgy.

'You never did like hard spirits much,' he observed.

He remembered.

How much else did he remember? Would he ever just remember the good times?

Quin took the glass out of her hand and said, 'Another?'

Sadie shook her head. 'No, that's enough.'

He put the glasses back and turned around again, folding his arms. 'Well?'

It was unbelievably daunting, having to launch into explaining everything while Quin exuded such remoteness.

'Can you...not look at me like that, please?'

'Like what?'

Like we weren't making love just twenty-four hours ago.

Sadie shook her head. 'Nothing. It's just...a lot to tell you. And I'm nervous. Can we sit down, or something?'

'Of course.'

Quin felt so tense he thought he might crack. He had to consciously breathe and relax his muscles, but it was hard when all he could do was look at Sadie and want her. In spite of what he'd just told her.

'It won't happen again.'

His brain might have formulated those words but his body did not agree. His blood was hot and heavy in his veins. And his groin.

She looked incredibly fragile right now. Pale. She'd changed into soft, worn sweat pants and another non-descript T-shirt, with a cardigan pulled across her chest. Her hair was still messy from earlier. But she was no less alluring than she'd been last night, when they'd come together like two starving people in the desert finding water.

When she hadn't come for dinner he'd told himself it was a good thing. Since she'd reappeared in their lives he hadn't felt fully in control. He'd been behaving instinctively. Reacting. The previous night was proof of that.

So he'd ignored the urge to go and get her, and had told Sol she needed to have some time for herself. He had done his best not to notice his son's disappointment. But he'd been conscious of the guesthouse lights through the trees.

He'd had to shut himself away in his office after he'd put Sol to bed, because the urge to go to her again had been so strong.

And even now, when she was about to tell him why she had walked out of their lives, he still couldn't focus fully. Damn her.

He forced his blood to cool and said, with as much civility as he could, 'Please, sit down.'

He pulled out a chair and Sadie sat, stiff. She was obviously as tense as him. He forced himself to sit too, on a chair near her, and rejected an urge he had to tug her onto his lap and feel her close to him, to reassure her that she could tell him anything.

This was why he couldn't touch her again. It clouded his brain. And he needed to be very clear now, when she was about to tell him why she'd walked out on her newborn baby and him. As far as Quin was concerned there was no reason on earth that could justify why she'd done that.

'Can you stop glaring at me? This is hard enough.'

Quin cursed silently and forced himself to relax. She was clasping and unclasping her hands. She was nervous. She was avoiding his eye now.

'Look, what I'm going to tell you is going to be a lot to take in and it's going to sound…ridiculous.'

She looked at him, and Quin's insides clenched at the sight of those amazing eyes.

'But it's all true. I promise you.'

The only true thing Quin knew in that moment was that, no matter what lurid tale fell out of this woman's mouth now, he would never trust her again.

He sat back and forced his tense limbs to relax. 'Go on, please.'

CHAPTER SIX

NOW SADIE COULDN'T sit still. She stood up and started to pace. Where did she even start?

'Sadie?'

She looked at Quin, who was leaning forward. This was it. No more hiding or procrastinating. She stopped pacing and took a breath.

'In the year before we met…before I came to Brazil… I was working in a big house in London for a very rich man. I was a housemaid—one of dozens. The house was huge…luxurious…like nothing I'd ever seen. The owner wasn't English, his accent hard to place. We hardly ever saw him. We weren't allowed to look at him, in any case.'

She started to pace again.

'One evening, I thought I'd forgotten to check that the lunch things had been taken out of his office—he was a stickler for that kind of thing. I was due to go home, and I didn't want the girl taking over from me to get in trouble, so I went back to the office before I left, to check.

'When I got to the door, it was partially open, and I pushed it open all the way. I saw that the owner was inside, with his back to me. It took me a minute to understand what I was looking at. There was a man on the floor in front of him, on his knees, with his hands tied behind his back. He was begging, pleading… I could see his face…

he was young… I didn't recognise him. I saw my boss… the owner…take something out of the back of his trousers and hold it to the man's forehead. And then there was a sound…like a loud but muffled crack. I didn't recognise it at first—it was such an odd thing to hear. But then I re-alised that he'd shot him. Just like that. Without even hes-itating. I'll never forget the mark on the man's forehead, or the way he fell backwards. And then the blood…bright red…so much blood…all around his head, on the floor…'

Sadie stopped pacing and looked at Quin, not really registering his expression.

'I must have made a sound, or something, because my boss turned around. He was still holding the gun, and it was pointing at me now. I could see him taking in that it was me, just a member of staff. Maybe he knew who I was…maybe he didn't. But somehow I felt in that mo-ment that he knew exactly who I was, and that I had no family, no ties. He could shoot me and no one would ever know. So I ran. All the way out of the house, out through the gate, onto the road. I kept running until I ran straight into a man who bundled me into a van. I thought it was someone attached to him. I was terrified. But it was the police…or not the police…a specialist unit. They'd been watching the house…they saw me run.'

Sadie stopped. She felt a little light-headed. She'd only ever told this once to the police, and then again for her video witness statement. She'd never told another soul.

Quin was looking at her. His face was hard. 'Is there more?'

Sadie swallowed. He didn't believe her. But she'd started now.

She sat down again on the edge of the chair, hands clasped in her lap. 'The police…detectives…whoever they were, took me to a police station—except it wasn't like any I'd seen before. It turned out the man I worked for was a well-known name in the organised crime world. Up to that point he'd never been caught doing anything himself—he was too powerful. The fact that I'd witnessed him murdering someone himself, on his own property, turned out to be their big break. But he fled the country before they could catch him.'

Sadie stood and paced again.

'I knew there was something off about the house—and the people in it but I didn't take much notice because I was only there to work part-time, to help pay for my hairdressing course. The man's wife looked perfect, but brittle—as if she'd break into pieces if you touched her. His children were never there…always in boarding school. The people who worked for him never really joked around or chatted, like normal staff. The boss wasn't even there most of the time, so we were cleaning a pristine house.'

Sadie's mouth twisted now.

'We got paid in cash. If I'd been less naive, and hadn't been so broke, I might have questioned that.'

She sat down again.

'Because I'd witnessed the murder, and could identify the victim when they showed me pictures, the police asked me if I'd be a witness if they ever caught my boss and got him into court. By now, there weren't just British detectives talking to me—there were detectives from France, Spain, America… They told me that even if I said no, I'd still be in danger. My boss would be coming after me. So I agreed to put my statement on video, so it could be used as evidence someday. And then the only way they could protect me was if I went into a witness protection programme.'

Sadie stopped talking. Her mouth was dry. Quin was just looking at her. Then he stood up and walked over to the drinks cabinet and poured himself another shot of whatever he'd poured before. He swallowed it down. He looked at her again, and held up a glass in question.

She shook her head. 'Just some water, please.'

He brought over a glass. She took a sip. Now Quin started to pace back and forth. Sadie could feel the volatile energy crackling around him…between them. Eventually he stopped and turned to face her, shaking his head.

'You've had four years to come up with a story and you couldn't come up with anything better than a plot straight out of a soap opera?'

Sadie felt deflated. And then angry.

She stood up, clutching the glass. 'I told you it was a lot.' Then she thought of something and said, 'Those nightmares I used to have—remember? They were actual memories of watching that man being murdered, except I had no idea what they were about.'

Quin's jaw was hard. 'Easy to say now…'

Sadie's hand was clutching the glass so tight her knuckles were white. 'Why do you think I didn't want to go on a date with you when you asked me out? Because I couldn't. I wasn't allowed to get close to anyone.'

Quin looked at her. 'So you're saying you only had a relationship with me because you couldn't remember that you were in a witness protection programme.'

'Exactly.' Sadie had to admit that it did sound fantastical. But that had been her reality.

Quin asked, 'When did your memory return?'

Was he starting to believe her? It didn't look like it. If anything, his expression was even more obdurate.

'The day Sol was born. That was when I remembered

everything. It was as if a veil had been pulled back, revealing the past. I think going into the city sparked something… I knew instinctively that going into a city was dangerous…so much CCTV. I'd been told to move around—to stay in places big enough to get lost and not so small that I'd stand out. Sao Sebastiao was perfect.' Before Quin could say anything else she asked, 'Why do you think I had no personal effects in my apartment in Sao Sebastiao? Why was there no trace of me online?'

'What's your real name?'

Sadie's chest tightened. 'It's Lucy White…but I haven't been Lucy for years now. I'm Sadie.'

Because she'd been Sadie when she'd met Quin and had Sol that was who she was. Who she wanted to be.

'You mentioned family…where *were* your family?'

'My parents died when I was a baby—in a car crash. I was unharmed. I was adopted, and lived with a family until I was around five. But then they had problems and handed me back into care. I was brought up in foster homes after that. It's harder to get adopted the older you are.'

Sadie tried to hide the lingering pain of knowing that she hadn't been enough for her adopted parents. She'd carried that feeling of being excluded all her life, like a stubborn wound. It had only been when she'd met Quin that she'd felt as if she'd found a home.

She could see now that it was part of the reason she'd fallen so hard for him—instinctively relishing the safe harbour of his love without understanding why until after her memory returned. Her upbringing had been a far cry from Quin's.

That reminder made her feel exposed and vulnerable, she said, 'I'd lost my memory. I had no idea who I was.

You did know who you were, but you kept your past from me as much as I kept mine from you.'

Quin's mouth tightened. 'You looked me up?'

Sadie nodded. 'Afterwards, yes. Primarily to see if I could find you online, so I could keep tabs on you and Sol.'

Quin sounded a shade defensive. 'I never lied to you.'

'Maybe not,' Sadie conceded, 'but I never lied to you either. Maybe I would have had to if you'd pursued me and I hadn't had the surfing accident and lost my memory.'

Quin sounded weary. 'Why don't you cut all this melodrama and tell me what really happened? You had the baby and you realised that you weren't really cut out for the domestic life so you ran. And when you realised that I'd made my fortune you came back to see what you could get out of it. Why not just admit that and save us all some time? I'd respect you more if you did.'

Quin's words landed like stinging barbs all over Sadie's skin. The hurt landed heavily in her gut. 'Because that's not what happened.'

There was only one way to prove her story. 'Can I use your computer?'

He frowned a little. 'Okay.'

Sadie loosened her grip on the glass, only realising then how tense she was. She put it on the desk, and went around to the other side of the desk and sat in Quin's chair.

She opened up the internet search engine and searched for a name and accompanying news articles. Then she wrote a name and a number on a piece of paper, and pulled up a biography of that person. She left the tabs open and stood up.

She pointed to the screen. 'You can read news articles about the murder and the implosion of the organised crime gang that was run by the man who owned the house

I worked in—the man I saw murder another man. Then you can ring the person who was my witness protection case officer. If you don't believe she's real, you can see her Scotland Yard biography, which I've also pulled up.'

She came around the desk again and stood in front of Quin.

'That's why I left that day, Quin. Because if I hadn't, and if they'd tracked me down, we'd all be dead now. The only reason I'm here at all is because all the people involved with that man and his gang—anyone who would have needed to kill me, or anyone close to me—is now dead.'

Sadie turned and walked to the door, but before she opened it she stopped and turned back.

'For what it's worth, I haven't been with anyone else since you. I wanted you to know that.'

Then she turned away again, opened the door and left.

Quin wasn't sure how long he stood looking at the door. At the empty space Sadie had left behind.

Not Sadie. Lucy.

What she'd just told him was like something from a lurid American daytime soap script. Ridiculous. A fantasy. And yet the words that reverberated in his head were, *'I haven't been with anyone else since you.'* As if that was the most important thing.

And yet he couldn't deny the frisson of satisfaction he felt at hearing that admission.

He shook his head. *Focus.*

Maybe, he thought now, *maybe she's actually mentally unwell.*

Maybe she'd created this fantasy explanation and perhaps she even believed it—because she certainly seemed genuinely invested in it. So much so that he'd doubted his own disbelief a couple of times.

What was it they said? The more elaborate the story, the more likely it was to be true, because no one could remember that amount of false detail.

Quin shook his head. No. It was nonsensical. He'd never heard such a labyrinthine story in his life.

Eventually he broke out of his stasis and went and sat down behind his desk. He looked at his computer screen and saw a slew of press headlines and images of a crime scene. Men on the ground. Dead.

Notorious crime boss living in plain sight SLAIN by his own gang!

Quin got a jolt. He'd heard of this man. He'd been a well-known billionaire businessman and philanthropist. There'd always been murky rumours about where his wealth had originated and whispers of links to criminal activity, but nothing had never been proven.

There was mention of him being on every Interpol list, with a high reward for any information. And there was a small paragraph about an anonymous witness who had been put under protection for their own safety. A witness who could place him at the murder of Brian Carson. Another well-known criminal.

Breathless column inches described how the crime boss had lived in one of London's leafiest and most exclusive suburbs—how he'd even socialised with royalty and sent his children to the best schools in Europe. How the authorities had watched him for years but hadn't been able to pin anything on him because he'd had such a vast network of people to do his dirty work.

Lucy White. Had she really just been an innocent, naive young woman who'd unwittingly worked for a notorious criminal gang boss? Maybe she'd been part of it and had taken a deal to get out if she confessed what she knew?

Quin's head throbbed. He made a call to Claude, an old friend who worked in security. He was someone he trusted, because he had helped him stay off the grid when he'd wanted to escape the furore around his family five years ago, after it had been revealed that his 'father' wasn't his biological father. When he'd walked away from everything he'd known and taken control of his own destiny.

He greeted his friend with the minimum of niceties and gave him the details. 'Can you look into this?' he asked. 'And also Lucy White? Let me know what her involvement was, if any.'

'Sure… This is an…unusual request…is everything okay?'

Quin clamped his mouth shut, to stop himself from revealing that the mother of his child might possibly be linked to a major crime syndicate. He just said, 'Everything is fine, thanks, Claude. I owe you.'

'No problem. I'll get back to you ASAP.'

Quin terminated the conversation. He felt edgy, restless. Didn't know what to think. All he could see were Sadie's huge eyes and how innocent she'd looked. Had she even really lost her memory? But then his conscience pricked. He recalled the headaches she'd get—so painful that they'd leave her pale and sweating. And the nightmares, when she would wake, sitting bolt-upright in the bed, screaming, her body slick with perspiration, eyes huge and terrified. He remembered cradling her in his arms as she said, over and over again, *'So much blood… I've never seen so much blood.'*

She couldn't have faked that.

Or maybe she could, and he was just a supremely gullible idiot taken in by a huge pair of eyes and a lithe body.

She'd been a virgin.

He could still remember the spasm of pain that had flashed across her face as he'd breached her tight body. The way she'd resisted him before her body had softened and moulded around his, giving him the most erotic experience of his life. Blood was pumping to his groin just at the memory.

Quin surged to his feet. *No.* He would not do this—sit here and torture himself. Tomorrow he would quiz Sadie about everything and look for chinks and holes in her story, and when Claude came back with the inevitable proof that she was indeed not what she seemed Quin could wash his hands of her for good.

The following day Sadie was cleaning Sol's bathroom, going through the motions automatically, avoiding thinking about last night. She needed to keep busy. She hadn't seen Quin yet—he'd taken Sol to school that morning. She felt curiously empty. Flat. Anti-climactic. She might have expected to feel somehow more…relieved, or even happy after finally telling Quin what had happened. But clearly he had viewed her explanation with outright suspicion.

Would it change anything?

But at least she'd done it. Told him the full truth. He would have to believe her eventually.

But would he ever forgive her? Maybe in his mind even the threat of death wasn't a good enough excuse for her leaving.

All she'd known at the time was sheer terror at the prospect that she might be the cause of any harm coming to Quin or Sol. She would do the same today if she needed to.

She heard a sound nearby and turned her head to see Quin appear in the doorway, as if manifested straight out of her thoughts. He took her breath away before she could try and control her response. He was dressed in dark trousers and a shirt. Open at the neck. The casual clothes did little to hide the powerful musculature of his torso and wide shoulders.

She only realised belatedly that she was still on her knees and she stood up, very aware of her hot face and perspiration from working.

He said, 'We're going out for lunch.'

Sadie struggled to understand why he was announcing this. 'Okay... You and Lena? Or Roberto?'

After all, they were the only other people she'd met so far.

Quin frowned as if she was being dense. 'No, you and me.'

'Oh...'

Sadie's insides fluttered, but then she told herself she was being silly. Obviously he just wanted to talk to her about everything she'd landed on him the previous evening. This wasn't a date.

She said, 'We don't have to go out if you're busy.'

Maybe it would be better to talk in a private space rather than out in public.

'You haven't left this house and gardens since we arrived,' he pointed out.

Sadie hadn't even realised that. But it was true. She remembered how, when she'd been with Quin before, she'd never wanted anything much more than to be with him. In their modest beachside house. She could appreciate now that part of that must have had to do with the danger she'd known was out there, but cloaked by her faulty memory.

Quin was looking at her. 'Okay, then, that'd be nice,' she said.

'Leave the cleaning things there. Sara will be back later—she's recovered from the accident.'

Sadie took off the cleaning gloves and took a second to check her reflection. She groaned slightly. As she'd feared, a shiny face, and hair scraped back to stop it getting in her way.

She released her hair from the clip she was using to hold it and quickly ran her fingers through it, to try and make it look a tiny bit presentable. She left the room and made her way to the front of the house, where Quin was waiting by a small, sleek sports car in the main courtyard.

Sadie came down the steps. Her chest felt suspiciously tight. 'You got your dream car.'

'I did.'

From what Sadie remembered him telling her about this particular car, it was fully electric. She reached out and touched the sinuous line of the roof. 'It's beautiful.'

'Sol loves it.'

Sadie looked at Quin, delighted by that fact. She wanted to hoover up every piece of information about her son.

Quin came around and opened the passenger door. Sadie had to contort herself slightly to get in, but the seat seemed to mould itself around her body like memory foam.

Quin got in and started the engine. Sadie could barely hear it as they made their way down the driveway and out into the suburban Sao Paulo streets. She felt a bit like an alien, beamed down onto planet Earth. She'd spent so much time hiding in the shadows that she'd never luxuriated in just being driven down a sunny street, looking at people going about their business.

Her life had been on hold and now, finally, it was beginning again. She was here with Quin, and whatever this was between them might be complicated and gnarly and prickly, but she was also with her son and that was the main thing.

Absurdly, emotion sprang up and made her eyes water.

Quin glanced at her at that moment and asked sharply, 'Are you okay?'

'Fine...fine,' Sadie said quickly, blinking her eyes. 'It's just the sun.'

Quin reached over and pulled down the sun visor. He said, a little gruffly, 'I didn't think to let you get your bag or things.'

Sadie shrugged. 'It's fine. I don't have much anyway.' She thought of something and said a little stiffly, because she was suddenly embarrassed, 'I'll pay you back whatever I owe you when I can.'

Quin's hands tightened marginally on the steering wheel. 'You've been cleaning the house. I shouldn't have let you do that.'

'I didn't mind,' Sadie admitted easily. 'I don't like being idle. Anyway, it's what I've been doing for the last four years, in between some hairdressing jobs, so I'm used to it.'

She felt Quin looking at her as they pulled to a stop at some traffic lights. They were getting closer to the city centre, and Sadie could feel her heartrate inevitably rise at the thought of all those people and the proliferation of CCTV cameras. She took a breath. It would take her a while not to worry about that any more.

'So how did it work, then?' Quin asked.

He sounded mildly interested, but Sadie could still hear a trace of scepticism. It hurt that he didn't trust her, but she couldn't blame him. In a way, she was lucky he hadn't just thrown her out on her ear after hearing her story.

Sadie had to consciously relax her hands, which were clasped tightly together. 'I moved around a lot. Stayed away from big cities.'

'Aren't they easier to get lost in?'

'Surprisingly, no. There's so much CCTV. I stuck to big towns, but not cities. I took menial jobs—cleaning offices and hotels. And I'd ask busy hair salons if they needed extra help at Christmas—things like that. Places that had enough foot traffic that the customers wouldn't strike up a conversation or get to know you as a regular stylist.'

'Where did you live?'

'Hostels, mainly. Sometimes hotels, if I was lucky enough to have the funds. Sometimes I even got a short let.'

'Didn't the police give you any money?'

Sadie shook her head. 'You're expected to get a job and provide for yourself. They paid for my ticket to Brazil, and some modest funds to help me disappear, but that was it.'

'You said you weren't with anyone…?'

Sadie looked at him. Did he doubt what she'd told him? His profile was so hard.

'No one. I couldn't afford to get close to anyone.'

'Did you want to?'

Sadie shook her head. 'No, there was no one.'

How could there have been? she wanted to say to him. All she'd thought about was him and Sol, going into internet cafés when she thought it safe enough and looking Quin up online, hoping for a glimpse of her son. Hoping for a glimpse of Quin. Hoping she wouldn't see him with another woman.

Quietly, Sadie said, 'If I'd felt I had a choice, of course I wouldn't have walked away. But I knew Sol was in good hands…you've been an amazing father.'

Quin was pulling into a valet parking area outside a

building on one side of a pretty leafy street. When the car had stopped he looked at her and said, 'That's probably because I had to become mother and father overnight. I had no choice but to step up.'

Because she'd stepped out.

He didn't say it, but he obviously meant it. She was tempted to defend herself by pointing out that she hadn't had a choice either, but she said nothing. Clearly her explanation had fallen into some space between them where Quin was not ready to believe her. Yet. She couldn't necessarily blame him—it was a lot to take in.

He would have to believe her eventually, though, because there was no other explanation. But right now she couldn't imagine that even then there'd be much of a thaw in the air.

CHAPTER SEVEN

IT BECAME APPARENT as soon as they walked into the restaurant—impossibly sophisticated, with soft music playing, big open spaces and tables arranged around a central open-air pond where exotic fish swam lazily, all overlooked by a wall of green foliage—that Sadie was woefully underdressed.

It was in the raised brow of the impeccable maître d' and in the looks of the other diners as they were led to their table in a—thankfully—discreet corner. The clientele was sleek and beautiful, casual but elegant, the women in silk and linen, men in suits. By the time she was sitting down opposite Quin her face was burning with humiliation.

He glanced at her as he flicked out a linen napkin. 'What's wrong?'

'What do you think?' she hissed, wishing she could wrap her own napkin around her, to hide her tatty T-shirt. 'I'm completely out of place here. I can't believe they let me come in with you.' She added, 'If it was your intention to humiliate me then it's worked beautifully.'

Quin put his napkin down and looked around, and then at Sadie, whose face was still burning. He had the grace to look guilty. He said, with genuine contrition, 'That wasn't my intention at all. I'm not so petty. It just didn't occur to me… I should have given you time to change.'

Sadie looked at him. She believed him. Her anger fizzled out and she made a face. 'I'm not sure I have anything smart to change into, except for that dress I wore the other night, and that's not appropriate either.' She seized the moment and pointed out, 'Maybe it didn't occur to you because you're used to walking into places like this without a second thought.'

He looked at her sharply. 'What's that supposed to mean?'

'The fact is that you were born into this world. You take it for granted.' She shook her head. 'Why didn't you tell me about your family? About where you came from? You never even mentioned your brother.' She hoped the lingering hurt wasn't apparent in her voice.

He looked at her. 'You really want to talk about this now?'

'Why not?'

She'd laid herself bare last night, but Sadie held her breath, not sure if Quin would comply.

But eventually he said, 'Because I was escaping them—and that world. Being with someone who didn't know who I was with all its accompanying noise was…a novelty. I liked being anonymous.'

Sadie absorbed that. 'Why did you need to escape?'

A muscle pulsed in his jaw. He didn't look at her now. He said, 'Because I'd found out that everything I'd grown up taking for granted was a lie.'

'Do you mean about your father not being your biological father?'

He nodded. 'I only found out when we had an argument because I didn't want to go into the family empire, like my brother did. It explained why I'd always felt like an outsider in my own family. He'd tolerated me for the sake of the family reputation.'

'The articles I read said you were disinherited.'

He looked at her. Proud. 'I disinherited myself, and that's when I went to Sao Sebastiao to work on my own tech stuff.' His gaze narrowed on her. 'And then I met you.'

Back to her. Obviously his omission wasn't as big a sin as her actions.

Sadie suddenly had so many questions, and was determined not to let him change the subject, but at that moment she registered a prickling sensation at the back of her neck. Someone appeared at her shoulder. She nearly jumped out of her skin, inadvertently knocking over an empty glass with her hand.

It was only the waiter. Heart pounding, she apologised and righted the glass. She realised her hands were trembling with the sudden rush of fright and adrenalin.

The waiter poured them water and left again.

Quin was frowning. 'What was that about?'

Sadie looked at Quin, mortified. 'I'm sorry, it's just that I'm not used to sitting with my back to the people around me.'

Quin looked at Sadie. She was pale. Her hands were trembling slightly. She glanced over her shoulder again and he noticed how she let her hair fall so that her face was hidden. It was a move that had obviously become habitual.

He stood up. 'I'll switch with you.'

Sadie looked up at him, eyes wide. 'Do you mind?' Quin shook his head. She stood up and they moved around the table. She sat down in his seat. It was only when Quin sat down that he was suddenly aware that he felt a prickle of discomfort.

He suddenly recognised that very primitive instinct that must be within everyone—to feel a sense of danger at not knowing what was behind you. It did make him feel a little vulnerable…

'I'm sorry,' Sadie was saying. 'You must think I'm being ridiculous, but I've just got used to always being aware of my surroundings. I had to.'

'If what you say is true.'

The words came out before Quin had a chance to fully think them through. He registered the look of hurt on her face, but something inside him had hardened. He pushed down the urge to trust her—because if he believed her that would send his world even more off its axis.

He suspected rather uncomfortably that having to let go of the anger that had felt so righteous for so long would expose more uncomfortable things that he'd never really dealt with. Like the sheer hurt. Pain. Loss. Sense of betrayal. A betrayal made worse because his own mother had abandoned him too. It had been so much easier when Sadie had been the straightforward villain and not a potential victim.

Sadie sagged back in her chair, as if she might be feeling the weight of his thoughts. 'Why would I make such a story up?' she asked. 'It would have been easier to say that I thought I couldn't cope.'

'But not as sympathetic.'

Sadie's eyes flashed, but before she could say anything the waiter was back to take their order. Quin noted that some of the colour was back in Sadie's cheeks, and something in him eased a little. He scowled at himself. They ordered, and the waiter left again.

Quin sat back. He was prepared to indulge her for now, at least. 'So, tell me, then, how did you end up in Brazil?'

Sadie's mouth compressed for a moment, and Quin had to restrain himself from reaching across the table and touching his finger to her soft lower lip. Before, they'd touched each other all the time, and that tactility had been a revelation for him after growing up with little in the way of open affection. It had been impossible not to respond to Sadie's irrepressible nature, and the affection—physical and emotional—that she'd given so freely.

'Why should I tell you anything more when you don't believe me?'

'I'll suspend my disbelief.'

He saw how Sadie's glance flicked past him to the restaurant behind him and then back. He hated to admit it, but such a reflex could only be borne out of an ingrained habit. When they'd been together before she'd used to dislike going out to bars or restaurants, preferring to stay in and cook for them.

'I picked Brazil to come to because I couldn't think of anywhere further. I figured I could get lost in a country like this.'

'And your witness protection team just agreed?'

Sadie nodded. 'I didn't have any family or relationship ties. Once they'd furnished me with a new identity and new documents they were happy to get me out of their hair. They already had my video deposition, so if anything did happen to me it wouldn't ruin their case. They liaised with the police here, but only so far as to let them know my background. After that I was on my own. I had to find a job and support myself.'

'Why didn't the police here or back in the UK try to track you down when they didn't hear anything from you after losing your memory?'

'I found out when I contacted them after my memory returned that they *had* been trying to track me down. But my mobile phone was gone, and a lack of resources and lack of personnel meant they were limited in what they could do to find me. I hadn't been in Sao Sebastiao for long before we met, so I hadn't yet checked in, telling them my latest location. The onus on keeping myself alive and safe was really on me. They didn't have any obligation beyond being a place for me to call in case I needed help or to find out information—like how the case was going...'

Their starters arrived, and Quin forked some salad absently into his mouth as he said, 'So what happened when your memory returned?'

Sadie swallowed her food. 'I knew I had to check in with them. I had no idea what was going on. When you'd gone to the hotel for the night, after Sol's birth, I got in touch. They'd received intel that my old boss *had* actively been looking for me in North America... They couldn't be sure that he hadn't extended that search further to South America. They'd started looking for me in lists of missing people when they couldn't find me.' When Quin stayed silent, Sadie continued. 'The fact that he was actively looking for me... I knew I had no choice. I had to go.'

The waiter returned and removed their plates as Quin absorbed this. Eventually he asked, 'Why didn't you just tell me?'

'I agonised over it. That whole night. It would have been the easiest thing in the world... But I kept looking at Sol, and all I could see was how small and vulnerable he was. It wasn't just about me. It was about you and him. I couldn't take the risk of telling you, just to make myself feel better, and risk your lives as well as mine. The witness protection team had been very clear that *anyone* I got close to would be a target too.'

Quin sat up straight. 'But I could have done something... I could have taken us somewhere else—somewhere safe.'

Sadie looked at him. 'First of all, I didn't know that. I didn't know you had access to any resources. But that wouldn't have changed anything. These people have access to information that you can't even believe. They have access that goes beyond the scope of any police force. If they'd tracked me down they wouldn't have hesitated to kill you too. And Sol.'

Sadie's eyes were wide now, her face leached of colour again. It was as if she was reliving a nightmare, and Quin had to concede that, whether she was telling the truth or not, she believed her own story. Or else she should be on the stage, winning awards for her acting skills.

Hurt at this reminder that Quin hadn't confided in her while they'd been together, no matter what he'd just revealed about liking his anonymity, made her say, 'There's no point talking about it any more—not until you're prepared to accept it's what actually happened.'

With perfect timing the waiter returned with their main courses. Sadie looked stupidly at her plate. She hadn't even registered what she'd ordered, but apparently it had been fish, artfully arranged on the plate on a bed of herbs, with a seasonal salad and baby potatoes.

For the next few minutes she avoided looking at Quin and focused on her food. Even though her appetite had fled, to some extent, she'd learnt the hard way not to skip a hot meal if it was handed to her.

To Sadie's surprise, the tension defused a little and they ate in silence. If not companionable, then at least not overtly antagonistic.

She glanced up and saw Quin's muscled forearms, exposed where he'd rolled up his sleeves. Her insides twisted with awareness. He had big hands with long fingers. Blunt nails. Masculine.

Their plates were taken away and coffee and biscuits delivered. Sadie took a sip of the fragrant, rich drink and closed her eyes, appreciating the aroma. She could feel the constant inner tension and vigilance she'd carried around for years slowly starting to unwind within her. In spite of Quin's anger and distrust.

When she opened her eyes again Quin was studying her. Her cheeks grew warm. She put her cup down. Quin didn't look away. He'd always had that confidence. No shyness. Not like her. He'd used to look at her intently before, until she'd start laughing or try to break his focus.

Once, when they'd been in bed, she'd asked, 'Why do you look at me like that?'

'Like what?'

'Like you want to see all the way inside me.'

'Maybe because I do…maybe because I wonder who you really are.'

The memory made Sadie shiver a little.

'Cold?' Quin asked.

Sadie shook her head. 'No, just a memory…' Impulsively she said, 'I'm glad Sol had you.'

'He will always have me.'

There was a clear warning in Quin's tone.

Sadie looked at him. 'He also has me now. I'm not leaving again.'

The air quivered between them. But the tension was broken when Quin said, 'Come on—we've a stop to make before we pick up Sol from school.'

Sadie's heart jumped. She would get to see her son at school! She stood up and followed Quin out of the restaurant, noting how the manager practically bowed to him on the way out. A far cry from their very humble life together in the beach house in Sao Sebastiao.

Back in the luxurious confines of the car, Sadie noticed they weren't going back towards the suburb. 'Where are we going?'

'You need some clothes.'

Sadie opened her mouth and was about to protest, but nothing came out. She did need clothes. She still felt self-conscious. The restaurant had highlighted her shabbiness. No doubt Quin was wondering how on earth he'd let lust overwhelm him the other night, now he'd seen her in the harsh light of day against a sophisticated backdrop and in comparison to other women.

'I don't have money to pay you back now, but I will as soon as I get a job.'

Quin made a sound that was somewhere between a sceptical noise and *'whatever'*, which made Sadie even more determined to do what she could to get her life back on track as soon as possible. There was bound to be a hair salon looking for a stylist in the city somewhere.

Quin was slowing down now, and expertly parking in a space outside what appeared to be a very upmarket boutique, with mannequins in the window wearing long sheaths of glittering dresses.

Before Sadie could say anything, Quin was out of the car and opening her door, extending a hand to help her out. She was loath to touch him when he'd all but told her that making love to her had been a huge mistake, but there was no other way to get out of the low-slung car gracefully, so she put her hand in his and gritted her teeth against the all too predictable reaction in her blood.

She pulled away as soon as she was standing up straight,

and studiously ignored Quin as he gestured for her to pre-cede him into the boutique. Once inside, Sadie immediately wanted to turn and leave again—but she couldn't, because Quin was right behind her, saying something over her head to the very elegant manager. His Portuguese was so fast, Sadie couldn't keep up.

He pushed her gently towards the woman, who was now smiling and saying, 'Come with me, please.'

Sadie had no choice but to let herself be led into a luxuriously carpeted inner room, where there were rails of clothes—everything from jeans to evening gowns.

The woman stood back and looked Sadie up and down assessingly. Then she said, 'Okay, let me see what we have for you…'

'Her story stacks up, Quin. She is who she says she is, and it's a miracle she survived. This organised crime gang was one of the most sophisticated and deadly in the world. They signed their own death warrants, though, when Almady murdered someone in his own home. He was getting complacent…arrogant…and that led to his ultimate downfall.'

Quin was standing outside the boutique, where he had gone to take this call from his friend. A heavy weight lodged in his gut. Sadie's story was true. He would trust Claude with his life.

But not the mother of your own child? prompted a voice.

Quin pushed it aside.

Quin had told his friend that Sadie was Sol's mother. He asked, 'Is there any danger now?'

His friend sighed. 'No—and I've checked it out thoroughly, with contacts who would know. Anyone who wanted her gone is dead or disappeared now. She has no relevance any more, thankfully. But I should tell you that one of Almady's associates was in Sao Paulo just over a year ago, sniffing around, showing people her picture, so they were intent on finding her. She did the right thing, leaving.'

Quin went cold. It had come that close? The danger? 'Could I have protected her and Sol?' he asked. 'If she'd told me?'

Claude was deadly serious when he answered, 'Three moving targets are easier to find than one.'

For the first time Quin had to wonder what he would have done in Sadie's situation. The thought of harm coming to Sol—his skin went clammy. Of course he would have done whatever it took to ensure his son was safe.

Even if that meant walking away?

His friend's voice cut off that uncomfortable question.

'Quin, I can't emphasise enough how real the threat was. And she'd witnessed a murder, so she had the trauma of that on top of the trauma of being on the run. If the gang hadn't imploded the way they eventually did, who's to know if she could have ever settled down again? The fact that she lost her memory and was blissfully unaware of the danger she was in, unwittingly putting you and her baby in, is frankly a little terrifying. It's sheer luck they didn't track her down in that year.'

'I swear it could have been made just for you. I knew you'd look amazing in it.'

Sadie smiled weakly at the boutique owner—Monica. She'd already tried on an array of day wear, and the woman was so nice and friendly that Sadie hadn't had the heart to refuse when she'd said she had an evening dress for Sadie to try on.

Sadie was almost afraid to look at her reflection in the mirror, very aware that the dress was made of some kind of gold lamé and clung to her body like a second skin.

But the other woman said, 'Look at yourself, please… you are stunning.'

Sadie gave in, and for a second didn't recognise her own reflection. She'd never worn an evening dress in her life—apart from when she'd gone to that party to try and see Quin. And calling that dress an 'evening dress' had been a stretch.

But this…this was Cinderella territory.

Sadie glowed with a golden light. Her skin looked almost translucent next to the gold. The dress was simple, with two thin straps and a low-cut vee that ran between her breasts, making them look more ample than they were. It was a feat of engineering that Sadie would never be able to figure out.

It hugged her neat waist and clung to the flare of her hips, making her look far more shapely than she really was, and then fell in what could only be described as a waterfall of gold to the floor in soft, shimmering folds.

Her back was bare to the top of her buttocks.

Sadie had never been a girly girl, but this dress was evoking a multitude of things inside her. Yearnings and memories. The only other dress she'd ever had was the simple white broderie anglaise sundress she'd worn on the beach, while pregnant with Sol, when she'd married Quin.

Or, as he'd reminded her, *not* married Quin.

A sound came from behind them—a discreet cough. Monica went to the curtain and pulled it back, saying, 'Senhor Holt, please tell your girlfriend how stunning she looks.'

Girlfriend.

Sadie immediately froze. That couldn't be further from the truth of what was happening here. She was already anticipating the censorious look on Quin's face—he hadn't brought her here to play dress-up in gold lamé dresses! Maybe he'd suspect that she'd introduced herself as his girlfriend.

At the last second she reached for her neck, where her engagement ring would be hanging from the chain she'd put it on. But she let out a breath of relief when she remembered she'd left it in a drawer by the bed in the guesthouse for fear she'd lose it while cleaning.

Quin appeared in the space where Monica was holding open the curtain, blocking out all the daylight behind him with his wide shoulders, and all Sadie could do was look helplessly at him through the reflection in the mirror.

At first he was frowning, stern, but then he looked at her and his expression was wiped blank. And then…it changed. The only way Sadie could describe it was…*arrested*—as if someone had just punched him in the back. His eyes were glued to hers. And then moving up and down, taking her whole body in from bare feet to the top of her head. The look on his face was so intense…and something else…*hungry*.

Sadie's skin prickled. She had to be imagining it. He was angry, not hungry. And then his phone rang again, and he said something to Monica before turning away to take the call.

Monica came back, all business, helping Sadie out of the dress.

When Sadie went to look for the clothes she'd been wearing she couldn't find them. Monica made a face and handed her some of the new clothes, saying, 'I think these might be more comfortable for now. I'll get the rest packed up.'

Sadie took the clothes, and when she was alone again saw that there was a new pair of jeans and a loose silk shirt. A very luxe version of the casual style she liked. There was a pair of soft slip-on brogues. And—her face coloured—underwear. It was as if Quin had surmised that her underwear would be as tatty and cheap as the rest of her very limited wardrobe.

In any case, she was pretty sure he wasn't investing in new undergarments for his benefit. He'd made that clear.

When she'd changed—underwear and all—she caught her reflection in the mirror again and had to make a wry face. Even with unkempt hair and no make-up she could see that the quality of these clothes added an elegance that couldn't be manufactured any other way except by money.

She sighed. She'd never be able to afford to pay Quin back for this—an entirely new wardrobe of clothes.

She went out of the changing area into the main salon. Quin was off the phone now. He had his back to her, arms folded, looking out of the window. Legs planted wide. She could tell he was brooding from his stance.

He turned around then, and said, 'Ready?'

Monica reappeared, smiling—and no wonder. Quin had just dropped a small fortune. 'I'll have everything sent over today,' she said.

'Thank you. I appreciate it, Monica. *Adeus.*'

'*Obrigado.* Goodbye, Sadie.'

Sadie forced a smile. 'Thank you.'

At the last moment, Monica said, 'Wait!' and Sadie turned around at the door. The woman handed her a pair of sunglasses and said, 'On the house.'

Sadie smiled for real. 'Thank you,' she said, and slipped them on, appreciating the protection from the afternoon sun outside. And, more importantly, the protection from

Quin's dark gaze that kept flicking to her as he manoeuvred the car out of its parking space and into the traffic.

There was silence between them. Tension was growing and becoming suffocating.

When they were stopped at some lights, Sadie blurted out, 'I never said I was your girlfriend, and I didn't ask to try that dress on. She insisted, and I didn't have the heart to say no...'

Quin looked at her. 'What?' He frowned and then he seemed to absorb what she'd said and waved a hand. 'I didn't even hear her say that.'

Sadie felt a little deflated. 'What is it, then?' she asked. 'You're tense enough to crack.'

A muscle pulsed in his jaw. The car moved forward again with a little jerk. Eventually Quin said, 'Not here. We're almost at the school. We'll talk later.'

Soon they were pulling up outside a big modern building. Small children were coming out of the gates, being greeted by parents and carers. It was a happy throng, and for a moment all Sadie could do was blink to try and keep her emotion back.

Quin must have noticed, because he took her by surprise, touching her hand in a fleeting movement. 'Okay?'

Sadie shook her head and nodded at the same time, and tried to swallow the lump in her throat. 'It's nothing. I just... I used to fantasise about this—about someday being able to collect Sol from school. A normal thing that most people take for granted with their kids.'

She didn't look at Quin, afraid of what his expression might say, so she didn't see the way he looked at her thoughtfully.

He got out of the car and came around to help her out. Sadie stood beside him and pushed the sunglasses onto her head, straining to see Sol's distinctive reddish blond hair. And then there he was—a blur of energy, colliding with his father.

'Papa! I missed you.'

And then he noticed Sadie, and took her completely by surprise.

'You came too!' he said, as he threw his arms around her waist.

Sadie's legs nearly buckled at his easy and open gesture.

He pulled back, unaware of the emotional earthquake he was causing, and looked at Quin. 'Papa, can I show Sadie my classroom?'

'Sure, let's go.'

Sol took Sadie's hand and pulled her towards the school. A woman who must be a teacher was standing talking in the doorway and Sol said, 'Miss Diaz, this is my friend Sadie. I'm showing her my classroom.'

'Okay, Sol, that's fine.'

The woman smiled at Sadie, and then seemed to do a double take when she saw her similarity with Sol. Sadie pretended she hadn't noticed.

Quin stayed behind, talking to the teacher, and Sadie savoured every second with her son, chattering nineteen to the dozen as he showed her where he sat, where his locker was, and where he put his shoes and which artwork was his.

When they got back to the house Sol was despatched to change out of his school clothes and Sadie finally met Sara the housekeeper—a friendly, no-nonsense woman. Roberto had left snacks, and when Quin disappeared to his home office to make some calls Sadie sat with Sol and ate them, helping him with the little piece of homework he'd brought home.

She was so engrossed that at first she didn't notice when Quin arrived back into the main living area. He'd changed into board shorts and a T-shirt. He looked like the man she'd first met, and her heart flipped over in her chest.

She realised then that he was looking at her with a strange expression—as if he'd never seen her before, or as if she was about to do something outrageous.

His gaze went to Sol. He said, 'Enough books—let's get outside and play some football.'

Sol was outside like a shot.

Quin looked at Sadie. 'Are you coming?'

The way he said that, so easily, made something cave inside her. Some of the wall she'd erected to protect herself in the last few years. It had been the only way she could survive.

'Okay,' Sadie said quickly, and tried to hide how pathetically seismic it felt to be invited to play with her son.

She stood up.

'I'll just change into something a bit more casual.'

When she went down to the guesthouse she found Sara putting away the new clothes that must have just been delivered.

Mortified, she protested, 'Please, don't. I can put them away myself.'

The woman smiled. 'It's no problem…it's almost done.'

Sadie sat on the bed when Sara was gone and looked into the dressing room, now full of brand-new clothes. And then she noticed something hanging at the back…a glimmer of…gold.

She got up and went into the room, reaching for the glimmer, sucking in a breath when she pulled out the stunning gold dress. It slid through her fingers like liquid. It must be a mistake. Sadie made a note to let Quin know.

She had no doubt a dress like that must have cost a fortune. Even she recognised the designer's name, and she'd been more or less living under a rock for the last half a decade.

There was a shout from outside and Sadie went through to the main living area to see a red-faced Sol, standing in the door with mud streaked across his legs.

'What's taking you so long?'

The dress was forgotten as a surge of emotion gripped Sadie, bright and pure. But she managed to get out a strangled-sounding, 'Nothing...give me one minute.'

CHAPTER EIGHT

QUIN COULDN'T FOCUS on the game. He missed another pass from Sol, who groaned. But Quin's vision was filled with a pair of long, shapely pale legs, expertly dribbling the ball to the goal, followed in hot pursuit by Sol.

Sadie was wearing short denim shorts and a loose T-shirt, which she'd not long before carelessly tied up into a knot at her waist, revealing the smooth skin of her back and lower belly. Her hair was pulled up into a messy knot, tendrils escaping. No make-up, just a sweaty face.

Something in Quin's chest ached, and he absently put his hand there, as if he could soothe it. He realised that in this moment Sadie looked more or less exactly as he remembered her when they'd first met. But that had been before she'd walked away from him and her newborn son and all the good memories had become toxic.

And yet...as much as he'd love to cling on to that outrage and anger, as he had for the last few years, cultivating it like a cold, hard diamond in his chest, he knew he couldn't. Not now that he *knew*. Not now that his friend had told him Sadie had had nothing to do with the gang. She'd been an unwitting bystander, caught in the crossfire. Living on the run to stay safe. To stay alive.

Quin still couldn't quite grasp the full significance of what that had meant for her.

At that moment the ball landed at his feet, but before he could react Sadie was hurtling towards him and colliding with him full force, driving him backwards.

He landed with an *oof*, and with Sadie still welded to his body, because he'd automatically put his arms around her. There wasn't a point where they didn't touch. Thigh to thigh, hip to hip, chest to chest. And also, as Sadie drew her head back slowly, breathing harshly, practically mouth to mouth.

'I'm sorry,' she gasped. 'I thought you were going to move.'

But Quin hardly heard her. All he could see were those blue-green eyes. His son's eyes.

A rogue thought popped into his head: if they had another child, would it too inherit her eyes? The thought was so unexpected that Quin felt a little winded.

And then, predictably, a certain part of his anatomy started responding to Sadie's proximity.

Her eyes widened and her cheeks went pink. She said, 'I thought you said…' She trailed off.

'I said it wouldn't happen again,' Quin gritted out. 'Not that I didn't want it to.'

'Are you gonna kiss Sadie, Papa?'

They both turned their heads at that moment, to see Sol crouching down beside them, watching with open curiosity.

He said, 'If you want to, it's okay. I've seen Maria's papa kissing her mom.'

Immediately Quin stiffened and put his hands on Sadie's arms, to push her up and away from him as he said, 'No, I am not going to kiss Sadie. We just fell, that's all.'

Sadie scrambled to her feet and Quin could see the red of her cheeks, even though he wasn't looking straight at her. This was exactly what he wanted to avoid—confusing Sol. Although Sol had already started kicking the ball again, oblivious to the tension in the air and, it would seem, to any confusion.

Quin opened his mouth to say something, but at that moment Roberto called out from the house.

'Dinner is ready.'

Sadie said, 'I'll just wash my hands first.' And she fled towards the guesthouse.

Quin had to curb the urge to follow her and—

And what? asked a voice. *Punish her for turning you on so easily by making love to her? After telling her it wouldn't happen again?*

Thoroughly flustered, frustrated, and feeling as if the ground was shifting underneath him, Quin went straight to his own room to freshen up—starting with a very cold shower.

Sadie was still trembling under the shower spray a couple of minutes later. Trembling from the way Quin's body had felt underneath her. All hard sinew and steel and muscle and beating heart, thumping unsteadily against her chest. She'd wanted to put her head down, put her ear close to that strong beat. As she'd used to when they'd lain in bed.

Before.

And then she'd felt another part of his anatomy stirring against her, and any thoughts of listening to his heart had melted in a flash of heat. To her shame, she'd even forgotten that Sol was there, watching them. Until he'd spoken.

Quin had moved so fast to push her off him that her head was still spinning.

He did still want her. But he didn't want to want her. Well, he'd made that clear the first time they'd made love. Disappearing like a thief in the night.

Sadie turned off the spray and stepped out of the shower,

drying herself briskly and putting a towel around her head and another around her body. She went into the dressing room, but instead of gravitating towards the jeans and shirts, she found herself moving to the dresses and pulling out an olive-green silk shirt dress with a slim gold belt.

She let the towel drop and pulled on some of the new underwear—wispy pieces of silk and lace that felt far too flimsy and decadent. Frivolous… It had been a long time since she'd felt frivolous.

But she couldn't deny that here in this place, when she was with her son at last and had told Quin the truth of what had happened, she felt lighter. Buoyant. Hopeful. In spite of the ever-present undercurrents.

She towel-dried her hair, leaving it in damp waves, and then slipped on the dress and a pair of flat sandals. She made her way up to the main house. The early evening air was warm and balmy.

When she went inside Quin and Sol were already sitting at the table.

Sol saw her and jumped up. 'You sit here, Sadie, beside me.'

Sadie's heart spasmed. She smiled and sat down, and only then risked a glance at Quin, whom she fully expected to be looking stern. But he wasn't. He was looking at her with that half-arrested expression again. Like the one he'd had when he'd seen her in that dress in the shop. Which reminded her…

She said, 'They sent over that gold evening dress with the other clothes from the boutique. It must be a mistake. I'll pack it up so it can be sent back.'

Quin shook his head. 'Leave it…it's fine.'

Sadie would have protested, but Sol had started chattering as he spooned some of the delicious pasta into his mouth, and Quin reminded him not to talk with his mouth full.

Sadie let the incredibly soothing chatter of her son wash over her, making the appropriate responses when he looked at her with those wide eyes, pasta sauce around his mouth. Without thinking she took a napkin and dipped it in a glass of water, before using it to wipe his face.

Sol merrily went back to eating. Sadie looked up and saw Quin staring at her. She immediately felt self-conscious—she hadn't even considered that maybe she didn't have a right to touch Sol as a mother would, without thinking. But when she looked at Quin again it was as if she'd imagined it. He was smiling at Sol indulgently and her heart turned over again. She remembered that expression because he'd looked at her like that.

Before.

When they'd finished eating, Quin stood up and said to Sol, 'Bath time and bed.'

The little boy's lower lip protruded almost comically, but Sadie could see that the day's activities had worn him out.

He got up and followed his father, but then stopped and came back to Sadie. 'I had fun today. Will you play with me again tomorrow?'

Sadie smiled. 'I'd really like that.'

Then Quin spoke. 'Can you wait for me to put Sol to bed? I want to talk to you.'

A quiver of tension lanced Sadie's belly. 'Sure,' she answered, feigning nonchalance.

Quin and Sol disappeared. But before Sadie could start clearing the table Sara came in and said, 'Make yourself at home in the lounge, Miss Ryan. Would you like tea or coffee?'

'No, thank you—and please call me Sadie.'

The woman smiled and got on, clearing the table with brisk efficiency.

Feeling a little redundant now that she didn't have anything to occupy her time or justify her existence here—because being a mother to her son was still an unspoken quantity—Sadie did as she was bade and made her way into the lounge. A room she hadn't spent much time in at all.

She surveyed it now. The soft, comfortable furnishings were very elegant, but not intimidating. She could see scuffs and marks on the furniture. Children's books on the lowest shelves that made up one wall. All signs that a child lived here.

She crouched down and picked out one of the books. It was a classic that even she remembered: *Guess How Much I Love You.*

She sat down and flicked through the pages, and her vision blurred a little as she looked at the pictures and followed the story, thinking helplessly of the amount of times she'd lain in a lonely bed somewhere and wished with all her heart that Sol and Quin could feel the love she had for them.

'I would have thought you're a little above that reading level.'

Sadie tensed and looked up, blinking rapidly. She'd got lost in the story. She forced a smile. 'This was one of my favourites. It's a classic.'

'Yes, it is. Sol loved it.'

Sadie bit her lip in case she blurted out her sad story of sending them both her love from afar for all those years.

She got up and put the book back and faced Quin. He was obviously determined to ignore the electrical current that sprang into action whenever they were close.

She would do her best to ignore it too. Even though she couldn't help but be aware of his tall, lean body encased in low-slung denim jeans and a short-sleeved polo shirt.

Again, he reminded her of the surfer boy tech nerd she'd first met. But then, he'd never actually been either of those things. She had to remember that and use it as a shield. He'd never fully trusted her.

She said, 'You wanted to talk?'

Quin went over to a cupboard that Sadie realised was a drinks cabinet when he pulled back a sliding door.

He looked at her. 'Drink?'

Sadie felt she might need some sustenance for whatever it was Quin wanted to talk about. 'Sure—whatever you're having.'

'I'm having whisky.'

'I'll have a little. Maybe I'm developing a taste for it.'

Quin poured her a drink, and then one for himself, and brought over two crystal tumblers, handing her one.

'I've watered it down.'

'Thank you.' Sadie accepted the glass and took a sip. It didn't taste as strong as it had last night. It trickled down into her stomach and sent out a warming glow.

Quin faced her, and after a moment said baldly, 'I know you're telling the truth.'

Something bubbled up inside Sadie: relief.

Quin went on. 'I spoke to a friend of mine. He owns a security company and I asked him to verify what you told me.'

The bubble of relief burst. So Quin hadn't come to believe she was telling the truth because he trusted her. He'd had her story verified. But she'd more or less instructed him to do that, so she shouldn't really be feeling hurt.

'What did he tell you?' she asked, as if there wasn't a great gaping chasm opening up in her chest.

'He confirmed what you told me. He told me the gang were notoriously dangerous. He told me that you were an unfortunate victim, in the wrong place at the wrong time. He also told me that one of them appeared in Sao Paulo as recently as last year.'

Sadie could almost feel the blood rushing out of her head before dizziness took hold.

Quin was by her side in a second, taking her arm and saying, 'Sit down.' He cursed softly as she did so, and said, 'I shouldn't have told you that.'

Sadie had gone cold all over at the thought of one of those odious men here. So close to Quin and Sol in spite of everything she'd done. Her huge sacrifice. Her hand gripped the glass.

Quin crouched beside her. 'Take a sip of your drink.'

He took the glass out of her hand and held it to her mouth. Sadie obediently opened her lips and let him pour some of the alcohol into her mouth. Her eyes watered a little, but the drink revived her.

Quin put the glass on a table and she looked at him. 'Now can you see? They were actually here! Looking for me! What if they'd found out who you were? Everything I'd done would have been for nothing—'

'Claude has assured me that there were no links to me or Sol. We weren't officially married, and Sol was registered with my name when he was born.'

'Yes, of course. Thank God…' breathed Sadie. Then she asked, 'Did your friend say if there was still any danger? The detectives in London told me that every threat was gone, but I feel like I can't ever fully relax.'

Quin moved back to sit on the edge of a couch, near the chair. Their knees were almost touching. Sadie ached to reach for Quin and climb onto his lap. Just have him hold her, tightly, making her feel nothing could harm her, as he used to, before her memory had returned and she'd run… The more she thought about it now the surer she was that she must have known of the threat in some dim recess of her damaged memory and she'd relished his ability to make her feel safe. But inevitably their close contact would lead to far more incendiary things than feeling safe…

'Claude has assured me that anyone who would have wanted to see you…' Quin faltered.

'It's okay,' Sadie said. 'You can say it. See me *gone*. I lived with it for four years.'

His jaw clenched. The fact that he was obviously having trouble saying it out loud—that she could have been killed—provided her with some level of vindication. But it was small.

Quin went on. 'He assured me there's no threat, but I've asked him to make absolutely sure of that. He'll let me know if he finds anything.'

'Thank you,' said Sadie.

For the first time in four years she had someone else who knew. Who cared. Except Quin didn't care about her…

She shook her head. 'You don't have to do that—it must be costing a fortune.'

Quin stood up and moved towards one of the windows, hands in his pockets. He turned back and his mouth was quirked up slightly. That tiny hint of lightness was enough to take Sadie's breath away.

He said, 'Yes, Claude is expensive, but he's thorough.' Then the quirk in his mouth disappeared. He was serious. 'There's no way I won't make sure that you're safe. You're Sol's mother. He's lost you once. I won't let that happen again.'

Emotion was back, swelling inside Sadie's chest. She

fought it down, not wanting Quin to see how vulnerable she felt. 'Thank you…for saying that. After losing my own parents and spending so much time in foster care, the last thing I would want is to put Sol through losing me again.'

Quin turned and faced her fully. 'You said you were adopted after your parents died?'

Sadie nodded. 'Until I was five. But then the marriage broke down, and neither one could afford to keep me, so they sent me back into care. I was in foster homes until I left school.'

'How was that?'

Sadie looked at Quin and then quickly looked away again. She felt exposed. 'It wasn't ideal… No matter how nice the families were, it was always very apparent that I didn't belong to them. They were mostly kind, though. I was one of the lucky ones. Some foster kids have much worse experiences than me.'

'"*Mostly* kind"?'

Sadie repressed a shiver. 'There was one home…where the son was a few years older than me. He came into my room one night but his mother caught him. I was moved within a week.'

'Sadie…'

She looked up and saw that Quin was pale.

'You were almost—'

'Nothing happened,' she said quickly, trying to forget about that moment when the teenager had been looming over her in her bed. She could still remember the terror robbing her of her voice. She took another sip of her drink to try and calm herself.

Quin asked, 'After everything you'd experienced, weren't you tempted to take Sol with you when you left?'

Sadie put down the glass and stood up too. The traumatic memory of those days after giving birth was never too far away. She'd been so exhausted, and full of raging hormones and instincts—chief of which were to clamp her baby to her chest and never let him go.

'Of *course* I wanted to take him—it went against everything in my body to leave him behind. But then I remembered watching that man execute someone right in front of me. As if it was nothing. The easiest thing in the world. The man was begging for his life and my boss just…shot him. I knew that if he ever found me a baby would be nothing to him. No deterrent. That's what stopped me from taking him. And knowing that he would be with you. I trusted you, Quin. I knew you'd be a good father.'

And I loved you. I still love you.

She didn't say those words, even though they were high in her chest, begging to spill out. She would always love this man—even like this, when things had changed so irrevocably between them. But she knew he wouldn't appreciate hearing it now. Maybe never.

'I knew you'd be a good father.'

The way Sadie had just said that with such conviction, as if there had never been any doubt in her mind… It robbed Quin of breath for a moment. She'd already told him she thought he was a good father, but this was different. She'd not hesitated to leave their days-old baby with him, and he was only fully appreciating the significance of that now.

Up until he'd held tiny Sol in his arms he'd not really understood how on earth he could be a father, not having experienced that bond with his own. He hadn't shared his fears with Sadie, too ashamed to admit that he might not be able to do it.

But as soon as the soft, vulnerable weight of his son had been handed to him his knees had almost buckled with the weight of love and awe slamming into him. He'd made a vow to love and protect his child with every atom of his being.

The fact that she must have felt that too, and yet she'd walked away from her baby, made Quin say now, 'I haven't acknowledged how hard it must have been for you.'

She looked at him from across the room, and even now, in the midst of this conversation, he was supremely aware of how strong her pull was. She'd changed for dinner into a silk shirt dress, and all evening he'd been aware of the way the belt encircled her narrow waist. Of the buttons, open to the point where he could just make out the shadow of her cleavage. He'd imagined her breasts encased in silk and lace…felt his body responding against his will.

He could still feel the weight of her body on his when they'd collided earlier. The press of her breasts against him. Her breath on his mouth. He'd *ached* for her. For four years…

She was shaking her head now, and saying with tell-tale huskiness, 'It was the hardest thing I've ever done.'

Quin resisted the effect her voice had on him. 'It's a lot to take in. To undo four years of suspecting you'd just walked out on a selfish whim.'

Sadie let out a surprised sound, halfway between a laugh and a sob. She put a hand to her mouth and then took it down again. Shaking her head, she said, 'It couldn't have been further from "a selfish whim". There were so many moments when I almost turned around and came back, telling myself that one more day wouldn't hurt. All I wanted to do was confide in you, have you tell me it would be okay…but I knew that was selfish and potentially fatal.'

Quin had a sensation that he was free-falling into a massive void with nothing to hold on to. There was no escaping it now, he could no longer cling to the anger and the rage that had felt so justifiable for so long. In the absence of any explanation. Now he *knew*. But, if anything, it didn't seem to make things feel clearer or easier—things felt more complicated.

You loved her and she hurt you in the worst way possible. She walked out on you just like your mother did.

He *had* loved her. Much as he might have tried to deny it since her return. He'd loved her more than he'd believed it possible to love another human being. But that love was gone. And even though she might have had very compelling reasons for leaving him and Sol, he knew he would never be able to trust her enough to revive those feelings. Falling for her had shown him how vulnerable he still was, and he'd vowed never to allow himself to be vulnerable like that again.

The attraction that had driven him to her the other night...the attraction he still felt...was borne out of frustration and anger. But surely that volatile mix would lose its potency now that he had all the facts?

Because the thought of allowing himself to cleave so fully to Sadie again was...frankly terrifying. And she was looking at him now as if she could see all the way into his head. He had to push her back, establish boundaries, find a path forward so they could co-exist and parent their son.

Before he could say another word, though, Sadie was speaking. 'It's been a long day and I'm tired. I think I'll say goodnight.'

Immediately Quin felt remorse. What was it about this woman that scrambled his brain so effectively?

'Of course. We can talk again about where we go from here.'

She looked about as eager for that conversation as he was. She just nodded and left, and Quin watched her slim, pale legs through the window as she walked down the garden. She cut a lonely figure, and he couldn't help but think of the life she'd lived—essentially on her own, always.

He could empathise. Even though he'd grown up within a family, he'd always felt somehow apart. He'd had no mother and a distant father who hadn't been his father at all. A brother who had been invested in taking over the family business. He couldn't even blame his brother, because they'd never really been encouraged to bond.

Quin had to curb the very strong urge to follow Sadie.

And do what? asked a voice. *Make love to her again and muddy the waters even more?*

Quin turned away from the view of Sadie disappearing into the trees. No. The attraction would fade. He needed to put down boundaries but he also needed to think about the best way to move forward while incorporating Sadie into their lives.

Sadie had had to leave quickly. The air between her and Quin after that conversation had been taut with tension and a million swirling things. The attraction she'd felt, and the need for him to touch her and take her into his arms, had been so overwhelming that she'd been terrified he'd see it on her face, or she'd blurt something out...

She'd not really felt tired when she'd used that as an excuse to leave, but a wave of weariness moved through her now. It had been a tumultuous twenty-four hours.

Clearly it was going to take time for Quin to absorb all this. She could understand that. She'd had four years to deal with it every day and she still couldn't quite believe what she'd had to do, or how she'd had to live.

But hopefully, after tonight, they could leave the past behind and start to move on. To where, Sadie had no idea. But as long as she got to be a mother to her son—that was the most important thing.

Yet when she went to sleep that night, her dreams were filled with images of her and Quin at the beach house. And when she woke the next morning her cheeks were damp from shed tears and her heart was sore.

'I have to go to San Francisco tomorrow, for a conference where I'm a keynote speaker. I'm taking Sol and Lena— she has a daughter there, so it's an opportunity for her to pay her a visit too. You're welcome to come with us.'

Sadie looked across the lunch table at Quin. It was the weekend, and Sol was outside kicking a football around with some friends who had come to play. She'd been enjoying the banal domesticity of it all after the intensity of the previous day and evening, but now her insides clenched a little.

She couldn't read Quin's expression. Did he want her to come? After all that had transpired?

'I don't mind staying behind if you want to have some time with Sol on your own.'

As much as she would have loved to suggest leaving Sol here so she could look after him, she knew that would be a step too far, too soon.

'Actually,' he said, 'I have a favour to ask.'

Sadie blinked. She could do something for Quin?

'Of course. What is it?'

He made a face. 'There's a social event that I have to host. I set up a charity foundation a few years ago, to help kids from disadvantaged backgrounds get scholarships into tech courses. But every year the speculation about my relationship status, or lack thereof, overshadows the work of the charity. I could do with a date.'

Sadie blinked again. 'You're asking me to be your date?'

Her silly heartrate went up a notch.

'If you don't mind?'

Sadie was confused. 'But… I thought I'd be the last person you'd want to be associated with?'

'There's a little more to it… I think we need to tell Sol who you are. He's already growing attached to you, and he'll start to get confused. I thought it might do no harm for us to be seen in public together. We can put out a statement saying that you are Sol's mother, and then we can suggest at a later date that our brief reunion is over. But by then it'll be established that you are Sol's mother, and hopefully the story will die a quick death in the social columns.'

This was almost too much for Sadie to take in. She stood up from the lunch table and started to pace back and forth. She tried to articulate her tangled thoughts.

'So…we'll appear in public? Pretending we're together?'

She looked at Quin and he nodded.

'But what will we say when they ask where I've been?'

Quin shrugged lightly. 'As little as possible. We won't suggest that you haven't been in Sol's life…we'll keep it vague. If anyone looks you up they won't find much—just like we didn't when we looked you up after you lost your memory. I've been largely off the social scene's radar, living here in Sao Paulo, so for all they know you could have been here all the time—just not with me.'

So, Sol would know who she was… That made Sadie's heart expand with a mixture of joy and trepidation.

What if he didn't like the idea of her being his mother? And what about the other stuff? Appearing in public as Quin's girlfriend? Lover? Partner? Only to be excised 'at a later date'...

But could she really complain? As he said, this would establish her as Sol's mother. It would put her firmly in his life. If not Quin's life.

It would be easy for Quin to keep Sadie at a distance. But he wasn't doing that. He was giving her a chance to step into their world and take her place there. This was huge.

She looked at him. He was sitting back in his chair, long legs spread under the table, one arm across the back of the chair beside him. Supremely relaxed. As if he wasn't wielding a high level of control over her life like some kind of a puppeteer.

He frowned a little as he registered her lack of response and leaned forward, taking his arm down. 'I thought this would be what you wanted?'

Sadie clasped her hands. 'It *is*. I want Sol to know who I am—and thank you for that... I want everyone to know. But it's just a little daunting...the thought of being thrust centre-stage after four years of being anonymous and living in the shadows.' She shook her head. 'I've dreamt of this moment for so long... I thought it might never come. But now it's here it's just a little overwhelming.'

An expression Sadie couldn't decipher crossed Quin's face, and then he said a little sheepishly, 'I'm sorry. I didn't really take all that fully into consideration. If you'd prefer to wait until another time—?'

'No,' Sadie said quickly, terrified of letting this moment slip out of her grasp. 'I've spent four years in purgatory. I can do this.'

CHAPTER NINE

'I'VE SPENT FOUR YEARS in purgatory. I can do this.'

Quin hadn't been able to get those words out of his head for the last twenty-four hours because they'd resonated inside him, touching too many chords. He'd been in purgatory too but he had to admit that he hadn't fully appreciated how daunting it would be for Sadie to step out in public as Sol's mother.

His purgatory had been that of not knowing why she had left. The purgatory of her betrayal. But he knew now that it hadn't been a betrayal. It had been the absolute opposite, in fact, of what he'd experienced with his own mother.

His mother's act had been selfish. Cruel.

Sadie hadn't been cruel or selfish. She'd sacrificed her own happiness and risked her life to protect them.

His anger at her might be gone, but Quin couldn't deny that the memory of the pain was still there. Like scar tissue. Warning him to be careful. Not to be susceptible again. Because all he wanted now was to be able to co-exist with Sadie. To have her in their lives, but not in Quin's gut any more. Making him feel…too many conflicting things. Making him *want*—

No. He shut that down.

All he needed was for equilibrium to return. Sanity.

So he could start living his life again, perhaps even take a lover—as he'd planned to do the evening Sadie had appeared before him like a genie out of a bottle. Bringing the past with her. A past that he could finally start to move on from.

That's why he knew this was a good idea, bringing her front and centre into his life, publicly. It was the most expeditious way of establishing their relationship and her as Sol's mother, even as they both knew that it was just a façade.

She would also have to get used to a certain level of public interest as the mother of Quin Holt's son. There was no getting away from his family legacy.

Then, when the time was right, they'd announce their amicable break-up and could then get on with independent lives, co-parenting their son.

Quin watched Sadie across the aisle of the plane, where she sat with Sol, their strawberry blonde heads close together. Sol was looking at a book and pointing things out to Sadie, who was smiling.

They'd planned on telling Sol last night about her identity, but he'd been so exhausted after playing with his friends that he'd practically face-planted into his dinner.

Sadie had hidden it, but Quin had noticed her disappointment.

He checked his watch. They had at least another six hours' flying time. They'd stopped for a short refuelling break in New York.

Quin said, 'Sol?'

His son looked up. 'Yes, Papa?'

Quin's heart turned over at his son's open trust and love. He held out a hand. 'Come here. I want to tell you something.'

Sol put the book aside and jumped off the seat. He came over to Quin, who pulled him up between his legs. Sadie looked at Quin and he sent her a nod of his head. She went pale, but nodded back. She understood.

Quin looked at his son. 'You know how you were asking about your mother a while ago, and I said she'd had to go away?'

Sol nodded, looking serious.

'Well, when I said Sadie was a colleague from work, it was not really true.'

Sol frowned. 'Did you tell a lie?'

Quin nodded. 'I did. And I know that's wrong, but I did it because it was too big a secret to tell you straight away.'

'What secret?'

'That Sadie is your mother.'

Sadie was holding her breath so hard that she had to force herself to breathe. Her heart was thumping. Her eyes were glued to Sol, who looked over at her now, suddenly shy, cleaving closer to his Papa. Her heart ached.

He looked up at Quin. 'Sadie is my mom?'

Quin nodded. 'Yes she is.'

'But where was she?'

Quin looked at her. 'I think you should ask your mother that question.'

Sadie got off her seat and went over to kneel down near Sol. 'Sol…?'

The little boy looked at her warily. She mentally sent up a prayer for forgiveness and understanding.

She said, 'When you were born, I had to leave. Someday I'll explain why I had to go, but I really, *really*, didn't want to go. Leaving you was the most horrible thing I've ever had to do. And for the last four years I've been on a really long journey to come back to you.'

Sol's eyes widened again. 'Like a magical adventure?'

Sadie felt like smiling sadly. She nodded. 'Something like that.'

'That's cool.'

Sadie couldn't help smiling at her son's interpretation of her absence as some kind of epic adventure. He was too young to feel the more adult emotions of anger and betrayal. Like his father.

Sadie continued. 'What's most important for you to know is that I won't ever be leaving again, and even if I'm not living in your house with you I'll be somewhere very close. I promise.'

'You can stay with us—can't she, Papa?' Sol looked up at his father.

'We'll have to see. Sadie might want her own space.'

'But she has the garden house by the pool.'

'Don't worry. No matter what happens, you'll still see her as much as you want.'

Sol looked as if he was going to say something else, but he actually said, 'Okay, Papa. Can I watch a movie now?'

'Yes—in the bedroom, in your pyjamas. You need to sleep before we land.'

'Okay, Papa, I'll change.'

Sol sped off, seemingly not all that fazed by the momentous news he'd just received.

Lena appeared. 'I'll get him changed and washed and settled.'

'Thanks, Lena.' Quin smiled at her.

Sadie got up off her knees and sat back down on the seat. She felt a little dazed. Winded. Now her son knew who she was.

She looked at Quin. 'Do you think he took that in?'

Quin nodded. 'He's processing the information. He can bring stuff up from a year ago as if it happened yesterday. It's just how they do it at that age.'

'I hope he's not upset.'

Quin shook his head. 'He's not upset.'

Sadie's emotions were suddenly surging upwards and bubbling too close to the surface. She stood up and mumbled something, then fled to the bathroom, locking the door behind her just as the emotions erupted out of her with a huge sob. She couldn't breathe or see. Everything was blurry.

'Sadie, open the door.'

Quin. She'd thought the knocking on the door was her heart.

There was no hope of her regaining control. Reluctantly she opened the door, and then Quin was in the small space and she was enveloped in his arms—the safe harbour she'd longed for every night for the past four years.

Sadie wasn't sure how long she cried and how long he held her—it could have been minutes or hours. When she finally pulled back from Quin's chest all she could see was a massive damp patch. Mortified, she said, 'I'm so sorry—'

'It's fine.'

Quin's voice had a rough quality. She was afraid to look at him, but he tipped up her chin with a finger and she had no choice. She was sure her face and eyes must be swollen and blotchy, but remarkably she felt better. At peace. Lighter.

'Thank you,' she said huskily.

Quin's gaze moved to her mouth, and even in the aftermath of her emotional storm Sadie could feel her blood spike with heat. Mortifying… He couldn't have made it clearer that he would not touch her again, but she was too weak right now to pull back.

'For what?' he asked.

'For telling Sol… For not casting me away on sight as you had every right to do.'

Quin rubbed his thumbs across her cheeks, wiping her tears. 'I'm sorry that I'm only realising now how hard it must have been for you, and how strong you've had to be to get through the last four years.'

Sadie's heart hitched. 'And for you too.'

A moment quivered between them, delicate and fragile. For the first time since she'd come back into his life Quin wasn't looking at her with that mixture of distrust and antipathy. It was something altogether…*warmer.*

Sadie looked at his mouth. She desperately wanted him to kiss her… Even as she had that thought his head started to lower towards hers—just as a sound came from behind Quin, and then a voice.

It was Lena. 'Sorry to interrupt, but Sol is asking for Sadie to watch the movie with him.'

Quin stopped moving. His eyes met Sadie's. She trembled with the heated intent she saw there. It didn't mean he'd act on it. She needed to be strong. To protect herself and not let him see how much she ached for him.

Quin spoke. 'Okay, she'll be right there.'

He took his hands down and stepped back out of the cubicle. The moment was gone.

Sadie forced a watery smile. 'I'll just freshen up.'

Quin left her, closing the door behind him. Sadie heard his and Lena's voices fading as they walked away. She turned around and looked at herself in the mirror—and gasped. Her cheeks were bright pink, with traces of her tears in salty tracks. Her eyes were overbright, and still a bit bloodshot from crying. Hair in total disarray. And here she was thinking he'd looked at her with desire. She was delusional.

No. She was in love, and aching for something that had been lost for ever.

Sadie groaned softly and turned on the tap. She had to try and minimise the damage of her overflowing emotions. She would just have to hug the thought of how good it had felt to be held in Quin's arms again close to her, like a guilty secret.

A couple of hours later, Quin pushed open the bedroom door on the plane. The light was dim. A tablet lay on the bedcovers, upon which lay his son and Sadie.

Sol was curled into Sadie and her arm was around him. They'd fallen asleep.

He could still hear her gut-wrenching sobs and feel the racking shudders through her slim body as he'd held her in his arms. No one could manufacture that kind of raw emotion.

Quin felt grim. He now knew—had known in that moment when he'd almost kissed her—that in spite of all the revelations and the tangle of emotions in his gut—each one screaming at him to not let her get too close—that the thought of not touching her ever again was simply not an option.

He'd been ready to make love to her back in that bathroom, and probably would have if they hadn't been interrupted. Their attraction was undeniable. Unavoidable. Clearly the hope that it would fade after the truth had come out had been futile. A fantasy.

So it would have to be allowed to run its course—be-

cause only then would Quin finally be able to put Sadie to
one side so they could all get on with their lives. Together
but apart. He had his son. He didn't need anything more.

Sadie looked at the clothes that had already been hung
up by some invisible person in the hotel suite's dressing
room. They'd arrived a couple of hours before, and were
now in one of San Francisco's most exclusive hotels, with
views that stretched all the way to the Golden Gate Bridge
from the terrace that wrapped around this penthouse suite.

Sadie had a bedroom to herself, as did Quin and Lena.
Sol was in a room that connected with Lena's. There was
a kitchen and a dining room. A media room and a gym.
And a lap pool outside, heated. The sheer scale of the opulence was breathtaking.

She spied something familiar hanging up and reached
for it, pulling out the gold evening dress. Had Sara packed
this under instruction from Quin? For the event he had
mentioned? Just the thought of wearing it made her feel
self-conscious. But then she imagined Quin looking at her
the way he had in the boutique—

There was a light knock on her door and she whirled
around to see the object of her thoughts standing in the
doorway. He was wearing a suit, no tie.

'Sorry to disturb you.'

She shook her head. 'You're not disturbing me.'

Things had felt stilted and formal between them since
she'd been woken by Quin on the plane some hours ago.
She'd still felt very mussed-up and a little fuzzy after her
crying jag. He, on the other hand, had looked pristine. He'd
obviously showered and changed into this suit.

She asked, 'Are you going out?'

They'd had a light lunch when they'd arrived, and Lena

had gone out to do some shopping. Sol was in the living room, reading comics.

Quin nodded. 'I have a meeting at my office.'

'Do you need me to look after Sol?'

'If you don't mind… Lena should be back soon, in any case, and she's going to take Sol with her later this afternoon to her daughter's place. They'll stay there overnight. Lena has a grandson around Sol's age, and they've met before and like each other.'

Sadie felt simultaneously thrilled at the thought of being allowed to stay with Sol on her own, and also a little bereft at the thought of him leaving for the night.

'Oh, okay… Well, you don't need to worry about me. I can amuse myself. You must have meetings and things planned.'

Silly to feel somehow excluded, but for Sadie it touched on that very old wound of never feeling she'd belonged to anyone or anywhere. The man in front of her was the only one who had ever made her feel a sense of *home* and *belonging* and she had no right to ask that of him again.

He said, 'That event I mentioned…it's actually this evening.'

Sadie's hand tightened on the dress—she hadn't even realised she was still holding it. She let go.

'This evening?' Her heartrate sped up a couple of notches.

He nodded. 'Is that okay?'

'I…guess.'

Trepidation filled her belly. Why had she agreed to this?

She gestured to the dress. 'Sara packed this. I'm not sure it'll be appropriate, but it's the only evening gown here.'

Sadie stopped talking, afraid Quin might think she was fishing for more new clothes or something.

But Quin just said, 'The gold dress will be perfect. Lena

will help you get ready before she leaves with Sol. I'll see you later. Feel free to explore and do whatever you like when Lena comes back…use the pool, or head into the city.'

Quin had left before Sadie could formulate a response. She went out through the French doors to the terrace and looked out over the city. For so long she'd seen cities as malevolent places, full of dangers, but now she would have to get used to letting all that go. It was exhilarating and terrifying all at once.

She turned away from the view. But for now she had her son to look after, and she was going to savour every moment she had with him like this. Because she had no idea what the future with him would look like once this period of pretending to be *with* Quin was over.

A few hours later, Lena's daughter Beatriz stood back and said, 'You look like a million dollars, Sadie.'

Beatriz had come to pick up Lena and Sol, and had been roped into turning into a stylist for Sadie. She was about Sadie's age, and disarmingly friendly and sweet. Sadie had had no choice but to let herself be swept along on her wave of enthusiasm.

And then a much smaller voice—Sol's—said, 'Wow, you look so pretty.'

Sadie forced a smile. She didn't see what they seemed to see in the mirror. She saw a stranger, wearing a dress that was far too revealing and far too…*gold*. She looked as if someone had poured a bucket of it over her head and it had fallen over her body, covering only strategic bits.

One aspect she didn't need help with was her hair, but Beatriz had suggested leaving it loose, saying, 'We're in California. I think casual is more suitable—and your hair is gorgeous.'

Her skin looked milk-white next to the gold.

'Now, what about this ring around your neck? I think you should wear it on your finger.'

Sadie had completely forgotten about the engagement-wedding ring. She touched it now, just as the small hairs went up all over her body. She realised Quin was in the doorway of the dressing room, dressed in a black tuxedo. How long had he been there?

She barely noticed Beatriz and Lena melting away, taking Sol with them. He was looking at her neck, where she was now clutching the ring.

'You still have it?'

'Of course I have it.'

I wear it every day.

'Why is it around your neck?'

Sadie swallowed. 'I wasn't sure how you'd feel if you saw me still wearing it.'

His eyes met hers. 'It's just a ring.'

Sadie shook her head, everything in her resisting that provocative implication that it was nothing remarkable.

Memories swamped her of how Quin had got down on one knee and presented it to her, saying, 'It reminded me of your eyes…but if you don't like it you can choose another one.'

Sadie had shaken her head, tears blurring her vision. 'No, this is perfect.'

'No,' she said now, a little defiantly, 'it's not just a ring. I wear it every day.'

She unlocked the chain and the ring fell into her hand. She put it back on her finger, where Quin had put it all those years ago. She wasn't going to let him diminish the significance of the ring that had bound them.

Quin said nothing, but Sadie could see a slash of colour

in his cheeks. Eventually he said, 'If you're ready to go, my driver is waiting.'

Sadie lifted her chin. 'I'm ready.'

She wasn't ready at all, but she felt a little more empowered now that the ring was back on her finger. Quin mightn't like the reminder that he'd once professed to love her, but that was his problem.

The ring kept catching Quin's attention, twinkling in his peripheral vision. Mocking him. When he hadn't seen it on Sadie's hand since they'd met again, he'd been surprised at the sense of disappointment he'd felt. He'd seen it as an added layer of betrayal. But she *had* kept it, and worn it every day.

This further evidence of her innocence made him feel a little unmoored. Exposed.

He could recall how the ring had caught his eye in the window of a jewellery shop in Sao Sebastiao one day. Its blue and green stones. Emeralds and sapphires. He'd immediately thought of Sadie's eyes.

In spite of the gems being real, it wasn't a sophisticated ring. It certainly wasn't the kind of ring that he would ever have presented to a woman from his old social peer group. It hadn't come with an iconic name like Cartier or Tiffany.

He'd also realised in that moment that he had never really articulated the fact that he wanted to marry her—even though obviously he saw his future with Sadie, and not just because of the baby on the way. For ever. To create a family. A home. A life. For the first time, with her, he'd had a sense that that might be possible for him. The kind of life he saw people living every day but hadn't ever experienced himself.

He'd told her he loved her. He'd told her that way back—

before she'd even got pregnant. The words had flowed out of his mouth as if it was the easiest thing to say in the world—when in fact he'd never said it to anyone else. It was as if when he'd met Sadie she'd unlocked something inside him. A need to be loved and love in return that he'd pushed down. Ignored. Because first his mother had abandoned him and then his father had turned his back, treating him with a disregard that had only made sense once Quin had found out he wasn't even his natural-born son.

But it had been easy to say to Sadie…and necessary.

And she'd looked at him and smiled and said, 'I love you too,' as if it was the most obvious thing in the world. As if she'd had no idea what a gift she'd just given him. Accepting him so unconditionally.

So he'd proposed to her with the ring. He'd offered to change it if she didn't like it, but she'd told him it was perfect.

And then she'd looked at him, concerned. 'Can you afford this?'

Not for the first time he'd felt his conscience prick hard—because he hadn't ever told her about his family history. He'd known he would have to one day but, shamefully, he hadn't wanted to risk her looking at him differently. Especially not at that moment.

He'd liked the person he was with her. Anonymous. No ties, no toxic family baggage, and so he'd just said, 'Don't worry about the cost. I used some savings.'

That moment when Sadie had accepted his proposal had been one of the happiest moments of his life. Happiness. He'd never truly understood that emotion until he'd experienced it with her.

Quin had waited for something terrible to happen—because he'd grown up in a world where emotions weren't permitted, where awful things happened—abandonment and emotional neglect. But nothing awful had happened and he'd forgotten about the danger. Until the day she'd disappeared. Then all the declarations of love and their promises to be together for ever had curdled in his gut, turning to acid and then to ice.

But the ice was in danger of melting now. Had been as soon as Sadie had said, just a short while before, *'I wear it every day'*, and slipped the ring back on her finger with something almost like defiance.

That moment had almost eclipsed the dress—the dress that made her look like she'd been dipped in liquid gold. But now, here in the back of his car, with a mere foot between them, the ring could no longer eclipse the dress.

Her scent—delicate, but with undertones of something potently sexy—permeated the air around them. The dress clung to every curve and dip. Cut down low between her breasts. Baring her back and the vulnerable length of her spine.

Quin had never seen Sadie like this because when they'd been together they'd lived a very simple life. No social engagements. Certainly not ones like this, where the paparazzi lay in wait. He could see them now, up ahead, cameras flashing as various celebrities and VIPs emerged from their cars, as they were about to do.

As if following Quin's line of thought, Sadie turned to him, her hair falling around her shoulders in soft waves. She wore hardly any make-up, but she *glowed* and her eyes looked huge, her lashes so long. But her mouth was tense. It made Quin's fingers itch to touch it…make it lose that line.

When she spoke, she sounded nervous. 'Quin, I've never been to anything like this in my life… I only got as far as meeting you at that party in New York. I don't know what to do.'

A surge of protectiveness rose up in him before he could stop it. He said gruffly, 'Just follow my lead. Stay in the car until I come and get you.'

The car came to a stop. Quin got out and opened Sadie's door, putting out his hand.

He saw her reluctance, but he said, 'It'll be fine—trust me.'

She looked up at him and he saw the way her expression had gone blank, as if she was retreating somewhere inside herself. As her hand met his, he wondered if this was what she'd had to do for four years. Hide behind a mask as well as a fake identity.

She stood up and they walked towards the steps that led up into one of San Francisco's oldest and most iconic buildings, where the exclusive charity event was being hosted.

As soon as the paps realised who he was, they went into a frenzy.

'Hey, Quin! Over here...'

'Who's your date? Quin!'

Sadie was gripping his hand so tightly her nails were digging into the back of his hand, but Quin just smiled and stopped for some photos. He looked down and saw Sadie's dazed expression.

He extricated his hand from hers and put an arm around her waist. She looked up. He said, 'Relax...they can't touch you.'

She smiled weakly. 'This situation is literally my worst nightmare...nowhere to hide.'

He shook his head. 'There's no more hiding.'

He knew that the statement he and his team had prepared, stating that Sadie was the mother of his child and that they were reunited, would be dropping just about now, to coincide with their appearance together tonight. And a sense of satisfaction that he didn't want to investigate too closely rolled through him.

Sadie felt giddy, but she put it down to the sparkling wine that had fizzed up her nose and down her throat. She gazed around in awe at the decadent surroundings of one of San Francisco's most gilded buildings. She needn't have worried about her dress standing out. With all the gold on the walls and muraled ceilings, she positively faded into the background.

Quin hadn't let her go—either keeping an arm around her waist or holding her hand. She relished the contact, greedily and guiltily soaking it up, knowing it was only for appearances. He'd told her about the statement now being released, revealing her identity as Sol's mother.

Maybe her giddiness was also due not only to Quin's proximity, but to the fact that her past on the run was well and truly behind her. She couldn't be more visible now. People were looking at her and whispering, but Sadie couldn't care less. She felt safe beside Quin.

There was a steady stream of acolytes wanting to speak with Quin, and Sadie couldn't help but feel proud of all that he had achieved—even if he hadn't come from an impoverished background like her, as she'd imagined. He'd turned his back on a vast inheritance and that had taken guts.

After a little while, Quin took two fresh glasses of wine from a waiter's tray and led her out to a fragrant outdoor terrace. Sadie took one of the drinks and breathed in the evening air. The city skyline twinkled in the distance… it was magical.

'Thank you.' She raised her glass at him before taking a sip. He loosened his bow tie a little. 'You don't like dressing up?' Sadie observed.

Quin made a face. 'Not really. I never did.'

Sadie put her back to the wall and looked up at him, her gaze taking in the hard, lean planes of his face. Her conscience pricked. He looked so much less carefree than he had when she'd known him before. Was that her fault?

She pushed aside the ever-present guilt and asked, 'Were you ever going to tell me about the world you'd been born into?'

Quin glanced at her, clearly reluctant, as he was whenever his past or his family was mentioned. But eventually he said, 'Of course. I would have had to—we were having a child together.'

'I know you said you liked the anonymity, but why was it so important for you to keep your background from me?'

'I liked the version of me that you saw. Someone who didn't have a massive legacy. I'd grown up with everyone knowing who I was. Looking and judging and whispering. It was a novelty to be free of all that. You weren't tainted with any of the toxicity.'

Sadie absorbed this. 'Your brother...he's older?'

Quin nodded. He turned away from the view and rested back against the wall of the terrace, like Sadie. She turned side on to face him. The rest of the party had faded way into the background. There was only her and him.

'Primo... He was born first, hence his name. Our mother was Brazilian. There's no ambiguity about *his* paternal lineage, he resembles our—*his*—father, albeit just physically. He's a much better man. He has integrity.'

Sadie frowned. 'There are other brothers? Sisters?'

Quin shook his head. 'No, our mother had three miscarriages after Primo—that's why I'm called Quinto. Number five.'

Sadie thought of something. 'That's why you were so insistent on me going to a big hospital for the birth, isn't it?'

Quin nodded, looking slightly uncomfortable. 'I hadn't thought about it like that, but maybe it was a subconscious fear of what might happen.'

Sadie was filled with compassion. 'So many miscarriages… That must have been traumatic for your mother. Are you in touch with her?'

Quin let out a sound that was meant to be a laugh but sounded more like a snarl. 'No, we're not close. I haven't seen her since the day she left us when I was a toddler. Needless to say I don't remember much about her.'

The words landed inside Sadie, softly at first, but as she registered their meaning they detonated inside her like little bombs. She put a hand to her mouth and Quin looked at her. She took her hand down.

'I had no idea…that she walked out on you…and then…' Sadie stopped. It was too huge, the meaning of this. She turned around to face the view, seeing nothing but the enormity of what Quin had just revealed about himself.

She shook her head. Her insides were collapsing in on themselves, her guts twisting with remorse and regret.

She looked at Quin, eyes stinging, and whispered, 'I had no idea… How could I?'

'Would it have changed things? If you'd known that you were repeating the betrayal of my mother?'

Sadie shook her head. 'Please don't say that…it wasn't the same. If I'd known… It would have made it so much harder, but I wouldn't have wanted you to torture yourself, thinking that I'd done it for any other reason than out of—'

'Don't say it!' Quin said harshly.

He shook his head, tension emanating from his tall, powerful body. Sadie could feel it.

He said tautly, 'I can acknowledge that what happened with you was different…but it didn't feel different to me. All I could think about was the fact that my son was going to experience the very same act of betrayal as me. I thought that I'd somehow caused it to happen, made history repeat itself.'

Sadie's throat ached with the effort to hold back her emotion. She knew he wouldn't appreciate it. 'Of course that's not true, Quin. It wasn't your fault at all. I'm so sorry… Please believe I never wanted to betray you and Sol. It was an act to protect you.'

Because I loved you.

But he wouldn't want to hear that. Not yet. Maybe not ever.

The moment hung between them. Tense. Fraught. And then Quin's shoulders dropped.

He said, 'My mother never returned. You did. There's that, at least.'

'I came back the minute I knew it was safe to do so. And I'm not leaving ever again. I know you might not believe me yet. But hopefully you will one day.'

CHAPTER TEN

QUIN LOOKED AT SADIE. Her eyes shone with emotion and a plea. For him to trust her. To believe her. But a weight was lodged in his chest. He had accepted that she was telling the truth about the past, but he knew that he still couldn't fully trust that one day she wouldn't just leave again.

The trauma of her disappearance, compounded by the fact that his mother had done it too, was just too huge to forget—even if their motivations had been very different.

He felt exposed. He hadn't ever fully admitted to himself that he'd blamed himself on some level for Sadie's disappearance. As if he'd brought it on himself, as a kind of punishment for believing himself worthy of love. Worthy of a normal life. Worthy of not being abandoned.

And she was looking at him now as if she could read every exposing thought in his head. Thoughts that led directly to the weight in his chest, making it feel heavier and tighter.

He said abruptly, 'We should go back inside. I need to give my speech.' And then, even though every instinct in him warned him to push Sadie back, he found himself reaching for her hand and keeping her close by his side and it had nothing to do with projecting a united front for the sake of appearances…

* * *

For the rest of the evening Sadie's head reeled with the revelation of Quin's mother's actions. He didn't seem remotely inclined to forgive her, and Sadie could understand why, but she knew better than anyone that things weren't always what they seemed.

Quin had given a passionate and articulate speech about the need for everyone to have access to tech education. Sadie couldn't help feeling proud of his work to extend a hand to those who hadn't had his advantages.

After they'd dined and listened to other speeches from the charity directors, who had then auctioned off various lots, they'd been asked to move into the ballroom, where a band were playing soft jazz. Now people were starting to dance. The lights were dim, candles flickering, sending out a golden glow that made everyone look even more beautiful. Women's dresses shimmered, jewels blinging. Sadie had never witnessed such a glamorous scene.

'Shall we?'

Sadie looked down and saw Quin's hand extended towards her. Her insides plummeted.

She looked at him. 'I can't dance, Quin.'

He took her hand. 'There's nothing to it. Just follow my lead.'

She tried to resist but he was an unstoppable force, and before she knew it they were on the dance floor and he was swinging her into his chest, one arm firm behind her back, fingers splayed across her bare skin. It was enough to distract her from the fact that they were moving—largely propelled by him.

She was pressed against him, and all she could feel was the whipcord strength in his body. She wanted to close her eyes and revel in this moment, but what he'd told her kept whirling in her head, making her chest ache.

She looked up. 'Quin—'

He took her hand in his and put a finger to her mouth. 'Is this about what we spoke of earlier?'

She nodded.

He said, 'I don't want to talk of the past any more. What I'm interested in is the present moment.'

Sadie's heart skipped a beat. He took his hand away. He arched a brow in question.

Sadie half shrugged, half nodded. 'Okay. The present.'

Maybe he was finally ready to move on with a view to the future?

But then he tugged her even closer, and Sadie's cheeks flamed when she felt the burgeoning press of his very *present* arousal.

Their gazes locked. Sadie couldn't have looked away even if she'd wanted to. She felt utterly exposed, bared in her desire for him, but he was equally exposed.

He said, 'I want you, Sadie.'

There was nothing she could do except say, 'I want you too.'

'Clearly we have unfinished business.'

'We have a child—that's the definition of unfinished business,' Sadie observed, even as her heart thumped.

What did Quin mean? Was he saying that—?

'I'm not talking about that. I'm talking about *this*.'

Quin's head lowered to hers, and there on the dance floor he kissed her—a long, slow, drugging kiss that left Sadie's head spinning when he finally drew back.

Yes, resounded in Sadie's head. He was saying he wanted her and he wasn't going to fight it.

Reluctantly she opened her eyes and all she could see was the heated intent in Quin's expression, his face stark.

He said, 'Let's get out of here?'

Sadie nodded, even though she wasn't sure if her legs would function properly. But somehow they did.

Quin didn't even stop to speak to anyone. He had a tight hold on Sadie's hand and all she could do was try to keep up with his long-legged pace. She lifted the folds of the dress in one hand as they went down the steps to where Quin's driver was waiting, holding the car door open.

The journey back to the hotel was swift. Quin didn't let go of her hand all the way up to the suite, and the air vibrated between them with an electrical charge.

Once inside the vast empty suite, Sadie took her hand from Quin's. He was undoing his bow tie fully and pulling it off. He looked a little wild, and every cell in Sadie's body clamoured for her to throw herself at this man right now.

She forced herself to say, 'Are you sure this is a good idea?'

She couldn't bear it if Quin went cold with her again after making love, as if he was punishing himself, and her, for being weak.

He came towards her, all dark, heated intensity. 'Like I said, we have unfinished business. We can't move forward until we've got this desire out of our systems.'

Something inside Sadie cracked a little at the hint of desperation she heard in his voice. Her heart. He believed this was finite—or at the very least he obviously hoped it was finite. And maybe it would be for him. But not for her. She knew that.

But she also knew she didn't have the strength to resist Quin. Not when he was looking at her as if she was the only thing in the world right now. And not when she craved his touch so badly. For four years she'd been in the desert, living a physically and emotionally barren existence. She needed him now. He and Sol were bringing her back to life, restoring her faith in humanity and her sense of home. Because no matter what happened with Quin, Sol would always be her home.

But some small, self-preserving part of her made her ask, 'What if we can't get it out of our systems?'

'I believe we will. It's just lust. Chemistry.'

There it was: the confirmation that Quin didn't want anything more. Didn't expect anything more.

She felt like pointing out that four years and his hatred for her hadn't killed their chemistry. But she didn't say that. She gave in. Succumbed.

'I want you, Quin. Make love to me.'

He came close and surprised her by taking her head in his hands and tipping it up. He looked at her for a long moment, as if learning her face, and Sadie's heart was beating so fast she thought it had to be audible. She'd expected him to take her straight to the bedroom, but if he was going to be like this…he would kill her before they even got there.

'Quin,' she said weakly. 'Kiss me, please.'

He took his time, until Sadie was quivering with need—so much that by the time his mouth covered hers a shudder of pure pleasure went through her whole body. She wound her arms around his neck, opening herself up to him, and his hands splayed across her bare back, hauling her closer.

Sadie wasn't sure how long had passed by the time they'd pulled apart again. Her blood was on fire, her vision was blurry, and she was gasping for oxygen.

Quin lifted her against his chest and walked down the corridor to his bedroom. Low lamps sent out pools of light.

He put her down and Sadie had to lock her knees to stay standing. He stripped with an efficiency that she knew she didn't possess right now and stood before her, tall and powerful. Proud. Virile. She drank him in greedily, stretching out a hand to touch him, tracing over his muscles and blunt nipples, making his breath harsher.

Then he was at her feet, and Sadie put her hands on his shoulders for balance as he removed her high heels, before running his hands up her legs under the dress until he got to her underwear. He tugged it down, and she stepped out of the flimsy lacy briefs.

But Quin didn't get up. He looked up at her and pushed her dress up her legs. He caught one leg behind her knee, lifting it so that it draped over his shoulder. He kept her steady when she would have fallen at the explicit intent in his gaze.

He drew her to him with a firm hold on her waist and bottom. Then he found where she was so exposed—literally—and put his mouth to her, tasting her desire for him…the desire that beat between her legs, hot and urgent.

Sadie gasped when she felt his tongue against her, exploring, licking its way into her and finding that cluster of nerves that throbbed with exquisite pleasure. He reached up and tugged down one strap of the dress, so it fell, exposing her breast. He palmed her flesh, finding her nipple and trapping it between his fingers.

That was all it took to make Sadie fly so high that she couldn't speak or breathe or think. She could only stand in Quin's embrace as she shattered against his mouth.

Quin was drowning in Sadie's scent and taste. He'd dreamed of this on long nights when he'd wake filled with frustration and a kind of pain he never wanted to experience again.

He stood and gathered Sadie into his arms, feeling a rush of emotion that he ruthlessly pushed down. Not emotion. Just sex.

He put her on the bed and looked at her. The dress was like a golden fountain around her body. Her hair was loose and wild. Mouth swollen from his kisses. Cheeks flushed. One breast was exposed, its nipple hard, making his mouth water all over again.

He would never get enough of this woman.

The assertion slid into his head before he could stop it or refute it. But he was too wound up to care right now.

He came down over Sadie, hiking the dress up over her waist, exposing her to his gaze. He pulled down the other strap to expose both breasts and lay beside her, using his hands and mouth to make her ready again, because he knew he wouldn't last long.

She was panting, legs moving, her hands finding every piece of skin she could touch on his body, finding where he was so hard and wrapping her hand around him.

Quin reluctantly took his mouth from her plump flesh, where the hard tip of her nipple was an incitement never to stop feasting on her, but she was going to send him over the edge before he'd even found the bliss he was craving between her legs.

He moved over her and she took her hand off his flesh. With one smooth thrust he was seated inside her, all the way to the hilt, and it was an exquisite torture to exert all the control he had to move in and out and not explode on contact, to eke out the pleasure until their skin was slick with perspiration and Sadie's nails were clawing his back like a hungry cat. But finally he gave in to the gathering storm, letting it wash them both away...

Sadie wasn't sure how long they lay entwined, but she savoured every moment. Quin's big powerful body was in hers, on hers, crushing her. It was a beautiful crush as their hearts finally returned to regular rhythms.

Quin seemed as loathe to break the embrace as she was, only moving after long minutes. Sadie winced a little, but it wasn't from pain—it was from breaking the contact.

Quin lay on his back beside her. The silence was only punctuated by the sounds of sirens, distant and far below, and their breathing. Sadie turned her head to look at Quin and took in his noble profile. It made her think of something.

She pulled the sheet up to her chest and turned on her side. 'Do you know who your real father is?'

Quin said nothing for a long time, and his eyes were closed, so Sadie assumed he must be asleep.

But then he said, 'No. I'd have to ask my mother, and I have no intention of pursuing any contact with her. The rumour mill has it that he was either the pool boy or her personal trainer.'

Sadie's heart clenched for him. She knew he wouldn't want to hear it, but she said, 'She had a lot of miscarriages...she might have been traumatised.'

Quin opened his eyes and turned his head to her. 'Not so traumatised that she didn't seek solace in the arms of another man. Under her husband's nose.' Quin let out a harsh laugh. 'God knows, he was no saint either, and he pretty much abandoned us emotionally, but at least he didn't actually leave.'

'I'm just saying that perhaps things aren't so black and white. Do you even know where she is?'

Quin shrugged. 'Primo mentioned something a while back about her being in Italy with a new husband.'

'Are you close to him?'

'Probably closer than most brothers in our situation. It helped that I never had any desire to go into the family business. We never had to compete. I think he respects what I've achieved on my own.'

'So is he in touch with your mother?'

'No, but I think their paths have crossed at an event.'

'It must have been so confusing and devastating when she left…'

'Yes, it was.'

His meaning was clear: Sadie should know that because she'd done exactly the same thing. Except…she hadn't.

Emotion made her voice thick. 'If I'd known… I can't believe that I re-enacted the worst thing that ever happened to you…and did it to Sol…'

Sadie half expected Quin to get up and leave, but he rolled towards her and put a finger over her lips. He said, 'No more talk of the past. Like I said, all I'm interested in is the present.'

He covered her mouth with his, pulled the sheet down and lifted her bodily, so that she lay on top of him. Sadie weakly gave in to his desire to push the past back, but she knew that they'd never really move on unless Quin realised that it was still casting a toxic shadow over the present—and their future.

They stayed a few more days in San Francisco, while Quin was at his conference. Lena spent a lot of time with her daughter, so Sadie got to spend more time with Sol alone.

They went to the zoo and to parks. And they went to the cinema on the third afternoon—the last day of Quin's conference—to see a charming and heartwarming animated movie about dogs, which had Sol asking Sadie if she thought they might be able to get a dog.

She'd smiled wryly and told Sol that *that* question would have to go to his father.

Sol had sighed dramatically and said, 'It was worth a shot.'

It was only when they were walking back out of the cinema that Sadie noticed the shaven-headed man in dark jeans and a utilitarian-type jacket who was hovering nearby. She'd noticed him earlier that day, and she had a sudden terrifying suspicion that he'd been at the zoo the previous day.

Sadie took Sol's hand and tried not to let him see how panicked she was. She walked away from the cinema quickly and moved down a side street, then ducked into a bookshop.

'Cool,' said Sol, pulling away. 'Can I look for a new comic?'

Sadie said yes, keeping an eye on Sol in the children's section as she pulled out her phone with trembling hands. She dialled Quin's mobile and he answered straight away.

'Is everything okay?'

Sadie was trying to put her back against a bookshelf, so she could see outside the shop, and her insides liquefied with fear when she saw the same man standing at the corner, staring straight at her. He looked terrifying.

'No, it's not. We're being followed by a man.'

Sadie's head was spinning with the implications of this. The police had been wrong. There *was* someone still out to get her—and to get anyone—

'Sadie! *Sadie!*'

Quin's voice broke through the panic but she could hardly get her words out because fear was strangling her. 'Did you hear what I said? We're being followed. The man is looking at me right now.'

'Okay, I'm sending you a photo. Please look at it and tell me if it's the man.'

Somehow Quin's calm voice managed to bring Sadie back from the brink of full-blown panic. She took her phone down from her ear as a photo pinged onto her screen. A photo of the man she'd just been looking at.

She frowned and lifted the phone to her ear again. 'Yes, that's him. But how do you—?'

'He's Security, he's been hired by me.'

'I… Oh.'

Quin said, 'Look, you don't have to worry, okay? He's meant to be there. I have to go now, but I'll talk to you later.'

And then he was gone.

Sadie and Sol got back to the hotel a couple of hours later and she did her best to stay calm during his bedtime routine. He went out like a light, clearly happy and exhausted, but Sadie took little comfort in that.

By the time Quin arrived back to the suite she was keyed up and practically pacing the floor.

He came into the living area and stopped when he saw her. He frowned. 'Is everything okay? Where's Sol?'

Sadie stopped pacing and said tightly, 'He's fine. He's in bed, asleep.'

'So what's wrong?'

Sadie looked at him and folded her arms over her chest, as if that might hide the sense of hurt and betrayal she'd felt since talking to him earlier.

'I know you don't trust me, but I didn't think you would actually hire someone to make sure I don't disappear again, this time with Sol.'

He looked at her as if she'd grown two heads. 'What gave you that idea?'

Sadie unlocked her arms and flung out a hand. 'The man who looks like he's come straight out of Central Casting for Scary Guy. The kind of man I've had nightmares about for the last four years.'

Quin shook his head. 'He's a bodyguard—highly recommended by Claude, my friend who works in security.'

'To protect Sol from…me? In case I try to take him?'

'No!' Quin slashed a hand through the air. 'To protect you *and* Sol. Claude has assured me that you're safe from any threat, but I didn't want to take any chances—especially since we've now appeared in the press and your face is out there.'

Sadie sat down on a chair behind her, her legs giving way.

She felt like saying, *You can say that again.* She'd nearly passed out with shock when she'd seen her face staring back at her from the front page of a daily newspaper with the lurid headline: *Quin Holt's baby mama! Who is Sadie Ryan?*

She looked at Quin, feeling a little chastened. 'I'm sorry… When I saw him and realised he was following us, I got such a fright. Then, when you said he was Security, I just assumed…' She trailed off. She'd assumed the worst. That Quin was protecting his son—from her.

'No,' Quin refuted. '*I'm* sorry. I should have told you. I meant to earlier, but I…forgot.'

Sadie's face grew hot as she thought of that morning, when Quin had stolen out of her bed as dawn was breaking, leaving her in a sated slumber. He hadn't wanted to risk Sol waking and looking for him.

They hadn't spent a night apart since making love after the charity function. Gravitating towards each other without saying a word. Making love with an intensity that left Sadie breathless and trembling but hungry for more.

It hadn't been like this before. Back then there'd been a lazy indulgence to their lovemaking; they hadn't known they were on borrowed time. But now it was as if they were up against a ticking clock that Sadie couldn't see. The ticking clock of Quin's desire for her.

'Have you eaten?' he asked.

Sadie shook her head. 'No, but I made Sol a burger.' She hadn't had the appetite, too wound up after what had happened.

'Come into the kitchen. I'll make something.'

Sadie's mouth fell open. 'You? Make something?' It had been a running joke between them that Quin couldn't navigate his way around a kitchen.

He looked sheepish. 'Yes, me. Let's just say I've had to cultivate some rudimentary culinary skills since Sol was born.'

Sadie stood up and followed Quin into the small kitchen. She sat on a high stool and watched with interest as he took out some eggs and an array of other items, proceeding to chop and whisk with enviable skill for someone who four years ago hadn't been able to boil an egg.

Sadie remarked, 'I just assumed you'd had an indulgent mother.'

'Not an indulgent mother—just an army of staff. I don't think I ever stepped foot inside the kitchen in any of our houses.'

Curious, Sadie asked, 'Has your father—?' She broke

off. 'I keep referring to him as your father...what is your relationship with him now?'

She saw tension come into Quin's body even as he said lightly, 'As minimal as possible. It's not as if he was ever a hands-on father anyway. He treated me and my brother more like staff, and his relationship with me was strained because even before it was confirmed he'd always suspected I wasn't his.'

'So he hasn't met Sol, then?'

'No interest.'

'Poor Sol...no grandparents to speak of.'

Something hissed in the pan on the stove, breaking the moment, and Quin attended to it.

When he turned back, he shook his head. 'You had no one.'

Hearing him acknowledge that fact, Sadie felt something deep inside her—a part of her that had always felt jagged—suddenly wasn't so sharp. 'Like I said, others had it much worse than me.'

'You're a survivor.'

Sadie blinked. No one had ever said that to her before. She shook her head. 'Really, I don't think I am. I just dealt with the circumstances I found myself in.'

'Your first instinct today was to protect Sol.'

'Of course,' she breathed. 'He's the most important thing.'

'Yes, he is.'

They looked at each other for a long moment, and then Quin seemed to break out of a trance.

'Let's eat.'

He plated up a delicious fluffy omelette and some bread. He opened a bottle of white wine and they sat and ate and drank in a companionable silence that Sadie didn't want to risk by opening her mouth again.

Quin was the first to speak when he'd cleared the plates. 'Sol has a half-term break next week. After we've dropped Lena back to Sao Paulo, I was thinking of taking him to Sao Sebastiao for a few days.'

'Sao Sebastiao…?'

Sadie wasn't even aware she'd spoken out loud. It was the most cherished place to her, but also a place of heartbreak, because that was where she'd left Quin and Sol behind.

'You still go there?' she asked.

Quin nodded, suddenly looking a little guarded. He took a sip of wine and put the glass back down. Sadie felt a little confused. Surely after what had happened the place would have bad connotations for Quin? Or…

Her insides shrank as something else occurred to her.

Perhaps it was no hardship for Quin to return precisely because it *didn't* hold any emotional pain for him. Because when she'd left he'd realised that he hadn't really loved her at all? To Sadie's mind, that suddenly seemed all too plausible.

'You're welcome to join us, of course,' he said.

Sadie thought of going back to where she'd been so happy and where she'd been so heartbroken. Bittersweet… If it wasn't a chance to spend more precious time with Sol she'd almost be tempted to decline, but of course she wouldn't.

She couldn't help feeling a sense of disquiet, though, that the place where they'd been so happy would ultimately make them again…or break them.

She forced a smile. 'I'd love to come.'

CHAPTER ELEVEN

SAO SEBASTIAO WAS exactly as Sadie remembered, its buildings with their colonial era architecture spread out between the mountains and the ocean. It was all at once sleepy and beachy, but also busy. This was why she'd got off a bus here one day—because she'd deemed it the perfect place to hide out for a bit.

Little had she known how her life would change here.

They'd arrived at a private airfield shortly before, and now Quin was driving a slightly battered open-top four-wheel drive, with their luggage in the back.

Sol was jumping up and down on the back seat with excitement. 'Can I go straight over to Joao's house when we get there?'

Quin glanced at his son through the rearview mirror. 'After you unpack and show Sadie around.'

'Okay, Papa.'

Sadie smiled and looked back at Sol from where she sat in the passenger seat. She was enjoying the salty sea breeze in her hair and the sun on her skin. 'Who is Joao?'

'My best friend. He lives right along the beach—practically next door.'

Sadie had absorbed the word *beach*, but never thought for a second that Sol was talking about—

But now they were turning down a road towards a beach that looked all too familiar.

Except Sadie could see changes. There was a high fence now, where there hadn't been a fence before.

Quin was turning the vehicle towards a set of discreet gates that almost disappeared into the lush foliage.

He pressed a button on a key chain and the gates opened. Sadie held her breath as he drove onto a short driveway that opened out into an open space where a simple beach house stood. The faint sound of crashing waves could be heard in the distance.

The house had been extended, she could see that—to the sides and to the roof. But it was unmistakably the same beach house where she'd lived with Quin. Except he'd only been renting it at that time...

Sol was already out of the car and running towards a woman who'd appeared in the main doorway and was hugging him with great affection.

Sadie got out, feeling a sense of déjà vu, and slightly dizzy.

Quin met her at the front of the car and said, 'Come and meet Fernanda. She and her sister take care of the house and gardens when we're not here, and they stock up when we come.'

Sadie couldn't move, though. She just looked at him. 'It's the house. Our house.'

Quin's jaw was tight, and then he said, 'I bought it and did some renovations.'

Sadie wanted to ask *why*, but the young woman was coming towards them now, holding out her hand.

'You must be Sadie. It's nice to meet you. I'm Fernanda.'

Sadie smiled at the friendly woman, who was very pretty, with dark brown eyes and crazy corkscrew curls in a soft halo around her head. Sadie couldn't help but respond to her easy warmth even in the midst of her shock, and smiled back, shaking her hand.

After greeting Quin with warm and easy affection, the woman led them in, saying to Quin, 'I've put out some snacks and drinks, dinner is in the fridge, and there are enough supplies to last a month.'

'Thanks, Fernanda. I appreciate it, as always.'

'No worries, boss—you pay me more than enough to make it worth my while!' She winked at Sadie, then addressed Quin again. 'Elena will come over at some stage to talk through some changes she wants to make to the garden.'

'Okay.'

Sadie turned to Quin. 'How much land is there?'

'About an acre.'

'Wow.'

Sol appeared in the room. 'Come on, Sadie. I want to show you everything.'

She did as she was bade and let Sol take her by the hand and show her around the house, almost thankful for his distracting chatter when a slew of memories rushed back at her on seeing the familiar rooms and then the new ones.

Downstairs, the house had been opened out into a huge living/dining area, and there was a beautiful kitchen overlooking the verdant back lawn where Sadie could see a pool. She noted that Sol was now in what had been her and Quin's bedroom upstairs. She was glad he didn't want to linger there too long. It was too full of memories. The master bedroom suite was now in the dormer extension. There was a balcony, with stunning views of the beach and the sea.

Tears pricked Sadie's eyes as she remembered being on that beach and looking back at this house, catching her first glimpse of Quin on the porch.

'And your room is over here.'

Sadie turned around to see Sol trying to haul her wheelie suitcase into a bedroom across the hall from Quin's. It was almost a mirror image of Quin's, but with no balcony—just windows overlooking the pool and beautiful gardens.

Sadie followed Sol into the room, and to her surprise he ran over and wrapped his arms around her waist. She hugged him back, bending down and pressing a kiss to his head.

He looked up at her. 'I'm glad you're my mom. I knew you were special when I first saw you.'

Sadie's heart swelled at his sweet words. She smiled. 'The minute I saw you, I knew *you* were very special.'

His eyes widened. 'When I was a baby?'

She nodded. 'When you were born, you didn't even cry. You just looked up at me and it was as if you'd been here before—do you know what they call that?'

He shook his head, fascinated. 'No, what?'

'An old soul.'

'Wow, cool.'

And then, like most children, Sol was already moving on, pulling away.

'Come on! Let's find Papa and go to the beach!'

'I'll follow you down.'

But Sol was gone.

Sadie took in a big shuddery breath.

'Okay?'

She whirled around at the sound of Quin's voice. He was wearing jeans and a T-shirt. Relaxed. Sexy. At home here.

She forced her mind away from all Quin's attributes and nodded. 'Fine… You've done an amazing job on the renovations.'

'They were your suggestions, remember?'

Sadie nodded slowly. Yes. She remembered it now. A conversation when she'd listed all the things she'd do if she owned the beach house. She'd been the one who'd said that she'd love a dormer room with a balcony, so she could sit and watch the dawn breaking. Her favourite time of day.

Maybe that was why she hadn't remembered at first—because it was so utterly bittersweet to see that Quin had gone ahead and done it. *Ready for someone else?* Because sooner or later he would move on, and be with another woman. Perhaps marry her. Have more children—siblings for Sol. And where would Sadie fit into that equation? The thought of being further and further sidelined as his new family formed made her feel a sharp pain in her chest.

She realised Quin had walked into his own room and was standing on the balcony. She joined him, still feeling emotional.

Sol's and Fernanda's voices floated up from downstairs.

'Why did you buy it, Quin? After what happened, I would've thought you'd never want to see this place again.'

He didn't answer for a long time, and then he spoke almost as if to himself. 'I stayed here for a month afterwards, with Sol. Expecting that you'd just reappear. I thought maybe you'd suffered some sort of post-partum depression or something. I thought if I waited...'

Sadie said nothing—just looked at Quin's profile.

He went on, 'And then... I think I knew. I couldn't feel you any more. Somehow I knew you were far away. But even when I knew I had to leave—because I had to work and I needed support for me and Sol—I just couldn't let the house go.' He made a little huffing sound. 'You see, even then—as angry as I was—I imagined you returning to the house, finding new people living here and not being able to contact me even though you had my phone number. It was irrational, but I kept on paying the rent after we left. And when the lease was due for renewal I found myself offering to buy it.'

He finally looked at Sadie, and she almost recoiled at the bleak pain she saw in his eyes. She knew it instantly. *He had loved her.*

'Even though I hated you for what you had done to us, I couldn't bear the thought that you might come back and find the place taken over,' he said. He shook his head at himself. 'How messed up is that? In the end I decided we'd use it as a holiday home and had it renovated.'

Sadie looked blindly out at the view, tears blurring her vision. She blinked them back. When she spoke her voice was rough. 'I can't keep saying I'm sorry, Quin. Sooner or later you'll have to accept that we can't go back. I did what I did at the time because I was terrified I would bring harm to you and Sol…and your friend Claude has confirmed how real the danger was…'

She looked at him. The enormity of being back here was dissolving every wall she'd had to build to protect herself in the last four years. She had nowhere to hide.

She could only say, 'But you need to know that I never stopped loving you, Quin. I still love you. The first thing I did when I learned that I could have my life back was come to find you and Sol.'

If Sadie had hoped that Quin's features would melt at hearing those words and he would gather her into his arms, then she'd been a fool. Still some part of her dared to hope…but he was like stone.

And then he shook his head. 'I'm sorry… I can't…'

Sadie's insides curled in on themselves. Ice went into her veins as some sort of self-protection.

Before she could figure out how to respond, how to get

out of this conversation with any shred of dignity, Sol appeared in the doorway of the bedroom.

'Come on, guys…hurry up!'

Sadie looked at her son. He was her focus now. The centre of her world.

She moved away from Quin and went back to her room on wooden legs, somehow forcing a brightness she did not feel into her voice. 'Okay, give me two minutes.'

'I never stopped loving you, Quin… I still love you.'

Quin had heard the words, but it was as if they'd hit a glass wall before they could impact him. In spite of knowing that Sadie had never meant to hurt him, or Sol, he still couldn't seem to let go of the cold, hard pain inside him.

All he could think of—especially here and now, in this place—was that awful moment when he'd returned to find the house empty. Sadie gone. And then…as the minutes and hours had passed…mild concern had given way to confusion, building panic. He'd found her note just when he'd been contemplating calling the police.

He'd gone out into the streets to look for her, not understanding what on earth the note could mean. Surely she was joking? Or maybe she was just unwell.

He'd had Sol strapped to his chest as he'd walked for hours. But there'd been no trace of her.

An awful, liquefying panic had settled into his limbs, making him feel weak. Reminding him of how he'd felt when he'd realised his mother had left him. When he'd found no trace of her left in their house because their father had had all her things removed.

He'd had to sit down on a bench. An old woman had been there. She'd looked at Sol and heard him fretting a

little, and she'd smiled and said, 'His mama will be needing him back soon.'

He'd told Sadie just now that he'd kept the house and had
it renovated in case she returned, but he knew it went deeper
than that and he couldn't ignore it. He hadn't been able to
let go of it, in spite of what had happened, because this was
where he'd been happiest. And somehow that had eclipsed
the pain. But it exposed him now. Exposed his weakness.
Just like she'd exposed his weakness before. Making him
fall for her. Making him vulnerable. Exposing him to pain.

Quin was still standing on his balcony a few minutes
later, when he saw Sadie emerge onto the beach below him
with Sol. Her hair was pulled up in a ponytail and she was
wearing denim cut-off shorts and a singlet, under which
he could see a turquoise bikini top. Her feet were bare.

Something inside him cracked. Like this, even with
her paler skin and lighter hair, she looked exactly like the
Sadie he'd first met. Shy and blushing. And then bolder,
more confident. Chattering non-stop about everything and
everything. Passionate. *Loving.*

Sadie might still love him, but her words couldn't even
make a dent in the solid wall he'd had to build inside himself to weather the pain of her abandonment. Opening himself up to Sadie again emotionally...*no*. The mere notion
made Quin's hand grip onto the railing of the balcony, so
tight that his knuckles shone white.

He wouldn't survive. And his son needed him.

His future could not be with this woman, even though
he knew she had a right to be in Sol's life. That way lay
certain pain. Because he would never not be waiting for
the day when he would return to find her gone again. And
that made a vice squeeze his chest so hard it hurt.

Sadie and Sol were further down the beach now, kicking a ball. Sol stopped suddenly, and turned and looked back. He saw Quin. He raised his hands to his mouth and shouted something, but Quin couldn't hear what he said. He raised his hand to indicate that he would join them.

It had been a mistake to come here—especially with her. The place was too full of ghosts and memories. He hadn't needed love in his life until he'd met Sadie, and he would never forgive her for making him fall for her. Nor would he ever be so weak again.

A sense of desperation filled him. Surely he would be able to find a way to minimise their contact? He would help set her up in her own place. Find her independence. There would have to be a way. And then this constant craving he felt would surely diminish.

He turned from the view and felt a sense of bleakness lodge in his gut. But bleak was good—better than pain.

That night, Quin woke to sounds of moaning...anguish. Assuming it was Sol, he checked on him—but his son was sleeping soundly in his bed, covers kicked aside, legs askew. Quin pulled the sheet back up and went out into the hall, closing the door softly behind him.

Maybe he'd imagined hearing the—

But it came again, and this time he realised it was from Sadie's room. Afraid she'd wake Sol, Quin went to her room and pushed open the door. Her covers were off too. She wore only sleep shorts and a vest top.

She was moving restlessly. He could see that her skin was slick with perspiration and her head was moving back and forth.

She moaned again. 'No...please, no...don't go away... come back...'

The sense of déjà vu was strong. She'd had nightmares when they'd been together.

Quin went over and put his hands on her arms, holding her gently but firmly. But it seemed to make her worse.

She started thrashing and mumbling incoherently. 'Please…don't try to stop me… No… *No!*'

She shouted that last word and, acting on instinct, Quin bent his head and covered her mouth with his to swallow her cries. He could feel it when her body relaxed under his hands…under his chest.

He pulled back. She was looking at him, eyes wide.

'Quin? Are you…? Am I still dreaming?'

Quin could fee her breasts moving against his chest, the sharp points of her nipples. He said, 'You were having a nightmare.'

She seemed to look beyond him and said, 'I was… I was on the beach, and you and Sol were really far away, and I was calling you but you couldn't hear me, and you wouldn't turn around, and then someone was holding on to me, stopping me from getting to you…'

Quin felt a shiver down his spine. For a while after Sadie had left he'd had exactly the same dream—except he was the one trying to reach her and she couldn't hear him.

He moved further back, but her hands clasped onto his arms. 'Please, don't leave me yet, Quin.'

Quin gritted his jaw. He'd ignored the temptation to come to her after Sol had fallen asleep earlier; he knew he would never be able to move on if he touched her again. But now his resolve was fast melting into the heat haze clouding his brain and the rising of his blood.

Sadie whispered, 'Can you just stay with me for a bit, please?'

Quin said, 'Move over.'

Sadie scooted into the middle of the bed and Quin lay down behind her, wrapping his arms around her. Holding her. Her backside nestled into his groin, fitting like a missing jigsaw piece. His body responded to her proximity at once, but he exerted every ounce of control to keep it at bay.

Eventually he could feel Sadie relaxing against him, her breaths evening out. He told himself he'd move soon... once he was sure that she was asleep. But, frankly, it felt so familiar and good to hold her like this that he gave in to the impulse and let his own muscles relax...until he too found himself drifting off.

Quin was gone when Sadie woke the next morning. But her body was still humming in the aftermath of what had happened when they'd both woken in the night to find themselves entwined. They'd moved to turn face to face. Sadie had pressed a kiss to Quin's mouth—a *thank you* for comforting her as much as anything else. She'd craved his touch so much after that awful dream...she'd felt so cold.

When she'd kissed him, she'd half expected him to pull away—because it had been clear he'd had no intention of staying earlier in the night, until she'd begged him. But after a long moment he'd kissed her back, and a slow but intense frenzy had overtaken them as they'd mutually combusted.

She'd told him she loved him.

She waited for a sense of regret and embarrassment, but it didn't come. She felt lighter. There was no way she could have kept those words inside—not here in this place where they'd been so happy. Where they'd made their beautiful son.

She knew she faced certain heartache now, but it would be nothing compared to the agony she'd endured for four years.

Birds tweeted outside. Sadie could hear Sol's voice downstairs, and she revelled in a brief moment of appreciating where she was, in spite of the realisation that since they'd arrived here whatever accord she'd reached with Quin had taken about four steps back.

She got up and showered in the generous en suite bathroom and dressed in a pair of indigo blue shorts and a matching sleeveless shirt. Sara had packed her bag in Sao Paulo before they'd come here, and it was still such a revelation to be wearing clothes that weren't falling apart at the seams from over-washing.

Tying her hair back roughly, Sadie went downstairs to find Sol seated at the dining table, with his mouth full and a delicious smell of…

'Is that pancakes?'

Sol swallowed his mouthful with comic facial expressions and said, 'Papa made them—they're amazing.'

Quin was behind the kitchen island in a T-shirt, avoiding direct eye contact with Sadie. Her face grew hot just remembering the previous night…

Sol addressed his father. 'Papa, can Mom have pancakes too?'

Sadie's heart stopped and Quin's hands stopped. Now he looked at her, but she couldn't read his expression. She looked at her son, who had no idea what he'd just done by calling her *Mom* for the first time.

Sol looked from her undoubtedly shocked face to Quin. 'What's wrong?'

Quin recovered first, saying briskly, 'Of course she can—and you can have one more and then you need to change for the match.'

A lock of Sol's hair fell forward and he pushed it back. 'Stupid hair… It's getting in my eyes, Papa.'

'You need a trim. We can find a barber shop here later on.'

'I can cut his hair,' Sadie offered, without thinking. She'd used to cut kids' hair all the time.

Sol's eyes bugged. 'You can cut hair?'

Sadie nodded. 'I'm a hairdresser…among other things.'

Jill of all trades… She'd had to be to blend into different places.

'Wow! Papa, did you hear that? She can cut my hair. That's so cool!'

Quin was looking at her. 'Are you sure?'

Sadie shrugged. 'Of course. We can do it after breakfast if there's time. It won't take long.'

'Yes, please. Papa! Can I? Then my hair won't get in the way when I'm playing football.'

Quin shrugged too. 'Sure.'

They had breakfast, Quin serving up more fluffy, light pancakes with fruit and syrup…fragrant coffee. But it was as if last night hadn't happened. For her own sanity Sadie knew she needed to talk to him about it, and what she'd said yesterday, to see if there was any hope at all for them. For a future.

She had to know, because she needed to be able to move on and carve out an existence for herself if Quin really didn't see her in his future.

She took Sol up to the bathroom after breakfast and sat him in a chair, with a towel around his shoulders. Luckily she'd got used to carrying her hairdresser's kit with her, because it was always an easy means to make money.

Sol was looking at her in the mirror with wide eyes, as if fascinated by this creature who was also his mother. She gave him the smallest of buzz cuts around his ears, and then trimmed and styled his hair into a baby Mohican, like the one she'd seen on his favourite football player.

Sol looked at himself. 'I can't wait to show Joao!'

Sadie took off the towel and shook it out over the bath, and then Sol threw his arms around her waist and buried his head in her belly.

He looked up. 'You're so cool, Mom.'

Sadie said carefully, 'You don't have to call me Mom yet, if it feels weird.'

He shook his head. 'I waited for you for a long time.'

Sadie's heart split open at this unwittingly poignant assessment, but before she could respond Sol was gone again, saying, 'I have to get changed for the match.'

Sadie sat down on the chair she'd used to cut Sol's hair. She had to force herself to remember that it had only been a couple of weeks since she'd come back into Quin's and Sol's lives. Surely this sensation of being on a rollercoaster wouldn't last for ever?

She could hear Quin shouting up the stairs. 'Come on, Sol. Joao will be wondering where you are.'

'I'm coming!'

Even that banal domestic exchange was enough to send her insides swooping with emotion again.

When she'd cleaned up, and felt a bit more together, she went downstairs to find Quin tidying up. Sol had obviously gone to get his friend.

He glanced up. 'Thank you for cutting his hair. He loves it.'

Sadie felt self-conscious. 'Kids that age love a buzz cut.' She could feel the tension in the air and blurted out, 'Look, about last night—'

Quin cut her off. 'I shouldn't have let it happen.' He put down a plate and looked at her. 'I think the shock of seeing you again, and the fact that the chemistry is still there, has blurred the boundaries… But it's not fair on you, me or Sol. He'll get confused if he senses that we're…together.'

Now Sadie felt guilty.

But Quin said, 'It's not your fault.'

The unspoken words were very clear. He was blaming himself for being weak.

'I was the one who had the nightmare. I asked you to stay.'

Begged. Her face grew hot.

A muscle in his jaw popped. 'I could have controlled myself better. I think it was a mistake coming here… I'm not sure if it's a good idea to stay. You've been established now as Sol's mother, so there's no real need to keep up any pretence that we're together.'

Sadie went cold all over. 'If this is because I told you I loved you… Don't ruin your holiday because of me. I can go back to Sao Paulo.'

He looked at her, and then he said, 'That might be for the best. We need to put down some new boundaries. I can arrange transport.'

Sadie's insides were plummeting into a deep void of pain. So this was it. The briefest of fraught honeymoons was over. She chastised herself. She'd known that they needed to talk about this. She just hadn't been prepared for Quin's brutally rapid response and rejection.

'No,' she said, feeling sick. 'I can go to the bus station and get the bus.'

His gaze narrowed on her. 'Is that what you did that day?'

Sadie's gut churned. 'Yes.' And then, before the past could reach out its tentacles to poison the present even more, she asked, 'Is there no chance at all of us trying… to be a family?'

An expression somewhere between anger and pain flashed across Quin's face. 'I grieved for you, Sadie,' he said roughly. 'I've never grieved for anyone in my life—

not even my own mother. But I grieved for you. And I won't ever risk that kind of hurt or loss again.'

Sadie's heart ached. 'I love you, Quin, and I never want you to be hurt again. I never wanted to hurt you in the first place. You gave me the only sense of belonging and home that I've ever had. *You* are my home. You are my world. You are everything that I love and adore, and I will never, ever leave you and Sol again if you give me a chance.'

Sadie stopped talking. She was raw.

Quin just looked at her, and she could see the pain in his eyes. The pain she had put there. The pain she feared was insurmountable.

And he confirmed it when he shook his head. 'No, I can't do it, Sadie.'

She couldn't breathe. And then, in the distance, she heard Sol's excited voice, and suddenly knew she wouldn't be able to keep it together if he saw her.

So she said, 'I'll go upstairs and start packing. Just tell Sol I had to go back early.'

Quin nodded. 'I'll be gone for the day too.'

So this was it.

Sadie looked at Quin, feeling as if her heart was being ripped out of her chest, still beating. It was agony, being sent away like this, but she couldn't argue with him. Sol had to come first, and if there was any danger of him getting too attached, and then confused by their actions, Sadie would never forgive herself.

The last four years had strengthened her in ways that she was only appreciating now. She could do this. She had no choice.

'Goodbye, Quin.'

His face was like stone. 'We'll discuss what happens next back in Sao Paulo.'

CHAPTER TWELVE

QUIN'S VERY BRITTLE sense of satisfaction lasted until about half-time in the football game—not that he'd been able to focus on it up to that point. All he could see in his mind's eye was the pale set to Sadie's face and the pleading look in her eyes for his understanding when she'd disappeared before Sol returned.

And then the look of abject disappointment on Sol's face when she hadn't been there.

Quin had felt like the lowest of the low, knowing he was hurting his son, but if anything Sol's disappointment only proved that he was doing the right thing in setting down boundaries.

He pictured her now, getting on the bus to Sao Paulo, repeating the journey she'd taken that fateful day four years ago.

And suddenly the flimsy, brittle facade of control he'd been clinging on to fell apart like shards of glass falling out of a window frame, cutting him so deep that he realised this was the first time he'd felt such pain in four years.

The kind of pain he'd thought he'd avoid because he was in control here.

Hadn't he'd just demonstrated that by sending Sadie away? Before she could leave again and rip his heart out and tear it to pieces.

But it hadn't worked. Because he was no more in control of his pain now than he'd been in control of anything since he'd laid eyes on her again and his life had been spun off its axis—much like the way it had when he'd first laid eyes on her.

She'd told him she loved him. That she'd never stopped. Her words had been lying in wait inside him and were now detonating like bombs, intensifying that pain, mocking him for believing that he was impenetrable.

Quin felt as if he was unravelling at the seams. Cracking open. Losing his bearings. Everything he'd clung to for the past four years was dissolving and being replaced with a vast abyss, into which he was falling with nothing to grab on to.

Suddenly he knew what he had to do. He felt wild, desperate. Urgent.

It was half-time. Sol was there in front of him. 'Did you see the goal I nearly got? I wish Mom was here—maybe then I would have scored.'

Quin knelt down on one knee. He said, 'There's something I need to go and do, so I'm going to arrange for you to go home with Joao afterwards. Is that okay?'

Looking wise beyond his years, but also very much like a little boy who had just got his mother back, he said, 'If it's to do with Mom then, yes, that's okay.'

Quin kissed his son and made a phone call. He left the football ground and went straight to the bus station.

But the bus to Sao Paulo had already left.

He felt sick. He'd just put Sadie through the cruelty of repeating the horrific journey she'd made when she'd left them, all because Quin was determined to beat her with the stick of his mother's sins. And his own cowardice.

Enough. It was time to move on.

All he could think of to do now, though, was to go back to the house. He would have time to think while Sol was with his friend.

When he got back to the house he stopped at the door, the pain in his chest intensifying. He knew he was about to walk into an empty house. And this time he couldn't blame Sadie for leaving because he was the one who had engineered this painful re-enactment.

He deserved every ounce of pain he was feeling.

He opened the door and went inside, steeling himself for the house to be empty. And it was. But then Quin noticed that the door leading out to the porch was open, the warm sea breeze making the curtains move.

He frowned. He was sure he'd closed the door, but maybe Sol had run back out to get something just before they'd left.

He went over and stopped on the threshold. Because someone was outside, standing at the railing. *Sadie*. Here. Not gone. Was he hallucinating? Conjuring her up? Like he had so many times in the past? Like in the dreams he'd had?

She turned around and saw him. Her eyes were huge and suspiciously red. She shook her head and said brokenly, 'I'm so sorry, but I just…couldn't get on the bus. I couldn't do it, Quin. I couldn't take that journey again… away from here, away from you and Sol.'

Quin closed his eyes for a second and sent up a silent promise to every deity that he would spend his lifetime atoning for this if he was lucky enough to get the chance.

He moved forward and touched Sadie. She was real.

He pulled her into his arms and said, 'I'm so sorry for doing that to you…please forgive me.'

Sadie revelled in the way Quin was holding her for a long moment, not daring to breathe in case this was a cruel mirage and he disappeared. But he felt so solid, and his heart was beating so steadily. Maybe a tiny bit fast.

She knew she should pull away before she dared to hope…*anything*. But Quin was the one to put his hands on her arms and put some distance between them. She couldn't look at him. She was sure she must be a sight. She hadn't stopped crying since she'd let the bus go, anticipating Quin's anger that she was still here. But he didn't seem angry.

He tipped up her chin and she had to look at him. There was an expression on his face that she hadn't seen since they'd met again. *Open.* Contrite.

He said, 'I need to say some things, okay?'

Sadie just nodded. Quin led her over to one of the recliner chairs and gently pushed her down. She welcomed it; her legs were like jelly. He stayed standing, then he moved away and stood with his back to the railing and the view.

He looked at her and said, 'When my mother left, I blamed myself.'

Sadie wanted to go to him, but she was aware of the fragility of this moment. 'You were only a toddler.'

'Yes, I was only a baby. But I remember holding on to her, begging her not to go. Crying. Afterwards I thought it was my fault because I'd been too emotional, too over-wrought, so after that it became habitual for me to ignore my emotions and to compartmentalise things.'

'And then you came along,' he went on, 'and with one look at you, before we'd even spoken, I felt every single wall I'd built up inside me to keep me safe start crumbling to pieces.'

Sadie felt shy. 'I was a nobody…'

Quin shook his head. 'No. You were amazing.'

Hope sparked inside Sadie, but she tried not to let it bloom. 'But then I lost my memory… I didn't even know who I was.'

Quin's mouth tipped up. 'You were probably more authentically you precisely *because* you had no memory of who you were. You weren't like any woman I'd ever met. There was no artifice. No games. Everything you felt showed on your face. You found joy in everything. It was so obvious that you loved me—'

'Stop!' Sadie ducked her head, letting her hair fall down.

But Quin came over and sat down near her. He took her hands and made sure she was looking at him before he said, 'I couldn't help falling fathoms deep in love with you. It would have taken a force stronger than I was capable of to resist you.'

Sadie bit her lip and then said, 'I wasn't sure if you ever *had* loved me.'

Quin's gaze was on her mouth, then it moved up to her eyes. 'More than I'd loved anyone else in my life. I hadn't truly loved before, and it was only when you left that I realised how much you'd changed me. It compounded my feeling of betrayal. I felt so naked...exposed.'

Sadie tensed. Nothing had changed. She pulled back from his hands. 'I can't keep apologising, Quin—

But he stopped her words as he reached for her and covered her mouth with his. Surprise and shock made her go still.

He pulled back. 'I don't want you to apologise ever again. You have nothing to be sorry for. It's only now that I'm a father that I can appreciate the selfless bravery it took for you to do what you did. And you shame me— because I'm not sure if I could have done it.'

Sadie was confused. 'Quin...what?'

'If anyone owes apologies, it's me.'

'But you didn't do anything.'

Quin let out a short, harsh sound and stood up from the

seat. He went back to the porch railing. Sadie got up too and went to stand beside him. He wouldn't look at her.

'I let you clean my house, Sadie…'

'I offered to clean. I wanted to feel useful.'

He looked at her and she saw the shame in his eyes.

'You offered to clean because I made you feel like an unwanted guest.'

'You were shocked to see me.'

Quin let out another harsh sound, half a laugh and half something else. Anguish. 'Why did you let me treat you like that?'

'Because I was finally back with you and my son. And, frankly, cleaning a bathroom was nothing compared to what I'd endured for four years. I was willing to do anything to absolve the horrible guilt I felt.'

Quin took her by the hand again and led her over to the recliner, sitting down and pulling her onto his lap, wrapping his arms around her. Sadie knew something momentous was happening, but she was too afraid to call it what it was. It didn't necessarily mean what she hoped it meant.

Nevertheless, she let herself melt into him, his strong, powerful body holding hers. She felt the ever-present hum of desire between them, but she also felt something infinitely deeper that transcended desire. After a long moment he spoke, and she could feel his chest rumbling under her cheek.

'The whole time I told myself I was hating you, I still loved you. The whole time I told myself I should never have trusted you, I was really angry for trusting myself— for letting myself fall so hard for a woman who would cruelly re-enact the worst betrayal I'd ever experienced.'

Sadie opened her mouth—but, as if reading her mind, Quin put a finger to her lips.

'I have to say this,' he said. 'That was just a tragic co-incidence, but I clung to it for four years, because hating you and blaming you was easier than admitting how much I loved you and how hurt I was. It helped me survive, I'm ashamed to say.'

Sadie tipped her head back and looked up at him. 'I'm sure I would have done the same.'

Quin looked down at her and shook his head. 'No way. You weren't cynical, like me. I'd forgotten how cynical I was—I thought that was your fault too. Believe me, anything I could have blamed you for I latched on to it like a drowning man to a buoy in the middle of the ocean.'

'If it helped you survive, then I don't mind.'

Quin's fingers traced her jaw and his mouth quirked. 'No, you wouldn't. Because you're a far better person than me, Sadie Ryan.'

Sadie's heart hitched. She came up higher and rested her hand on Quin's chest. The way he was holding her… the things he was saying…she was too afraid to let this go further if his endgame was still to send her away.

'What are you saying? Do you still want me to leave?'

His jaw tightened, and then he said, 'Have you not noticed that since the moment you appeared in front of me in New York I pretty much haven't let you out of my sight? And that we were in bed again within days?'

'Yes…but—'

'And that when I do send you away I last for approximately three hours before my world implodes and I have to get you back? I went to the bus station and the bus had gone…' He shook his head. 'I'll never forgive myself for making you do that.'

Sadie caught his hand and kissed it. 'But I didn't go. I'm here.'

Quin's eyes looked suspiciously bright. 'That's because you're brave and loving and kind and—'

She stopped his words with her mouth, and when she pulled back she said, 'I was too scared to get on the bus—afraid that if I did, something would happen and I'd never see you again…or Sol.'

Quin pulled her close again. 'Thank God for that.' He cupped her jaw. 'And you are an amazing mother—you protected him, and me, by risking your own life.' A shudder went through his body and he said, 'Jesus, Sadie, if anything had happened to you…'

She put her hands on his chest. 'It didn't. And the danger is gone. We're free now.'

Quin took one of her hands and held it to him. With emotion thick in his throat he said, 'I love you, Sadie… can you forgive me?'

The emotion she'd been so carefully holding back threatened to burst like a dam. 'Forgive you for what?'

'For being so hard on you…for asking you to leave…'

Tears pricked Sadie's eyes. 'Forgiven, my love.'

He smiled. 'Say that again.'

Sadie smiled too, and it was wobbly. 'Which bit?'

His eyes flashed. 'You know.'

She kissed him and then pulled back. 'My love…'

'I love you too—so much. And if you'll let me I want to spend the rest of my life showing you how much.'

Quin lowered his head to hers, sealing his words with a kiss that was so tender, and so full of all the longing Sadie had lived with for four years, that emotion ran over and leaked out of her eyes.

When they stopped kissing, Quin wiped her tears away. He said, 'No more tears, okay?'

Sadie half chuckled. 'I'll try my best.'

They sat in harmonious silence for a long time, watching the afternoon turn into evening and dusk. Eventually Sadie asked where Sol was, and Quin told her he was sleeping over at his friend's.

He stood up and held out his hand. She put her hand into his and let him lead her up to the bedroom as the dusk disappeared into the moonlight outside and the waves lapped against the shore.

They made love and talked and drifted into a doze, before making love again and finally falling into sleep.

When Quin woke he looked up and saw Sadie standing on the balcony with a sheet around her, watching the sunrise. He got up and went over to her, naked, and she leant back into his embrace. For the first time in four years he felt whole again. At peace.

She looked up at him and smiled. 'Come for a walk?'

He nodded. 'Anywhere, any time.'

They'd used to say that to each other. She'd stop him working on his laptop and say, *'Come for a walk?'* and he would take one look at her and say, *'Anywhere...any time.'*

They showered and got dressed and then walked along the shore, hand in hand, close together, not even speaking, just letting the moment wash over them and through them, healing all the pain and loss that they'd endured for four years.

They walked all the way to the end and then started back. Other people were on the beach now, jogging or walking their dogs before the heat of the day set in. There were some early surfers.

About halfway back, Sadie stopped. 'This is where we got married.'

Quin looked to the spot where she was pointing. 'How do you know?'

'Because it was the best day of my life, and thinking about it sustained me every day for the last four years. I can remember Sol kicking in my belly as we were making our vows.'

Quin turned to face her, pulling her close. He smiled. 'I remember him kicking too…and I remember how we celebrated.'

Sadie blushed and buried her head in Quin's chest. He smiled at the memory. She'd been very…amorous in her pregnancy.

He lifted her chin with his finger and she looked up at him. Such joy filled him that it almost scared him with its intensity. Had last night really happened?

As if reading his mind, Sadie whispered, 'I'm afraid this isn't real. That this is just a dream.'

Quin pushed the doubts and fears away. *No more.* 'It's real. We're here, together again. Please reassure me that no matter what happens in the future we'll deal with it together, as a team.'

Sadie smiled. 'I promise.'

'And will you marry me? Officially?' The words flowed out of Quin's mouth.

Sadie didn't skip a beat. 'Of course.'

'How about we go and get our son and have breakfast, and then start living the rest of our lives together?'

Sadie's eyes were suspiciously bright. 'I'd really like that.'

So they went to get their son—who squealed when he saw Sadie and ran straight into her arms. They held a hand each as they walked back to their beach house while Sol chattered happily. They looked at each other over his head and smiled, and then they did start living their lives again…together for ever, in love and at peace.

EPILOGUE

Three years and nine months later, Sao Sebastiao

'THERE ARE TOO many women in this family,' Sol grumbled good-naturedly as he moved his younger charges away from the danger of the open gate that led onto the beach, taking care to close it behind him. He really adored his three-year-old twin sisters, Luna and Stella, but he'd never let on—because at the grand age of nearly eight he was far too grown up to be mushy.

The girls were non-identical, their colouring closer to Quin's than to Sadie's this time. Dark eyes full of mischief.

Quin's voice was close to Sadie's ear. 'Do you think we should put him out of his misery and tell him he'll soon have a baby brother?'

He patted Sadie's sizeable bump under her one-piece swimsuit. She was lying with her back to his chest, his long legs spread out each side of her.

She squeezed a firm, muscular thigh and chuckled. 'No harm in letting him appreciate his outnumbering by women for a little longer.'

They'd been officially married in Sao Paulo, with Sol as their very proud ring-bearer, not long after that first trip back to the beach house.

In spite of her protestations that she didn't need one, Sadie now had a wedding band that was the perfect accompaniment to her first wedding ring, inlaid with diamonds, emeralds and sapphires.

She'd almost forgotten the pain of their four years of forced estrangement. Only very rarely now did she have a bad dream, and Quin was always there to wake her, and remind her that she was safe and loved and at home.

At home. With her family. Safe and loved.

They were literally creating a life full of love and happiness, giving their children all the things they hadn't had, and not for one second did they take it for granted.

Sol stomped up the steps to where they were sitting on their beloved porch and sighed dramatically before saying, 'I think we need to take the girls for a walk on the beach. Or they'll never go down for their afternoon nap and I will have no peace.'

Sadie could feel the effort it took for Quin not to laugh out loud as he gently disentangled himself from her. She sat up with a *huff*, feeling more and more like a beached whale every day.

He pulled her up from the seat and they donned hats and more suncream and set off to the beach—just one family among all the others, no more remarkable than anyone else. Except they *were*—because of the trials they'd endured and survived. And because of their rare love.

Quin wrapped an arm around Sadie's waist and they followed in the wake of Sol and his little sisters, who trotted devotedly in his wake on their sturdy little legs.

'Happy?' Quin asked, looking down at Sadie.

She looked up and grinned. 'So happy.'

A few weeks later Kai was born, and their love and happiness was multiplied. But, much more importantly, Sol was no longer outnumbered by women.

* * * * *

Did you fall in love with The Heir Dilemma*?*
Then don't miss out on these other fabulous stories
from Abby Green!

His Housekeeper's Twin Baby Confession
Mistaken as His Royal Bride
Claimed by the Crown Prince
Heir for His Empire
"I Do" For Revenge

Available now!

THE TWINS
THAT BIND

JACKIE ASHENDEN

MILLS & BOON

To all the heroes I give weird names to. Sorry (not).

CHAPTER ONE

ARISTOPHANES KATSAROS, BILLIONAIRE owner of one of Europe's most influential financial companies, had every minute of his phenomenally expensive time planned down to the last second. His schedule was his bible, his compass, and if something wasn't in his schedule then it was irrelevant. He liked the certainty and he liked the control it gave him.

He was a man for whom control wasn't simply vital, it was a way of life.

So as he exited the gala he'd been attending in Melbourne, a dull affair that he didn't enjoy—social engagements were the bane of his existence—he checked his watch to make sure he was on time for the meeting he'd planned at the penthouse apartment he'd bought three years ago and never visited. A meeting he was sure would *not* be dull in the least.

Angelina was scheduled to join him for the night, as per his instructions to his personal secretary. She was tall, blonde, elegant, a professor of literature at an elite American college, and in Melbourne for a conference. She, like he, had a very tight schedule and one night was all she could do.

Not that he minded.

He had a revolving schedule of lovers, women who wanted only a night and nothing more, and he liked to make sure he had at least a couple of evenings each week with one in whichever city he was in at the time.

Sex was necessary and it helped him let off steam, but he didn't prize it above anything else he had scheduled. It was a bodily requirement that he paid attention to as he paid attention to every bodily requirement in order to keep himself in optimum health.

He was looking forward to the evening, because he liked Angelina. She was cool, fearsomely intelligent and could more than hold her own in conversation with him. She was also uninhibited in bed and he was very much looking forward to that as well.

Beauty was not a requirement in his lovers, but intelligence was mandatory. Chemistry, too, was vital. His time was expensive and if he'd put aside the time for sex, then he wanted it. He also required that it should be as pleasurable as possible for all concerned.

That was all he was thinking as he came down the steps, his limo waiting for him at the kerb, and he wasn't paying any attention to the light drizzle coming down from the sky, or the slick stone of the footpath, or the small figure hurrying along said footpath.

Hurrying too fast, in retrospect.

Aristophanes had his phone out of his pocket and was in the process of texting Angelina that he was on his way, when he heard a cry and the sound of someone hitting pavement. He jerked his gaze from the screen, startled, only to see the small figure crumpled on the pavement directly in front of his limo.

It wasn't moving.

Aristophanes wasn't a man who acted without thinking. He considered all his options carefully. He took his time. But now, faced with an unmoving human being lying prone on a slick street, he didn't hesitate. He strode over and knelt on the wet stone, heedless of the rain on his immaculate black suit trousers.

The person was swathed in a cheap-looking black coat, what seemed to be miles of a woollen scarf, and he couldn't tell if it was a man or a woman until he'd managed to pull away all that fabric.

The loveliest woman he'd ever seen lay on the footpath in front of him.

For long moments he crouched there, ignoring the drizzle, almost transfixed.

She wasn't a conventional beauty, he supposed, though beauty didn't interest him the way it obsessed other people. He prized intelligence and self-control above all things, yet even he couldn't deny that the woman lying unconscious on the pavement was exceptionally pretty. Her features were delicate and precise, a small chin, finely arched brows, and the sweetest pout of a mouth. Thick, dark red lashes feathered her cheeks.

A couple of months ago he'd been forced to go to a gala at an art gallery in New York, and there had been an exhibition of Pre-Raphaelite painters. The gala had been as dull as expected so he'd busied himself by looking at the paintings instead, particularly those by Burne-Jones.

She reminded him of the women in those paintings. A Pre-Raphaelite beauty fallen on a wet pavement.

Not that he should be staring at her. She was unconscious, which meant she'd hit her head on said pavement, and what he should be doing was checking she was okay, not staring at her like a fool.

His driver had got out of the limo and was at his elbow, but Aristophanes didn't turn round. Instead he held a couple of fingers against the pale throat revealed by the plunging neckline of the black dress she was wearing. Her pulse beat strongly beneath her warm skin.

Thank God.

'Call an ambulance,' he said roughly to his driver. 'Now.'

He had other places to go tonight and this would put him behind schedule, but even he couldn't leave an unconscious woman lying on the pavement in the rain.

He stared down at her, frowning. The black dress she wore looked as cheap as her coat, but it clung to every curve, outlining a body made to fascinate a man for days. Full, luscious breasts, rounded hips, an elegant waist... and unless he was very much mistaken, she wasn't wearing any underwear.

A pulse of desire shot through him, making every muscle clench tight.

Disturbing. He'd never felt such an instant physical attraction to a woman before. He preferred conversation first before anything else, because it was always the mind that drew him, not the body.

But this woman's body...

He forced the thought away, hard. She was lying unconscious in the rain and he should be thinking about getting her warm, not noting her lack of undergarments.

Since moving her would be a mistake, he shrugged out of his handmade black cashmere overcoat instead, and laid it carefully over the top of her. She was so small the coat covered her.

'Ambulance is on its way, sir,' his driver said.

'Good.' Aristophanes didn't move from where he crouched beside the woman. 'Get an umbrella to shield her from the rain.'

The driver did so and, rather to his own surprise, Aristophanes found himself grabbing the umbrella from him, and holding it over the unconscious woman himself.

She was breathing, which was good, though she was very pale.

He checked his watch again. Time ticked by. The ambulance was coming. He could hear the siren. He should probably finish that text to Angelina to let her know he'd be delayed, yet he made no move to get his phone out. He kept holding the umbrella, crouched beside the woman, keeping the rain off her.

As the siren got louder, the woman made a soft sound and Aristophanes glanced down. Her eyelashes glowed reddish in the streetlights and were fluttering as she gave a moan. Instinctively, he put a hand on her shoulder to keep her still. Moving wasn't a good idea when the ambulance hadn't even arrived.

He'd never been a gentle man, never been one for kindness, but with an unconscious stranger on his hands, he made an attempt at both.

'Keep still,' he murmured. 'You have fallen and hit your head. An ambulance is coming.'

Her lashes fluttered again, then rose, revealing liquid dark eyes that met his unerringly. They were full of confusion and shock, and he wasn't sure what happened then, only it felt as if something large and solid had hit him squarely in the chest.

The ambulance sirens echoed.

He shook off the strange sensation and made as if to get to his feet—the paramedics would need room to work—but at that moment, a small hand crept out from under his coat and gripped his with surprising strength.

He froze.

Her eyes had closed again, but she didn't let go of his hand.

A long time ago, when he'd been on his fifth—or maybe his sixth?—foster family, he'd discovered a stray kitten underneath some stairs in the dusty concrete apartment block in Athens where he'd been living at the time. He'd been about twelve, or thirteen, and at that stage had still been bothering trying to make a connection with his current foster family. But his foster parents hadn't been interested, not when they'd had five other kids they were also fostering. So Aristophanes had been left to his own devices. Out of boredom and loneliness, he'd decided to adopt the kitten himself.

It had been wild, but he'd been patient, and eventually, using pilfered pieces of fish and crumbs of cheese, and little saucers of milk when he could get them, he'd got the kitten to begin to trust him. And the moment the kitten had allowed him to pick it up, he'd felt such a sense of achievement, as if there was something good about him after all.

It felt like that moment now, with this unknown woman clinging tightly to his hand. As if he were all that stood between her and destruction.

Aristophanes Katsaros was known as one of the brightest and best financial geniuses on the planet, and the financial algorithm he'd created had sent his fortunes into the stratosphere. He was a shark when it came to money, and numbers were his playground, his happy place. People, however, were far down on his list of priorities.

So he should have shaken her hand off, risen to his feet, and let the paramedics do their thing. Then he should have got into his limo and driven away to meet Angelina, and had the night of pleasure he'd allowed himself.

Except he didn't.

For no apparent reason that he could see, he stayed where he was, reluctant to pull his hand away from the small, slender fingers clutching his own. He couldn't recall a time anyone had reached for him, let alone some complete stranger in considerable distress.

Five minutes earlier, if anyone had told him that he'd be kneeling in the rain next to an unconscious woman and unable to pull away because she was holding his hand, he would have laughed.

Well, he might have laughed. If laughter were something he indulged in, which it wasn't. At the very least he would have ridiculed the idea.

Now, though, as the ambulance pulled up and the paramedics leapt out, he found himself staying exactly where he was, keeping hold of her hand. Eventually, he had to move though, so he eased his fingers from hers and stepped back to give the paramedics room to work.

It was time to go. Time send that text to Angelina and let her know that he was on his way.

But he didn't. He stood there, watching as the paramedics checked her over, shone a light into her eyes and murmured reassuringly to her.

She was awake again, her gaze darting around as if she was looking for someone.

Was it him? Though he couldn't think why she'd be looking for him, since she wouldn't know him from Adam. Still, he stepped closer and when she looked around again, her dark eyes met his. 'You,' she whispered and again reached out a hand to him.

The paramedics were putting her onto a wheeled stretcher and, once they'd strapped her in, he stepped in close and took her reaching fingers in his. They closed convulsively on his hand, gripping tight, and so he had no choice but to follow as they wheeled her to the ambulance.

'Will she be all right?' he asked one of the paramedics.

'She has a concussion,' the man said. 'We need to get her to hospital to get her checked out. Are you her next of kin?'

'No.' Aristophanes' attention was consumed by the woman and the grip she had on his hand. She felt so warm.

They were preparing to put her in the ambulance.

'I'm sorry, sir,' the paramedic said. 'If you're not her next of kin, you can't come with her.'

He hadn't planned on going with her. His plan for the evening was Angelina and her slender, supple body. Yet now the woman's grip tightened, as if she was trying to hold onto him, and he realised suddenly that he wouldn't be able to give his full attention to Angelina until he knew this complete stranger was okay.

She probably had next of kin somewhere, but she'd slipped over next to his limo and now he felt responsible. Also, she was holding onto his hand very tightly, making it clear—in his mind anyway—that she wanted his presence.

'I am coming with her,' he said flatly, using the same tone he always used when people disagreed with his wishes.

The paramedic shook his head. 'I'm sorry, sir. You can't.'

Aristophanes, who didn't hear the word no very often and never liked it when he did, focused on the man. 'I don't care.'

'Sir, you can't—'

'Yes, I can,' Aristophanes cut him off with all the force of his considerable authority. 'Or do you really want me to go to the trouble of buying your hospital just so I can fire you?'

The paramedic opened his mouth. Shut it. Then shrugged and muttered something Aristophanes decided not to catch.

They loaded the woman into the ambulance and let Aristophanes climb in beside her, and he continued to hold her hand as the sirens started and they sped towards the hospital.

She sighed, settling on the stretcher, her eyes closing.

Angelina was going to have to wait.

Nell was having a lovely dream. She'd been running from something very upsetting and had fallen over, and then the most beautiful man she'd ever seen had grabbed her hand to help her up. He was holding onto it now and she didn't want to let him go. She didn't want to let him go ever. He was so strong and reassuring and she was sure that nothing could touch her while he was here.

Now they were dancing and…no…wait…they couldn't be dancing because she was lying down and not moving, and her head was hurting, and she felt dizzy. Had she been drinking? Had she got really, really drunk?

Then again, no, she couldn't be drunk because she didn't drink much and, anyway, she had work the next day and she never missed work. She loved her job at the preschool, and she loved the kids. So not drunk, then. Perhaps she was sick and that was why her head was hurting?

If felt like an effort to open her eyes, but she managed it, expecting to find herself in her little flat in Brunswick with the morning light coming through the window.

Except she wasn't in her bed or in her flat.

She was lying on what looked like a hospital bed with a curtain drawn around it, and someone was holding her hand.

Wait, what? A hospital bed? What on earth was she doing in hospital?

Desperately she tried to remember what had happened. Things were a little hazy, but she'd got to the bar where she was supposed to meet Clayton—she'd been seeing him for about a month—and had sat there waiting for him. She'd dressed up specially, because she'd decided that tonight was the night she was going to sleep with him. She hadn't yet, wanting to wait until she was sure he was someone she could see having a long-term relationship with, and only in the past couple of weeks had she decided that, yes, he was.

So she'd worn a slinky black dress that clung to her generous curves and, in a fit of daring that wasn't like her at all, she hadn't put on any underwear. He'd been getting impatient with their lack of physical contact, so she'd wanted to make sure he knew that she was ready and willing right now.

Except then he hadn't turned up. At first she'd thought he was just late. But then late had turned into *very* late, and then, an hour after that, she'd got a text from him saying he was sorry, but he didn't think this would work between them. She was too uptight, he'd said, too many hang-ups about sex, which wasn't what he was looking for.

After the text, she'd walked out of the bar into the drizzly night, upset and full of embarrassment that she'd put on a sexy dress and no underwear for a man who hadn't wanted her. Who in the end had left her to wait in the bar for an hour then not even turned up.

She'd been determined not to cry as she'd walked blindly through the drizzle and then…something had happened and she'd woken up here.

At that moment someone bent over her and she found herself looking up into a pair of eyes the dark grey of thunderclouds, framed by long black lashes and straight black brows.

Her breath caught.

It was the man. The beautiful man from her dream. Except apparently he wasn't a dream after all.

His face was all rough angles and chiselled planes, his mouth hard, his cheekbones high, and he had the most impressive jaw she'd ever seen.

No, perhaps beautiful wasn't the right word for him. Compelling, maybe. Or magnetic.

Electric.

Nell stared at him, her voice vanishing somewhere she couldn't reach.

He was very tall, wide shoulders and broad, muscled chest encased in an expertly tailored white shirt that looked somewhat damp. He also wore black trousers that highlighted a narrow waist and powerful thighs and…

Lord. What was she doing? She never gazed at men like that. She'd certainly never gazed at Clayton like that. Then again, Clayton didn't look like this man and, also, Clayton had ghosted her in a bar the night she'd planned on sleeping with him.

Clayton, who she'd thought was the perfect man for her. Who worked for a bank, owned his own home, and was good-looking. Whom she'd had fun with and—

And who didn't want you.

Nell swallowed, a hot wave of remembered embarrassment washing through her, but she forced the thought away, concentrating instead on the man at her bedside and not the man who'd left her high and dry.

He looked expensive, this man in his damp evening clothes, and he radiated authority, as if he were one of the doctors who ruled this ER. No, as if he were one of the people who ruled the entire hospital, or possibly even the entire city itself. Maybe even the whole country…

Then something else interrupted the rush of chaotic thoughts. He was holding her hand, his fingers warm and strong, and somehow reassuring. She wanted to tighten her grip, as if he were all that stood between her and a hundred-foot drop.

'Are you well?' His voice was deep and a touch rough, with a hint of an accent she couldn't place. Definitely not Australian.

Nell tried to find her own. 'Um… My head hurts.'

'Yes,' the man said. 'You had an accident. You slipped

on the wet pavement and hit your head, and so I called an ambulance. You are in hospital.'

Oh, God. She must have been more upset than she'd thought if she'd slipped. She was normally pretty careful on the bluestone paving of Melbourne's streets, especially when it was raining. It had better not be serious. Sarah, her manager, would be extremely annoyed if she couldn't go to work the next day, since they were already short-staffed.

At that moment the curtain was pushed back and a doctor came in, looking harried. 'Miss Underwood,' she said. 'How are you feeling?'

'A bit woozy,' Nell replied.

'Of course, you've had quite the knock on the head. Luckily, Mr Katsaros here was able to call an ambulance and get you in to see us.'

'It was nothing,' the man—Mr Katsaros—said dismissively. He released his grip on her hand and glanced at her. 'You'll be looked after here.'

Her fingers tingled from where he'd been holding them, and his grey gaze was very sharp, very intense. It was as if all the air in the room had been sucked away when he looked at her, which was disconcerting.

'Thank you,' she said, trying to sound her usual calm, firm self since that was her default setting whenever she was disconcerted. Being calm and firm also worked extremely well with small children, animals and overbearing men.

'We'll need to do a brief examination,' the doctor said, 'but first I need to know if you have anyone at home who can look after you.'

Nell swallowed, her mouth a little dry. 'No, I live alone.'

'Friends or family?'

She shook head again. The only friend she could call on was Lisa, who also worked at the preschool, but she was on holiday in Bali. And as for her family... Her parents had died when she was a child, and there was no point asking her aunt or uncle. Or her cousins. She hadn't been in contact with them for years and didn't know how to reach them even if she'd wanted to. Which she didn't. They'd never been interested in her and the feeling was mutual.

The doctor frowned. 'You need to be with someone for at least twenty-four hours. Are you sure you don't have anyone you can call?'

Nell's head was starting to feel a little better so she sat up, taking it slow, pleased to find the dizziness receding. 'I'm sure I'll be fine,' she said. There was her neighbour, Mrs Martin, who could look in on her. No need to put anyone else to any trouble over a silly bump on the head. 'I have a neighbour who can—'

'I will look after you,' Mr Katsaros interrupted unexpectedly, his voice like stone, heavy with authority.

Nell blinked.

He'd turned to look at her again, his dark grey eyes boring into hers, radiating that peculiar intensity that sent a hot, electric feeling through her. It was disturbing. *He* was disturbing.

Rattled, she dredged up a sunny yet impersonal smile. 'Thank you. That's a very kind offer, but I couldn't possibly put you to the trouble.'

His gaze remained unblinking, making her feel as if

she were a specimen on a slide put under a very powerful microscope. 'It is no trouble.'

The electric feeling intensified, which disturbed her
even more, so she smiled harder. 'As I said, it's very kind
of you, but…well. You're a complete stranger and I have
no idea who you are.'

'Aristophanes Katsaros,' he said without hesitation, as
if he'd been waiting hours for her to ask. 'Google me.'

The doctor, who was checking her phone and now looking even more harried, glanced at Nell. 'I need to do a few
checks before we can let you go, Miss Underwood. But I
can't release you if you don't have anyone to be with you.'

The pain in Nell's head receded to a dull ache. 'As I
said, I have a neighbour who can—'

'You will be in no danger,' the preposterously named
Aristophanes Katsaros interrupted yet again, that storm-
grey gaze not moving from hers. 'Not from me. I have a
doctor on my staff who can keep an eye on you.'

At that moment an alarm sounded from somewhere
beyond the curtain around her bed, and people began
shouting. The doctor pulled a face, then vanished back
out through the curtain without another word.

Clearly some emergency was happening.

Mr Katsaros didn't move, making the confined space
seem even smaller than it was already, filling it with a
tense, kinetic energy that made her heart beat hard. And
it wasn't with fear. She didn't know what it was.

'I'm sorry,' she said, going into firm teacher mode
automatically. 'But I don't know you from a bar of soap.
And while I'm grateful for you coming to my rescue, I
don't understand why you'd suddenly want to spend the
next twenty-four hours looking after me.'

He stared down at her from his great height, standing quite still and yet somehow making the air around him vibrate with that strange electricity. His gaze flicked along the length of her body stretched out on the bed then came back to her face, the dark storm grey turning to silver. 'Do you have anyone else?'

Abruptly, she became conscious that her slinky black dress was damp and clinging to every single curve she had and that…oh, yes, she wasn't wearing underwear.

Her cheeks burned. How bloody mortifying. Here she was in this stupid dress that she'd put on for Clayton, with no underwear, lying in hospital because she'd knocked herself out. And this man had rescued her. He likely already knew what she had on underneath, or rather what she *didn't* have on underneath. What must he think of her?

Nell wanted to grab a blanket and pull it over herself, hide away from this far too magnetic man's gaze, but there wasn't one. All she could do was brazen it out, pretend she was wearing a suit of armour instead of a layer of cheap black jersey.

She gave him a very direct, quelling look. 'I've already said I have a neighbour.'

'Will they be able to stay with you the entire time?' he asked. 'A head injury can be very dangerous.'

Nell gritted her teeth. He was being very…insistent and she couldn't fathom why. The real problem, though, was that Mrs Martin, her neighbour, was eighty-five and had a bad hip. She used a walker, too, and, while Nell thought she could manage to pop in a couple of times over the course of twenty-four hours, Nell certainly couldn't ask her to stay.

Which meant Nell was in a difficult position.

She stared at Aristophanes Katsaros, who stared back intently, silver glittering in his eyes. It made her skin feel tight, that look, made her feel restless in a way she couldn't pinpoint. As if she were excited or thrilled by the way he looked at her, which couldn't be right. Why would she be excited about that?

Clayton never looked at you that way.

No, he hadn't. He'd been patient with her at first when she'd refused to sleep with him, telling her that it was fine, he'd wait. But then he'd been less patient, more irritated, making vague comments about his 'needs' and wasn't she being a little selfish?

Anger flickered at the memory and, briefly, she thought about lying to the demanding Mr Katsaros, but a lie involving a head injury would be very stupid and she wasn't stupid.

'No,' she said with a bit of bite in her tone. 'No, they will not be able to stay with me the entire time.'

'In that case you will come with me.' He said it as if that were the most logical thing in the world.

'I don't know you from—'

'Google me.'

'But I—'

'Do it.' He handed her his phone, his gaze relentless. 'I'll wait.'

His insistence made her bristle. 'Forgive me, but I'm not sure why you're insisting on looking after a complete stranger. I can arrange my own babysitter, believe me.'

His straight black brows drew together slightly, but the intense look in his eyes didn't waver. 'You slipped beside my car. You are my responsibility, and I take my responsibilities very seriously.'

A pulse of inexplicable heat went through her, though she wasn't sure why. She didn't want to be his responsibility. She'd been other people's responsibility for years after her parents' deaths, and it hadn't turned out that well, at least not for her.

Clearly impatient with her silence, he nodded at the phone. 'Search my name.'

Nell was tempted to tell him very firmly that he couldn't tell her what to do, but that wasn't going to help matters and, anyway, she abhorred a fuss.

Reluctantly, she opened the web browser in the sleek black piece of technology in her hand.

'Do you need me to spell it?' he asked.

She gave him a look. 'Aristophanes. Like the ancient Greek playwright?'

'Yes.'

'Fine.'

'Katsaros is spelled K-A-T—'

'I can manage,' she said coolly, interrupting him for a change as she entered his surname—it was Greek, she thought—into the web browser.

Hundreds of hits came up. Newspaper articles, magazine articles, think pieces, opinion posts, essays, interviews, videos… A bewildering array of information about Katsaros International, a huge finance company, and its mathematical-genius founder, who'd invented a financial algorithm that did something to the stock market.

Aristophanes Katsaros was that powerful billionaire founder, and he was currently standing at her hospital bedside in the busy ER of a public hospital, staring at her as if he wanted to eat her alive.

You would like him to.

The pulse of heat became a flame flickering inside her, and she couldn't keep telling herself that she didn't know what it was, not this time.

It was physical attraction, pure and simple.

She didn't understand. Why on earth would she be attracted to this stranger? She didn't know anything about him and, given how insistent and overbearing he seemed to be, she wasn't sure she'd like him even if she did. There was no way on earth she could be *attracted* to him. Yet, she couldn't deny that she felt hot when he looked at her, restless too, a million ants under her skin.

She'd had a grand total of one lover in her life and Clayton was to be the second, but even Clayton had never made her feel like this. That was the issue. Clayton had made her feel…well…nothing. If this was indeed attraction, and she'd never felt it before so she wasn't entirely sure, then Clayton hadn't made her feel even a tenth of what Aristophanes Katsaros made her feel.

Bewildering. She didn't like it. She *wouldn't* like him to eat her alive, and what she actually wanted was to be out of his disturbing, electric presence.

Also, she didn't need him to make such a fuss. If he was indeed the founder of Katsaros International, then he had much better things to be doing than looking after a lowly preschool teacher. Why on earth was he making all this effort for her?

'I see,' she said after a moment, gripping her self-possession as tightly as she could. 'May I ask why?'

His straight dark brows twitched again. 'What do you mean why?'

She gestured at the phone. 'You're very rich and obviously very important. Why on earth would you waste time looking after me?'

'Waste time…' he echoed, looking puzzled, as if the words meant nothing to him. 'No, you do not understand. I never waste time. Every second is accounted for, and I can assure you that I have rearranged my schedule to account for looking after you.'

Nell blinked. He had a strange way of speaking, as if his words were precious and he was doling them out one at a time. His accent was tantalising though, making soft music out of his deep voice, making her want to hear him speak again just for the pleasure of it.

Still…he'd rearranged his schedule? For her? Why would he do that?

She stared at him blankly, not knowing what to say.

Apparently, though, he didn't need her to say anything, because he checked the heavy-looking watch on his left wrist then reached for his phone, plucking it out of her hand. He glanced down at the screen and began to type one-handed, his thumb moving deftly.

'I will have you examined by my doctor. It will be quicker,' he said, still typing. 'It is pointless to wait further here.'

Nell opened her mouth in an automatic protest, but then he lifted the phone and spoke into it in a language that wasn't English. Maybe Greek, given his last name? He was short, to the point and devastatingly authoritative, before ending the call abruptly. 'Come,' he ordered, holding out a hand to her. 'I have my doctor waiting.'

The air of authority with which he spoke, as if the world were his to command, shocked her. She'd never met anyone with such a sense of their own importance.

Well. He might be a very famous, very rich, very powerful billionaire, while she was only a preschool teacher who was neither rich, famous nor particularly powerful, but she still wasn't going to go with him just because he said so.

'I don't care who you have waiting,' Nell said with the same gentle firmness she used with particularly recalcitrant children. 'But I'm not going with you and that's final. As I keep saying, I have a neighbour who can—'

'I don't care about your neighbour.' He didn't take his gaze from hers. 'Do you know how serious a head injury can be, Miss Underwood? The paramedic explained it to me on the way to hospital. You might feel fine now, but you could have a blood clot or any one of a number of serious complications. He was very clear that someone needs to be with you for the next twenty-four hours. So unless you fancy a hospital stay, in which case you'll be taking a bed from someone who might need it more than you do, I suggest coming with me now.'

CHAPTER TWO

ARISTOPHANES WAS VERY conscious of the seconds ticking by, of the further rearrangements in his schedule he might need to make. He'd already wasted hours at the hospital and he did not want to waste any more. His assistants had organised his doctor and his doctor had begun the process of handling the hospital bureaucracy. She would meet him at the penthouse apartment. Everything was being handled. There was nothing money and power couldn't arrange for him if he required it.

However, apparently the one thing his money and power couldn't arrange was Miss Underwood's consent to go with him, and she was currently being difficult. It was annoying. While he hadn't expected her to fall in with his wishes immediately, he'd thought she might take one look at his Wikipedia page and *then* graciously agree.

But she had not. What she'd given him was a look of brief shock, then, to his surprise, had doubled down on her refusal.

He found that inconceivable.

He wasn't a household name, it was true, but most people, in his experience, knew who he was. Knew the story of the company he'd started building when he was a teenager, already playing the stock market with his frugal earnings from a job in an Athens fast-food outlet.

He hadn't gone to university. He'd found school dull and had left as soon as he could, which had been at fourteen. Numbers had been his delight, his music, and he'd created symphonies with them. He made money obey his every wish, doubling, tripling, moving from place to place, fluid as water. Sometimes he lost it, but that didn't matter, because he could always make more and he did. Effortlessly.

People called him a genius, but for him that was merely the way he was. As long as he kept to his schedule. Time was money. Seconds were euros that he poured into something productive, because if he wasn't productive, he was nothing. And he couldn't be nothing. He'd been nothing once before, to the woman who'd called herself his mother and yet who'd never been any kind of mother to him. She'd taken him to church with her when he was eight, and then after the service she'd told him to sit still and be quiet and then she'd left. Without him.

He'd still been sitting there an hour later when the priest had found him. They'd searched for his mother for days, but she was long gone by then. That had been the beginning of his climb from the nothingness of being abandoned, and he would never allow anything like that to happen to him again.

Now this lovely little woman was sitting up in the hospital bed, staring at him with those dark, dark eyes, her delicate features set in stubborn lines, and she seemed to be hell-bent on wasting his time with her arguments. Yet all he could think about was not his wasted hours, minutes and seconds, but how beautiful she was. How she irritated him with her refusals and how mystified he was that he cared so much about them.

Possibly he was irritated because of the constant ache of physical lust that dragged at him whenever he looked at her, which had never happened to him before. Not without a meeting of minds first. He resented it. She was a complete stranger to him, he knew nothing of her mind and how it worked, and that was not the usual order of things for him. It further irritated him that he couldn't understand why he felt that way, either.

A fascinating mind was of the utmost importance to him, and then physical attraction. The chemistry of bodies was nothing compared to the intrigue of how a woman thought. But he had no idea how Nell Underwood thought. What he wanted was her body.

Annoyed with himself and his physical feelings, he stared stonily back at her. He just couldn't understand why she was protesting. She'd read his history; it was all there in black and white on the Internet. He wasn't a serial killer or an axe murderer. She had nothing to fear from him, so why was she arguing? Yes, he was a stranger, but he was hardly some random passer-by.

He was Aristophanes Katsaros. One of the richest men in the world. Some would argue that rich men weren't exactly pure as the driven snow and that maybe she was right to be apprehensive of him. But he'd never hurt a woman in his entire life and he wasn't about to start. That wouldn't be a productive use of his time anyway.

Tonight, his body had expected sex and that was still his plan—Angelina had some work to do and she hadn't minded waiting—but he needed to make sure Miss Nell Underwood was taken care of. His doctor would keep her under observation for the requisite number of hours. It would not be a problem.

Her cheeks had flushed prettily and he found his gaze drawn yet again to the deliciously feminine lines of her body. There were no bra lines, no panty lines showing under the cheap, clinging black jersey. She wasn't wearing a stitch beneath it, and he was inexplicably intrigued by that. Where had she been going wearing no underwear? Was she a sex worker? A high-end escort? Had she been going to meet a lover?

He didn't understand why he wanted to know. He didn't understand why her body fascinated him. Because it wasn't as if he didn't know what a woman looked like naked. He knew very well about breasts and hips and the soft, wet, hot place between a woman's legs.

Yet it seemed to him as if he was intrigued by *this* woman and *her* body, and he wasn't sure why. All bodies were the same and they all worked the same, too, but it was the mind that was different. It was the mind that fascinated him.

'No,' she said, calm yet firm. 'I don't think so. Your doctor can come to me instead.'

Her voice was huskier than expected and it stroked over his skin in a velvet caress. He wanted to hear it again. He wanted to hear it moaning his name as he made her come, as he—

Aristophanes gritted his teeth, dragging his thoughts away from that particular track.

No wasn't acceptable. He didn't like. He didn't like being unable to fathom why his body wanted her so very badly. And he *really* didn't like that a part of him didn't want to let her go. A part of him felt that she was his obligation now, his responsibility. Absurd to liken a woman to the kitten he'd once rescued, but still, that was how he felt. He'd witnessed her getting hurt and he'd looked after her until the ambulance came. She'd reached for his hand, had held it as if she hadn't wanted to let him go and yet apparently now his doctor was preferable to him.

Logically it made sense, so why was he feeling the need to argue with her? His doctor would be there, his sense of obligation duly discharged. He didn't need to be there himself, and besides, the longer he stayed, the more the seconds poured through his fingers, becoming minutes, turning to hours, time sliding away into nothing.

He had places to go, people to see. This strange fascination with her had already cost him a few hours of his evening and he didn't want it to cost any more.

Yet as she sat there in the hospital bed, he found his gaze returning yet again to her delicious curves. Full breasts, the perfect dip of her waist, rounded hips to grip and grip tight. That glorious mane of thick auburn hair, long enough to wind around his wrist to tug her mouth close. And her mouth... Yes, there were so many things he could do with that beautiful, full mouth...

Her eyes went wide and she tore her gaze away, her skin flushing the most beautiful shade of pink.

She'd seen what was in his eyes. She'd seen the hunger there. He'd betrayed himself, which was unconscionable, and yet still a part of him had noted the blush in her cheeks, the racing pulse at the base of her throat.

He wasn't the only one who'd betrayed themselves.

You should go. Now.

He gave a soundless growl. Yes, he should. If she didn't want him there, that was fine. He wouldn't insist. He had

Angelina to quench the curious flare of desire that had sprung to life inside him, and she was always appreciative of his attention. He wanted more from his partners than just sex anyway. Sex was easy and cheap and he disdained easy and cheap. Sex could be had from anyone. Time was precious, so why would he spend it satisfying only his body, when he could also satisfy his mind?

He would have his night with Angelina and he would forget about Miss Nell Underwood.

'Very well,' he said coldly. 'If that's what you prefer. Give me your address and I will have my doctor escort you home.'

She did and then he forced himself to leave her bedside and wait for his doctor away from her.

Things moved with their usual smoothness after that.

His doctor arrived, leaving Aristophanes to finally go to the penthouse apartment he owned, where Angelina was waiting for him, and once there, he should have forgotten about Miss Nell Underwood completely.

But he didn't. He couldn't.

His normal plan for an evening with a lover was an excellent meal, a very good glass of wine, an interesting conversation and then some mutually satisfying sex.

However, when he got to the apartment, the meal his favourite chef had prepared was lukewarm, the wine subpar, and Angelina irritated at being made to wait. Then, to make matters even worse, he couldn't stop thinking about the woman he'd left back in the hospital ER. His brain kept reminding him of the shape of her body underneath that clinging dress, and the way her gorgeous auburn hair had curled in the rain. How soft her mouth had looked. How she'd gripped his hand so tightly, as if she couldn't bear to let go of him. How, after she'd fallen, her beautiful deep brown eyes had opened and he'd looked into them and felt something deep and profound shift inside him.

He was furious. His evening plans had been blown to smithereens and it was all her fault.

Angelina, sensing his distraction, tried her best to engage him. He'd been neglecting his sexual needs for a couple of months because he'd been fine-tuning an update to his algorithm and when business called, he was consumed by it. So his body should have been primed and ready for sex from the moment he'd walked into his apartment. But when Angelina kissed him and he prepared for the usual rush of lust, there was nothing. And when she ran a hand down the front of his trousers, caressing him through the fabric, he didn't get hard. Even when he kissed her back and slid his palm down her spine, touching her skin…

He felt nothing.

His body wanted sex, but not with Angelina. His body wanted the Burne-Jones angel he'd left in the ER, and it didn't care what his mind wanted.

Aristophanes had never been turned inside out by physical desire. He was always in complete control of himself physically and emotionally, because only then could he set his mind free. The body and its needs were an inconvenience that he tolerated and managed accordingly, but this… He could not tolerate this and most especially not when he didn't even understand why she'd got so completely and thoroughly under his skin.

Which meant that there was only one thing he could do.

The answer to his problem didn't lie with Angelina.

It lay with Miss Nell Underwood.

And fortunately, he had her address.

Mr Katsaros' doctor was nice and a complete profes-
sional, much to Nell's annoyance, since she didn't want
to like anything associated with the disturbing, kind of
rude, yet also mesmerising man who'd left her in the ER.

The doctor gave her a thorough examination, before
dealing with the hospital paperwork. Then a car arrived
for them, delivering them back at Nell's small but cosy
flat in Brunswick.

Nell, going automatically into hostess mode, tried to
make the doctor some tea, but was then told in no uncertain terms that the correct behaviour after a knock to
the head was rest.

That was annoying too, because she wasn't good with
rest. She liked to be doing something, so, instead of going
into her bedroom and lying down, she went to have a hot
shower. She was cold, her head ached, and she wanted to
get out of her damp dress.

She also felt oddly…abandoned.

Aristophanes Katsaros had left her in the ER. After
first arguing with her, then staring at her as if he wanted
to eat her alive, he'd agreed to her wishes without another
protest before turning around and leaving.

And she'd felt deflated, which was ridiculous because
what more had she expected? If he truly was who he'd
said he was, then why on earth would he want to stay
in the ER with her? She was merely a random stranger
that he'd helped, and he'd already helped as much as he'd
been able to. There wasn't anything more he could do.

Yet still, her heart pinched tight at the memory of his

powerful figure disappearing through the curtains around her bed. He hadn't looked back and she hadn't realised she'd wanted him to until he didn't.

It was the way he'd looked at her just before he'd left that was the issue. His gaze burning bright silver as it followed the line of her body before coming to rest on her face once again. She knew what a man wanted when he looked at a woman that way. Clayton had looked at her in a similar way, yet his gaze had never been as hot, never been as hungry. And more importantly, she'd only felt… warm in return. Warm, not burning hot. A bit peckish, not starving. Pleased that he wanted her, of course, yet…

If she was being really honest with herself, she'd never felt the rush of sudden, hot physical desire for Clayton. Had never been so breathless in his presence that all thought had left her head. Never felt as if her cheeks were on fire whenever he'd caught her looking at him. In fact, she couldn't remember looking at him the way she'd looked at Aristophanes Katsaros.

God, it was stupid to be thinking about him. It didn't matter how he looked at her. He was too disturbing for her peace of mind anyway, and she should be glad he'd walked away.

Peeling off the embarrassing, ridiculous dress, Nell stepped into the shower, sighing as warm water ran over her chilled skin. Apart from a painful lump at the back of her skull, the ache in her head had receded and she was feeling a lot better. The doctor had given her a list of concussion symptoms to watch for and Nell was to let her know if she felt woozy or dizzy. Some people didn't develop concussion, though, so she might be fine, especially if she'd only been out for a couple of seconds.

Nell wasn't sure how long she'd been unconscious, but she had none of the symptoms the doctor had mentioned. Maybe she'd be one of the ones who didn't develop any. She hoped so. She didn't want to annoy Sarah by not coming into work tomorrow.

Once she'd showered, she stepped out of the stall and dried herself off, then reached for the thick pink fluffy robe she always wore when it was cold, wrapping herself up in it. Humming softly, she towel-dried her hair to get most of the water out before winding the towel around her head turban-style.

Then she opened the bathroom door, stepped out into the hall, and came to a dead stop.

A man stood in the middle of her tiny, narrow hallway.

A familiar man.

Aristophanes Katsaros.

All the breath left her body in a wild rush, an electric thrill shooting straight through her, and her first thought was, *Thank God.* He hadn't abandoned her after all. He'd come back.

He stood with his arms folded across his muscular chest, filling the hall with his compelling physical presence. His height and the broad width of his shoulders, the flickering silver fire in his storm-grey eyes. A crackling energy seemed to leap between them, rooting her to the spot.

He seemed to be furious about something and, given the way he was looking at her, that something appeared to be her.

Her mouth became a desert. She had no idea what he was doing here.

'I have dismissed the doctor.' His deep rough voice was

a shock to her system, as if she'd been fast asleep and the sound of it had woken her up. 'I said you were my responsibility and so you are. For the next twenty-four hours.'

She struggled to find her own voice. 'But…why? Don't you have better things to do?'

'I did.' His gaze slid over her and she was very aware that she was naked underneath her fluffy pink robe and… oh, yes, she was wearing a fluffy pink robe. And a towel turban. Sexy. 'Until you interrupted my evening with your accident.'

There was definite accusation in his tone and her cheeks heated. She was shocked he was here, embarrassed to be caught in her dressing gown with a towel around her head, and already angry with herself for thinking about him. Him getting angry with her for having the gall to slip in front of him was the last thing she needed.

'I'm terribly sorry your evening was inconvenienced by my head injury,' she snapped. 'I'll be sure to watch my step better next time when incredibly rude, overbearing men are in my vicinity.'

His black brows twitched again, his gaze sharpening. 'I am *not* overbearing.'

'Really? Then maybe I imagined you flinging your phone at me and ordering me to google you. I probably imagined you ordering me to come with you back to your residence, and being petulant when I refused, too.'

He said nothing, yet she could see the temper glittering in his eyes.

She shouldn't have spoken to him that way. Why had she? She was always patient, always caring and considerate. Never rude. It was just… Everything about him rattled her.

Still, she handled some of the worst nonsense humanity was capable of every day in the form of four-year-olds. She would not let a confrontation with one adult man get the better of her.

Nell lifted her chin, determined to show him that she was not intimidated by him and his silly little male temper, not one bit.

He glowered, obviously unimpressed by this show of defiance. 'Do you know what I had planned for this evening?' he bit out.

'No.' Nell lifted her chin even higher, ignoring how her heart beat far too fast and her skin was tight and hot. 'I can't imagine how your evening plans would be at all relevant to me.'

He did not like this one bit, something hot leaping in his eyes, and he took a step towards her, his arms still folded, his stare relentless. 'Sex, Miss Underwood. That's what I had planned for my evening. Dinner, conversation and sex. But because I couldn't stop thinking about you, I could not pay proper attention to my date.'

'That sounds like a you problem,' she said coolly. 'I didn't ask you to come here, Mr Katsaros, and if you're so concerned about your date, perhaps you should be with her instead of standing in my hallway being annoyed with me. Certainly you'll get more sex that way.'

His glower turned into a scowl and she *really* didn't like how hot that made her feel. As if part of her was pleased she was getting under his skin as much as he was getting under hers.

'I *tried* being with my date,' he growled. 'It didn't work.'

'Inside voice, please,' she said automatically.

'Excuse me?'

Nell knew a moment's fierce embarrassment as she realised what she'd said, then shoved it away. He couldn't blame her for treating him like a four-year-old when he was acting like one.

'It's what I tell the children in my preschool class,' she said, meeting his hot gaze head-on. 'When they are throwing tantrums.'

For a second something tense and electric crackled in the air between them.

'Your preschool class,' he echoed as if he'd never heard of such a thing.

'That's right.' She didn't look away. 'I'm a preschool teacher.'

'Good God,' he muttered with some disgust. 'Then what is the point of all of...*this*?' He flung out a hand, clearly indicating her.

Nell stiffened. 'All of what? What are you talking about?'

'All of you.' He virtually spat the words. 'You are the most beautiful woman I've ever seen and I have not been able to stop thinking about you since I left you in the ER.'

Nell blinked. No one ever complimented her. Clayton had told her she was pretty a couple of times when they'd first started going out, but then the compliments had stopped, and he'd started complaining about her more than he'd praised her. And as for her aunt and uncle, who'd taken her in after her parents had died... They hadn't complimented her either. They'd been resentful they'd had to look after her in the first place, and had made no secret of the fact.

Yet now this maddening man had called her beautiful and seemed to regard this as a personal affront, and she didn't know whether to be complimented or insulted.

'Fine,' she said, struggling to hold onto a patience that was usually limitless. 'You're upset about the interruption to your evening and I'm truly sorry about that.' She wasn't and made sure that her tone indicated that she wasn't. 'I'm also sorry my appearance is such an aggravation. But you really don't have to stay.' She gave him one of the sunny smiles that always cheered the children she taught. 'I'll be fine. So why don't you go off and have your little evening, and enjoy your date, hmm?' She'd wanted to sound calm, firm and authoritative. Yet she had a horrible suspicion that the words that had escaped were the ones she'd usually use with Dylan, one of the naughtiest boys in her class. Dylan. Who was four.

Aristophanes Katsaros, who was definitely not four, stared at her as if he couldn't believe what she'd said. 'My little evening?' he repeated. 'My *little* evening?' He took another step forward, and then another, and another, stalking down the hallway towards her, and Nell found herself backing up and up, until the closed door of her bedroom was hard at her back, stopping her.

He towered over her, so much bigger and more powerful than she was. If he decided to do anything to her, she wouldn't stand a chance. She should have been terrified.

Yet she wasn't. She was…exhilarated almost. This man was a billionaire. The founder of a huge company. He was a mathematical genius and he hadn't been able to stop thinking about her. He'd dismissed the doctor so he could look after her. He'd said she was the most beautiful woman he'd ever seen.

Yes, he seemed angry about that, but he'd also called

an ambulance when she'd been unconscious and injured. He'd held her hand and come to the hospital with her.

He wasn't going to do anything to her; she knew that as well as she knew her own name.

But he was certainly angry, which was fair since she probably shouldn't have used quite that tone with him. And maybe she was crazy, but she found it unbearably exciting. When she'd gone to live with her aunt and uncle, they had never taken much notice of her. They'd already had four other kids and hadn't wanted a sixth, especially one who wasn't theirs, so she'd been forgotten, ignored. Her middling marks at school and her middling performance at the outdoor activities they preferred had ensured her place as the most mediocre of their brood. Or perhaps the cuckoo in the nest was a more apt term, since the rest of their kids were blonde and tall, while she was dark-haired and short.

She'd once tried a bit of rebellion as a teenager by sneaking a cigarette or two and going to a couple of parties, but even doing that hadn't earned her their attention. They hadn't even yelled at her. They'd shrugged their shoulders and ignored her, deeming her so unimportant they weren't even going to waste their anger.

But this man was wasting his anger on her, and God help her, but she liked it.

He was inches away, staring down at her, and she could smell his aftershave, spicy like sandalwood or frankincense, and it made her mouth go even drier than it already was. His body was large, hard, and powerful and he was hot; she could feel the heat of him radiating through his clothes.

His attention was fixed wholly on her as he put one

hand on the wall beside her head. 'I don't want my date,' he said roughly, putting his other hand on the wall, caging her against it. 'I want you.'

Her heart thumped hard, deafening in her ears, electricity dancing like static over her skin. She looked into his eyes, the grey light in the centre of his iris darkening to charcoal around the edges. Fascinating eyes.

She wasn't afraid, even though he was crowding her. No, she was excited. Excited that she'd got to him, that she'd bothered him. Amazed that he found her beautiful. And thrilled beyond measure that he wanted her.

Because she wanted him too.

Nell took a sudden, shuddering breath and then, holding tight to her courage, she put out a hand and brushed her fingers along one of his high cheekbones. His skin was warm beneath her fingertips, whiskers making it slightly rough. 'Then what are you waiting for?' she said.

CHAPTER THREE

ARISTOPHANES DIDN'T KNOW what was happening to him. He'd expected to come into her flat, dismiss the doctor, then perhaps order her to bed—rest was important— while he stayed up all night working. However, it was only once he'd arrived that he realised he hadn't brought anything to do his work on, and so he was looking at an entire evening of wasted time. An abhorrence that had made his already foul temper even fouler.

Dismissing the doctor hadn't been an issue, but then he'd heard the bathroom door open, so he'd gone into her tiny hallway only to find yet another aggravation: her standing there staring at him, wrapped up in the most ridiculous dressing gown he'd ever seen.

It was pink and fluffy, and she had a towel around her head, and she should not have looked so completely and utterly adorable. In addition, everything male in him knew she was naked beneath that dressing gown, and wanted to see if her skin was as pink as the robe and what would happen if he pulled at her towel and her hair tumbled down her back.

He wanted to know what would happen if he kissed her.

An absolutely unacceptable situation.

He'd been telling himself on the way over to her flat that it was only because he was worried about her, that was why he'd been drawn back to her. Nothing to do with the softness of her mouth, or the darkness of her eyes. Nothing to do with her delectable curves or the silkiness of her hair.

Physical attraction was nothing. It happened all the time. It wasn't special or singular.

It was the attraction of the mind that fascinated him, that drew him. He'd much rather have an interesting woman over a beautiful one any day of the week.

Yet right now, with her backed against the wall, looking up at him with darkened eyes, he didn't care about her mind. What he wanted was to rip aside all that fluffy pink and find the beautiful body beneath it. Touch it. Kiss it. Taste it.

Bury himself inside it.

It was the stupidest thing he'd ever felt and he was appalled by the baseness of his own desires. By how he seemed to have no control over them whatsoever.

He'd never, for example, become so angry with himself that he'd crowded a woman up against a door, or flung her own beauty back in her face. He'd never let himself care enough to even think about doing that.

Yet here he was, doing all of the above.

She should have been scared, since he was clearly behaving like a lunatic, yet instead she'd reached up and touched his face, her fingers soft against his cheek.

What are you waiting for? she'd said, the words hitting something deep inside him.

As if he'd been waiting indeed and now here she was, ready for him.

A preschool teacher… Not inherently bad, yet not on a par with Angelina, a professor at Harvard. Why had he left her for this woman? Why was his body insisting that Nell was what he wanted, when his head was positive it was Angelina?

'I don't know you,' he ground out, wanting her to understand. 'I don't do this with women I don't know.'

There was something soft in her eyes, something hot that sent fire all the way to his groin. She stroked his cheekbone lightly, as if he were hers to touch however and whenever she wished, and that didn't make any sense either. He didn't like people touching him when he wasn't in bed with them. He found it distracting.

Yet her touch… He wanted it. He *wanted* it.

'I don't do this with men I don't know,' she said in her husky voice. 'So, I suppose that makes us even.'

He should shove himself away, put some space between them. She'd hurt herself, for God's sake. What was he doing holding her against the door like this?

Yet he couldn't bring himself to move. His body wanted him to stay right here, where he could smell the soap and shampoo she'd used, something sweet and simple that made him ache for reasons he couldn't name. And she was so warm. He wanted to pull the tie of that ridiculous dressing gown, discover if she tasted as sweet as she smelled.

'Then why?' It was rapidly becoming difficult to think, which *never* happened to him, and he hated the feeling. Yet he seemed to be powerless against it. 'Why do you want me?' It was obvious to him why she'd want him— he was, after all, who he was. Yet he wanted to hear her say it. 'Why do you want *this*?'

Her silky red lashes lowered, fanning against her pink cheek. 'I... You're...' She paused, as if searching for the words, then her lashes lifted once more, her eyes wide and dark. 'When I was out, I dreamed of you, and when I woke up, you were holding my hand. And you're...beautiful. You're not like anyone I've ever met.'

He wanted to growl with satisfaction, an unbearably primitive response. Women wanted him, it was true. The lovers his assistants scheduled for him always, without exception, wanted him. He took it as read most of the time.

But the way Nell said it made him fierce and triumphant and feral.

It made him want to ravage her right here against the door.

He eased closer, so the pink fluffy edge of her dressing gown was brushing against his shirt. 'To be clear, I wanted sex tonight,' he said. 'So is that what you're offering?'

She flushed almost as pink as her robe, and yet she didn't look away. 'As it happens, I wanted sex tonight, too. But the man I was going to have it with ghosted me.'

Another thing he didn't understand. How could anyone have ghosted her?

'Why?' he demanded, suddenly enraged at the thought.

'He said I was too uptight.' She kept on staring at him, throwing the words at him like small hard stones. Challenging him, he thought. 'That I wasn't what he was looking for.'

For once, Aristophanes didn't think about the words that came out of his mouth and asked the question that had been taunting him all night. 'Was that why you weren't wearing any underwear? Was that for him?'

She flushed even deeper, making the darkness of her eyes even more apparent. 'Yes. But he never got to see under my dress because he ghosted me before I could show him.'

'Good,' he said fiercely. 'His loss is my gain. Why don't you show me, instead?'

She searched his face for one long moment, an emotion he couldn't name flickering in her gaze. Then her hand dropped from his cheekbone to the tie of her robe and she pulled it. The fluffy fabric of her robe slowly slid open.

And she was indeed as pink as her gown, her skin gloriously flushed from her shower, all freshly scrubbed and glowing and silky. Her breasts were as full as her curves had promised, and everywhere else she was gently rounded. She was biteable, lickable, and the sweet little thatch of auburn curls between her thighs...

God save him.

Satisfaction unfurled in him, lazy and hot, and he almost bared his teeth in yet another primitive growl. Yes, she wanted him. She wanted *him*.

She had her head half turned away, as if afraid to see his expression, so he reached for her chin and gripped it, turning her back to face him. 'Don't look away from me,' he ordered. 'You have nothing to be ashamed of.'

Instantly that little chin hardened in his grip. 'I'm not ashamed, I'm—'

'You're as beautiful as I said you were.' He wasn't sure why it was so important that she understand that. Perhaps it was only that the thought of a woman as gorgeous as this one being ghosted by some bastard who didn't realise what he had was insupportable. 'Shall I prove it to you?'

She took a breath, the pulse at the base of her throat

racing frantically. Her eyes were dark as midnight and he couldn't stop himself from closing the gap between them, easing himself against her silky little body.

She shivered all over at the contact. 'Yes.' The word escaped on a breathless puff of sound, and he'd never heard anything so sweet. 'Please.'

He took one hand from beside her head then reached for one of her own, drawing it between them, looking into her face as he held her palm down over the front of his trousers, where he was so hard he ached.

Her eyes widened and her full mouth opened, her fingers giving a small convulsive squeeze that sent the breath from his lungs.

All rational thought had left his brain, all his higher thought processes non-functional. He was nothing but primitive hunger and base instinct now, and, for once in his life, he didn't care. So he didn't hide his reaction. She should know what she did to him. Especially when he was going to do the same to her.

Holding her gaze, he lifted his other hand from the wall and gently laid it at the base of her throat, fingertips brushing the frantic beat of her pulse. She shivered, gasping softly, her head falling back slowly against the door, lashes lowering as he let his hand slide from her throat to the luscious curves of one breast. Her skin felt like silk, smooth and warm, the soft weight of her breast as his palm cupped it literally perfect.

She made a sound deep in her throat, her back arching as she pressed herself into his hand. Her nipple was hard and when he stroked his thumb slowly back and forth across it, teasing it, she made another of those passionate, wanton sounds.

Beautiful little woman.

Perfect little woman.

He bent his head and kissed her, taking one of those breathless moans into his mouth. She tasted exactly the way he'd thought she would, so sweet. No, she tasted even better, and now he was hungry. Starving.

He kissed her deeper, hotter, and she let him, arching against his hand as he teased the taut peak of her breast, and then kissing him back. She was unpractised, but that only added to the sweetness, and when she squeezed him again, slightly harder, the last trace of rational thought left his head.

There was only one thing he wanted now. Only one.

He wanted to be inside her and as quickly as possible.

Nell had no idea how it had happened. How she'd got herself to this point, her dressing gown open, pressed up against a door as the world's most incredible man cupped her bare breast, turning her into a starving beast. But, however it had happened, she didn't care.

She should be resting and nursing her head, yet all that pain had vanished, lost under the onslaught of the most overwhelming tide of pleasure. She'd never dreamed her body would be capable of this, and yet she couldn't deny what she felt now. It was glorious.

Aristophanes Katsaros was better than any drug.

His hand gently stroking her, the press of his muscular body. The heat of him. The hard length of his shaft pressing against the material of his trousers and into her palm. A big man in every way.

She'd lost her virginity to her first boyfriend in her last year of high school. It had been a very disappointing and

embarrassing ten minutes in the back of his car and she
hadn't been in any hurry to repeat the experience. But
then she'd met Clayton and…

Well. She and Clayton had never got this far, and she'd
told herself it was because she'd wanted to wait, but now
she knew that was a lie. She'd never wanted to wait. She'd
never wanted Clayton at all. Not as she wanted this man,
this stranger who'd rescued her unconscious from a rainy
street. Who'd held her hand and cared enough about her
to make sure she was okay. Who'd made her feel more
wanted than anyone else ever had in her entire life.

Perhaps that was why she'd found the courage to pull
the tie on her dressing gown, baring herself to him. That
and the look in his eyes. *Why don't you show me, instead?*
he'd ordered and all she'd been able to think about was yes,
yes, she wanted to show him. She wanted him to see her.

Her courage had left her for a second the moment her
gown had fallen open, but then he'd taken her chin in his
hand and turned her back to face him, his silvery gaze
electric, blazing with fire. There had been no doubt that
he'd liked what he saw and he'd wanted her to know that
too.

Now she couldn't imagine anything she wanted more
than to strip away the confining material of her dressing
gown. Pull open his shirt, touch his skin. Be naked with
him. They'd both been intending to have sex so why not?
They could have it now, right here, she didn't care. She'd
have him any way he wanted it.

Nell moaned into his mouth as his hand slid from her
breast down over her stomach, fingertips grazing the
curls between her thighs. 'Yes,' she breathed, hardly
aware she'd even spoken. 'Oh, yes, please…'

He gave another of those deep, sexy growls and then his fingertips were sliding over the slick, sensitive skin of her sex, exploring, stroking, teasing. She shuddered and, without thought, reached for the button of his fly, desperate to touch him as he was touching her. But then he growled again, pulling away, and before she could process what was going on, he'd dropped to his knees in front of her.

She barely had time to gasp before his hands gripped her hips, pinning her hard against the door, and his mouth was on her stomach, licking a slow, lazy path down to where she was hot and wet, and so needy she thought she'd die.

He held her against the wood, nuzzling against her, licking, exploring, tasting. Then his tongue found the most sensitive part of her and flicked over it, making her shudder and shake. Her hands were buried in his hair, the thick black strands silky against her fingers, and she gripped him tight, unable to hold in the sounds he brought from her.

No one had ever touched her like this, tasted her like this.

No one had ever made her the sole focus of their attention.

No one had ever made her feel as if she was being slowly and thoroughly worshipped, as if they couldn't get enough of her.

No one had ever made her feel as if she might die from pleasure.

Her eyes drifted closed, colours swirling behind her closed lids as everything inside her drew tight, as if she were an arrow about to be launched into the sky.

'That's it,' she heard him murmur, his breath against her skin as she trembled. 'Scream for me, woman. Scream, so I can hear it.'

Then he did something with his tongue and she did scream, pleasure unleashing in a wild storm through her body, her cries echoing in the small space of the hallway as the orgasm took her.

She was still panting, wondering how on earth she was standing upright, when his hands slid beneath her thighs and she was lifted against the door as if she weighed nothing. He pinned her there with his body, holding her pressed to the wood effortlessly, and his hand was back between her thighs, touching her, stroking her back into trembling hunger once again. Then he pulled open his fly, spread her delicately with his fingers before pushing into her slowly, so very slowly.

His silver gaze didn't leave hers, pinning her as surely as his body, holding her mesmerised as she felt her body open for him, stretching to take him. She groaned, nothing but the feel of him inside her, a heavy, aching fullness that made her want to pant and claw at his back.

'You are perfect.' His voice was raw, guttural, and he bent, his teeth grazing the tender skin of her shoulder, making her shiver in delight. 'Absolutely perfect.'

She had never felt perfect. She'd always felt as if there was something missing, something that made her less interesting, less intriguing, less worthy almost, than her cousins. They were mystified by her, and so were her aunt and uncle. Sometimes she felt as if they didn't know what to do with her and—worse—weren't interested in finding out, so they just left her to her own devices.

Now, even though her towel had fallen from her head

and her wet hair was draped like seaweed across her shoulders, and her dressing gown was half off, she didn't feel uninteresting or unworthy. She didn't feel as if she was missing something.

She felt beautiful. As if she really was as perfect as he'd told her she was.

Nell squeezed her legs around his waist, pulled his shirt half open and slid her hands inside it, feeling the hot velvet of his skin. He was all hard muscle, the crisp brush of hair, and he smelled spicy and musky and male, and she was desperate for him.

He was perfect too.

Then he began to move and everything slid away. Her embarrassment and shame at Clayton's no-show. Her anger at Aristophanes' overbearing manner. Her self-consciousness and fear that this would end the way so many of her relationships with people had ended, with her not being enough for anyone... They all vanished. There was no room for them, not when the pleasure inside her was growing and filling every space.

A part of herself she'd never realised she had, a more primal part, began to take over. It was hungry and passionate, with no inhibitions. It only wanted more of the pleasure he was giving her, making her sink her nails into his back and moan as he moved deeper, harder.

But while she might have lost all sense, he apparently hadn't, because she felt him slide one of his hands behind her head, cupping the base of her skull in his large, warm palm, projecting her injury as he moved inside her.

For a second Nell loved him for that. Then the knife edge of pleasure grew sharper, and she felt again the tightness gather, the bow being drawn back, ready to launch her into the sky. He shifted, changing his angle, the friction so perfect it brought tears to her eyes, and then the tightness inside her was released and she was flying, soaring into the sky in a wild, glorious rush. Dimly she heard him say her name in a low, guttural roar before he too joined her in the sky.

Time passed as she floated slowly back down to earth, both of them still leaning against her bedroom door locked together as if nothing could tear them apart, their breathing slowly easing.

This moment, too, was perfect, and she didn't want to move. Yet then she felt him shift his grip on her, lowering her to the floor, cold air moving over her heated skin as he pulled away. His hands gently pulled her robe closed, wrapping her up, and it hit her suddenly that he was preparing to leave.

Nell didn't think. Operating entirely on instinct, she reached out and grabbed his hand, holding on. 'Don't go,' she said and if it came out sounding a little more desperate than she wanted it to, she didn't care.

He went still, his gaze full of storm clouds. 'I'm not. I have to stay with you for twenty-four hours, remember?'

'That's not what I meant.' She took a little breath. 'I meant stay with me.'

His beautiful face was unreadable, yet there was lightning in his eyes as he looked at her. 'There can be nothing more than this, Nell,' he said after a long moment. 'Only a night. We can never see each other again after that, understood?'

There was a second where she wanted to know why, but then dismissed the thought. It didn't matter why. The only thing that mattered was that he was here and he wanted her, and that once wasn't enough for either of them.

'Understood,' she said hoarsely.

The quality of his attention changed then, sharpening, focusing on her, studying her as if she was a complex problem he was desperate to solve. 'How are you feeling?'

She felt something inside her release then, in a silent exhale. 'Pretty good. Though… I could always feel better.'

His gaze became pure silver. 'The doctor is gone, but perhaps you need my help?'

'I do,' she agreed, her heartbeat already ramping up.

His fingers tightened around hers. 'Then come here, woman. Show me where it hurts and I'll kiss it better.'

CHAPTER FOUR

THE ELEVATOR DOORS opened and Aristophanes stepped inside. He'd just finished up a meeting in his New York office in downtown Manhattan, and, according to his schedule, he had half an hour to get uptown to meet Claire, an astrophysicist who'd been working with CERN, and whom he'd been trying to match schedules with for the past week.

Or at least, his secretaries had been trying to match schedules. This was their third attempt to find an evening that suited both him and Claire, and, if this fell through, Aristophanes was thinking he might not bother at all. They'd met at a fundraiser and she'd been interesting, and there had been enough chemistry between them that he'd told her that if she'd wanted a liaison, he'd be happy to oblige. She had and so his secretarial team had swung into action.

Yet he was feeling restless and off kilter, and strangely enervated at the thought of sex with Claire. Almost as if he didn't want her, which would be the fourth time this month that he hadn't wanted a woman. It had been the same the month before that too.

If he really thought about it, he'd felt the same since

he'd had that one night in Melbourne three months earlier, with the perfect little preschool teacher.

He didn't like to think about that night. He didn't like to think about what they'd done in her small bedroom in her small, cluttered flat. They hadn't talked. They hadn't had any kind of conversation at all; they'd let their bodies talk instead, their conversation wild and passionate, without boundaries or limits. They'd done everything and anything, and, for once in his life, his brain had gone quiet and still. Silenced by raw hunger and need.

He'd left her fast asleep the next morning, organising his doctor to give her a final check-up. Then he'd pushed her to the back of his mind as far as she would go. As far away from his consciousness as possible.

He'd been busy these past few months, flying between his offices in various countries, never staying too long anywhere, which was his preference. He'd paid a visit to Cesare Donati, a good friend—possibly his only friend—whom he'd known for years, and who was the owner of one of Italy's largest private banks. Cesare had recently married a lovely Englishwoman called Lark, and had spent Aristophanes' visit proudly showing off his little daughter, Maya, whom Aristophanes, who'd never had anything to do with children, found rather more interesting than he'd expected. The little girl had even lifted her arms to him, wanting to be picked up, so he had, then had felt oddly at a loss as to what to do next.

Maya had looked at him with big blue eyes, babbling on about something, and he, who knew many different languages and a lot of them fluently, hadn't understood a word. He'd found himself staring at her in stunned silence, a nagging sensation in his chest that didn't make any sense. The child was a mystery, and he loved a good mystery, a good, complicated puzzle, yet there was another part of him that wanted to put her down and get as far away from her as he could.

Having children of his own had never occurred to him and if he'd ever thought deeply about it, he would have said he didn't want them. Children could not operate on his schedule, for a start, and he didn't have enough time for them even if they could. They demanded too much, and he was a man who demanded of others. He did not meet *their* demands.

Still, he couldn't deny that having Maya and Lark had changed Cesare's life and for the better. His friend had found happiness, it was clear, and Aristophanes was pleased for him.

But family life was not and could not be for him.

He was a man of the mind, of the intellect, and it was cerebral topics that interested him, not home and hearth.

Aristophanes hit the button for the first floor and the elevator moved smoothly into life, descending through the sleek steel and glass skyscraper that housed the New York office of Katsaros International, and down into the vast, glass-ceilinged hall that was the foyer.

As Aristophanes stepped out, a gentle commotion at the imposing front desk caught his attention. A woman was standing on her tiptoes, her hands on the edges of the desk as she tried to make herself taller, leaning into it and saying something urgently to Karina, who managed the front desk.

A small woman. Wearing a voluminous black coat against the early spring New York weather, the shoulders of which were wet with rain. As was her auburn hair, hanging down her back in a thick braid.

Karina was shaking her head with emphasis, then she glanced over to the security guards near the entrance and gestured to them.

Aristophanes should have continued on. He should have walked right past the little woman making a fuss at his front desk. Many people wanted entrance to his building and many people were turned away. Certainly, if it was him they wanted to see then they were out of luck. His schedule was full for the next month.

So he wasn't sure why he stopped dead in his tracks, his gaze fixed on the woman at the desk. There was something familiar about her. Something familiar about the thick auburn hair hanging down her back. It reminded him of that night in Melbourne, of Nell, his Burne-Jones angel with her thick and silky hair that he'd gathered in his fist as he'd driven inside her from behind, making her bed shake…

The woman turned her head slightly and an arrow of desire so intense it stopped his breath pierced him.

It *was* her.

Nell.

She hadn't seen him, still talking urgently to Karina, who was now shaking her head as a couple of security guards came over. Clearly they were on the point of escorting Nell from the building.

His thoughts seemed to stop in their tracks, overwhelmed utterly by the reality of her, and then, with the same abruptness, they began to move again and this time at lightning speed.

She was here. In New York. In his building. Which

must mean she wanted to see him. Why? He'd told her it could only be one night and she'd agreed. He'd left her sleeping and she'd been as good as her word. He hadn't heard from her since.

Something must have changed, something urgent enough that she'd come to see him herself. Something important enough that it required a face-to-face meeting and out of the blue.

For a second his brain furiously sorted through all the possibilities until there was only one left. One that made him go icy with shock.

He'd thought they'd been careful with protection that night. Every time, he'd used a condom. Also, she'd told him she'd been on the pill in preparation for giving herself to that pathetic, ungrateful boyfriend of hers.

But…now he thought about it, he couldn't remember using protection that first time up against her bedroom door. He'd been so hungry for her, so desperate, so motivated by his own base instinct, he hadn't even thought about it.

There was a failure rate for the pill. It was slim, but it was there, and it only took once…

The shock penetrated the whole way through his body and then something else seemed to ignite in his chest. Smouldering, leaping into flame, burning hot…

She *must* be pregnant. That was why she was there, that was the only reason he could think of, and it would certainly explain the urgency with which she was talking. And how she gripped onto the front desk with her fingers as one of his security guards took her arm, trying to urge her away, then pulling…

'Stop,' Aristophanes said coldly, his voice echoing in the vaulted spaces of the foyer.

Everyone standing at the front desk froze, then turned.

And the fierce burning in his chest shifted and changed as Nell Underwood's dark eyes met his then widened, her creamy skin flushing with colour. His body hardened almost instantly, his brain no help at all as images of their night together began playing in his head.

Ruthlessly, he shoved them aside, ignored the demands of his body, and strode over to where Nell was standing, staring at him like a deer in the headlights of a car. 'Leave this to me,' he ordered to the security guards and Karina, who all obediently went back to their posts as if nothing had happened. Then he looked down into Nell's beautiful face. 'You,' he said. 'You're coming with me.'

It wasn't a question and he didn't give her a chance to protest. He took her arm in an unbreakable grip and urged her over to the elevators.

'I'm coming, I'm coming,' she said irritably, though she didn't resist him. 'You don't need to manhandle me. I was actually here to see you.'

'I thought as much.' He hit the button for his private elevator and, though every base instinct in his body was screaming at him to keep hold of her, he released his grip on her arm. 'You didn't have an appointment.'

The doors opened smoothly and he ushered her inside. As they shut, he pressed the button for his office and the elevator began to rise.

'No, I didn't.' She'd taken a few steps away from him, as if she wanted to put some distance between them. It grated on his nerves for reasons he couldn't have explained. Her hands moved restlessly, adjusting her coat and smoothing her damp hair. 'That woman at the front desk told me it was impossible to see you,' she said, her familiar voice clear as a bell. 'That you were booked up for an entire month, and even if there was a space in your schedule, you wouldn't be able to see me, because you were far too important.'

'I am,' he said without irony, because it was no less than the truth. 'However, I find I have some time now.' He didn't, of course. Claire was waiting for him. Yet Claire seemed to be the least important thing to him in this moment.

Nell's dark gaze was wary, but that little chin of hers was stubborn. He remembered taking it in his fingers, remembered how warm her skin had been and how silky it had felt. 'Why now?' she asked.

'Because you are here.' He met her gaze head-on. 'I thought I told you that you weren't to contact me again.'

'You did.' She made another nervous adjustment to her coat. 'And believe me, I wouldn't have done so. But…' A breath escaped her and she swallowed. 'I need to tell you something.'

He could smell her scent, sweet and tantalising, and the fire in his chest seemed to burn brighter, hotter. He was going to be so late for Claire, but, now that he was here in this elevator with Nell, he couldn't think of anything he wanted less than to leave and find a different woman. A woman who wasn't Nell.

Remember why she's here.

Ah, yes. There was that.

'Yes,' Aristophanes said. 'You're here to tell me you're pregnant.'

* * *

Nell had no idea how he'd guessed. She was too busy trying to get some air into her lungs, an impossible task when Aristophanes seemed to take up every square inch of the extremely small space of the elevator. And not only with his tall, muscular body, but also with the electrical charge of his magnetic presence.

He was so very intense.

She hadn't forgotten how beautiful he was, but she *had* forgotten how physically devastating he was in the flesh. She could almost feel her body readying itself for him, which was disconcerting in the extreme, especially since it had been three months since she'd last seen him. Apparently, though, it didn't matter how long it had been. She still wanted him with the same hunger as she had back then.

The past six weeks had been such a roller coaster. First there had been the shock of discovering she was pregnant and then a barrage of appointments to make sure everything was looking as it should. Then there had been the nausea and exhaustion of early pregnancy, as well as the uncertainty of what she was going to do about the baby.

That she was going to keep it had never been in doubt—she'd always wanted children and, despite the timing being horrendous, she desperately wanted to keep this one. However, she felt very strongly that a child should have two parents. She'd lost hers so early and it was a constant grief to her, and she couldn't imagine her own child not having them.

It made letting Aristophanes know he was going to be a father imperative. She'd decided to wait until after the twelve-week mark just to be sure, but after emails, phone calls and requests to speak with him had all fallen through, she'd eventually booked a ticket to New York since that was where he apparently was for the next month. She hadn't had much in the way of savings, but it had been enough for a flight and some cheap accommodation, which wasn't very cheap because it was New York.

She'd debated about how to tell him, because he'd been very clear he didn't want to see her again and likely wouldn't welcome the news he was going to be a father. But that was too bad. She didn't want his money; she wanted only his presence in their child's life. That was all.

So all the way on that long, interminable flight from Melbourne to JFK, she'd gone over and over in her head what she was going to say to him. How she was going to tell him. Then, in the end, he'd taken the words straight out of her mouth.

The pedantic fool.

She stood in her damp coat, in the too-small space of the elevator, staring into his silver eyes. Conscious once again of his physical beauty. He was even taller than she remembered, his magnificent physique clad in what had to be a handmade suit of dark grey wool that seemed to highlight every inch of his broad shoulders and wide chest. His pristine black shirt was offset with a silver silk tie the exact colour of his eyes, and she wished she'd chosen something better to wear than the cheap rust-red dress she'd bought at a chain store because it was stretchy and would go over the little bump that was beginning to show.

Sadly, it was too late for that. She hadn't had the money to buy anything decent anyway, not after the extortionate flight had been paid for.

She shivered as his intense silver gaze scanned her from the top of her damp head to the wet black leather of her pumps, and back up again. The elevator seemed to get smaller and smaller, the air in it thicker and thicker.

'Thanks for completely ruining my announcement,' she said, unable to hide her irritation. She hadn't been in his presence more than a minute and already he was getting under her skin. How he managed to do that, she couldn't fathom.

The first few weeks after their night together, she'd pushed him firmly to the back of her mind, because he'd said they'd never see each other again, and she'd agreed. Then after she'd discovered she was pregnant, the night they'd spent together had flooded back into her consciousness and had been taunting her ever since.

She'd thought she wouldn't want him again. She'd thought that one night was enough. Yet here she was, cold and jet-lagged and irritable, and all she could think about was putting her hands on his broad chest and pulling the buttons of his shirt open, pressing her mouth to his skin, tasting him…

Aristophanes tilted his head, the silver in his eyes glittering brighter as his gaze roved hungrily over her. And yes, it was hungry. The three months since she'd last seen him might as well not have existed. He might have been standing once again in the hallway of her small flat, staring at her as though he wanted to eat her alive.

Nell swallowed, her irritation turning into something more intense yet no less unsettling, her heartbeat thumping loudly in her ears.

The tension filling the elevator car felt almost unbearable.

'Mr Katsaros,' she began determinedly.

Abruptly and without a word, he dropped the briefcase he was carrying and took two steps towards her, forcing her back against the rail that ran around the interior of the elevator at waist height.

The look in his eyes burned, making an intense burst of wild excitement flood through her in response, an excitement she'd only ever felt once before: in his arms.

Oh, Lord, he wanted her and badly.

Slowly and with intent, he put one hand on the rail next to her, then the other hand, caging her against it the way he'd caged her against the door back in her Melbourne flat. And now, as then, she was acutely conscious of his warmth, of the musky spice of his aftershave.

It was intoxicating. She hadn't realised how cold she'd been until he was here.

He didn't move, only stared at her, his gaze searching her face as if looking for something. She couldn't get enough air, the only sound her heartbeat thumping crazily in her ears.

'Don't,' she breathed shakily, even though he hadn't said anything or moved another inch. She only knew if he did, she'd be lost, and she didn't want to be lost, not with this baby literally between them. Also, they needed to talk, not do…*this*.

'Don't?' he echoed, a thread of heat running through his deep, dark voice like fire in a coal seam. 'Don't what?'

Her breathing was getting faster and faster, the physical electricity he was throwing off making it difficult to think. He was standing so close, the gap between them mere inches.

'This,' she breathed, her voice husky. 'Don't do…this.'

Again, he didn't move closer, only lifted a hand and took her chin in his large, warm fingers, tilting her head back to look at him. His gaze burned so brightly she couldn't look away.

'Three months,' he murmured, his attention dropping to her mouth and then back up again. 'That's how long it's been since I've had a woman. And that's all your fault.'

Something inside her dropped away.

He hadn't slept with anyone in three months? Was he serious? There really had been no one since her?

'M-my fault?' she said unsteadily.

'Yes, yours.' His thumb stroked over her bottom lip, making her tremble. 'Every woman I have tried to spend time with hasn't interested me, and I thought it was because I've been working too hard. I thought it was because I was tired.' He paused, a flame in his eyes. 'Then you suddenly appear in my goddamn building, and now all I can think about is how to get you naked as quickly as humanly possible.'

The warmth of his touch was radiating through her entire body, chasing away the cold and the irritation, and somehow the jet lag too. She felt like a sunflower starved of light, turning towards the sun.

You didn't come here for sex, remember? You came here to talk.

That was true, but she'd felt nothing but uncertain for weeks and weeks. She'd been physically sick and anxious, and afraid of what would happen with the baby, what her life would look like after it was born. And now he was here and he wanted her with the same fierceness as he'd wanted her three months earlier. He'd made her feel so good, so beautiful and sexy, and desirable, and she wanted more of that; she couldn't deny it.

So why couldn't she have it? Have one more good experience before reality hit. A few more moments of pleasure, before her child arrived and took over her world.

He was still a stranger to her as much as he had been that night, but she didn't care. She hadn't realised how badly she'd been craving his touch until now.

'I…' She couldn't stop looking at his mouth, remembering how it had felt on her skin. Remembering its softness and the dark taste of him. 'I…don't think this is a good idea.'

'I disagree.' His head dipped, his mouth inches from hers. 'Did you know I was on my way to see someone else tonight when you turned up?'

'No.' The word escaped her on a sigh, the only thing of any importance his mouth so close to hers. 'I didn't know.'

'Woman, this is the second time you've ruined my evening plans.'

Nell wanted him to kiss her more than she'd wanted anything in her entire life. 'Perhaps it's fate,' she breathed.

'I don't care what it is.' His voice had deepened into that low growl that stroked over her skin like a hand. 'But if you don't want to have sex in this elevator, I suggest you tell me now.'

It was the raw note in the words that got her. The desperation that turned her inside out. She hadn't been able to resist his hunger for her all those months ago and she couldn't resist it now. She lifted her hands, took his face between them and pulled his mouth down on hers.

The kiss was blinding, a fire that once ignited couldn't be put out and it blazed high.

He made a rough sound in the back of his throat and abruptly his hands were on her hips, lifting her effortlessly onto the rail at her back. Then he glanced down, touching the little bump of her stomach almost in greeting, before pushing up her dress and spreading her knees wide so he could stand between them.

She gasped as he caressed the outside of her thighs then shuddered as his fingers slid inward, seeking more sensitive parts of her. A harsh sound of male satisfaction broke from him as he pulled aside her underwear and stroked over the slick heat of her sex, discovering how wet she was already for him.

She liked that sound. It thrilled her, as did the pleasure flooding through her, saturating every cell, making her arch back against the wall, glorying in his touch.

He bent his head then and kissed her again, devouring her utterly as his fingers teased and caressed her slick flesh, making her shift and move against his hand, desperate for more.

'Tell me where you want me,' he demanded, low and rough against her mouth. 'Tell me exactly.'

Nell was trembling, remembering how he'd demanded similar things from her that night they'd spent together and how she'd given them to him. Every single thing.

She wanted to do the same now.

'I want you inside me,' she said huskily, unable to hide the desperation in her voice.

He lifted his head, silver eyes burning. 'Now? Here?'

'Yes,' she whispered. 'Now. Here. Please…'

He didn't wait.

Almost in one movement, he turned, hit the stop button on the elevator, then turned back to her, tearing open his trousers and freeing himself. Then he gripped her hips and pushed hard and deep inside her, making her groan at the delicious burn and stretch of him.

It was too good. Too perfect. He made all her jet lag and cold and exhaustion just disappear and she didn't know how, but she didn't question it. She felt better than she had for months and she wanted more.

He'd paused, deep inside her, and she didn't look away as he stared at her, letting him know how good he was making her feel without words. Then she lifted her hand and touched his face, her fingers trembling, mesmerised by the feel of his skin. Warm and smooth, and yet some parts of it rough with whiskers.

He'd been beautiful back in Melbourne and he was still beautiful now.

He began to move, a slow rhythm that made her twist and arch against him, the fever beginning to build inside her until she had no idea where she was or even who she was. She only knew the pleasure growing wider, deeper, vaster than space.

'You,' she whispered to him, falling headlong into the melted silver of his eyes. 'What are you doing to me?'

'Only what you're doing to me.' He took her mouth again in a raw, demanding kiss that sent every last remaining thought from her head.

There was nothing after that. Nothing except the bonfire of pleasure they built between them, the flames leaping high. Then a final blaze into the sky with a wild rush of sparks before falling back, leaving both of them nothing but glowing embers.

She rested her forehead against his shoulder, panting as her heartbeat began to slow, the aftershocks still rocking her. He didn't move, a warm wall of hard muscle for her to rest against, and so she did.

She didn't want to think about what would happen next.

She didn't want to think at all.

She'd just had sex with the father of her child within minutes of meeting him for the second time. And she had no idea at all what she was going to do with that.

CHAPTER FIVE

ARISTOPHANES STARED AT the slightly reflective steel wall at Nell's back, thanking God he couldn't see his own reflection. Because he was pretty sure he'd find himself looking into the eyes of a complete fool.

A fool who'd thrown both his intellect and self-control straight out of the window in favour of parts located below his belt.

He was appalled at himself. Again.

What magic did this woman possess that she made him lose his head every time he saw her? The smallness of the elevator hadn't helped, it was true, making it impossible to put distance between them. And all he'd been conscious of was the scent of her, so sweet and feminine, and that yet again she was wearing a dress that outlined every luscious curve of her body, including the little bump of her stomach where his child lay.

A heated, raw feeling had flooded through him then, primitive and possessive, that had made him want to back her against the wall and claim her, make her his in every way.

He'd fought the urge, battled it hard, yet he hadn't been able to drag his gaze from hers. Her dark eyes had been velvet soft and he'd seen them heat in response to him, getting even hotter the longer they stared at each other. Then the tension had pulled tighter and tighter until he'd known he had to take some kind of action, otherwise he'd go mad.

He shouldn't have backed her up against the wall, but he had. And then she'd reached for him, drawing his mouth down on hers and…he'd lost himself. Lost himself as completely and utterly as he had that night with her three months earlier.

Perhaps he should have done what he'd intended to do tonight, sent Nell away and gone to see Claire. But…he couldn't even remember Claire's face or the sound of her voice, not with Nell slumped against him, her forehead resting against his shoulder, her face pressed to the cotton of her shirt, the warmth of her breath soaking through the fabric and into him…

She's pregnant with your child. If you claim her, you could have her close whenever you needed her. You wouldn't have to do all that matching schedules nonsense…

Aristophanes went very still as the thought struck him and echoed.

What if he could have her—have this—any time he wanted? He'd still have to schedule time with her, but it would be much more efficient to schedule it with a woman he knew he wanted and who would satisfy his bodily needs.

As for his child, he already knew that he wouldn't abandon it. He'd never do to his own son or daughter what his mother had done to him. He was a better man than that.

Of course, he had no idea how to be a father, but surely

it couldn't be too hard. Cesare had managed it and his little girl seemed to be a happy, normal child despite having him for a father. That might have been down to Lark, Cesare's wife, but that was why a child had two parents. He'd only ever had one since he'd never known who his father was and he felt no urge to find out. Any man who abandoned his child was as bad as his mother, in Aristophanes' opinion.

He wasn't sure if Nell was here for child support or something else but, given their physical chemistry, he'd already decided what he was going to do. She might not be open to it, but he was confident he could convince her. He could be persuasive when he wanted to be.

Time was passing, the minutes ticking by, and now was not the time to be standing here. They needed to talk. Also, he needed to tell the secretaries who managed his diary to arrange an appropriate apology gift for Claire, since he wouldn't be meeting her after all. It was also likely that they were going to have to rearrange his schedule to accommodate…other things. A child, for one. Possibly a woman for another.

Now, though, Nell had to be dealt with, so he eased himself away from her, obtaining yet more satisfaction from the slight sound of protest she made at his retreat.

'We need to talk,' he murmured as he helped her down from the rail so she was standing, unable to resist tracing the curve of her stomach where his child lay, a fleeting, possessive touch before he rearranged her clothes and dealt with his own. 'I have made some decisions.' He turned to the elevator doors, hitting the button once again.

The elevator shuddered into life and resumed its climb to his office.

'What decisions?' she asked, her clear voice pleasantly husky.

The sound of it shivered over his skin, the knowledge that she sounded like that because of the orgasm he'd given her making him hard all over again.

Yes, this was clearly something he was going to have to deal with. His physical response to her either needed to be nipped in the bud or indulged to its fullest extent until he didn't feel it any more.

Since she was pregnant and he would not abandon his child, indulging it seemed to be the best course of action.

He turned and looked down at her.

She was in the process of smoothing down the dress she wore, the fabric clinging deliciously to her curves, and he couldn't help raking his gaze hungrily down her body. If he kept her for a time, he could dress her in expensive gowns, of the finest material, that he could then tear off. Or maybe he would simply cover her naked body in jewels. He had more money than he knew what to do with… Why not?

Her cheeks were flushed and as he stared at her, she went an even deeper shade of rose.

'Decisions about you,' he said as the elevator arrived at his floor and chimed. 'About the child.'

She blinked, clearly still coming back down to earth. 'What about me and the child?'

The doors opened then so he turned back, taking her hand and stepping out directly into his vast office.

It occupied one corner of the top floor of his skyscraper, a huge, open-plan space with little islands of furniture dotted here and there. A desk positioned near the acres of floor-to-ceiling windows with a chair on the other side of it. Then across the pale carpet stood a meeting table surrounded by chairs. Near one of the other windows was a sectional couch of bone-coloured leather. A huge whiteboard covered in complicated maths equations stood by itself in the centre of the space.

The whiteboard and the desk were the main things he used, the space between the other bits and pieces of furniture where he paced up and down while he ran projections and equations in his head.

She came with him as he went over to his desk, her hand in his small and warm, and didn't resist as he guided her to the chair that stood in front of it.

'Sit,' he murmured.

He didn't want to release her, but he forced his fingers to uncurl from hers, helping her into the chair, even though she didn't need him to. It was difficult to keep from touching her, a light hand on the small of her back, a passing brush to her elbow.

She glanced up at him as she settled, dark eyes burning. Some of her hair had escaped its braid and was curling around her face, her cheeks still stained the prettiest shade of pink. And again he felt the same burst of satisfaction as he had when his fingers had quested between her thighs and found her warm and wet and ready for him.

He'd put that flush in her cheeks. He'd put that dark passion in her eyes.

It was primitive, that satisfaction, and he should be wary of it. Should be forcing it aside, along with all those other bothersome biological responses.

It wasn't that he denied his body—it was, after all, the vessel that contained his mind and so he looked after it, made sure it stayed in optimal condition. But he resented anything that distracted his intellect, and most especially when he was working.

A child is certainly going to distract your intellect.

The thought crept through him, making every muscle get tight, a burning sensation in his chest. No, a child would not distract him. He wouldn't let it. He'd keep both the child and the woman close, keep them near so he could keep any such distractions to a minimum.

Forcing his recalcitrant feelings back into the box he kept them in, Aristophanes strode around the side of the desk then sat down in the vast black leather chair behind it.

'So,' he said. 'These decisions. The child is mine, correct?'

Nell's eyes widened slightly in surprise then narrowed, her full mouth compressing. 'Of course the child is yours. I haven't been with anyone else since you.'

For a moment a weighted silence hung between them and he found himself staring into those velvety eyes of hers, the memories of that night filling the vast space of his office with heat and desperation, and the most intense physical pleasure. It was clear she was sharing in those memories, too, because her gaze darkened even further, turning smoky, the tightness leaving her lovely mouth, her lips parting just a touch.

They'd had sex mere moments before and yet he could feel his desire rising yet again, heating the blood in his veins and making him hard. If he let this silence go on too much longer, he wasn't going to be able to stay in his chair. He was going to lunge across the desk and grab her, drag her into his lap like a lion with an antelope.

She took a soft breath. 'Mr Katsaros—'

'I have many houses scattered across the globe,' he said abruptly, forcing the desire away, trying to get some control back. 'You choose which one you prefer to bring our child up in.'

Nell blinked. 'Excuse me?'

'You will live with the child in one of my houses. I don't care which it is.'

'I… I don't—'

'If finances are a problem, I will take care of it.' He found himself gripping the arms of his chair as if that were the only thing stopping him from reaching for her. 'You and the child will want for nothing.'

The smoky look had vanished from her eyes and they sharpened. 'You…want me to live with you?'

'No, not with me.' He wasn't used to having to explain himself. He'd always thought it a waste of precious time, and he resented having to do so now. It was this need, though, that was the problem. This desire wrapping its hands around his throat and squeezing him, choking him, making it difficult to think. He never found it difficult to think. 'I do not live anywhere in particular. You will have one of my houses and the child will be raised there.'

The desire had vanished utterly from her gaze, giving way to shock. 'You're joking,' she said. 'I mean, seriously?'

Annoyance started to bite. At himself and the desire that wouldn't seem to leave him alone, that he couldn't control. At her and her beauty, and the way his body had fixated on her for some reason. At how she clouded his mind and made it difficult to think.

His mind had been his sanctuary, the perfect escape from the drudgery of living ever since he'd been a child.

An escape from loneliness, from anger, from longing. A private world where he was the master. That mastery now extended into the real world and he would allow no one to compromise it, still less one little preschool teacher from Melbourne, no matter how lovely she was.

'No,' he said flatly. 'I am not. The child is mine, my heir. He or she will also need a mother, therefore your presence will be required.' He paused, his fingers clenched around the arms of his chair. 'Your presence will also be required in my bed.' His jaw felt tight, a muscle leaping there. It felt as if he were trying to hold back the tide. 'And that, Miss Underwood, is non-negotiable. Do you understand?'

Nell stared at the man sitting across the acres of dark oak.

He sat like a king, the vast black leather chair his throne, his gaze boring into hers. It burned that gaze, nothing but molten silver, making her feel hot all over.

She'd thought that maybe those feverish frantic moments in the elevator would have blunted the edge of her own desire, but they hadn't. If anything they had only intensified it, made her hungry for more. It hadn't been water on a fire but gasoline, and now she felt as if he'd burned away some vital part of her, a layer that had been protecting her, leaving her vulnerable and raw and, yes, still desperate for him.

Perhaps it was a combination of pregnancy hormones and shock. Or maybe it was just him. Him and the all-consuming way he looked at her, as if he was as hungry for her as she was for him.

Still. Even after three months had passed.

God, she couldn't look away.

Tension radiated from him, a muscle leaping in the side of his strong jaw, his hands gripping the arms of his chair as if he was afraid what he might do if he let go.

You did that to him. That was all you.

He wanted her and she'd loved that hunger of his. She hadn't had to do a thing. She'd just been herself and now she had this powerful man, this billionaire who owned the towering skyscraper she was sitting in, ravenous for her.

It was intoxicating, a welcome respite from the months of uncertainty and fear and constant exhaustion, and she wanted more of it. She hadn't tested the boundaries of her effect on him back in Melbourne that night, not when they'd been too busy with their basic hunger for each other, but now she wanted to. She wanted to test her power.

Get it together. He's basically demanding you sleep with him again, remember?

Nell took a sudden breath. What had he said? That he wanted her and the baby to live in one of his houses, and she would be in his bed. And that was non-negotiable.

Awareness flooded back in, cold as ice, washing away the heat and the pulse of desire.

She struggled to shake off the force of his intense gaze. 'That's…not why I came here,' she said, trying to get rid of the husk in her voice. 'I don't want your money.'

He didn't move, his beautiful face set in hard lines. 'Then why did you come?'

'You know why. I told you.'

'The baby, yes. But that could have been a phone call. What else did you want?'

'I didn't have your number and no one would give it to me, and I thought…this was a conversation we should have face to face.' Her hands twisted in her lap, the adrenaline coursing through her making her feel restless and antsy. 'Our baby needs a father and I wanted to give you the chance to be one.'

His gaze roved over her face, her hair, her shoulders and down over the curves of her breasts, and she knew she should draw her coat around herself, that she shouldn't pour any more petrol on this particular fire, yet she didn't move.

There was something powerful in his hunger. Something that made her feel as if she, the mediocre cuckoo in her aunt and uncle's nest, was beautiful and mysterious. A femme fatale who could make a man do anything. Perhaps she could make *this* man do anything.

Before she knew what she was doing, Nell leaned back slightly in her chair, allowing her coat to fall open so that the curves of her body were clearly visible beneath her clinging dress.

As she knew it would, his gaze followed those curves, igniting little fires inside her everywhere it went.

'I will be a father,' he said roughly. 'I will be anything you want. As long as you and I sleep together as much as possible. I'll have to rearrange my schedule, of course, but I can make it work.'

Sleep together as much as possible sounded good, yes—

What are you doing? Did you fully comprehend what he's asking you to do? You didn't come here for this. You came for the sake of your baby.

Nell gritted her teeth, attempting to put aside the heat rising inside her, trying to focus yet again on what he'd said. He would be a father. Also, there was something about a schedule…

'Schedule?' she asked. 'What schedule?'

'The schedule I use to run my life,' he said. 'My time is expensive and so I schedule every minute of it. That includes any time I take to spend with lovers. I will add the baby to the schedule and I will definitely be adding time for you.'

A little shock went through her, though she wasn't sure why. Important people were often very busy, so it made sense to have a schedule. Then again, scheduling lovers? That seemed over the top.

Aristophanes Katsaros *was* over the top though. Everything about him screamed intensity. The vivid silver of his eyes. His deep, rough voice. His compelling, electric presence. A genius. A billionaire. Head of a global finance company. Powerful. No part of him was middle-of-the-road.

And *this* man was the father of her baby.

There was such satisfaction to be had about that particular fact. That this man was her child's father and that she, as mediocre as she was, had attracted his attention.

In a dim corner of her brain, a warning sounded. Because no matter how pleased she was that he wanted her, he was also a stranger to her, despite how many times she'd had sex with him. And now he was demanding that she live in one of his houses. Demanding that she be put in his schedule so they could have sex.

What on earth was she doing even contemplating it? She'd slipped up back in the elevator and made a mistake, giving in to the power of their physical chemistry. It couldn't happen again, not given how much it clouded her thinking. She had a child to consider now and that baby was more important than anything else in her entire life.

Taking another slow breath, she dug her nails into her palms, the slight pain an antidote to the heat in her blood. 'No,' she said. 'I don't want you to schedule me for anything. And I don't want to move into one of your houses either, not when I don't even know you.'

Instantly his dark brows drew down into a scowl, the silver glitter of his eyes becoming even more intense. 'That is not acceptable,' he growled.

'Which part is not acceptable?'

'All of it.'

Nell tried to keep a grip on her temper, meeting him stare for stare, because, while she might be only a lowly kindergarten teacher and he a powerful billionaire, she couldn't let him get under her skin. Not again. He might be used to getting his way, but she wouldn't let him this time. Stubbornness of the male kind was something she was used to dealing with—in boys, admittedly, not men—but fundamentally they were the same.

She needed to hold her ground, make him understand that he wasn't in charge of this.

'I don't care if it's acceptable,' she said evenly. 'The only thing I require of you is that you be a father to this child. Be part of their life.'

'So you've already said.'

'I only wanted to make sure you heard. Little boys have painted-on ears.'

His scowl became a glower, his gaze burning like liquid mercury. 'I am not a little boy, Miss Underwood,' he said in a voice like gravel. 'Shall I demonstrate how I differ?'

More heat shot down her spine. Oh, yes, she wanted him to demonstrate. She *badly* wanted him to demonstrate. But again, she couldn't give in. Sex with him wasn't what she was here for. Because while it had been amazing, the experience in the elevator had also reminded her of why surrendering to him was a bad idea.

She'd always wanted a husband and partner, a family, a chance to recreate the family she'd lost after her parents had died. She wanted that security again, the feeling of belonging, and she already knew she wasn't going to get that with Aristophanes Katsaros.

He was rich and powerful beyond her wildest imaginings. He belonged to a world she had no conception of and didn't want to be a part of anyway. And even aside from all of that, he was also incredibly overbearing and rude. A man like that would suck her in, chew her up, and spit her out, she had no doubt.

She shifted, holding his relentless stare. The glitter of heat still burned there, but there were shadows now as well. The storm clouds of his temper, tarnishing the silver to steel.

'If you don't want me to treat you like a little boy, then you'll have to stop acting like one,' she said with an attempt at calm. 'I am not having sex with you again, and I will not be moving out of my flat, and that's final.'

His eyes darkened further. He was clearly not a man used to being denied. 'I am very rich, Miss Underwood. You do understand that, don't you? If you don't want one of my houses, then I can buy you one. I can buy you a whole town if you prefer.'

'I don't want you to buy me anything.'

'But you *do* want me to be involved in my child's life, correct?'

'Yes. I believe a child should have two parents.'

'A child always has two parents.'

Nell gritted her teeth. 'That's not what I'm asking and you know it.'

'No, I do not know it. You wished me to be involved, so here I am, involving myself.' The tension in the air around him had thickened and pulled taut, and now she could feel it reaching her, an electrical field prickling over her skin.

He leaned forward, elbows on his desk. 'What, exactly, is your objection?'

She dug her nails into her palms harder. 'I'm not up-ending my entire life to go and live in one of your houses. I have a job. I have friends. I don't want to leave.'

'What? That cluttered little flat?' There was an edge of disdain in his voice. 'Hardly a suitable place for a child of mine to live in. There are security issues, for a start, and also I am not in Melbourne frequently. Not only would it be safer if you and the baby were in one of my residences, it would also make visiting more efficient.'

Now it was her temper starting to rise. 'I'm not giv-ing up my job to—'

'I will find you another job. It cannot be that hard to find something else to do.' There was an unyielding note in his voice, his gaze steel that felt as if it were running straight through her.

'But… I don't know you,' she burst out. 'Why on earth would I want to live with you when you're a complete and utter stranger to me?'

'That can be remedied.' He shoved back his chair and got to his feet in a sudden explosion of movement, stalk-ing with animalistic grace around the side of his desk like some great hunting cat.

Stalking to her.

She half rose too, her heart beating out of control, but by then he was standing in front of her, leaning over her, bracing his hands on the arms of her chair. He stared down into her face, his expression so hungry and fierce she almost went up in flames there and then.

'Tell me you don't want me,' he demanded, low and rough. 'Tell me that sex with me isn't all you're thinking about right now.'

Her mouth had dried. All she could think about was how warm his body was, how good he smelled. How she wanted to kiss him, rip off his suit, be naked with him. Have his hot skin sliding over hers. Have his mouth on her... God, everything.

'I... I'm not.' Her voice was a mere scrape of sound.

He lowered his head until his mouth was millimetres from hers. 'Liar,' he murmured. 'You're thinking about it right now. You're thinking about that night we had together and what happened in the elevator just before. You want it again. You want more. You want me.'

His lips were so close. All she'd have to do was lift her head and they would be against hers. She could taste him again. She could feel beautiful and wanted again.

He wasn't wrong. She did want him.

'You're asking too much,' she said huskily, trying to fight him and her own desire. 'You're asking me to change my entire life for you.'

'Your life is going to change anyway, and so will mine.' He bent a touch lower, his mouth even closer. 'Spend tonight with me. Help me get rid of this chemistry. Then perhaps we can have a rational conversation.'

It was difficult to think with him so close and her body

so hungry, but she tried. Spend the night with him… That didn't sound bad. And he was right that they needed to get rid of their chemistry. How could they have a discussion about their child with that getting between them and distracting them? They'd both underestimated how strong it still was.

She tried to get some moisture into her dry mouth. 'My flights… I have appointments…'

'I will handle it.' He brushed his mouth over hers in the lightest of kisses. 'I will handle everything.'

Nell shivered. She had no doubt that he would, just as he'd handled it when she'd slipped and hurt her head. He'd got her to hospital, organised a doctor, made sure she was cared for… And after all, they really did need a clear-headed discussion about the baby. He'd said he'd be a father…

His hand moved from the arm of the chair to her coat, pulling aside the fabric, then his fingertips grazed over the curve of one breast, her hip, her thigh, before lifting again, brushing down the side of her neck to her throat, settling on the frantic beat of her pulse.

'Say yes, Nell,' he murmured. 'The baby will be safe. *You* will be safe with me, I promise.'

It was strange to feel the tension slip away from her in that moment. She didn't know him, yet she believed him. In the same way as she'd reached for his hand when she'd knocked herself out that night in Melbourne. As if her body had known who he was before her mind had. Known that he wasn't a stranger to her, that she could be safe with him.

He meant what he said. So what would it hurt?

His palm was a tender weight at the base of her throat

and she could feel every part of her come alive once again at his touch.

She lifted her head, brushing his mouth in a return kiss, but he pulled away, just out of reach. Her breath caught as she stared up at him, at the burning intensity of his gaze. 'Say yes,' he repeated softly. 'If you say yes, you'll get everything you want.'

His hand slid from her throat, slowly down over the curve of one breast, and cupped it gently, his thumb teasing her aching nipple through the fabric of her dress.

She trembled, arching into the warmth of his palm.

Everything she wanted...

Right now, all she could think of was him.

A long breath escaped her and she reached up, sliding her fingers in his thick black hair. It felt like raw silk against her skin. She gripped it, drawing his head down, making sure he couldn't pull away.

'Yes,' she whispered against his mouth.

'Tonight.' It was a growl. 'You'll be mine tonight.'

'Yes.'

Then his mouth was on hers and all words were lost.

CHAPTER SIX

ARISTOPHANES TURNED OVER and opened his eyes. Half of him had been dreading that the night before had been a dream, that when he awoke he'd find his bed empty and the woman he'd been with, the warm, silky, beautiful little woman he'd spent the night exploring every inch of, would be gone.

But she wasn't gone. She was still fast asleep next to him in his giant bed, her thick auburn hair spread like kelp over the white Egyptian cotton pillowcase. Her hands were tucked beneath her chin like a child's, her auburn lashes lying still on her cheeks. The sheet had slipped down to her waist, exposing pale shoulders, the swell of her stomach and the graceful arch of her back.

She was lovely. So lovely.

Once she'd agreed to a night together the day before in his office, he'd been very tempted to simply lay her out on the carpet before his desk and have her there and then. However, he'd decided that there would be fewer interruptions if he took her back to his penthouse apartment on the Upper East Side, that looked out over Central Park.

So he had and they'd fallen into bed immediately, only surfacing for food and drink, before losing themselves in each other again. They hadn't talked. They'd let their bodies continue the same wordless conversation they'd first had back in Melbourne, communicating via sensation, with touches and licks, and caresses and bites, and pleasure.

It had been incredible. Maybe even more incredible than that first night they'd spent together, which was saying something.

He wanted to reach out and touch her, trace her little bump the way he hadn't been able to keep from doing in the elevator the day before, a rare experience for him since usually after a night with a lover, all he wanted to do was leave. Then again, they hadn't had much sleep and she was still jet-lagged. She really should have some rest.

Especially since she's pregnant.

An unwelcome arrow of reality pierced him, making his chest feel tight and uncomfortable. Yes, how could he have forgotten that? He was going to be a father.

It was hard thinking when he was right next to her, with her warmth and scent all around him, because she made him want to do things other than thinking. So, he slid out of bed carefully without waking her.

And he did need to think. She'd been very clear the day before that she didn't want to move into one of his residences, or give up her life in Melbourne, and why her feelings about this mattered to him, he wasn't sure. But they did, and he didn't like that they did.

Frowning to himself, he went into the en suite bathroom, stepped into the huge granite shower, and turned on the water, letting it slip over his naked body.

Logically it made sense to insist she move where it was easier for him to visit both her and the child. He could more easily care for her there—or rather have his staff care for her. Also, the more he thought about it, the more he realised he wanted his child to have one place to grow up in. A home.

He'd had one once, before his mother had abandoned him. A large house in Athens, with a garden he'd played in, but that was all he remembered about it. He remembered more of being shipped around the country, from one foster family to another, always a new house, always new family. He'd lost count of how many homes he'd had, which was why he'd used his mind to escape. In the privacy of his own head, there was familiarity, continuity. Control.

Yet while that had worked for him in many ways, he didn't want his own child to have that kind of childhood. It had been a lonely existence to be always left longing for a connection with someone, anyone. A longing that had never been fulfilled, since he'd never stayed with any family long enough to establish any kind of connection.

Eventually he'd excised that longing from his heart and taught himself not to want, never to need. But still…

His child should have better than that.

He stepped out of the shower, dried himself off and pulled on the first pair of trousers that came to hand. Then he went out of the bedroom, padded down the hallway and into the cavernous kitchen of his massive apartment, and began the process of making coffee.

Yes, logically the child should be accessible to him and he had to be close, or at least within easy reach should anything happen with Nell. A child cared for by only one parent was a child at risk; some people, for one reason or another, couldn't deal with the pressures of parenthood after all. His mother being a prime example.

There had been times in his life when he'd tried to understand why she'd left him the way she had, but that had been the one puzzle he'd never managed to solve. There had been no signs that he could remember, no hint that she'd suddenly found being a mother to him impossible. He'd loved her and he'd thought she'd loved him.

Not that it mattered now, since he'd put his fury at her away years ago. He only wanted to be sure that the same thing wouldn't happen to his child, which meant he'd need Nell to be situated closer to him. She wouldn't like it—she'd mentioned her job and her friends—but he wouldn't be moved on this particular point. Europe, Japan, and the States were his main bases of operations, and as such he couldn't base himself in the southern hemisphere.

After preparing himself a small cup of the thick black espresso he preferred, he took it out into the living area, the huge floor-to-ceiling windows giving a fine view over the large green rectangle of Central Park far below.

Aristophanes sipped his coffee, still thinking.

He could be ruthless when he chose—he hadn't got to where he was today by being kind or gentle—but he could offer Nell some incentives. Obviously, money wasn't going to work, since she'd told him she didn't want it, but he had plenty of other ways to leverage her agreement.

Sex, for example. One night had taken the edge off his hunger, but only slightly. He couldn't stand the thought of her going back to Melbourne right now. He wanted to keep her here, in his bed for the next few days, and, considering how passionate and wanton she'd proved herself to be, he thought she wouldn't refuse him.

She wanted him every bit as badly as he wanted her, and he was prepared to use their chemistry to get her to do what he wanted. Also, he could find her a job if that was what she needed, and as for her friends… He'd give her his private jet so she could fly them out from Melbourne whenever she liked.

She'd find that acceptable, wouldn't she?

He sipped again at his coffee, staring out through the glass, satisfaction gathering inside him. Telling his secretaries to amend his schedule to include Nell was his first order of business. In fact, he was even considering moving his morning meeting from eight to eleven, to give himself a few more hours with her.

Conversation wasn't his strongest suit, but business negotiations were. It wouldn't be difficult to change her mind about living in one of his residences. Certainly nothing a few good orgasms couldn't fix.

Speaking of which…

Inevitable physical desire began to rise again, so he downed the rest of his coffee, put it down on a side table, and turned from the windows. He was halfway across the room to the hallway that led to the bedroom when Nell suddenly appeared.

She was wrapped in one of his sheets, her hair a glorious auburn veil around her shoulders, and he opened his mouth to tell her to get rid of the sheet, then stopped.

Her face was very pale, almost as white as the cotton wrapped around her lovely body. 'I… I…' she murmured, took a step towards him, then staggered.

A fist closed around his heart, and he was moving before he'd even thought the action through, striding over to her and sliding an arm around her waist just as her knees went out from under her. She fell against him and he caught her, holding her fast.

'Nell,' he said urgently. 'What happened? What's wrong?'

Her pale face turned against his chest, her dark eyes suddenly full of fear. 'I'm…bleeding…'

The fist around his heart squeezed tighter. The baby…

Dimly he was aware of an unfamiliar feeling, something akin to fear, but he pushed it ruthlessly aside, sweeping her up into his arms and carrying her over to the sectional sofa near the windows. He laid her gently on it as adrenaline flooded his body, the way it had the night she'd fallen over on the pavement, but this time it was even more intense. He wanted to keep hold of her, use his body as a shield against anything that would hurt her or the baby.

His baby.

'Hush,' he murmured. 'And lie still. I'll get help.' As he reached into the pocket of his trousers to get his phone, Nell's fingers closed around his wrist and held on tight.

'I don't want to lose the baby,' she said hoarsely, her dark eyes full of desperation. 'Please don't let me lose it.'

In that moment certainty gathered weight and solidity inside him. A determination. She would *not* lose their baby. He'd move heaven and earth, bring down the sun if need be to ensure that she wouldn't.

'You won't lose it.' He held her gaze with his so she could see his conviction. 'I'll make sure you don't.'

The fear in her eyes eased a little and she nodded, releasing his wrist.

Ten minutes and some urgent calls later, his doctor arrived and organised for Nell to be transported via helicopter to a private hospital not far from his apartment. And as she had that night in Melbourne, Nell held tight to his hand the whole way, and didn't let go even when she was rushed into an examination room in preparation for a scan.

His whole body felt tight and that fist around his heart wouldn't let go, squeezing and squeezing. And as the doctor came in and sat by the bed, murmuring reassuring things as she prepared Nell for her ultrasound, he realised with a kind of shock that the baby hadn't seemed real to him before now. It had been an idea, a concept, a fact. He hadn't thought deeply about the reality of it, because he'd been too wrapped up in Nell and their intense physical chemistry.

Now though, as the doctor spread gel on Nell's stomach and positioned the wand, the reality of his child hit him over the head with all the solidity of a cricket bat. And along with it came the choking fear that it was too late, that she might lose it.

They might both lose their child.

He stared at the monitor beside Nell's bed, holding her hand, filled with the most intense helplessness. There was nothing he could do in this moment, nothing he could say that could affect the outcome. It was out of his hands.

It reminded him so powerfully of his childhood, of watching yet another social worker walk up to the front door of whichever house he was living in at the time, knowing that she was here to take him away again. That he was going to be moved again, given to a new family, living in a new house, and that there was nothing he could do to stop it.

His jaw was so tight it ached, and he had to use every

ounce of his considerable strength to force away the fear. Nell's fingers around his were tight too, holding his hand in a painful grip, and he had no idea why everything had suddenly changed.

Why he only realised now how much he wanted something when he was on the point of losing it. And he didn't know whether it was because of her or whether it had been there inside him all along, but that didn't matter.

What mattered was that he couldn't lose his child. He couldn't.

The doctor moved the wand a few times, frowning at the screen, while Nell sat in the bed, her face the colour of ashes.

'What is it?' Aristophanes demanded, his voice rough as gravel. 'Please tell me the baby is fine.'

'The baby is fine,' the doctor said calmly, still frowning as she ran the wand back over Nell's stomach. 'At least one of them is.'

Aristophanes was conscious first of a flood of relief then, hard on its heels, cold shock. 'What? What other one?'

'Oh, there's the other one.' The doctor made another pass with the wand then the frown vanished and her face relaxed. 'It was hiding. But both have got good heartbeats and don't look like they're in any distress.'

Nell's face got even whiter. 'I'm sorry, but what do you mean by "both"?'

The doctor glanced at her then at Aristophanes and smiled. 'Oh, you didn't know? There are two babies in there. Congratulations, you're having twins.'

For a long moment neither he nor Nell spoke as the words penetrated, the shock still echoing inside him.

'Twins,' Nell murmured blankly. 'We're having twins.'

'Yes,' the doctor said, turning the monitor around so they both could see. 'Do you want to know the gender?'

Aristophanes stared fixedly at the monitor and the two little pulsing heartbeats on the screen, then he glanced down at Nell, who was still holding his hand in a death grip. Her gaze met his, dark and velvety and full of shock.

Nell nodded mutely at him and he nodded at the doctor. Not that he cared about the gender of his child. Of his child*ren*. Not when he was still reeling from perhaps nearly losing one baby, unable to even get his head around the concept of two of them.

'A perfect pair,' the doctor said. 'A girl and a boy.'

That was when Nell promptly burst into tears.

A few hours later, feeling drained and not a little shell-shocked, Nell sat once again on the couch in Aristophanes' New York apartment, wrapped up in a cashmere blanket, staring at the pale carpet and wondering what on earth she was going to do.

The night before, all she'd been able to think about was him. She hadn't been able to get enough, and the more she had of him, the more she wanted. He'd been ravenous for her too, and she'd decided to allow herself the whole night of not thinking of anything else.

It had been amazing, magical. So when she'd finally woken up and gone to have a shower, she hadn't been thinking about the baby. Her head had been too full of him and what she was going to do now they'd had their night together.

She'd started to wash herself dreamily and only then had she noticed the blood. That, combined with the lack of sleep and heat of the water, had nearly made her faint. Somehow, dizzy and nauseated, she'd managed to get herself out of the shower and semi-dry, before stumbling down the hallway to the living area to find him.

Only then had she fainted.

He'd caught her though, the strength of his arms surrounding her as he'd carried her over to the couch. For a brief moment she'd felt safe and cared for. But after that…

She didn't like to think about the tense hour after that, of being rushed to a hospital and then waiting for the doctor to see if her baby was okay. She'd been numb with fear and dread, her only lifeline Aristophanes' big warm hand around hers.

She hadn't wanted to lose her baby. She couldn't bear the thought.

Finding out the baby was fine had made her dizzy with relief.

Finding out that there were two babies instead of one had been a shock. To put it mildly. Because at her first scan there hadn't been two. Apparently, though, one could remain undetected that early.

She'd felt ridiculous for bursting into tears, but the surprise of twins on top of everything else had been too much for her. Aristophanes' arms had gone around her once again, and she'd turned her face against his chest, the intellectual part of her wondering why it was that she felt so much better when she was in his arms. Especially when she knew nothing about him. Yet in that moment, she hadn't been thinking intellectually. She'd been nothing but rubbed-raw emotion as the doctor had said a lot of stuff that had gone over her head and was only now sinking in.

For the health of her babies, she had to rest. Not complete bed rest, but she had to limit her activities. No lifting heavy objects. No standing upright for longer than twenty minutes. No walking longer than twenty minutes. And definitely no sex.

Now here she was, in this stranger's apartment, expecting not one but two of his babies, and the health of those babies was dependent on a support system at home that she didn't have.

She didn't know what to do.

How was she supposed to return to Melbourne? She couldn't work, that much was certain, and she'd need someone to look after her, and, given that she had no one to do that for her, there was only one solution.

Aristophanes and his demand that she live in one of his residences.

Before he'd made her lose her mind in his office, he'd suggested it, yet she'd been barely able to take it in, too blinded by her need for him. There had been a momentary spark of temper then…well. She hadn't been able to think more about it.

Now, though, she was staring that demand full in the face.

She liked her job and her flat, and her life in Melbourne. After she'd left her aunt and uncle's house at eighteen, she'd shifted cities from Perth where she'd grown up, to Melbourne across the country, wanting to get as far away from childhood as she could. She'd been determined to make a new life for herself, in a new city where no one knew her and she wasn't bound by the limitations her aunt and uncle had put on her.

She'd always wanted to make a difference to people,

to help them, and while she hadn't been smart enough for med school or nursing, or social work, being a preschool teacher had fulfilled the nurturing, protective need in her.

No one had looked after her as a child. No one had cared after her parents had died. The kids she looked after obviously still had parents, but someone needed to watch over them during the day, and she'd be that someone.

She loved the work and didn't want to give it up. Yet there didn't seem to be a lot of choice, not if she wanted to put the health of her children first. That was if Aristophanes Katsaros' offer was still open. She assumed it was, since she was still pregnant, and he'd been very clear the day before about what he wanted. Then again, who knew? He might have changed his mind since sex was off the table.

She lifted her gaze from the carpet to where he stood in the middle of the vast minimalist living area, all pale carpet, pale walls and black leather furniture. He was pacing back and forth, talking on his phone. She wasn't sure what language he was speaking—it was too fast for her to guess—but it definitely wasn't English.

He'd told her to sit and rest while he 'organised' some things, but she hated sitting still. She also wanted to know what he was organising. She wanted to know what he thought about the fact that they were having twins.

In the hospital, his face had been set in granite lines, his whole body radiating tension. Yet his long fingers around hers had been gentle and firm, holding her with intent. He clearly hadn't been about to let her go and she'd liked that. His grip had felt like an anchor, holding her steady against a powerful current.

She'd seen fear in his eyes, though, and for some reason it had been comforting that he'd been scared for their baby too. But then had come the revelation of the twins and his eyes had gone dark with shock.

Did he want them? She didn't know. They hadn't talked about it. They hadn't talked about anything, and, despite her spending all of the previous night with him, she still knew nothing about him.

Today he was in another grey suit with a white shirt. His jacket had been thrown carelessly over one of the chairs, his shirtsleeves rolled up, exposing strong tanned forearms. Even now, after everything, her heart beat fast and her mouth dried as she looked at him move with careless, athletic grace.

What was going to happen? Whatever it was, she wasn't going to like it, she just knew. Perhaps there was another option that didn't involve throwing herself on his mercy, or upending her life, yet if one existed, she couldn't think of what it might be.

It was times like these, bad times, that she wished desperately her parents hadn't died, especially her mother. She wished she could talk to her about her pregnancy, about how she was going to be a mother too, but...that was impossible. She had only her aunt and her aunt hadn't cared. Her aunt had four other children of her own and she'd never shown much interested in her husband's brother's little girl.

For a second Nell closed her eyes, trying to recall her mother's face, but there was only a faint blur in her memory. It had been too long. All she had left now was the faint scent of her mother's favourite perfume and the gentle warmth of her hugs.

Nell's stomach hollowed, her throat feeling thick, but

she forced away the rush of emotion. God, she didn't have the energy to cry again.

In front of her Aristophanes stopped pacing and pocketed his phone. 'It is arranged,' he said, striding over to where she sat.

'What's arranged?' she asked.

He came to a stop in front of her, folding his arms over his broad chest, his gaze the colour of steel. 'You will not be returning to Melbourne. At least not until our children are born.'

A little shock went through her. She hadn't known what to expect from him, but she hadn't thought he'd take charge so immediately. There was no denying the authority in his voice though, the tone of a man used to giving commands and having them obeyed.

Deep down she was conscious of something tight and afraid relaxing, but her temper flickered. He hadn't even asked her what she wanted; he'd simply decided all on his own. 'Thank you for asking my opinion,' she said acidly. 'Always nice to have what I want completely disregarded.'

Storm clouds gathered in his eyes. 'What you want is irrelevant. You are carrying two children—*my* children—and the best thing for their welfare and therefore yours is to be properly cared for by me.'

Her temper, already frayed by the day's emotions, flickered higher. She was tired. So very tired. 'They're also *my* children,' she snapped. 'And since when did their welfare suddenly become of the utmost importance to you?'

'Since sleeping with you almost lost them,' he snapped right back.

Her anger leapt, and she half rose from the couch. 'So this is my—'

But before she could finish, he was suddenly there, reaching for her and gathering her up in his arms like a child. For a moment she lay still against the hot wall of his chest, too surprised to move. Then her anger redoubled, and she twisted. 'Let me go!'

His grip on her tightened. 'Keep still,' he growled, his stormy gaze full of steel. 'This will not help the babies.'

At that, all her fury abruptly flickered then went out. He was right, of course. Getting angry and arguing wasn't exactly the rest the doctor had ordered. Her children mattered more than her anger.

She took a breath, willing herself to relax. 'Fine. But if you don't want me to argue with you, don't make me the bad guy.'

He scowled. 'I am not making you the bad guy.'

'Yes, you did. You made it sound as though I somehow nearly lost the babies on purpose.'

'I… I did not mean that.' His mouth tightened. 'I just did not like the idea that we put them at risk for something as meaningless as sex.'

This time it was hurt that echoed through her. 'Meaningless? Is that what you think last night was?'

'It was pleasurable,' he said tightly. 'But hardly the most important thing in the world.'

The splinter of hurt slid deeper inside her. It *had* been pleasurable, he wasn't wrong about that, but it had never been meaningless, not to her. He'd made her feel, for the first time in her life, beautiful, desirable, and…special. It had deeply affected her. But clearly it hadn't been the same for him. Pleasurable, he'd said. Not that important.

Stupidly, her eyes filled with tears, which she hated. She hated, too, that somehow she'd given him the power to hurt her in this way, because what did it matter that it hadn't been as earth-shattering for him as it had been for her? Did she really care what he thought about it anyway?

Since she'd left her aunt and uncle's, she'd told herself that she didn't care about other people's opinions of her. That she was tired of caring. Tired of wanting more than she'd ever been given. Tired of feeling so insecure all the time.

Yet here she was, expecting twins with this scowling man, and she was hurt that he hadn't thought that sex with her was as great as she'd thought it was herself.

Stupid of her. She didn't care what he thought, not one iota.

'That not-very-important sex created these babies,' she said coolly, blinking away the tears and leaning her head against his shoulder. 'But I'm glad it was merely "pleasurable" for you.'

He stared down at her, his eyes narrowing, and it was downright unfair how that scowl made him look even hotter than he already was. 'You are tired,' he said abruptly. 'You were jet-lagged when you arrived, and then I kept you up far too late. You have had so little sleep and today has been full of too many surprises.' He turned and started in the direction of the hallway, still carrying her as if she weighed nothing at all. 'You should rest while I prepare everything for our trip tomorrow.'

That he was planning something else he hadn't told her about somehow didn't come as a surprise. 'What trip?' she asked as he carried her into the hallway.

'I own an island off the coast of Greece and the villa

there is perfect for convalescing. There is also a separate villa where the doctor can stay should any emergencies happen.'

Of course he owned a Greek island. And apparently she was expected to stay there like Napoleon on Elba, except pregnant and without the benefits of being the Emperor of France or of having an army.

She glared up at him. 'Did you even think to ask me whether I might like to go to Greece or was this just another thing that you decided?'

'I have some meetings in Athens,' he said, stalking through into the bedroom. 'I can make sure you're safely settled while I'm there.'

'What if I don't want to go to Greece? What if I want to stay here?'

The bedroom was huge, his vast bed pushed up against one wall, the sheets tangled from their activities the night before.

'What you want is irrelevant,' he said, carrying her over to the bed. 'The well-being of the babies is all that matters.'

That hurt too. To her aunt and uncle, all she'd been was an extra and very much unwanted child, but to Sarah at the preschool, she was a valued teacher. The children she taught loved her and missed her when she wasn't there. To them she was important.

So to be treated as if she were nothing more than a human incubator now made her feel like that unwanted child once again. She hated it. She hated, too, that he was right.

'Fine. But the well-being of the babies also depends on the well-being of the mother,' she said tartly as he set her down gently on the mattress. 'And being treated as if I'm nothing more than a vessel for your children does not exactly help my well-being.'

'You are not just a vessel.' He glanced down at the small bump of her stomach, then unexpectedly he reached down and touched it, his fingers tracing the curve.

A small arrow of surprise caught at her, because, as well as possession, there was reverence in the touch, and she hadn't expected that of him.

Then he spoiled it by straightening suddenly, his hand dropping away, storm clouds shifting in his eyes. 'Do not be difficult, Nell.'

'I'm not being difficult. You're the one being rude, hurtful and overbearing, not to mention ordering me around like a small dog.' She gripped the edge of the mattress. 'We were supposed to talk about this, remember? That's why I came here to New York in the first place, to have a conversation about what we're going to do, not for you to have a conversation with yourself.'

He was silent, clenching and unclenching his hands as if trying to relax them, and she suddenly had the impression that, for all his authority, all his apparent confidence, he was as much at sea about the situation as she was. Except he either didn't know he was at sea or couldn't admit it. And that was a surprise. He was a man used to being in charge and making decisions, and he needed to be considering the vastness of his company. He brought that natural authority to sex, too, yet she'd held her own against him there, matching him passion for passion. They'd found a natural equilibrium in bed, each of them the other's perfect match.

Out of bed, though, it was another story. He was just

as stubborn as she was, and what worked with physical passion didn't work when it was two people trying to negotiate a difficult situation.

She let out a breath. Arguing wasn't going to help and she didn't want to fight him anyway. She didn't have the energy for it. But still, one thing she'd learned dealing with both children and their parents was that sometimes hammering at someone wasn't the way to go. Especially when it only made them push back even harder.

Sometimes a different approach worked better.

With a conscious effort, she pushed aside her anger. 'Look, I'm sorry. But all of this has been a terrible shock. I was hoping to talk to you, not spend the night with you. I didn't even know if you'd welcome the idea of a baby, let alone be a father to it. And then to think I was losing it, then finding out it's twins…' She swallowed. 'It's a lot to deal with.'

His steely gaze flickered, as if he'd been expecting another attack, not her sudden honesty. 'Yes,' he said after a moment. 'Yes, it is. And I admit that the situation we find ourselves in is…difficult. My schedule is full for the entire month and I do not have a lot of leeway to include you and the babies, which is why I decided on Greece. I can visit you and make sure everything is as it should be.'

Well, at least he'd made a stab at explaining his reasoning, even if it didn't make much sense to her. Especially his ridiculous schedule. If he was the boss, couldn't he rearrange a few things?

She released her grip on the mattress. 'Why is me going home to Melbourne so difficult? Surely if you're the CEO of your company, you can do whatever you want?'

'Within reason,' he said. 'But I cannot stand wasted time or inefficiency, and Melbourne is out of my way.'

'Why do you need to visit me at all? You've only known you'll be a father for all of twelve hours. Also, we can't have sex, so what's the point of a visit?'

He glowered, as if she'd pointed out something he didn't like. 'I didn't lie when I told you that the welfare of my children became important to me the moment I thought I was losing them. In that examination room, looking at that monitor and seeing two heartbeats, that's when I decided. And as you've already pointed out, the health of the babies is dependent on the health of the mother. That's why I want to visit. I need to make sure you are well.'

Nell felt that little splinter of hurt work its way even deeper inside her, which was annoying. Why did it matter to her that he visit her for *her*, not simply because she was the mother of his children? Why did she want more than that? They'd spent two nights together, that was the grand total of their dealings with each other, and, while those two nights had rocked her world on its axis, the reality of the man standing in front of her was very different from the lover who'd made her see actual stars. Perhaps too different.

'In that case,' she said tightly, 'I'd imagine it'll be a very quick visit.'

'Yes. It will. Which is another reason for you to be close to where I do business. There's no point wasting time in idle conversation.'

Nell opened her mouth to tell him he was being an absolute bastard, but abruptly she didn't have the energy. All she wanted to do now was sleep. 'Fine,' she said wearily. 'I'm sure you have plenty to do. Don't worry about me. I'll be okay.'

He kept on frowning. 'You don't seem—'

'Please, just leave me alone,' she interrupted, the frayed tether she had on her temper snapping. 'I need to sleep.'

His mouth worked, as if he meant to say something. But then, clearly changing his mind, he straightened. Gave her a single nod, then turned on his heel and went out.

CHAPTER SEVEN

ARISTOPHANES WAITED UNTIL the rotors had slowed, then he opened the door of the helicopter, got out, then turned to help Nell disembark.

They'd just touched down on the helipad near his villa on Ithasos, a tiny green jewel of an island set in the deep turquoise blue of Mediterranean, near Mykonos.

His villa here was one of his preferred residences, and since it worked in well with his schedule for the next week, he'd decided it would be the perfect place for Nell. He'd have some time to spend helping her get settled in before he had to go on to London—he'd even managed to fit into his schedule a whole afternoon and evening to show her around his house and the island.

He knew she'd been unhappy with his decision back in New York that she should stay here for the duration of her pregnancy, but, really, it was the best solution for both of them. He didn't want her going back to Melbourne on her own, not when he had no idea of what kind of support she had there, and not when he couldn't accompany her because of his schedule—after the near miss with the babies, he didn't want to let her out of his sight if he could help it. Which meant taking her to Greece was the most logical decision, especially given her pregnancy restrictions.

He could have asked her, he supposed, as she'd flung at him back in New York, but then she'd argued anyway, and arguing was a waste of time. Especially when he'd already decided what was going to happen.

The potential loss of the babies had pierced him in a place he hadn't known he was vulnerable, a painful place. A place of fear. It was true what he'd told her, that he hadn't realised how badly he'd wanted those children until he'd nearly lost them.

Before leaving New York, he'd talked to Cesare on the phone for a long time about how Nell was pregnant and that it was twins. His friend had taken a good deal of amusement from that particular fact, but Aristophanes saw nothing amusing about it. Almost to his own surprise, when he'd told Nell he'd keep them safe, he'd meant it. He'd meant it more than he'd meant anything else in his entire life. The children were not abstracts any longer, not ideas. Not equations or problems to solve, but small lives under threat, lives that were precious. He would never allow them to be lost, which meant he'd do everything in his power to make sure that didn't happen. Even if it meant making decisions that Nell didn't like.

You didn't have to be so cold though.

The thought was an uncomfortable one and it had nagged at him ever since they'd left New York. It was true he'd been less…kind to her than he should have, and yes, probably cold. He'd just been operating on a threat response level, which didn't allow for anyone's feelings.

When he'd implied, for example, that the sex had been meaningless in comparison to the health of the babies, there had been a flicker of what he suspected was hurt in her gaze. The same when she'd asked what the point of him visiting her was, and he'd responded with the truth, to make sure she and the twins were healthy.

It had made him wonder what it was about what he'd said that had been painful for her. Certainly with the latter, it was almost as if she'd wanted him to visit her for *her*, which was odd when, as she kept saying to him, they were complete strangers. He didn't know her and she didn't know him.

Also, he was a billionaire financial genius and she was a preschool teacher. What on earth would they have to talk about? Sex had been the language they'd used for all their communications up to this point, and if they couldn't have sex then the only other reason to bother with a visit was for health reasons.

But why not make the effort? How can you know that you don't have anything to talk about, when you haven't bothered to initiate any kind of conversation?

The thought sat uncomfortably inside him as he turned to help her out of the machine. Her gaze was shuttered, giving him nothing, the way it had been ever since they'd left New York. He didn't like it. It made his chest get tight, made him wonder if he'd done something wrong, made the wrong move. He didn't like that either.

Nell was pale, with circles under her eyes, her hair flowing in thick auburn waves down her back, and she wore a pair of stretchy black pants and a loose sweatshirt in vivid emerald green. The colour made her eyes even darker, bringing out the red sparks in her auburn hair.

An inevitable punch of desire hit him as his hand settled on her hip to help her out of the helicopter, the feel of her so warm and soft, it was all he could do not to squeeze her gently then slide his hand between her thighs, see how warm and soft she was there too.

But he couldn't do that, not without endangering his children, so, with an effort that cost him far more than it should, he crushed the urge. It shouldn't still be so strong after their night in New York, yet it was, which meant yet more decisions needed to be made about what would happen after the babies were born. He already had a few ideas…

'Welcome to Ithasos,' he murmured as he helped her down onto the helipad.

The expression on her face remained guarded, her mouth tight. 'Thank you.'

She was still putting distance between them, clearly, and his patience for it was running thin. In his arms, she'd been unguarded and passionate, her dark eyes glowing with heat and desire, awe and wonder.

But now… Her lashes fell, veiling her gaze, and she turned her head away from him, shutting him out. A salty sea breeze lifted her hair from her shoulders, blowing it around her face, and again he experienced a fierce urge to touch her, push that recalcitrant lock of hers back behind her ears. Then maybe demand that she look at him, tell him why she was shutting him out.

He'd never wanted to know what someone else was thinking before, never been almost desperate to know. Yet he found himself staring at her, wishing he could see what was going on inside her lovely head.

Then the wind blew a lock of her hair across the sleeve of his suit, the strands gleaming red against the dark wool, and his thoughts shifted and changed. Would their children have auburn hair and dark eyes like hers, or would they have grey eyes like his? Would they be lovely, like her, or—?

Emotionally dead like you?

He gritted his teeth and forced the thought away. He had no idea where it had come from. He wasn't emotionally dead; he just preferred his emotions to be tightly controlled, which wasn't the same thing.

Their children would never be emotionally dead anyway, not with passionate Nell for a mother.

She could leave them, though, the way your mother left you.

Aristophanes slid his hand beneath her elbow and gripped it, mentally crushing the irrational fears that kept winding through his brain.

The children would be fine and Nell would be an excellent mother. She worked with small children after all.

Together, they walked up the white shell path that led from the helipad to the villa, threading through the olive groves that surrounded the house, along with lemon trees and lavender and other shrubs that grew well in the dry, rocky soil.

The villa itself was white plaster and on several levels, with windows that looked out over the sea, and large vine-covered terraces accessible by wide curving stone stairs. There was a pool area beside one wing of the house, with an infinity pool and sun loungers scattered about. He'd decided to put her in the bedroom next to it so she could access it more easily. A pool would be cooling and provide some nice gentle exercise.

She stayed silent as he showed her into the villa, introducing her to his housekeeper and some of the other staff, then, while the staff dealt with the luggage, he took her on a tour of the property, periodically checking on the time to make sure it would take no longer than twenty minutes as per the doctor's orders.

First, the wide salon, with doors that opened all the way out onto the terrace. Then down some stairs to the guest wing, with the big bedroom next to the pool and a wooden bed piled high with pillows. A big bathroom with a wide white porcelain bath she could lie in, and a large shower to stand beneath if she so chose.

As they came out of the bathroom, Nell went past him and over to the windows near the bed, looking out over the deep blue green of the sea. She hadn't spoken a word since they'd got out of the helicopter.

Impatience ran through him. Did she like it here? Was the bedroom to her taste or would she prefer another? He wanted to know what she thought of the island, which was strange, because why did he care about her opinion? He'd never cared about the opinions of others before. Then again, maybe it wasn't so strange. As she'd told him, her well-being was important to the lives of their children, and if he was going to look after her, then that was his responsibility too.

Not just her physical well-being. Her emotional well-being too.

Another thing he'd never been concerned about before—a person's emotional well-being. And why would he? When no one had ever considered his? Yet he was considering it now. On the plane on the way over, he'd been doing a lot of reading, research papers on pregnancy mainly, and he'd discovered that the emotions of the mother did affect her foetus, and if she was, say, depressed, then the baby had worse outcomes.

He didn't want that for her or for their children.

'Will this be adequate?' he asked at last, breaking the thick silence.

She didn't turn from the window. 'Yes.' The word sounded colourless. 'It's fine.'

He frowned, taking in the elegant curve of her obdurate back, a sudden frustration rising in him. Was this all he was going to get from her? Just this…silence?

Are you surprised? It's not as if you've given her anything but dismissal.

A memory gripped him then, of the hurt in her eyes as she'd said what was the point of a visit without sex, and he'd implied that the health of their children was more important. Which it was, but still… They were strangers, and yet…they weren't. He'd touched every inch of her body, he knew the feel of her, the taste of her. He knew what she looked like when she came, the noises she made when he gave her pleasure. He knew her kiss, the touch of her hand, the way her nails dug into his back…

He didn't know her mind, though, and perhaps he should. Especially when she was their children's mother and they'd be raising those children together.

'Do you need food?' he asked, at a loss for what else to say, but wanting to say something to break the ice. Small talk, though, had never been his friend.

'No, thank you.' She was scrupulously polite and still didn't turn.

'Perhaps you would like to rest?' He took a couple of steps towards her. 'The bed is very comfortable.'

'I'm sure it is.'

His jaw felt tight and he didn't know what else to say. Words were always a barrier. They got in the way, imperfect and inexact, a primitive vehicle when it came to expressing ideas and concepts. Apart from sex, though, he didn't know what other tools he could use to express himself. Mind to mind would be so much easier, and it was a constant aggravation to him that no one had yet invented telepathy.

If sex hadn't been forbidden, he would simply have crossed the space between them, taken her into his arms, kissed her thoroughly, then given her all the pleasure he was capable of to make her feel better.

But he couldn't.

So he stood there uselessly, impatient and annoyed with himself, until she finally turned around. 'I'm sorry?' she said coolly. 'Don't you have other places to be?'

'I want to know if you need anything,' he said, irritated by how inarticulate he was being, and how it almost made him feel stupid. Which he wasn't in any regard.

'I don't.' Her gaze was very level, telling him nothing.

'Do you like the villa?' he demanded, getting even more irritated with himself.

'Yes, it's fine. I said that already.'

'But do you—?'

'It's fine, Mr Katsaros,' she repeated, her voice cold as a splinter of ice.

'Aristophanes,' he growled, realising all of a sudden that she'd never said his name out loud, not once. 'You can't call me Mr Katsaros. Not when we will be having children together.'

At last, to his enormous satisfaction, tiny sparks of temper glittered in her eyes. The satisfaction was akin to when he gave her an orgasm, but sharper somehow. He liked that he could disturb her, that he could affect her in some way.

'I'm not calling you Aristophanes,' she said with some irritation. 'It's ridiculous and far too long.'

He glared at her. 'How dare you—?'

'I'll call you Dylan, after one of the naughtiest boys in my class.'

'You will *not* be calling me Dylan,' he forced out through gritted teeth.

Nell tilted her head and abruptly he realised that it wasn't only temper in her eyes, but something else, almost like…amusement. 'Bear, then,' she said. 'He's the second naughtiest and you're certainly bad-tempered enough to be a bear.'

'Bear?' he repeated blankly. 'You have a boy in your class called Bear?'

'Yes,' she said. 'So, thank you, Bear. That will be all.'

Nell watched Aristophanes' dark brows plunge into yet another one of his sexy scowls and felt extremely pleased with herself. It was a strange thing to discover that she could render this powerful, apparently humourless, billionaire genius speechless. Not to mention annoyed. And he was definitely both now, his mouth tight, his grey gaze thunderous.

It was satisfying. That she could get under his skin so easily made her feel better about being here, on this Greek island that she hadn't asked to be brought to and would effectively be imprisoned on for the next five months.

She'd thought that nothing she said would move him,

since it appeared he didn't care about her at all, except that she was the mother of his children.

And she'd thought that the case all the way over from New York, on the interminable flight to Athens, where he'd spent the majority of time either staring fiercely at his laptop or reading one of the hard science magazines he'd brought with him.

Then he'd showed her into the bedroom of this admittedly very pretty villa, on this admittedly very beautiful Greek island, and she'd thought he'd show her to the bedroom then leave immediately, yet he hadn't. He'd asked inane questions instead, wanting her opinion on the villa, wanting to know if she needed anything to eat, or if she needed rest. And even when she'd said no, he'd continued to stand there, looking incredibly annoyed yet resolutely not leaving.

She had to admit it was slightly amusing that such a self-proclaimed genius could be so inarticulate, and it made the bleak feeling in her heart feel a little less bleak. He was just a man, after all. As flawed as any other.

'You can't call me Bear,' he growled.

'Why not? You do growl a lot.'

He looked typically thunderous. 'I do not.'

She expected him to simply turn around and leave then, yet he didn't. He only stood there, glaring at her accusingly. And she had the odd impression that he didn't actually want to go. He was lingering here because he wanted to talk to her.

Nell studied him a moment. Was that what he wanted? And he just didn't know how? Seemed strange for a man who'd repeatedly told her that he liked having conversations with women. Then again, those women were also very smart, weren't they? And perhaps their conversations were smart also? Perhaps he didn't have normal, casual conversations. Perhaps he didn't know how.

'Didn't you ever have a nickname when you were a little boy?' she asked, after a moment. 'Or did everyone go around calling you Aristophanes?'

'No one called me anything as a little boy.'

'No one? Not even your parents?'

'I was raised in foster care,' he said. 'I was never with a family long enough to be called anything but "boy".'

Shock prickled over her skin. She hadn't expected him to reveal anything personal about himself, still less something so sad. Or so relatable. Because if he'd been in foster care, that meant something had happened to his parents and she knew all about that.

'Oh, I'm sorry,' she said impulsively. 'I lost my parents, too. I didn't go into foster care though. I was raised by my aunt and uncle.'

His gaze sharpened. 'You were lucky.'

Nell shook her head. 'No, I wasn't. I already had four cousins and my aunt and uncle didn't want another kid. I don't know why they took me in. My uncle only said it was because he owed my dad, but he made it clear it wasn't something *he* wanted. My aunt wasn't happy either. They just kind of ignored me.'

There was a steely glint in Aristophanes' eyes. 'Ignored you? How the hell did they ignore you?'

She shrugged. 'They just did. All my cousins were six feet tall and blonde. Sporty. Academically gifted. And I was…none of the above.'

'So, what happened?'

'What do you mean what happened?'

'I mean, how did it affect you? What did you do?'

It seemed a genuine question and, since he still hadn't left, and the sharp intensity of his gaze hadn't moved from hers, she had to assume it was.

'I…decided to carve out my own identity and my own existence, I guess,' she replied. 'I wanted to be a doctor, or maybe a nurse, but I wasn't academically gifted. I wanted to care for people, especially kids, because of my own experience, I suppose. So, I moved from Perth to Melbourne, and eventually decided on preschool care. I got a few certificates, found myself a job…and the rest, as they say, is history.'

He was still staring at her as if he'd never heard of anything more mystifying in his entire life yet was determined to understand. It made that horrible, bleak feeling inside her start to fade a little. 'Why?' he demanded. 'Why did you think you weren't academically gifted? Why did you want to care for children?'

'Are we having a proper conversation now?' The words slipped from her without her thinking, the urge she had to tease him irresistible. 'Is that what's happening?'

His eyes narrowed. 'Why is that amusing? I want to know.'

'As an aside, do you ever find anything funny?'

'I haven't found anything in life to be particularly amusing, no.'

Her throat tightened abruptly. He looked quite serious. 'Well, that's a tragedy.'

Something glittered in his eyes for a moment, then it was gone. 'Tell me why,' he insisted.

She sighed. 'I thought I wasn't academically gifted because I wasn't as intelligent as my cousins. They all got straight As while I was a steady C—B plus if I was lucky—student. I never excelled in anything, and I certainly didn't have the marks I needed to be a doctor or a nurse.'

He shoved his hands in his pockets, his shoulders still tense and stiff. 'Perhaps the school you went to wasn't a good one. Perhaps the style of teaching didn't suit you.'

This time it was her turn to look at him in puzzlement. 'Or maybe I'm just not smart enough. Why is that important?'

The muscle in his jaw flicked again. 'You're the mother of my children and intelligence is important to me. Perhaps you are smarter than you think you are.'

'Or maybe I'm as dumb as a post.' The words were tinged with a bitterness she'd thought she'd long since put behind her, and she wished she hadn't said them.

He stared at her a second, then abruptly came across the room to her, still scowling ferociously as if she'd done something to offend him. 'You are not,' he said with some insistence. 'I always wondered why I wanted you so badly. The women I take as lovers are all, without exception, gifted with high intelligence. But you're not a professor or a scientist. You teach small children. But you must be very gifted in some way in order to—'

'Or maybe you want me to be smart because you can't think of any other reason to want me?' she interrupted, her temper rising. 'Children are important. They're the society we'll have one day, so why are you looking down on my profession? I'm making sure that future society will be full of people who are empathetic and understanding. Who listen. Who build good relationships with others. It's not rocket science, but it's just as important, if not more so.'

He was silent a moment longer, then the hard lines of his face eased, as if she'd proved something to him. 'There,' he said softly. 'You see? You don't think you're as dumb as a post at all.'

Her cheeks heated and she had to glance away to hide the strange fluttering feeling in her stomach that definitely didn't have anything to do with her pregnancy. 'You didn't seem to think being a preschool teacher was so great compared to being a professor or scientist. Or a mathematical genius.'

'I didn't,' he said. 'But maybe I need to change my mind.'

'Why?' She glanced at him. 'Because of me?'

'Yes.'

'But how can you say that when you don't know me?'

'Perhaps I should know you.' He kept on staring at her as if she were a puzzle he desperately wanted to solve. 'You're the mother of my children. Don't you think you're worth knowing?'

You're not, not to a man like him. Mediocre, remember? That's what you'll always be.

The thought drifted through her brain, thorny and sharp. It wasn't anything her aunt and uncle had ever told her outright, but their silence when it came to her had left a void. A void that her own thoughts had filled for her. Because there had to be a reason that they'd never been interested in her. Never asking her if she'd done her homework, never wanting to know which part she'd got in the school play. Never remembering her birthday and never asking to see her school reports. Never really asking her about herself at all.

She'd been forgotten. She'd always thought that maybe it was because she wasn't that interesting. Nothing special about her, nothing that would catch anyone's attention. She'd tried not to listen to those thoughts, tried to prove to herself that she was better than what her aunt and uncle thought, that she was intelligent and strong and special. But she'd never really believed it.

Not until Aristophanes had come to her the night she'd hit her head, because he hadn't been able to stay away. Then he'd given her the most perfect night she'd ever had, and for that brief time she'd believed. She'd believed she was as special as he made her feel.

She looked up into his cool silver eyes. 'You tell me. Do you want to know me purely for the sake of the babies? Or for yourself?' She wasn't sure she wanted to know the answer to that question, but it had to be asked. For her own peace of mind if nothing else.

'What difference would that make?'

'It wouldn't in the greater scheme of things. But it would make a difference to me.'

'You don't think you're worth it,' he said slowly, staring at her intently, as if she were a difficult text he was translating. And it was not a question.

The heat in her cheeks intensified and a desperate vulnerability crawled through her, making her turn her head to look out of the window so she didn't have to look into his eyes. She didn't like that he'd managed to see that about her. Then again, should she really have been so surprised? He was a genius, while she...

His thumb and forefinger gripped her chin, forcing

her gaze back to his. 'Look at me,' he ordered softly. 'Is that what this is about?'

Unable to pull away, Nell could do nothing but stare back. 'I mean, would you think you were worth knowing? If no one in your entire life had ever shown any interest in you?' She threw the words at him almost defiantly.

He scowled again, but this time she had the odd sense that it wasn't her he was angry with. '*I* am showing an interest,' he said flatly. 'And if I am showing an interest then, yes, you are definitely worth knowing.'

A quiver ran through her, almost a tremble. 'But only because I'm the mother of your children. Not for any other reason, right?'

'Wrong.' His grip on her chin tightened. 'I want to know for myself. You are a puzzle, Nell. And I like puzzles. I like puzzles very much.' His thumb stroked her chin and before she could move, he'd bent his head and his mouth brushed over hers.

A shock of desire went through her and she couldn't stop herself from kissing him back, because she was hungry for this. For him.

He allowed the kiss for a second, then pulled away. 'No,' he murmured, his breathing fast. 'No, we can't do this.' He released her and stepped back. 'Rest now. I will have the housekeeper unpack your things. But tonight...' His gaze intensified. 'You will tell me everything about yourself over dinner, understand?'

CHAPTER EIGHT

ARISTOPHANES PACED OVER to the edge of the stone terrace and spent a moment gazing out over the olive groves
and the darkening sea beyond Ithasos' cliffs. The sun
was going down, washing the sky in oranges and pinks
and reds, an evening breeze carrying the scents of the
sea and sun-warmed rock, and pine.

He glanced back at the table that stood underneath the
vine-covered pergola. He'd had his housekeeper prepare
and arrange the table just so, setting the scene for dinner with Nell, the island scenery and sunset a perfect
backdrop.

It was all as it should be and he was pleased.

After the conversation they'd had in her bedroom on
their arrival, he'd been thinking. In fact, he'd spent the
whole afternoon thinking. About her and what she'd said.
About her childhood and how she clearly didn't view herself as being smart or intelligent or any of the things she
thought she should be. Then teasing him with that silly
nickname—'Bear', of all things—and then disagreeing
with him about the importance of her job. Telling him
why it was important, her dark eyes glowing with conviction...

He'd felt angry at her aunt and uncle for making her

think things about herself that weren't true, and then he'd been angry at himself for doing the same thing, because it was clear he had. He'd been less than complimentary about her job, but that was because he didn't know anything about it, nor had he thought about it until she'd told him what it meant.

He liked intelligence in a woman, but he was beginning to see now that it was a very specific sort of intelligence. An academic intelligence, logical and cool. Nell wasn't like that at all, but when she looked at him sometimes, he felt as if she knew things he didn't. Mysterious things he couldn't even conceive of, that made him uncomfortable and yet fascinated him at the same time.

She *was* smart, but not in the way he'd always thought about it.

That she seemed to doubt that she was worth knowing, though, had appalled him. He didn't know why it mattered, or why he felt so strongly about it, but he did. Perhaps because it was that she was the mother of his children and he didn't want her upset…

No. That wasn't the reason and he had to be honest with himself. It mattered to him because he didn't want her to think that way about herself. Because it hurt her, and he didn't like her being hurt. It also wasn't true.

He was interested in her and he was a genius, so of course she was worth knowing.

The way her mind worked intrigued him, and also she'd been brought up by people who didn't value her, yet she'd defied them. She'd left her home, gone across the country to a new city, and found a fulfilling life despite them. That spoke of a bravery and determination, and a strength of character he found admirable.

He wanted to know more, much more. Even though being near her and not being able to do more than kiss her was a constant test of his control. Really, he should be absenting himself, taking the helicopter back to Athens for the night, not staying here, so close to temptation.

But he wasn't going to. He wanted to do something nice for her, do something to make her happy since her well-being was his responsibility now, and he didn't think she'd appreciate being abandoned so soon after arriving here.

So he'd organised everything like one of his dates, with dinner and conversation, and then they'd go to bed separately. Not exactly what he wanted, but that was the way it would have to be for the moment.

It was an interesting situation and one he'd never been in before.

Just then, Nell appeared in the doorway of the living area, stepping out through the French doors and onto the stone terrace. Her hair was curling in thick waves over her shoulders, and for once she wasn't wearing a clinging dress, but a loose, cool-looking white linen caftan. It hid her body, including her little bump, but the wide neckline almost hung off one shoulder, revealing an expanse of creamy skin that made his fingers itch to touch it.

Ignoring the urge, he strode over to the beautifully set table and pulled out a chair for her. 'Please,' he invited. 'Sit.'

She hesitated, then came over to the chair and sat down, the sweet scent of her hair and body surrounding him for a moment, making his mouth water. Knowing that he couldn't take her to bed later seemed to make the desire sharper, deeper, and he had to fight to force it away.

Resolutely steeling himself, he pushed her chair back in and moved around the table to his own opposite hers, before sitting. The candles he'd ordered leapt and twisted in their glass holders, radiating a shifting golden glow. She looked beautiful in that glow, her skin gilded, her hair gleaming with red fire.

'This is lovely,' she said, glancing around at the candles, the light glittering off the crystal glasses, silver cutlery, and the elegant glass vase with sprigs of jasmine in it. 'Did you do all this?'

'My housekeeper did, but I decided to make an event of it, yes.' He stared at her, unable to take his eyes off her. 'This is just the setting though. The true beauty here is you.' It felt natural to compliment her, even though he'd never been one for compliments, and he got his reward when she blushed, her lashes falling, her mouth curving.

He knew sensual satisfaction. He experienced it whenever he made her gasp aloud. But right here, right now, he knew another kind of satisfaction that wasn't sexual. It was a pressure in his chest and the way his mouth wanted to curve as if her smile and the obvious pleasure she'd taken from his compliment made him want to smile too.

Emotional satisfaction. He couldn't recall ever feeling anything like it. Perhaps once when that little cat he'd tried to adopt had first started lapping at the milk he'd brought her. And perhaps again the first time she'd curled up in his lap, purring as he'd stroked her. Satisfied that his presence had made a difference to another living creature's life. That he'd given them some kind of emotional pleasure.

It was the most curious feeling. Addictive, even.

Nell's lashes lifted, her dark eyes flickering with gold

from the candlelight. 'I've decided something, Bear. I've decided that if you want to know everything about me, I want to know everything about you, too.'

That seemed logical and yet…he was conscious of a vague reluctance. His past wasn't a secret, and he wasn't ashamed of it, so he shouldn't feel…uneasy at the prospect of telling her. Then again, perhaps that had more to do with her clear-eyed gaze and that way she looked at him, as if she could read his mind.

He didn't like it, not at all. It unsettled him, made him feel as if he were an open book that she could read with impunity.

But he was *not* an open book. He kept his thoughts hidden, his emotions under control. They had no place in the mathematical world, the world of algorithms and money, and he liked it that way. He *wanted* it that way.

Yet he couldn't deny that, if she gave him pieces of herself, he would have to reciprocate. Perhaps he wouldn't have thought that three months ago, but he did now. She wasn't one of his dates, after all, but the mother of his children, and maybe it would even be a good thing if she knew his background. That would help her understand the things he *didn't* want for them. He certainly didn't want, for example, the kind of childhood Nell had grown up in for them. Not abusive, but traumatising in its own way.

'Very well,' he said, reaching across the table for the jug of home-made lemonade that sat next to the bottle of his favourite red wine. 'What would you like to know?' He poured the lemonade into a heavy cut-glass tumbler and pushed it over to her, before pouring himself some wine.

'You mentioned being brought up in the foster system.' She reached for the tumbler, took a careful sip, then looked at him in sudden delight. 'Oh, this is very good!'

Again, satisfaction tugged at him, that she was pleased with what he'd given her. It made his chest burn. He tried to ignore the feeling, but his mouth twitched all the same. 'Lemonade,' he said. 'My housekeeper makes it from the lemons in our grove.' He nodded to a small bowl in the middle of the table next to some fresh bread. 'That is olive oil from our olive groves.'

'Looks amazing.' She reached for the bread, tore a piece off it, then dunked an edge into the olive oil before taking a bite. 'Mmm… And tastes amazing too.'

'My housekeeper is an amazing woman.'

'She is.' Nell leaned forward, elbows on the table as she tore off another chunk of bread. 'Okay, so tell me about you, Bear.'

Bear yet again. She seemed wedded to it, which was ridiculous. Then again, a part of him liked it. Cesare called him Ari, but that was as close to a nickname as he'd ever had. He'd never been a man to invite anything more intimate than that.

Bear, though, he could live with.

'I was born in Athens,' he said. 'I never knew my father. He and my mother split up before I arrived. I don't remember much from my time with her, but we had a large house in the hills. It had a garden. My mother was kind and loving—I never knew a moment's unhappiness. Then one morning she took me to church and left me there.'

Nell, in the process of dunking more bread in the oil, went still. 'What do you mean left you there?'

'At the end of the service, she told me to sit still in the

pew and she'd be back soon, so I did. Except she didn't come back.'

Nell's eyes widened. 'What? You mean, not ever?'

'Not ever,' he confirmed, picking up his wine glass and leaning back in his chair. 'I was eight. Eventually the priest came over and asked me my name, and why I was sitting there. To cut a long story short, they eventually discovered that my mother had gone. The house was empty, there was no sign of her. I had no surviving grandparents, no other family, so I was made a ward of the state.'

A crease formed between her brows, her eyes dark and soft with what he very much hoped was *not* pity. 'Oh, that's awful,' she murmured. 'How could she have left you?'

A question he'd asked himself many times. A question he would never know the answer to.

Aristophanes lifted a shoulder. 'The why isn't relevant, only that she did. So I went into the foster system and my experience was…imperfect, to say the least. I never stayed long with a particular family. I was always being shifted around. Eventually, I decided I'd had enough. I'd taken part-time jobs here and there while I was at school, and I'd managed to save quite a bit of money. I made a few astute investments and soon found I had a knack. I'd always loved mathematics as well, and the two seemed to go together for me. That was the start of my company.'

She stared at him as if fascinated, making the pressure in his chest take on a kind of warmth and this time he liked the way she looked at him. He liked it a lot.

'You must have been very determined to leave all of that behind,' she said.

'Oh, I was. I wanted to leave my childhood behind, make my mark. I also liked numbers and the idea that you could make money with numbers. Money, too, is an interesting idea. You have physical money, obviously, but much of it exists in the ether. You have some, you lose some, you get more… It doesn't really matter, because it wasn't real to start with.'

'I know plenty of people who would disagree with you.'

'Of course. I'm talking about the idea of money, you understand. That's not really real or tangible, but the effects of it are. I like making it, I like controlling it, and I like doing things with it. It's a game.'

She leaned her chin in her hand. 'But it's not really about the money, is it?'

The question was unexpected and it made him think. 'No,' he said. 'It's not.'

Nell stared at him through the flickering candlelight. 'What is it about, then?'

'Challenging my mind, my intellect.'

'Why is that so important to you?' she asked. 'Genuine question.'

'Because there I have the most control,' he said slowly. 'I am the master of it. The numbers do what I say and on the rare occasions they don't, I make them.'

'Control is important to you?'

He shifted uncomfortably, finding the conversation vaguely unsettling. 'Yes.'

'I suppose it would be, considering how little control you had over your early life.'

'The past is irrelevant,' he said, a touch irritated and not bothering to hide it. 'It doesn't bother me. I didn't have a family, it's true, but I didn't need one. I only needed what I found in my own head to survive, and I did.'

The crease between her brows deepened and he didn't like the expression on her face, the pity in it. 'It sounds very lonely,' she murmured.

He shrugged. 'As I said, I survived. Your childhood doesn't sound any better, either, yet you survived too.'

'I did.' She took another sip of her lemonade. 'But when I said it must have been lonely, what I meant was I can relate to that. Because mine was. Not that no one spoke to me or anything, it was more having no one notice that you were maybe a bit quiet today. Or that you were pale. Or that you looked happy. The feeling that you could just…not exist and no one would ever notice you were gone.'

A sharp and painful feeling threaded through him, as if she'd touched on an old and still festering wound.

You felt that too.

He had. Once. He didn't feel it now, though, because he couldn't not exist without someone knowing, because everyone knew who he was. He'd made sure everyone knew. So any pain he felt now was merely an echo, phantom-limb pain from a part of himself he'd cut out years ago. As was the anger that used to overcome him every now and then, formless and hot, with seemingly no cause.

He hadn't felt that for at least a decade, not since he'd poured everything of himself into his business, using his ambition as the engine that drove his life. He'd needed a purpose and his life of numbers and money was it. That was why he had his schedule, so every second of his life was dedicated to using his intellect in the most efficient way and not getting sidetracked by…anything else.

'People would notice,' he said tersely. 'They'd certainly notice if you were gone.'

Her gaze was very dark and she looked at him steadily, and for a second there was pain in her gaze. 'Who would?'

At first he thought it might be another tease, but no, not with the way she was looking at him now, not with that pain. She really wanted to know.

'*I* would,' he said. 'I would notice you were gone and the world would be a poorer place for it.'

He meant it. She could see the force of his conviction in his steel-grey eyes, and a small hot glow started up in the centre of her chest.

At first, she'd wished the words back, because it had sounded too needy, too desperate. Yet he hadn't treated it that way at all.

She could feel the tension between them again, the force of their chemistry and the need in his eyes that he didn't hide from her. But they couldn't act on it, not with the health of their children at stake. 'You shouldn't say such things to me,' she said quietly.

'Why not?' His gaze didn't flicker. 'It's true.'

'Is it? You can't sleep with me, remember?'

'You think I'd only say that to sleep with you?'

She felt too vulnerable staring at him the way she was doing, but she was the one who'd started this conversation. The one who'd told him about her aunt and uncle, revealing much more than she'd meant to. She couldn't falter now. 'I don't know—would you?'

A spark of temper glittered in his eyes. 'I do not need to give a woman empty compliments to get her to sleep with me. I never give empty compliments, full stop.'

Of course, he wouldn't. He wasn't that kind of man. Every word he spoke was with intention and purpose, because he meant it. Which then must mean...

He was telling the truth about you.

She swallowed, her mouth dry. 'You really do think those things? That the world would be a poorer place without me?' Sometimes, in her darker moments, she'd wondered if anyone would care if she simply ceased to exist. Sometimes, she couldn't think of one person who'd care.

Aristophanes' gaze was almost ferocious. 'Of course it would. Your beauty is incomparable, and I have never wanted anyone the way I want you.'

'But those are just physical—'

'I haven't finished,' he interrupted sharply. 'You're also strong and determined, and very stubborn. Which is annoying, but you stand up for what you believe in and you've never once let me intimidate you, which is a feat, considering I am much more powerful than you are.' He paused a moment. 'I wondered if perhaps you would be like my mother, but you aren't. You would never abandon your child to its fate, which means you will be an excellent mother to our children. Also...' His gaze intensified. 'You are very perceptive, and I think you have far more intelligence than you give yourself credit for.'

Something quivered in her, something deep inside. It was ridiculous. She didn't need a man's praise to make her feel good about herself, yet it was *his* praise that made her feel as though she really was all those things he'd said. Not just any man, but him in particular.

You will be an excellent mother...

She'd wondered on and off, after she'd found out she

was pregnant, whether she, who'd had so little love in her life, could even be a good mother. Whether she'd know how to show them how much they mattered, how important they were, and how much she loved them. She'd tried not to think about it though, because if she did, the doubt would eat her alive. Now she felt it like a fault line running through an essential part of her.

'You really think I would?' she couldn't help asking, hating how needy she sounded and yet not being able to stay silent. 'Make a good mother, I mean?'

'I think,' he murmured, 'that a woman with as much to give as you have will make the most wonderful mother any child could ask for.'

Nell's cheeks burned and she had to look away at last, unable to hold his gaze. She didn't want to negate his praise by dismissing it or minimising it, but she wasn't used to compliments, especially about her most deeply held doubts, and couldn't think of a word to say.

In the end all she managed was, 'Thank you. That actually…means a lot to me.'

A weighted silence fell.

She hadn't realised until arriving here that the bleak feeling in her heart dogging her since leaving New York had been loneliness and doubt. And now he'd lightened that load somehow. Even though he'd insisted on her coming here, he'd taken time out of his schedule to show her around and then have dinner with her and while it might not seem like much, from what he'd told her about his schedule and about himself, she had the feeling that this was a big deal for him.

Perhaps he was lonely too. His childhood had certainly sounded as bleak as hers, probably bleaker since at least she'd had some sense of continuity with her cousins and aunt and uncle. But he'd had no one. No one at all.

Finally Nell lifted her lashes and looked at him again.

He'd leaned forward, elbows on the table, his wine in front of him, watching her. His grey gaze seemed unreadable and yet she could see the silver glitter of hunger there. Hunger for her, she knew, but that wasn't news. She knew all about his physical hunger. However, now she suspected that there might be something more underneath that. Not sexual hunger, but a hunger for something deeper and more profound.

He was a man who prized his intelligence, his mind. A cerebral man, yet one who also enjoyed his physical hungers. But his emotional hungers... Did he know about those? Did he ever acknowledge them or understand them?

You know he doesn't.

No, she was beginning to see that. And maybe that was where her power lay. She could see things in him that he couldn't see himself. She knew things about him that he didn't know.

He's lonely. Profoundly lonely.

The thought ripped a hole in her heart.

'If you don't have family, who do you have, then?' she asked softly. 'Friends? Colleagues?'

He lifted one powerful shoulder. 'I have one friend in Italy whom I've known for years, though I have seen less of him lately. He has a wife and a child now. As for colleagues, no. I have found it easier to work alone.'

'So you have no one?'

He frowned. 'In what way?'

'Someone to talk to. Someone to spend time with.'

'I have lovers whom I talk to. We have conversation over dinner, which is why I prefer an intelligent woman.'

Her heart squeezed tight. Not only was it clear he didn't have anyone, he didn't even know what she meant by that.

'I mean someone who knows you,' she said. 'Someone who understands you. Someone you trust. Someone you care for. Someone you can be intimate with.'

His features hardened and his gaze shuttered. 'No,' he said tersely. 'I do not. Nor do I need anyone like that.'

'Everyone needs someone like that.'

He abruptly lifted his wine and took a long swallow before putting the glass back down with a thump. 'I don't.'

'You had no one? Not one person?'

'No,' he said flatly. 'After my mother left and I went into foster care, people weren't interested in making connections with me. Which was fine. I was happier in my own head.'

She didn't think it was fine, though. There was an insistence in his voice that sounded as if he was trying to convince himself as well as her. 'What about friends at school?' she persisted.

'School was boring, the other children dull. They didn't like me anyway, and I didn't like them.'

An uncompromising man. Then again, she already knew that too.

She studied him, the hard lines of his beautiful face, the steely glitter of his eyes.

For a time she'd tried to turn herself into a child she'd thought her aunt and uncle would notice, such as being like her cousins. She'd dyed her hair blonde, taken up hockey. But it hadn't worked, and it wasn't until after she'd left Perth that she'd realised that she needn't have bothered. Being like her cousins wouldn't have helped, because she was still *her*. She was still the girl that had been dumped on them and nothing would ever change that.

But Aristophanes hadn't bothered to change himself to suit anyone. He'd remained steadfastly who he was, resisting any effort to make himself more palatable to anyone.

It had made him lonely, yes, but he was splendid in his isolation.

She admired him for it.

'That must have been hard,' she said.

'It was not,' he said. 'As I said, I survived.'

'Survival isn't living, Bear.'

He scowled. 'What are you trying to say?'

'Nothing,' she said without heat. 'I'm only sad for you that you had such a rough childhood.'

'I wasn't beaten.' His voice was hard. 'I wasn't abused in any way. I had a roof over my head and I was fed. What more could have been done for me?'

'You could have been loved,' she said, not even knowing where the words had come from.

He stared at her a moment, the look in his eyes difficult to read. 'Love,' he echoed eventually, the word tinged with bitterness. 'Love left me sitting alone in a church at eight years old after my mother abandoned me. I didn't need love. I was better off without it.'

Her heart squeezed even tighter. It hurt to think about him as a lonely little boy. A boy who'd decided that love was just another word for abandonment, and who could blame him? He had reason. No one had ever given him the love he'd deserved, and he had deserved it. All children did. At least her memories of love had been good ones, happy ones. Even if she'd lost it and never found it again.

'I don't think you were,' she said gently. 'And your children definitely won't be.'

A muscle flicked at the side of his strong jaw. 'Are you saying that I won't love them?'

'No. I only mean that all children need love.'

'And so I will,' he said flatly. 'Don't worry about them.'

'I'm not worried about them. I'm worried about you.'

'Don't worry about me.' He stared at her across the table. 'This topic of conversation is uninteresting, so let's leave it. What are your plans for the future? Have you thought about it?'

She didn't want to drop the subject, but it was clear she wasn't going to get anything further from him, so she let it go.

'The future? Uh…no. No, I haven't.' She really hadn't. She'd been too busy thinking about how she was going to get through the next five months trapped on this island, let alone what would happen when the babies were born.

'Well, I have,' Aristophanes said, picking up his wine again and taking another swallow. 'I think that we should get married.'

A pulse of shock went through her. 'What?'

'It's a logical step. The twins will need both parents and we're agreed on that, so why not make it official? Marrying me will give you some security and legal protection should anything happen to me, and it will give our children a family.'

He said the words with such dispassion, as if he was talking about a business arrangement. Which was perhaps what marriage meant to him. Certainly, from what he'd said about love, he wasn't asking her because he was in love with her.

This was what you wanted, though. You wanted a family.

She always had. But she'd thought it would involve finding a man she loved and who loved her, not after an accidental night of passion, and certainly not with a man who found the idea of love abhorrent.

He's not wrong, though. It will give you some security. And after the children are born, you will also have physical passion...

She took a breath. 'What about you? What will you get out of it?'

The flickering candlelight reflected the silver flames in his eyes. 'I will get a wife I very much want to spend time in bed with. Also, I will no longer need to schedule lovers to take care of my sexual needs so that will free up time to spend with the children.'

So. Sex and his damn schedule were all he cared about. She'd give him a couple of points for wanting to spend time with the children, but she had to deduct several million for being entirely blind to how it would affect her.

And how exactly will it affect you? You want what he wants, and this will be good for the twins. This is about them, not you. What more is there?

'I... I have to think about this,' she said uncertainly, her mind spinning.

'What is there to think about? You get my name, my money, and the children will be cared for. We will be a family.'

A family...

The words echoed through her. Yes, she wanted that.

She wanted a family like the one she'd lost when her parents died. A family held together by love.

A sharp, painful feeling gathered in her gut.

She'd spent her whole childhood mourning, not only the loss of her parents, but the loss of the love they'd had for her, leaving a void inside her that had never been filled by her aunt and uncle.

He won't fill it either, not now you know what he feels about love.

'It's just…' She paused, her throat tightening. 'It's not only children who need love.' She steeled herself and looked at him. 'I do too.'

Across the table, Aristophanes' beautiful face remained hard. 'You do?' he demanded.

'My mum and dad loved me,' she said, her certainty gathering more and more weight with each second that passed. 'I knew that before they died. And the day they died, I lost that love. I spent my entire childhood mourning that loss, and swore to myself I'd find it again. Find myself someone who loved me the way I loved them. So… Yes. That's what I want in my future, Bear. I want a family. I want to love someone and I want them to love me, too.'

Steel glinted in his eyes. 'And you will have that. The children will love you.'

'The purpose of children isn't so they can love you. The purpose of children is to have their own lives.'

He scowled, which she was starting to think meant he didn't understand what she was talking about. 'Does it matter what source the love comes from?'

'Of course it does.' She felt tired all of a sudden, her appetite gone, her patience with him running thin. 'But

I guess if you don't know what I'm talking about, then this is a pointless conversation.'

'Then explain it to me,' he insisted.

But Nell's energy had run out, and she didn't know why she was arguing with him anyway. After all, it couldn't be that she wanted love from him, it just couldn't. He was as in touch with his emotion as a rock and equally articulate, and she didn't want anything from him.

'No,' she said, putting down her lemonade glass. 'You know what? I'm tired and I can't be bothered, especially when you don't even have the slightest idea what I'm talking about.'

He gave her a ferocious look. 'Nell. Sit down.'

She ignored him, shoving her chair back and getting to her feet. 'Goodnight, Mr Katsaros,' she said.

'Nell!' he called after her as she strode towards the doorway to the salon. 'Sit down and explain!'

But she didn't.

She walked through the doors and back into the villa.

CHAPTER NINE

ARISTOPHANES SAT IN his Athens office, scowling at the schedule on his computer screen. His schedule. He'd thought he'd set aside ample time to help Nell settle in—an afternoon and an evening was plenty. Or so he'd thought. But given their conversation the previous night, he was now starting to wonder.

He couldn't believe she'd walked away from him the night before. He'd only asked a question, wanting her to explain what she meant about love, and she'd just... walked away. It incensed him. Didn't she know how rare it was for him to need something explained? Didn't it matter to her? He'd have thought she'd jump at the chance, but no, she'd only looked tired and told him she 'couldn't be bothered'.

Unacceptable.

Perhaps she was genuinely tired? She's pregnant with twins, remember?

That was true. Possibly he needed to be more under-standing. Still, he was trying. He wanted to give her what she needed for her well-being and for that of the twins, yet this love business mystified him.

Most people were in love when they got married, he knew that, but some weren't. For some it was an arrangement for legal purposes, which was what he'd been thinking when he'd asked her. He'd wanted some certainty for the future, and naturally legal protection and security for her, and he'd thought she'd see the logic behind the offer. But no, apparently not.

If he took into account her childhood and how miserable it had been, then he could almost see why it was important for her to feel loved. The difficulty for him, though, was that he didn't love her. He wasn't sure if it was even possible for him to feel love. He was certain he'd love his children—apparently that happened automatically the moment they were born—so he wasn't worried about that. It was she who concerned him.

He wanted her to say yes to his marriage offer. In fact, the more he thought about it, the more imperative it was that she accept. It would make things much simpler in the long run if she was his wife. He'd never have to bother with finding and scheduling lovers again, not with Nell in his bed, because their chemistry was still hot and strong. And she'd have the advantage of having his name. She'd never have to work again if she didn't want to, and if she did? Well, he'd create a school for her and she could run the place. Why not? The possibilities were endless.

Except if she didn't accept his offer, there would be no possibilities at all.

The tension in his gut twisted and he bared his teeth in a soundless growl.

No, he couldn't allow it. He had to get her to accept somehow and if that meant asking for some advice, then he'd ask for some damn advice.

Pulling his phone from his pocket, Aristophanes called Cesare.

'Another phone call?' Cesare said the minute he answered. 'And the second within two days of the first. Astonishing. Have you turned over a new leaf, Ari?'

Aristophanes glared out of the window and across the cluttered streets of Athens' downtown area. 'I need advice,' he said flatly.

'Intriguing. About your impending twins?'

'No, I'm sure that won't be an issue.' Aristophanes ignored his friend's slightly strangled laugh since there didn't seem to be anything amusing about what he'd said. 'It's about Nell. I have offered to marry her but...she refused.'

'I see.' Cesare's voice was suspiciously expressionless. 'How could that be? You're rich as Midas, have your health and all your own teeth. Not to mention a full head of hair. What more could she want?'

'I don't know,' Aristophanes replied, irritated. He *hated* not knowing something. 'I offered because we needed some certainty for the future. I thought it would also give her legal protection, not to mention creating a family for us. It's the next logical step.'

'Logical, hmm? That sounds like you. And speaking of, is this something you actually want? A wife, I mean.'

'Of course I want a wife. I wouldn't have asked her to marry me otherwise.'

'It's just that you've never professed any interest in wives.'

'I'm going to be a father, Cesare,' he said curtly. 'And you married Lark when you discovered she'd had your child.'

'True,' his friend admitted. 'Though it did take some time to learn how to be a proper husband and father.'

'I'm sure it will not be a problem for me,' Aristophanes said, because he was sure it wouldn't be. Again, if Cesare could do it, so could he. 'I only need her to accept my proposal.'

'Did she give you a reason for refusing you?'

Aristophanes was conscious of the ache in his jaw, a tight feeling running across his shoulders. 'She wants to be loved,' he said tightly.

Cesare sighed. 'Of course, she does. So I suppose this means you're not actually in love with her.'

'No.'

'And I suppose she's not actually Satan incarnate and thus completely unlovable?'

'Of course not,' he growled, bristling with defensiveness. 'She's the most beautiful woman I've ever met. She's intelligent, honest, stubborn, passionate and—'

'Yes, yes,' Cesare muttered. 'I get the idea. Are you sure you're not in love with her?'

'I'm not' he said, irritation becoming annoyance since this wasn't about him. It was about her. 'It isn't me we're talking about, Cesare.'

'Fine, fine. So she wants to be loved.'

'Yes. I told her that our children will love her, but apparently it wasn't enough.' He picked up a pen and toyed restlessly with it. 'I wanted her to explain what kind of love she wanted, but she refused and told me she "couldn't be bothered".'

'Hmm,' Cesare said. 'Difficult.'

'Yes. And now I am at a loss. I want to change her mind, I want her to marry me, except I don't know how to do it.'

'I see. Well, you're the genius, Ari. Why don't you work it out?'

'I have,' he snapped. 'If we could sleep together, it would be fine. I would just seduce her into taking my ring. But sex is forbidden until the babies are born.'

Cesare was silent a long moment and Aristophanes fiddled incessantly with the pen, impatience and frustration winding tight inside him.

'You need to spend time with her,' Cesare said at length. 'Do some nice things for her. If you're not in love with her, the least you can do is make her feel as if you are.'

'Is that what you did for Lark?'

'Yes. I spent time with her and our little one, took them all around Italy. Showed her some of my favourite haunts. Wandered around eating gelato, that kind of thing.' His voice warmed. 'It was wonderful, and she loved it.'

There were obviously happy memories there for Cesare, so Aristophanes tried to think about similar things he could do with Nell and failed. He didn't have any favourite haunts. He didn't like gelato. His life consisted of flying from office to office, playing around with numbers and attending the odd gala when he absolutely had to. Which was not, he suspected, what Cesare was talking about.

'I don't know…what she would like,' he said at last.

'Then, my friend, may I suggest you find out? Perhaps even have a conversation or two?'

'I could just insist,' Aristophanes muttered, even more aggravated. 'Make her do what I said.'

'Tell me, my genius friend, have you *ever* tried making a woman do something she doesn't want to do?' Cesare asked. 'Not something I would recommend, not if you value any part of your manhood. And seriously, that would *not* be good for her well-being.'

Aristophanes threw the pen down on his desk in a snit. 'Do you, in fact, have any suggestions? Or are you just wasting my time?'

'You called me, remember?' Cesare said calmly. 'Good God, man. It's like you've never seduced a woman before.'

'I told you. We can't have sex—'

'I'm not talking about sex. Look, a woman isn't an equation to be solved or an algorithm to compute. She's a person. A human being. Find out what she likes to do, what her interests are. Listen to her. Remember, Ari, sometimes the most important gift you can give to a person is your time.'

Time. A precious commodity and that he understood. But did Nell even want his time? He'd told her about his schedule, about its importance, but would she understand if he gave her some of that?

Why does it matter that she understands you? This is about her, remember?

The thought sat in his head after he'd ended the call, and he found himself sitting and staring out of the window once again, his mind working feverishly. Thinking about Nell. Thinking about her childhood, about her aunt and uncle. About how she'd been made to feel as if her existence was something that went unnoticed and unappreciated.

Nell had survived without love, it was true, as he had. But she'd also said that surviving wasn't living. And while he didn't quite understand what she meant by that, he did understand that she'd had love once, before her parents had died. For her, love had been a good thing and she'd mourned its loss.

He couldn't remember what love had been like for him. Perhaps the vague recollection of his mother's embrace. A kiss on the head. A smile. Yet every one of those things had been negated by what had followed it. Sitting in an emptying church pew, waiting, waiting. The gradual realisation that his mother wasn't coming to get him. The sense of a dark pit opening up inside him, a pit he was going to fall headlong into. Because she'd left him there. She'd left him there alone, unwanted—

He jerked his thoughts away. Again, this wasn't about him. This was about Nell. He didn't love her, but perhaps he could make her feel as if he did. Give her the things she'd missed out on in her life: attention and care and respect. Easy enough to do in bed, naturally, but he was going to have to think of different ways to do it now.

The thought galvanised him. He'd always loved a challenge and he had a couple of ideas already spinning in his head, so he leaned forward to his computer and, with a couple of mouse clicks, cleared his entire schedule for the next week.

Then he began planning.

Nell sat by the pool, on a lounger, trying to pay attention to the book she'd found in the villa's library, and failing. It was annoying that she felt just as miserable now as she had when she'd gone to bed the night before, hoping a good sleep would help. Except she hadn't had a good sleep. After leaving Aristophanes and the lovely dinner he'd laid out for her the night before, she'd gone to her bedroom and lain down, hoping oblivion would come. Instead, she'd tossed and turned, her head full of him and his marriage offer.

She shouldn't have walked away from him. She should have stayed and tried to explain what she wanted, because it was clear he didn't know, and that wasn't his fault.

It wasn't as if he'd had a normal childhood. He'd been abandoned by the one person who was supposed to love him, then gone from foster family to foster family, making no connections with anyone. Withdrawing into himself deeper and deeper, escaping into that wonderful mind of his.

A lonely man. A man who had no idea about love. And while he might be a genius with numbers and money, he was functionally illiterate when it came to emotions.

Last night it had all felt too much and she didn't even know why she was staying here. She wasn't a prisoner after all and, while he was offering a great deal of support for their children, it was obvious he didn't care that much for her.

She didn't know why she wanted him to, either.

Nell pulled the brim of the hat she was wearing down lower, so it shaded her nose from the hot Greek sun, and stared so hard at her book the print blurred.

Sex had blinded her, that was the issue. She'd been rendered so breathless by his touch and the way he made her feel physically that she'd expected the same feeling to follow on naturally out of bed as in it. And it hadn't. Their interactions were fraught and stilted when sex was taken out of the equation, and she didn't know how to make it better.

Yet you reached for his hand that night in Melbourne. And you reached for it again that day in New York when you thought you might lose the babies. And he took it. He held you as tightly as you held him.

This was true. As if something deep inside her, something wordless and instinctive, automatically reached for him in times of trouble, and found him.

She didn't understand it. Words were supposed to aid communication and yet with her and Aristophanes, they got in the way. They communicated far better in bed than they ever did out of it, but sadly a marriage was about more than sex.

Nell let out a breath, finally giving up reading and watching the sun glint off the water of the pool.

Would it really be so bad being married to him? You'd be looked after financially and that would mean great security for the twins. You'd have all the passion you could stand once the babies are born too. You could insist on a career, he wouldn't deny you that, and you could even have your own life apart from his.

All of that was true and all of it was attractive. Plus he hadn't been wrong when he'd said the children would love her. She'd have them, at least. Then again, she didn't want to put that kind of pressure on them. They didn't exist to fulfil her need for love. They existed for their own sake and she would love them. This was all, after all, for them.

Still, she wanted a marriage to exist for its own sake too. Not for legal reasons or because she was pregnant. She'd wanted the kind of family she'd lost, the kind of marriage her parents had. She'd been only a child when they'd died, so she'd had no idea what their relationship had been like, but she did remember her mother kissing her father. Her father holding her mother. They'd been happy together, she was sure.

Was it so wrong to want that for herself? After years of being resented for her mere existence?

'Nell.'

The deep, masculine voice cut through her thoughts, and she jerked her head up, her heartbeat going into overdrive as Aristophanes' tall figure stepped out of the French doors and into the pool area, striding over to her sun lounger with his usual animal grace.

She pushed her hat back on her head and looked up at him.

He stood beside the lounger, tall and dark, the sun outlining his powerful figure like streams of glory around a god.

You might be in trouble here...

'What are you doing back?' she asked, ignoring both the thought and the husk in her voice. 'I thought you were in Athens all week.'

'I was.' His eyes had taken on a familiar silver glitter, making her heartbeat even faster. 'But I have decided something. I have a gala in London I have to attend, and I wondered if you would like to come with me. I thought we could visit my good friend Cesare in Rome first, then go on to London. Perhaps we could do some sightseeing, if you are up to it.'

A little shock washed through her. He wanted her company? And to introduce her to his friend? That was definitely not about the pregnancy. 'Go with you?' she said, a little uncertainly. 'But I thought I was supposed to stay here. Be on bed rest.'

'You are not limited to lying in bed, and, in fact, some exercise is good for you. The doctor will accompany us to London.' He paused a moment, as if thinking something over. Then he went on, a little haltingly. 'I...don't wish to go to the gala. I get impatient with social functions and don't enjoy them. However, it's important for me to attend and so I would like…your company. We need only stay for a short time.'

Something in the region of her heart tightened. 'But…why?' she couldn't help asking. 'I mean, why do you want me there?'

Aristophanes' gaze abruptly became focused and intense, making her breath catch. 'Because you are beautiful and you are better with people than I am. I want you on my arm, dazzling everyone in a pretty gown and fine jewels, with your lovely smile. I want the entire world to know that this amazing woman is mine and no one else can have her.'

Her heart tightened even more, heat stealing through her cheeks at his praise, a bone-deep longing clutching inside her. To be on his arm in a wonderful gown, the centre of attention at an important party, in London. To be his…

'Is that what I am?' she couldn't help asking. 'Yours?'

'Yes,' he said without hesitation, an edge of finality in his voice that should have annoyed her, because she was no one's, surely. Yet she wasn't annoyed. For some reason it reassured her in a way she wasn't expecting. 'There will be media there,' he went on. 'And no doubt there'll be some speculation about who you are, but I want everyone to be in no doubt that you're mine. However, if you're concerned for your and the twins' privacy, I can make sure it is protected.'

She swallowed. 'So…how am I yours? Am I your girlfriend?'

Again, silver flickered in his gaze. 'What do you want to be? I would prefer you to be my fiancée, but I understand why you can't.'

'Do you?' she asked, searching the hard lines of his face. 'Do you really understand?'

Aristophanes stared down at her, quiet for a long moment. 'You want to be loved, Nell,' he said at last. 'And yes, I understand why. At least, I think I do. You want what you lost when your parents died, what you never had from your aunt and uncle. And I have to be honest, but I can't give that to you. I think when my mother left me, something inside me broke, something that can't be repaired.'

The tightness in her chest gathered into pain. 'Oh, Bear, I can't—'

'Hush,' he interrupted softly. 'I haven't finished. I want to say that while I can't give you what you want, I think I can make you feel as if you had it. I think I can make you happy.' A muscle in his jaw leapt. 'I'd like to try, if you'll let me.' His expression was intent, the full focus of his considerable attention turned on her, making her feel breathless. Making her feel as if she were the only person worth looking at in the entire world.

But it hurt too. Because perhaps it was true what he'd said, that he was broken. That when he'd been abandoned, a vital part of him had shattered, never to be repaired, and he certainly gave every impression of a man who'd had some vital emotional connection severed.

Yet, he wanted this; she could see it in his eyes. It was important to him; it meant something to him. *She* meant something to him.

She didn't want to be a woman drawn to men in need of fixing. She'd really rather the man came fixed already. Yet she was in deep now, perhaps too deep. She'd seen his loneliness, even if he didn't know the depths of it himself, and because she too was lonely, she knew how it felt. She knew how it hurt, and she didn't want that for him.

That was why it was too late to leave him, she realised with sudden insight. That was why she hadn't left the island already. Not only because of the lack of support and her anxieties about her pregnancy, but because of him.

And maybe he wasn't broken, maybe he'd only been wounded. Which meant she didn't need to fix him, but to heal him, and that was a different thing, that was something she could do. He obviously needed more than a kiss on the head and a sticking plaster, which was what she did for the kids she taught when they hurt themselves, but she could try. Perhaps even, in healing him, she'd find a measure of healing for herself too, such as being on his arm, in a beautiful dress, at an important party in London.

Perhaps he was even right that feeling loved was all she needed. It didn't have to be real in order for her to be happy, and, if nothing else, at least she'd get a trip to London. So, she might as well go with him. What else did she have to lose?

Nell stared up at him, drawing out the moment shamelessly, because it wouldn't do him any harm to wait a little for her answer, maybe even suffer a little. Then she eased herself out of the sun lounger and got to her feet, only inches between them. He smelled so good, making her breath catch and the hungry place between her thighs ache.

'Nell,' he murmured, soft and gravelly, the silver flames in his eyes leaping high. 'You should not get so close to me. Especially when you're only wearing a bikini.'

'But if I'm going to be on your arm,' she said, looking up at him from beneath her lashes, 'we're going to need to practise being close to each other, aren't we?'

He smiled then, quick and blinding, the charm of it stealing her breath clean away, and perhaps taking her heart along with it.

Then it was gone, his features reverting to a slightly less tense version of his usual stony expression. 'Good,' he said. 'I'll have the staff pack for you. We'll leave for Rome tonight. I'll show you the schedule I have planned on the plane.'

CHAPTER TEN

ARISTOPHANES SAT ON the terrace of Cesare's villa in Rome and watched as Cesare's daughter, Maya, ran over to where Nell was sitting at the other end of the long table with Lark. They'd been at Cesare and Lark's for a couple of nights on their way to London, and Aristophanes had felt a burst of possessive pride at how much both Cesare and his wife liked Nell, as did their daughter.

Now the little girl leaned against Nell as she showed Nell the picture she'd drawn. Automatically Nell had put her arm around her as she asked Maya questions about the picture, listening intently as Maya explained.

He could see why Nell was so good with children. She gave Maya all her attention and was endlessly patient with the little girl's chatter.

Cesare was talking to him about something, but Aristophanes wasn't listening. All he could see was Nell, imagining her with their own son and daughter, talking to them about the pictures they'd drawn or playing with them, or even just holding them. It made his chest tighten, made him feel possessive, hungry almost, wanting things he couldn't articulate.

Just then, Nell looked over at him and smiled before whispering something in the little girl's ear. Maya instantly picked up her drawing and ran over to where Aristophanes sat, clambering up onto his knee without any apparent shyness and demanding he look at her picture.

Nell leaned on the table, her chin in her hand, watching him with a kind of gentle amusement that held such warmth that for a moment he couldn't breathe. And he had the strangest sense that he knew exactly what she was thinking, and it was the same thing he was, about their children and what it would be like to have this. Them, together, with their son and daughter.

He smiled at her, he couldn't help it, and his heart clenched when she smiled back in a perfect moment of understanding.

How can *you understand, though? When you don't know what love is?*

The thought was an ugly one, so he ignored it, and concentrated on Maya and looking at her drawing instead.

That perfect moment of understanding he'd experienced, however, lingered, the warmth of it colouring the rest of their visit with Cesare and Lark, and it was still there a week later, when Aristophanes had the limo pull up outside the sweeping stone steps of the deconsecrated church that had been turned into a five-star event space. The gala—a charity fundraiser—was being held there and already a sizeable crowd of onlookers and paparazzi had built up around the entrance.

It was going to be an exclusive event and Cesare had informed him that it was one of the highlights of London's social calendar and thus well attended, which satisfied him immensely. He wanted the crowd to be large and the event important, so he could present Nell to as many people as possible. As he'd told her back in Greece, he wanted the world to see what a beautiful woman he'd managed to snare.

Now he stared out through the limo window, noting the press standing by the stairs, and feeling that same deep sense of satisfaction, plus an anticipatory thrill that he never experienced when going to social engagements.

It was her, of course. Tonight she would be on his arm, and for the first time in his life he found himself actually looking forward to getting out of the limo and walking up those stairs, to entering the venue, and having people notice him. Having them notice her.

Looking forward to showing her around and showing her off. Introducing her to people and having them be charmed by her instead of having to make awkward conversation with him. They would be captivated by her and how could they not? Especially when he was.

Completely and utterly.

He felt her hand rest briefly on his thigh and he turned to look at her, sitting beside him in the limo.

Good God, she was lovely.

He'd had gowns brought to his London residence in Knightsbridge for her to try on, and they'd all without exception been spectacular. But the one she'd eventually chosen was truly remarkable, of deep red silk that he'd thought would clash with her hair, yet somehow didn't. The gown had little sleeves that dropped slightly off her shoulders while the bodice gently cupped her lovely breasts, the skirts flowing down gracefully over her little bump.

Her hair had been gathered on top of her head, with one long lock curling around her neck and falling down to graze the rise of her breasts, and she wore the simple waterfall necklace of glittering rubies that he'd bought for her.

She looked beautiful. Exquisite. And so luscious he wanted to take a bite out of her.

'You really don't like these things, do you?' she asked quietly, a crease between her brows as she studied him. 'Why not?'

He didn't know how she managed to always know what he was feeling. It was as if she had some kind of inbuilt radar automatically attuned to him, and he should have found it as annoying as he had a couple of weeks earlier, when she'd first come to him in New York with news of her pregnancy. But for some reason, he didn't now. He had, after all, given her a little piece of himself back in Greece, when he'd first revealed his London plans to her, revealing that he didn't like social engagements.

You didn't have to tell her you were broken, though.

No, he didn't. But he hadn't been able to lie to her, tell her he could give her something that he couldn't. She had to know that there was a part of him that didn't work properly, that couldn't be fixed. It wasn't fair otherwise.

He put his hand over hers where it rested on his thigh, the warmth of her skin a comfort he hadn't anticipated. 'I find them a waste of time. Small talk is pointless and no one wants to talk about anything of any value.'

She smiled. 'You must be fun at parties.'

'I don't like parties,' he said.

Her dark eyes sparkled. 'I'm teasing you, Bear.'

He couldn't think when she smiled at him that way. There were literally no thoughts in his head right now except how velvety and soft her eyes looked, and how biteable her mouth was, and how silky her skin seemed.

How her smile made him want to check the sky through the window to see if the sun had somehow come out, even though it was night.

And a sudden realisation caught at him in an intense, breath-stealing rush: he couldn't let her go after this. Not after they got back to Greece, and definitely not after their twins were born. He couldn't let her go. Not ever.

He wanted to tell her, right here, right now, that she wasn't ever to leave him, that she couldn't, but he bit down hard on the words. Not now. Later, after the gala, he'd tell her. When they had some privacy enough that he could convince her to take his ring. He'd tell her anything she wanted to hear if it meant she'd agree to be his wife.

They couldn't stay long here anyway, not given her condition. The doctor had okayed the event, but told him that Nell could stay only a couple of hours at most, and that she wasn't to be on her feet the whole time.

So he didn't speak and instead gripped her hand, and when the driver opened the limo door, he got out first, then helped her from the car and into the glare of the paparazzi's cameras.

She was smiling as she stared around, gripping tight to his hand, and the paparazzi began calling his name and taking pictures. Wanting to know who she was and what she was wearing, all the usual things.

Strangely, he found himself smiling too, watching her excitement at all the fuss.

'Do I tell them who I am?' she asked as they walked up the stairs hand in hand.

'Do you want to?' he murmured back. 'Or would you rather be my mystery woman?' He'd thought she might prefer that, but he hadn't been sure. Yet her mischievous smile confirmed that he'd been right, which made him feel extremely pleased with himself.

'Definitely your mystery woman,' she said, and gave him a look from beneath her lashes that nearly incinerated him with desire on the spot. He didn't know how he was going to last the next few months of her pregnancy without touching her. It would likely kill him.

But while not touching her was a torture, the gala itself turned out to be the best he'd ever attended in his entire life. It had nothing to do with the venue or the occasion, and everything to do with Nell.

Nell's hand in his and her excitement as they went inside and she kept pointing out celebrities, politicians, and the odd royal. Then her asking questions about who the other people were—CEOs like himself and other industry leaders—and so he spent a good deal of time telling her who they were and explaining what industries they were in.

Nell, and how she glittered as brightly as her ruby necklace, catching fire from the auburn glints in her hair and the deep red of her mouth.

Nell, and how she somehow managed to make the conversation with people flow so easily and so naturally, it made him wonder why he'd ever found it so difficult.

Nell, who made him find out what charity this was in aid of and then, when he discovered it was a children's charity, wanted to be introduced to the CEO and then had a long discussion with them about children in need.

He stood by her side, watching her, unable to take his eyes off her. Listening to her talk confidently about kids and what they needed, and how important it was to the future of society to look after the children of today.

It mystified him how he could ever have thought that she was somehow less intelligent than any of his dates. Bewildered him how he could ever have looked down on her choice of career. Puzzled him how he'd managed to get this far in life without her in it.

Because if she wasn't in it, he didn't know if he could survive.

That's why you have to hold onto her. She can't leave you. She can't ever leave you, yet you know she might. After all, your mother left you...

Ice wound through him, turning his fingertips numb. No, that thought was wrong. Nell wouldn't leave him. How could she? He was the father of her children; she had to stay with him. She didn't have the support she needed at home and, also, she was happy; he was certain of it.

There was no way she could leave. He wouldn't allow it. He'd just keep on making her so happy she'd never leave him.

Yet no matter what he told himself, the icy feeling in his gut wouldn't go away.

A reminder on his watch went off, letting him know it was time for Nell to sit down again, so, gripping her elbow and murmuring a few excuses, he steered her away from the charity CEO and over to a comfortable-looking couch placed in a nook by a pillar.

'This is getting tiresome,' she said as she sat down. 'I was enjoying that conversation.'

'I know. But you will have plenty more opportunities to talk once the babies are born.' He sat down next to her, keeping her hand in his, not wanting to release it. 'We should probably go. You need rest.'

'I'm fine.' She squeezed his hand reassuringly. 'How are you?'

'Tonight's occasion has been surprisingly bearable,' he said, trying to force down the strange pressure that had been building in his chest. 'You will have to come with me whenever I'm invited to these interminable things.'

She smiled and the pressure increased, making his heart feel full of air, inflating hard against his ribs. 'Of course. Just buy me another pretty dress and a gorgeous necklace like this one, and I'll go wherever you ask.'

She was teasing him, making him feel as if living weren't quite as heavy as it was. As if there were something light to be found in it, something joyful.

Happiness. Was this what she meant when she said she wanted to be happy? This effervescent feeling, as if he were full of champagne bubbles, all rising and bursting and rising again. It made him want to keep this moment, lock it in amber somehow, her dark eyes full of warmth and tender amusement, her mouth curving in the most beautiful smile and all for him.

Your mother smiled at you, too, remember? Just before she walked away.

Ice pierced him and his fingers around hers tightened. 'You can't leave, Nell,' he said far too abruptly, the ice closing around his throat. 'You can never leave.'

A brief look of shock flickered through her eyes. 'What do you mean never leave?'

'You can never leave me.' He held onto her hand even tighter, feeling all at once as if he would drown if he let her go. 'You can't. I won't let you.'

She stared at him, her smile fading, the excitement vanishing.

This is what you will do to her. What you do to every-one. It's no mystery why your mother walked away. You lack something fundamental that makes anyone want to stay.

His heartbeat in his head sounded like a funeral march.

'Bear?' She looked concerned now. 'What's wrong? Why are you talking like this?'

He'd make her smile fade, make her go pale. He'd keep her on the island, imprison her so she'd never leave, yet in doing so, he'd suffocate her.

He would keep her from what she wanted most.

Love.

Pain knifed through him all of a sudden as another thought came to him.

The babies, his children. His son and his daughter. He'd thought loving them would be automatic, but what if it wasn't? Cesare loved his daughter, but then Cesare loved his wife too. What if Aristophanes couldn't? What if he couldn't love his children? He remembered that moment the week before, at Cesare's villa, when he'd met Nell's gaze and known that they'd both been think-ing about how they would be together as a family. But… what if he couldn't do that? If he couldn't love Nell, how could he love them?

Nell raised her free hand and laid her palm against his cheek. 'Bear?'

It took everything he had, but he managed it, opening his hand and letting her fingers slide from his. Then he took her palm from his cheek and laid it back down on the red silk of her lap.

'You were right,' he said roughly. 'You were right all this time.'

'Right?' Not even a ghost of a smile turned her mouth now. 'Right about what? What's going on, Aristophanes? You're scaring me.'

He'd never hated his name more than he did in that moment. 'You do deserve to be loved, Nell. You deserve to have the family you lost, and you deserve happiness. You deserve much more than anything I can give you.'

Her eyes went wide, as if he'd slapped her. 'What are you talking about?'

'I can't give you the love you want.'

'I know, you told me—'

'And I don't think I ever will,' he said, cutting her off. 'I told you: I'm missing something…inside me. Something important. Something vital.'

'You're not missing anything.' The rubies of her necklace glittered in time with her quickened breath, her dark eyes searching his face. 'You're just hurt. Wounded.'

He shook his head hard. 'No. It's not a wound, Nell. It was already there. It had to be. Why else would my mother have walked away?'

'You can't know—'

'I can't love you, Nell. I don't know how. I don't know if I can even love our children, and I can't—*won't*—allow that possibility.' He took a breath and steeled himself because he knew what he had to do now. The only thing he could think of that would save her. 'You have to leave me, understand? You have to walk away from me and never look back.'

Shock, cold as ice, seeped through her as she stared into his eyes.

He was so certain. She could see that. He believed

it totally. That there was something missing from him, something broken. He'd told her as much back in Greece, and it had hurt her then. It hurt even more now. More than she'd ever thought possible.

'You're wrong,' she said in a tight voice, emotion almost strangling her. 'I don't know why your mother walked away, but it was the worst thing in the world a mother can do to their child. You were eight years old and there was nothing wrong with you.'

'The other foster families—'

'You were traumatised,' she interrupted, reaching for his hand again. 'You were abandoned by your mother, then shipped to live with complete strangers. You were bounced from one to another, and no one made an effort with you. No one bothered to connect with you. But that's a trauma, Bear. That's a wound. It doesn't mean you're broken.'

But he was shaking his head, removing his hand from hers yet again, because she was wrong. 'I wasn't wounded when she left me in that church,' he said roughly. 'I was whole then. Or at least, I thought I was. Logic suggests otherwise.'

It felt as if he'd reached inside her and it wasn't her hand he was squeezing now, but her heart. Making it ache. Making it hurt. 'You can't think these things,' she said desperately. 'You can't ever know why—'

'No.' The word was a growl. 'I can't do it. I can't risk it. Something dark in me wants nothing more than to keep you and the twins, and it will do anything in its power to make sure you can never leave. But I can't do that to you, Nell. There will never be happiness for you if that happens.'

She swallowed, her throat thick, her chest aching at the desperation she saw in his eyes. 'You don't even want to try?'

'I could, but what if it doesn't work? What if there *is* something wrong? What if the babies are born and I feel nothing for them? What would that do to them? What would that do to you?' He shifted suddenly, putting some distance between them. 'I thought I would love them automatically, but I could be wrong. Some people don't love their children, Nell.' His gaze had darkened, going from brilliant silver to tarnished steel. 'My mother didn't love me, did she? If she did, she wouldn't have walked away.'

Nell had never wanted to slap someone as hard as she wanted to slap the woman who'd left her little boy sitting alone in a church. Left him to be given to one family and then another, like an unwanted present. Was it any wonder he felt this way? With a childhood like his?

She ached and ached for him.

He was so beautiful in the black evening clothes he wore. Simple, exquisitely tailored, showing off his broad shoulders and narrow waist. His black hair, his silver eyes. His focused intensity, his electric presence.

He'd been at her side all night, holding her hand, and she'd felt him watch her, as if he hadn't been able to look at anyone else. So many celebrities and famous people here at this gala, and all he'd been interested in was her.

He'd bought her the most beautiful gown to wear and the glorious necklace. Yet even without them, she'd still feel the way she had that first night together. Beautiful. Special. Like a treasure he'd uncovered and couldn't believe was his. Because it wasn't the gown or the jewels that made her feel that way. It was the glittering intensity in his eyes whenever he looked at her, the flickering heat, the desire. As if she was the only woman for him.

He'd cleared his schedule for her and she knew what that meant to him. He'd introduced her to his friend, Cesare, and his wonderful wife, Lark, and their adorable little girl. And she'd had a moment watching him as Maya had hauled herself into his lap, waving her drawing in his face, and the granite lines of his face had softened. Then he'd looked over at her and smiled, and she'd been able to see him all at once, with their own children, a patient, caring father.

He'd even handed her an organised itinerary of their visit to London, each part of the day set aside for different activities. It was very Aristophanes. But some blocks of time simply had 'Nell's choice' on them, which she'd been delighted by.

He'd made an effort, she understood. Made an effort to get to know her, to understand what she'd meant when she'd said she'd wanted to be loved. An effort to make her happy.

She still wanted those things. Yet she was also beginning to understand that it wasn't just any man she wanted those things from.

She wanted *him* to make her happy, because she wouldn't be happy with anyone else.

She wanted *him* to love her, because it didn't mean anything if it wasn't him.

No other man meant anything except him.

You love him.

Of course she did. Perhaps she'd loved him that moment she'd opened her eyes on the pavement in Melbourne, and found him leaning over her, her hand in his, the warmth and strength of him flowing into her.

He was aggravating, oblivious, arrogant, and wanted his own way far too much. But he was also caring, honest, protective, and, maybe even more than all of those, he wanted to understand.

This man wasn't broken. He was wounded. He'd put his emotions away in a box so they didn't hurt him any more and had carried on with his life as if they weren't there. But they were there, and now they were escaping the box and he didn't know what to do.

Her eyes filled with tears; she couldn't help it. Tears for him. For the little boy he'd once been, who'd been abandoned in a church. A church like the one they were sitting in right now. And for the man he'd become, armoured and closed off and yet, despite all of that, still caring. Still wanting a connection. Needing it. She could see the strength of that need in his eyes. Had felt it in his arms late at night too. He had love inside him, a whole ocean of it, but he couldn't access it, that was his problem. He didn't even know it was there.

'You can't let what your mother did define who you are,' she said. 'You're more than just a genius, Bear. You're kind and protective and caring. You have everything you need to be a wonderful father and I have no doubts at all that you will be.' Her throat ached. She could barely swallow. 'I don't want to walk away from you. In fact, I've changed my mind. I think I do want to marry you after all.'

The expression on his face lit with something so bright she could barely look at it, and then it vanished, gone as if it had never been. 'No. I can't allow it. I can't give you what you want, remember?'

'But what if I don't need it?' She blinked fiercely, not wanting to cry. 'What if me loving you is all I need?'

He stared at her. 'You love me?' he asked blankly.

There was no reason to deny it and she didn't want to. 'Yes. I think I loved you the moment I opened my eyes on that pavement in Melbourne and saw you leaning over me.'

'Nell—'

'It's enough. It's enough for both of us.' She reached for him a third time. 'Let's try. I want to.'

He'd gone very still, making no move towards her hand, the expression in his eyes one she couldn't interpret. Then abruptly, everything about him went dark, shadows in his eyes, across his face, his features hard as rock.

'No,' he said. 'There is no point in trying if you can't do it. And I can't do it.' He turned away from her, staring stonily ahead. 'Leave, please.'

She blinked. 'Bear, please—'

'Leave,' he said, with so much quiet emphasis he might have roared it.

Shaking in every part of her, Nell slowly got to her feet, looking down at the man she loved. And a sudden lash of anger caught at her. 'That's it,' she said. 'Make me be the one to walk away. Turn me into the bad guy, turn me into your mother. It's easier, isn't it, to order someone to leave you than ask them to stay?'

'You aren't the bad guy,' he said. 'I was the one who told you to go. It's better for you and for the babies. Better for all of us.'

'But you're not giving me a choice, Aristophanes. You're deciding for me.'

He turned then and looked up at her, his eyes nothing but dull grey iron. 'Now you know why I'm not the husband for you.'

'It's not better,' she said, trying one last time. 'It's not better for me or our babies if you're not there.'

'Yes, it is,' he said tonelessly.

She stood there for a moment, feeling as though her world were shattering slowly into pieces. 'For all that you're supposed to be a genius,' she whispered, 'you're actually a very, very stupid man.'

Then she turned and left him sitting there, on a bench in a church, alone.

CHAPTER ELEVEN

ARISTOPHANES HAD NEVER found alcohol to be all that enlightening, but by the time he arrived back at his London residence that night, he'd decided that perhaps he needed to try it. Anything that might blunt the sharp edges of the pain in his chest, a pain that seemed to grow wider and deeper with every passing second.

He'd done the right thing, he was certain. It had been the hardest thing he'd ever done in his life to make her walk away from him, but he'd managed it. He'd taken himself out of the equation and now there was nothing in her way to prevent her from having the kind of life she deserved.

As to their children, well, he would have to deal with that at some point. They were probably better off without him. At least they'd have one parent who wasn't irretrievably damaged by their past.

On arrival at his residence, he was informed that Nell wasn't at home, which immediately alarmed him, at least until one of his staff informed him that she'd taken herself off to a hotel for the evening.

That made the pain inside him grow teeth, long and sharp, and he sent a couple of staff off to check she was okay and to make sure she had everything she needed.

Really, it should have been him going to the hotel, not her. Then again, that was another reason why he would make her a terrible husband.

After that had been accomplished, he went into his study, shut the door, and conducted a very thorough investigation of a bottle of whisky, along with an experiment in how many glasses it would take to make the pain inside him go away.

When morning came around, he was none the wiser as to how many glasses since the pain was still there, eating away at him like rust in iron, and he was on the point of getting another bottle when the door of the study opened, and Cesare walked in.

Aristophanes, slumped in an armchair, scowled at him. 'What the hell are you doing here?' he demanded gracelessly.

'Apparently you're worrying people,' Cesare said, throwing himself into the armchair opposite, stretching his legs out and folding his hands comfortably on his flat stomach. 'People who shall remain nameless.'

Aristophanes didn't stop scowling. 'You're interrupting my drinking.'

'You do know you're expecting twins, right?'

'They are better off without me.' He lifted the bottle of Scotch and poured the last remaining drops into his tumbler.

Cesare lifted a dark brow. 'And who decided that?'

'I did.'

'So, you're already deciding things for your children.' He nodded. 'Spoken like a true father.'

Aristophanes, who'd never found his friend more irritating and his presence more pointless than he did right now, changed his scowl to a glare. 'You are mocking me.'

'You deserve to be mocked,' Cesare said unrepentantly. 'You're going to have twins and here you are, sitting in your study drinking and brooding like an eighteen-year-old. All the while, your lovely Nell is very upset and I'm not sure it's wise to leave her like that in her condition.'

His lovely Nell. Beautiful, wonderful Nell.

The pain reached epic proportions, but he shoved it away, and studied his glass of Scotch instead. It was distressingly almost empty. 'I am sparing her,' he said.

'And what exactly are you sparing her?'

'The pain of being with me.' He tossed back what little Scotch there was in the glass. 'You don't understand.'

Cesare shook his head. 'Of course, I don't understand. Me, who had no idea what to do with a surprise daughter and a woman who turned me inside out. Me, who now has the world's most wonderful wife and child, and who is now blissfully happy. No, I definitely don't understand anything about that.'

'It is not the same,' Aristophanes growled. 'You are able to love—'

'Everyone can love, you idiot,' Cesare growled right back. 'Unless you're a sociopath and I'm pretty certain you're not one of those. Also, I think you're already in love with her. The choice is whether you accept it or keep on being your usual grumpy self. Scheduling lovers when you have the time and scheduling father moments along with them. I'm sure you'll be happy doing that.'

Aristophanes gritted his teeth and stared at his friend. 'I am *not* in love with her.'

'Then why are you drinking?' Cesare's blue stare was

uncompromising. 'Why did you send her away? And why are you looking at me as if you want to kill me?'

'Because you're annoying,' he said, meeting Cesare stare for stare. 'Make yourself useful and get me another bottle of Scotch.'

'No,' Cesare said tersely. 'Do you remember what you said to me when I was agonising about being enough for Lark?'

Aristophanes shifted in his chair, not wanting to think about it. 'I do not.'

'You said, and I quote, "You have a beautiful daughter and a lovely wife. Be a shame to throw all that away because you're not brave enough to man up."'

'It's not the same,' he began roughly. 'It's different—'

'It's not different,' Cesare interrupted. 'You were right. I did have to man up. And so do you. You say you can't love, but that's just an excuse. You're as capable of it as any man, but you're afraid. Because love is vulnerability. Love is pain. Love is wondering if you're ever going to be enough for someone but choosing to try anyway, because they're worth it. Because love is worth it.'

His chest ached, agony echoing inside him. Was his friend right? Was that pain love? Was that why his life, which had kept him content for so long, suddenly seemed bleak and worthless? Had it always been like that and he just hadn't seen it? And if so, why did he only see it now?

But, of course, he knew the answer to that, didn't he? *You are afraid.*

The thought wound through his brain and his instinct was to shove it away, but now the words had been said, it was all he could think about. He'd told Nell he was broken, that love was impossible for him, but if that was true then why did he hurt so much? Why did he want to punch Cesare in the face for telling him he was afraid?

Because it's true. Because it's easier to tell someone to leave than to ask them to stay.

That was what Nell had said to him before he'd made her leave. And yes, he'd made her. She'd wanted to stay with him. She *loved* him.

Agony twisted inside him, and a suspicion began to grow. What if it was true? That the pain he felt now was actually love? And what if the fear that lay at the heart of him was love too? What if all the doubt and anger were also love?

'How?' he demanded suddenly into the tense silence. 'How are any of those things worth it?'

The look on Cesare's face softened slightly. 'That's just one side of the coin, Ari. There's the other side too. Which is knowing there's one person in the world who will be on your side no matter what, and who makes your life better just by existing. Who brings out the best in you. Who makes you happy. What's worth more than that?'

Aristophanes went very still as realisation came, slowly but very, very surely.

She made his life better just by existing. She made him happy. That was why his life felt bleak and meaningless now—because she wouldn't be in it. He'd sent her away.

You gave her nothing but excuses. You're afraid that, because of your mother, you're not enough for a woman like her and you never will be. And you're in love with her and you have been ever since you saw her.

And now he was hurting her.

'It's not better for me or our babies if you're not there.'
That was what she'd said to him the night before, and

there had been tears in her eyes, pain too. She loved him, even though he'd told her he was broken, that he couldn't give her what she wanted. She loved him anyway. She loved him in spite of that. She thought being with him was worth all the terrible things on the other side of that coin.

She'd chosen love.

His beautiful Nell. Braver by far than he was, braver than he'd ever be. And she was right. He was a stupid man.

Of course love was worth all the terrible things it also brought with it, the pain and the doubt and awful vulnerability. Because that was not all love was. There was the pleasure and intimacy he found in her arms. The happiness that filled him when he made her smile. The delight of listening to her talk to people and charm them and make everything less fraught. The joy of watching her with Maya and knowing that soon she would be that way with their own children and how he couldn't wait to see it. The wordless comfort he felt when she reached for his hand and held it, knowing she was with him and that, together, they could face anything.

She made his life better in every conceivable way. How could that not be worth it?

Aristophanes clumsily put down his tumbler on the floor, feeling strangely light-headed as a powerful feeling swept through him, burning, intense, like liquid flame.

'Did she call you?' he asked. 'Did she ask you to come here?'

'She wanted me to check on you,' Cesare said quietly. 'She was worried about you.'

'She loves me.' His voice sounded strange, hoarse and

half choked with the power of that intense emotion. 'She told me she loved me and I told her to walk away.'

'Sounds logical.' The words were oddly gentle. 'She's an amazing woman.'

'Yes,' he said simply. 'She is.' He looked up from the fallen tumbler and met his friend's gaze. 'You're right. I do love her.'

'Of course you do,' Cesare said and smiled. 'So now you're going to do what I did, which is try to be the husband she deserves and the father your children need. And if you fail, you try again and again and again.'

'Because she's important,' Aristophanes said roughly, the fire burning inside him, a fire he knew wasn't ever going to burn out. 'Because I can't live without her. Because she's worth it. She's worth everything.'

And she was, he knew that now. Which meant he couldn't let his fear guide him. Nell was having his children and she'd faced that with courage and strength. Faced him and his ridiculous demands with the same. She'd matched him will for will, and he knew now— perhaps too late—that in the end, for all his IQ points, it was she who was smarter than he was. She who was more perceptive, more brave, more honest, more compassionate.

Cesare was right. She was better than he was in every way and he couldn't live without her. He wouldn't.

Aristophanes shoved himself to his feet and stood there, swaying a little yet determined. Cesare also got up, putting a steadying hand on his shoulder. Then he frowned and sniffed theatrically. 'For God's sake, man,' he muttered. 'At least have a shower first before you go to her.'

* * *

Nell sat in the featureless hotel room, on the edge of the bed, staring down at the schedule in her hand. The schedule Aristophanes had given her when they'd arrived in London. Today was supposed to be a 'Nell's choice' day, yet the words made her eyes fill with tears.

There would be no choice today. Today was going to be filled with wondering what to do next and planning how she was going to cope. She didn't know how long it would last, him absenting himself. Would he contact her again? Would she ever even see him again? And what would happen with the children? What would she say to them?

So many unanswered questions. He'd told her to leave and she had. She'd gone to a hotel because she couldn't bear being at his Knightsbridge residence in case he came home. It hurt too much.

She had no idea what to do next.

A rush of sudden fury caught at her and she abruptly screwed up the schedule and threw the ball of paper at the nearest wall.

How dared he do this to her? How dared he abandon his children? How dared he leave her like this, weeping and feeling shattered in a featureless hotel room in a strange country?

How dared he make her fall in love with him and then tell her to walk away?

Stupid, *stupid* man!

Tears filled her eyes and she covered her face with her hands, allowing herself to weep for a little bit. Afterwards, she'd clean her face and have a shower. Get dressed and eat something. Then she'd try to figure out what the future looked like with twins if he refused to be a part of their little family, but until then, she was going to have a damn good cry.

There was a sudden, loud knock on the door.

Nell muttered a hoarse curse under her breath, grabbed some tissues from the table beside the bed and hurriedly wiped her eyes, before going to the door.

The knock came again, louder and more impatient sounding this time.

'Okay, okay,' she said tiredly, and, without bothering to check the peephole, pulled open the door.

Aristophanes stood in the doorway, his black hair standing up on end, no tie, his shirt crumpled. There was dark stubble on his jaw. He looked like hell. He was also the most beautiful sight she'd ever seen.

Her stomach dropped away, at the same time as her fury leapt high. 'What the bloody hell do you want?' she demanded. 'I thought you told me to leave.'

'I did.' His eyes were blazing silver, his voice rough with emotion. 'I was wrong.'

Nell's heart tightened. 'I don't know—'

'Let me in,' he said hoarsely. 'Please, Nell. Please let me in.'

She didn't want to and yet she found herself giving ground as he took a step forward and then another and another, backing her slowly into the hotel room, the door swinging shut behind them. Then he stopped and stared at her as if he hadn't seen her for years and years instead of only the night before.

Nell swallowed and folded her arms. She wasn't going to be the first one to speak.

'I was wrong,' he said starkly, obliging her. 'I shouldn't have asked you to leave. Because you're right, it *was* easier to make someone go than it is to ask them to stay. And I was just…terrified that I wasn't enough to make you stay. I'm a difficult man, Nell. I'm arrogant. I am not empathetic. And I do not like to be wrong.' His broad chest heaved as he sucked in a breath. 'I will make you a terrible husband and I hope to God I won't be a terrible father, and, quite frankly, that also terrifies me. I'm terrified of not being enough for you.'

He ran a hand through his hair. 'You're so amazing. You're a better person than I am in every way, smarter, braver, more honest. But… I want to try, Nell. I want to be worthy of you.' The look in his eyes blazed brighter. 'I'm in love with you and I don't know how this is supposed to work… All I know is that I can't live without you.'

There were more tears rolling down her cheeks. All her fury had died, vanished without a trace, leaving in its place something hot, something that felt suspiciously like joy.

He loved her. He really did. It was there, burning bright, in his eyes.

'You don't have to do anything to be worthy of me, Bear,' she said huskily. 'All you have to be is yourself, just as you are, arrogance, stubbornness, and difficult behaviours and all.'

He took another step towards her, and then one more, and then suddenly she was in his arms, held tight and close to his chest, his heat and his strength flowing into her. And something that had knotted tight and hard in her heart abruptly released, making her turn her face into his shirt to stem yet more tears that threatened.

'I love you,' he murmured into her hair. 'I can't live without you, Nell. Don't ever leave me, don't ever leave me again.'

She swallowed and lifted her head, staring up into his beautiful face. 'I won't. Not ever again.'

He bent and kissed her, and it went on for some time. Then she put her hands against his chest and said, laughing, 'You're very damp.'

'Cesare told me to have a shower before I came to you. I was too impatient to dry myself.'

She laughed. 'Idiot, Bear. Were you angry that I called him?'

'No.' He kissed her again, hungrier this time. 'I was glad. He can be very intelligent sometimes.' Another hot kiss, then he lifted his head, looking down at her, one hand curving possessively over her stomach. 'Nell, I know you didn't choose to be the mother of my children, but I would very much like it if you chose to be my wife.'

Her heart was full, a joy she'd never thought would ever be hers making a home for itself inside her. Making a home for him, too, and their babies. A family, together.

'Yes, Bear,' she said, smiling. 'Yes, I think I'd like that very much, too.'

EPILOGUE

'TWINS,' CESARE SAID through gritted teeth, as five children caused havoc in Aristophanes' previously immaculate pool area, 'are such a delight.'

Someone screeched, and there was a splash, followed by a howl of accusation.

'That's your son, I believe,' Lark murmured from the sun lounger, not looking up from her book.

Aristophanes tried not to smile as Cesare rolled his eyes, got up from his lounger, and went to deal with the offender. Then Aristophanes surreptitiously checked on Plato and Hypatia to make sure it wasn't either of his children causing the drama, since they were known mischief-makers. But it seemed not to be the case now, as they were playing an innocent game at the other end of the pool. A suspiciously innocent game.

Idly, he wondered if he should go and do something about it, then decided not to. He was enjoying sitting here, watching over the children with Cesare and Lark.

They'd come for a week's visit with their three children, filling his house with chaos and noise and laughter and happiness.

In fact, he wasn't sure he could get any happier. His life had become the most glorious thing. He was no longer tied to his schedule. He simply didn't need it any more. He knew what was important, and that was his wife and his children, and while his business had to be managed, he'd decided to delegate that to someone else, at least until the children were older. He hadn't regretted it.

After the twins had been born, Nell had decided to take a job at the charity the fundraiser they'd attended had been in aid of, which she did remotely. Because she too knew what was important. Then again, she'd always known that.

Thinking of Nell, he wondered where she'd got to. She'd gone into the house, muttering something about peace and quiet, and hadn't come out again.

'I'm going to check on Nell,' he murmured to Lark. 'Can you keep an eye on—?'

'Of course,' she said, still not looking up from her book. 'Cesare! Watch Hy and Plato for a minute!'

Aristophanes grinned as he got up from his lounger while his friend gave him a long-suffering look from the side of the pool. All a front, as Aristophanes well knew. Cesare loved watching the kids.

He stepped into the cool of the salon just as Nell came through from the hallway. She wore a white dress and her hair was loose and flowing over her shoulders, and desire hit him hard in the gut, the way it always did.

His beautiful, amazing wife.

He reached out to her and she came over, taking his hand and lacing her fingers through his. 'Where did you go?' he asked. 'I missed you.'

She looked up at him, her dark eyes sparkling. 'I have something to tell you.'

Aristophanes raised her hand to his mouth and kissed it. 'Oh?'

'Do you think we could do another philosopher name? Or is three in the family too much?'

His heart leapt. 'Nell…'

'Because if it's a girl, I like Theodora,' Nell went on. 'And if it's a boy, I was thinking maybe Aristotle—'

But she never got to finish, because Aristophanes had pulled her close and was now kissing her hungrily.

He'd been wrong after all.

It was perfectly possible for his life to get even happier.

* * * * *

Did you fall head over heels for
The Twins That Bind*?*
Then you're sure to adore the first instalment in
the Scandalous Heirs duet
Italian Baby Shock*!*

And don't miss these other Jackie Ashenden stories!

Pregnant with Her Royal Boss's Baby
His Innocent Unwrapped in Iceland
A Vow to Redeem the Greek
Enemies at the Greek Altar
Spanish Marriage Solution

Available now!

MILLS & BOON ®

Coming next month

ENEMY'S GAME OF REVENGE
Maya Blake

Jittery excitement licked through Willow's veins as she watched Jario stride to the edge of the swim deck. Like her, he'd changed into swimming gear.

She tried not to openly stare at the chiselled body on display, especially those powerful thighs that flexed and gleamed bronze in the sunlight.

She sternly reminded herself why she was doing this.

He'd finally given her the smallest green light, to get the answers she wanted. Yes, she'd jumped through hoops to get here but so what?

'Ready?'

Her head jerked up to the speaking glance that said he'd seen her ogling him. Face flaming, she shifted her gaze to his muscled shoulder and nodded briskly. 'Bring it.'

A lip twitch compelled her eyes to his well-defined mouth, and her stomach clenched as lust unfurled low in her belly. God, what was wrong with her? How could she find him—yet another man bent on playing mind and *literal* games with her, and the one attempting to destroy what was left of her family—so compellingly attractive?

Continue reading

ENEMY'S GAME OF REVENGE
Maya Blake

Available next month
millsandboon.co.uk

COMING
SOON!

We really hope you enjoyed reading this book.
If you're looking for more romance
be sure to head to the shops when
new books are available on

Thursday 16th
January

To see which titles are coming soon, please visit
millsandboon.co.uk/nextmonth

MILLS & BOON

LET'S TALK

Romance

For exclusive extracts, competitions
and special offers, find us online:

f MillsandBoon

X @MillsandBoon

◉ @MillsandBoonUK

♪ @MillsandBoonUK

Get in touch on 01413 063 232

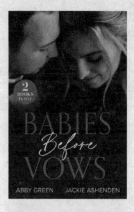
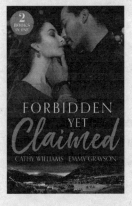

Afterglow Books is a trend-led, trope-filled list of books with diverse, authentic and relatable characters, a wide array of voices and representations, plus real world trials and tribulations. Featuring all the tropes you could possibly want (think small-town settings, fake relationships, grumpy vs sunshine, enemies to lovers) and all with a generous dose of spice in every story.

♪ @millsandboonuk

📷 @millsandboonuk

afterglowbooks.co.uk

#AfterglowBooks

For all the latest book news, exclusive content and giveaways scan the QR code below to sign up to the Afterglow newsletter:

SCAN ME

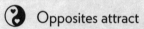

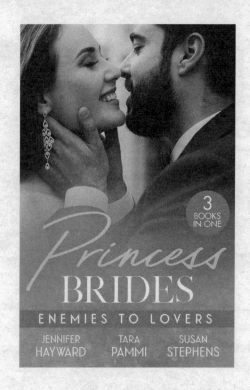